Resounding praise for
MATT HILTON's explosive
JOE HUNTER novels

"[Hilton] delivers a thrill a minute. Awesome!"
Chris Ryan, author of *Agent 21*

"Hard-hitting and fast-paced."
St. Augustine Record (FL)

"A dose of pure rocket fuel."
Christopher Reich, author of *Rules of Betrayal*

"Taut, thrilling, tense and sometimes scary. . . .
Loved it."
Richard Hammond, star of *Top Gear* and author of
On the Edge

"If it's straight-shooting machismo readers are
after, Hilton and Joe Hunter fit the bill."
Booklist

"Firmly in the mold of Lee Child's matchless
Jack Reacher. . . . Packed with ruthless, dramatic
violence from the outset. . . . Electrifying."
Daily Mail (London)

"Joe Hunter takes you in at the deep end . . . and
never lets up."
Adrian Magson, author of *Red Station*

W9-BHF-127

By Matt Hilton

CUT AND RUN
SLASH AND BURN
JUDGMENT AND WRATH
DEAD MEN'S DUST

MATT HILTON

JUDGMENT
AND
WRATH

HARPER

An Imprint of HarperCollinsPublishers

This book is a work of fiction. References to real people, events, establishments, organizations, or locales are intended only to provide a sense of authenticity, and are used fictitiously. All other characters, and all incidents and dialogue, are drawn from the author's imagination and are not to be construed as real.

HARPER

An Imprint of HarperCollins*Publishers*
10 East 53rd Street
New York, New York 10022-5299

Copyright © 2010 by Matt Hilton
Excerpt from *Slash and Burn* copyright © 2011 by Matt Hilton
ISBN 978-0-06-171826-7

First Harper premium printing: October 2012
First William Morrow hardcover printing: August 2010

Printed in the United States of America

Visit Harper paperbacks on the World Wide Web
at www.harpercollins.com

10 9 8 7 6 5 4 3 2 1

To my wife and best friend, Denise

The seventy-first spirit is Dantalion.
He is a great and mighty duke, who governs 36 legions of spirits.
He appears in the form of a man with many countenances, all
men's and all women's faces. Dantalion knows the thoughts
of all men and women, and can change them at will.

The Goetia: The Lesser Key of Solomon the King
A. Crowley

Hell is empty and all the devils are here.

The Tempest, act 1, scene 2
William Shakespeare

JUDGMENT
AND
WRATH

Prologue

CAITLIN MOORE OPENED THE DOOR TO HER LIVING room and stepped into Hell.

Or that's how it seemed to her for the remaining three minutes and twenty-seven seconds of her life.

The clock began ticking when she pushed the door to with a nudge of her hip and reached for the light switch with an expertly aimed elbow. It was the usual Friday evening routine. Coming home from high school with her arms filled with books and test papers for marking, she could hit the switch every time.

Except this time the click of the switch didn't correspond with the usual blinking and averting of her face while her eyes adjusted themselves to the glare.

Not to be outdone, she hit the switch a second time.

Blackness prevailed.

"Goddamnit," she muttered under her breath, swinging to place the papers down on the cabinet next to the door.

It was the creaking of the easy chair next to the TV that made her pause.

"Are you awake, Nate? How about giving me a hand here? The power's down."

Nathaniel Moore was also a teacher at Miami's Collinwood High. But unlike Caitlin, her husband was a track coach and didn't have to endure the Friday evening tedium of the faculty meeting. He always got away three hours earlier, picked up Cassie from the sitter, and arrived home. Once Cassie was tucked up in bed, and a couple of Jack Daniel's were residing in his belly, Nate would doze in front of the wide screen with the Discovery Channel doing its best to cover his snores.

Routine.

"Nate?"

But tonight's routine was blasted into smithereens.

There'd be no supper. No cuddling on the settee while watching a late movie. No fondling their way to bed where a rejuvenated Nate would prove he was still a jock when it came to stamina-based sports.

"Hello, Caitlin."

The voice was soft, but it was enough to shock her to the core. She jerked, her spine knocking on the cabinet, papers spilling from the pile. That wasn't the voice of her husband.

It wasn't the voice of anyone she knew.

The easy chair creaked again, and there was a shifting of the darkness around her, and Caitlin realized that the owner of the mystery voice was on the move.

She almost turned for the door.

Then she remembered Cassie.

Eight-year-old Cassie would be asleep in her room. If Caitlin ran, what would happen to Cassie? What *had* happened to Nate?

A flashlight was thumbed on, the beam stark in Caitlin's eyes. She croaked, throwing an arm across her face.

There was that rush of movement again and a hand clamped on her throat. The fingers were long and slim, but they felt like steel where they dug into her flesh. Caitlin's lungs bucked in her chest.

She had no way of resisting. Air gone, she didn't have the strength or the will to fight. She was turned in a lazy circle, then ushered to the center of the room. Sparks popped and fizzed behind her eyelids. Without air she'd be unconscious within seconds. Then the fingers were gone from her throat and she was retching: gag reflex on overdrive.

"Hello, Caitlin," the voice said again.

"Who . . . who are you?" Caitlin gasped. "What do you want?"

The light was still in her eyes. She couldn't make out the figure behind its beam. Did she know the voice after all?

"I want to give you a choice."

The flashlight went off and darkness slapped its hood over Caitlin's head. Around her a breeze eddied. The stranger was on the move again. Caitlin swung with the breeze, trying to determine where the stranger was now.

"Do you love your family, Caitlin?" The voice was barely more than a whisper.

"More than anything," Caitlin bleated. "Please! Don't hurt them. I'll do anything you say."

"Anything?" the voice asked, sounding strangely disturbed. "You'd debase yourself for them? You'd lie down and give yourself to a stranger?"

"Anything," Caitlin sobbed. "Money! You want money? I'll get you money."

"I don't want money," the voice said, "nor do I want your sex."

"Then what? What do you want?"

"I told you. I want to give you a choice."

There was a metallic click above her. A bulb being turned in its holder. Pearlescent light bathed the room.

And Caitlin saw the figure and knew that her life could now be counted in seconds.

He was tall. Slim almost to the point of emaciation. His face was too pale, a wax mask that made Caitlin think of a reflection in a steamed-over mirror. His hair was silk-fine, as pale as his skin, and hung to his shoulders beneath the wide, circular brim of a hat. His coat was shabby: a long, ankle-brushing raincoat that was missing all but the topmost button. A thin silver chain looped from one side to the other, where something bulged in the pocket. On his feet were grimy deck shoes that were threadbare where his overlong toenails pushed against the material.

The stranger had that look about him that spoke of sleeping under cardboard, drinking from bottles concealed within brown paper bags, and ranting at alcohol-induced phantoms.

But Caitlin knew: This was no street person who'd found access to her home. This man was the type that even the hardiest of the streetwise shunned.

Two things told her.

One, the silenced pistol he held loosely in his hand.

Two, the stone-killer intensity of his eyes.

"I'm going to give you a choice," the man offered again. "Who will you save, Caitlin? Nate or Cassandra?"

Caitlin followed his gaze. On the opposite side of the room, two wooden chairs had been dragged from the kitchen. In them sat the people she loved most in the world.

Caitlin croaked. Not knowing which of their names to call first. Nate was bound and gagged. He strained at his bonds, his eyes huge. In contrast Cassandra was very still, her features lax.

A wail swelled in Caitlin's throat.

"Make your choice, Caitlin," whispered the man.

How could she? How could she? How . . .

"Cassandra has been anesthetized," the stranger said. "If you choose Nathaniel she will never know. Do I kill her, Caitlin?"

Nate's veins were standing out on his temples like blue ropes. He was shaking his head in denial. Caitlin met his eyes and he sank back in the chair.

"Please," Caitlin said, "don't harm our daughter."

The stranger nodded. Then shot Nate in the forehead.

"You made the best choice. Your child will be safe now, Caitlin. You can rest easy."

Then the stranger lifted the gun to Caitlin's face.

1 SOMETIMES YOU MAKE RASH DECISIONS THAT you instantly regret. Then you just have to take the consequences and go with the flow.

Like when I walked into Shuggie's Shack—a roadhouse north of Tampa, Florida—and parked myself on a stool at the corner of the warped and stained bar.

Shuggie's was the kind of place that self-respecting souls avoid unless they're dragged inside by the hair. The tables were planks nailed to barrels, seats 1970s retro vinyl from the first time around. The atmosphere was redolent of beer fumes, cigarette smoke, and the stench of unwashed bodies. Tattoos seemed to be the order of the day. Muscles and hair, too. And that was just the women.

You finish your meal of grease over easy, and the kind of gratuity you offer the staff is thanks that you get out with your face still intact.

I was made as a cop by every man, woman, and beast in the place within the time it took me to catch the bartender's eye and nod him over. Every last one of them was wrong, but I wasn't averse to letting them wonder.

"Beer," I said. There didn't seem to be any other

choice. It was that or chance the brown liquid mas-
querading as liquor in the dusty bottles arranged on
the shelf behind the cash register.

The bartender moved toward me reluctantly. He
glanced around his clientele, as if by serving me
he was betraying their creed. Not that he looked
the type to worry about people's feelings. He was
a massive man in one of those cutoff leather vests
designed to show the size of his biceps. He had a
black star inked into the rough skin beneath his
right eye, and a scar that parted his bottom lip
and ended somewhere in the braided beard on
his chin.

"Don't want no trouble in here, mister," he
said as he set down a beer in front of me. "You'd
best drink up and get on your way."

Holding his gaze, I asked, "Is that what you call
southern hospitality round here?"

"No," he sneered. "In these parts we call that
good advice."

Besides the long hours I'd already put in at the
wheel since leaving Tampa, I could foresee a long
night. A relaxing drink would have helped my
mood. Maybe a little pleasant conversation, too.
Didn't look like I was going to find either in here.

"Thanks for the heads-up," I said.

Flicking dollars on the bar, I stood up and
walked away, carrying my drink. It felt warm in
the glass. Conversely, the barkeep's gaze on the
back of my head was like ice.

Passing a group of men sitting at a table, I inclined my chin at them. True to form, I was re-

garded with the dead eyes of men wary of the law. One of them shivered his overdeveloped pectoral muscles at me and they all sniggered.

In the back corner of the bar sat a man as incongruous with this setting as I was. A small, birdlike man with nervous eyes and a way of oozing sweat through his hair without it moisturizing the dry skin on his forehead. His right hand was in continuous motion, as though fiddling with something small in his palm. I may have caught a flash of metal, but his hand dipped to his coat pocket and it was gone.

Without asking, I placed my beer down and took the chair alongside him. The barrel made it awkward to sprawl, so I leaned forward and placed my elbows on the planks. I turned and studied the man, but he continued to watch the barroom as though fearful of who might walk in the door next.

"When you said I'd know you when I got here, I see what you mean," I said. "You don't strike me as the type who hangs out in biker bars."

"We agreed on this place for that very reason," the man said. "It isn't as if anyone I know is going to be here."

"It wasn't a good idea," I told him. "If you wanted anonymity, you should have chosen someplace where you'd blend in. Where *we'd* blend in. Check it out; we're on everyone's radar."

Maybe the bartender's advice wasn't so bad after all.

"We should go," I told him.

The men gathered at the table further along had turned their attention to the spectacle we presented sitting in their midst. They didn't seem pleased, as if we spoiled the ambient testosterone.

The man wasn't listening. He dropped a hand from the table and dug beneath a folded newspaper. I saw the corner of an envelope.

"Everything you need is in there." He quickly grabbed at his drink, taking a nervous gulp. "The balance will be paid as soon as I get the proof that Bradley Jorgenson is no longer a threat to me or any of my family."

Sighing at his amateurish game of subterfuge, I left my arms resting on the table. It gave me cover for when I dipped my right hand under my coat and caressed the butt of my SIG Sauer P228.

"I'm not sure I want the job," I said to him.

The man stiffened.

"I'm not who you were expecting," I said.

He finally glanced at me, and I knew what he was thinking: Is this a setup? Was I a cop, like everyone in the damn bar thought?

"You can relax, Mr. Dean. I'm Joe Hunter." I folded my fingers round the butt of my gun, placing my index finger alongside the trigger guard. "What I mean is I'm not a hit man."

"Jared Rington told me that you would help," Richard Dean whispered harshly.

"I will help," I reassured him. "I'll get your daughter away from Jorgenson. But I'm not going to kill the man without any proof that he's a danger to her."

Dean nodded his head down at the envelope. "Take it. You'll see what I mean. All the proof is there. Everything you'll ever need."

There was movement among the men at the next table. One man with jailhouse tats stood up. He picked up his beer, held it loosely in his hand, gave me a look that said we'd outstayed our welcome. He sniffed loudly, then jerked his head at the two men nearest him.

Oblivious, Dean said, "Please, Mr. Hunter, I need you to get my daughter away from that monster. If it means killing him to do that . . . well . . . I'll pay you any price you want."

"Pass me the envelope," I told him, "under the table. I've got your phone number. I'll be in touch with you, let you know my decision."

Dean had panic in his eyes. Whether it was about relinquishing the cash already in the envelope without a firm agreement or because there was a real possibility I was going to do as he asked, his nerves got a grip on him. He wavered, his fingers plucking at moisture on his glass.

"Two seconds and the deal is off," I warned him.

That said, he quickly slipped the envelope into my outstretched left hand.

"Okay. Now go."

He opened his mouth to speak and I gave a slight shake of my head. Suddenly he was aware of the Aryan Brotherhood approaching us. Coughing his excuses, he started from his seat, dodging round the tattooed man and his two compadres. They heckled him but allowed the little man to go.

Pushing the envelope into my waistband, I stood up.

"I'm going, guys. You can relax."

The man with the jailhouse tats barred my way. He lifted a grimy, nicotine-stained finger to my chest.

"You ain't welcome here."

"Didn't you hear what I just said?"

"Don't think I did. What's that funny accent?"

I get remarks like that occasionally. Comes with being English. And northern to boot.

"Look, guys, you've caught me in an awkward predicament," I said to Tats. "You don't want me here; I don't want to be here. Truth is, normally I wouldn't sully myself by entering a shithole like this. But here I am."

My words had the desired effect.

I got a laugh.

Stepping forward, I found they parted for me.

That should have been it. Playing on the paradox of self-deprecating humor, I should have got myself out of Shuggie's Shack and there'd have been no injuries. Only two things got in the way.

First, Tats's question: "What'd that little freak hand you under the table?"

Second was the surly mood I'd been in when I arrived. Which wasn't helped by the bullshit Richard Dean had subsequently laid on me.

"None of your fucking business," I told him.

The jukebox was spitting out heavy rock music. Ear-jarring stuff, but expected in a place like this. It played on. If there'd been a pianist in the bar he'd have stopped at that moment.

"You're in *my* place," Tats pointed out. "That makes it *my* business."

"Oh, so you must be Shuggie, then?" I swept my gaze around the barroom. Shook my head at what I saw. "You know, dump like this, you should be ashamed of yourself."

"I ain't Shuggie, asshole. And that ain't what I meant."

"Yeah, I know what you meant."

"I own this place. I own what goes on under this roof." He stuck out his grimy hand a second time. "Hand it over."

I shrugged.

"Okay."

The SIG was between his eyes before the smirk had fully formed on his lips.

Chairs scraped and there was a chorus of shouts as just about everyone leaped to their feet, pulling out guns of their own. A couple of the more delicate customers headed for shelter.

It was like Defcon Five had just been announced and anarchy was the new world order.

It kind of matched my mood.

"This is how it's going to be," I said. My words were for everyone in the room. "Everyone relaxes, puts away their weapons, and gets the hell out of my way. The alternative is that Biker Boy will be throwing his very own wake in the near future."

"He ain't but one fucking pussy," an anonymous voice shouted from out of the crowd. "We can take him."

"One pussy with a gun at your stinking boss's

head," I reminded the shouter. Turning my attention to Tats, I asked him, "How would you like things to go? Bit of a party animal, I guess. Should be a good turnout for your wake."

"Put down your goddamn guns," Tats yelled. "Any of you muthas get itchy fingers, you gonna answer to me!"

Smiling at him, I grabbed a handful of his denim cutoff.

"Me and you are going to walk out of here together," I told him.

He was shorter than I was but bulkier round the chest. Slightly awkward for getting a hold round his neck. Making do with bunching his cute little ponytail in my left hand, I stuck the SIG under his ear. That way we moved toward the door.

A man to my right maybe still had it in his mind that I was a cop. Cops will always warn before they shoot. He lurched at me, trying to grab the gun away from Tats's throat.

But I'm not a cop.

My sidekick found his knee. There was a tendon-popping twang and his leg now had a two-way joint. His face screwed around the agony, a good target for my elbow. He went down, but at least in his unconscious state he wasn't in pain any longer.

In the fraction of a second that it took to take the idiot out, the SIG had never wavered from its target.

"Any more of you assholes want to test me?" I growled.

They hung back like a pack of hyenas, wary of the lion in their midst, starving but too afraid to try to snatch away its kill.

Taking that as my cue, I dragged Tats backward and out the door. Arrayed along the road outside was a row of chopped and converted Harley-Davidsons and other bikes I didn't recognize. I shot at a few of them, putting 9 mm ammo through their gas tanks. One of them went up in the air like a space shuttle, trailing fire and burning fuel that splashed most of the others. Rapidly I dragged Tats away from the conflagration, even as others began to spill out of Shuggie's. Suspended between their desire to get Tats free and saving their beloved bikes, there could be only one winner. I was able to bundle Tats into my Ford Explorer without anyone else trying to play the hero.

Screeching out of the parking lot, I pushed the SUV into the eastern lane approaching eighty miles an hour and gaining.

"Fuck, man!" Tats said from the passenger seat. "You didn't have to blow the bikes to hell."

I smiled. The action had done a world of good to my bad mood.

"Had to make it look real, Ron. Otherwise they might've guessed you were a willing hostage."

2

I'M NOT A COP. I'M NOT A BOUNTY HUNTER. But I didn't mind the cash kicked back my way for taking Ron Maynard in.

He was grateful for the service, even thanked me for my help as I passed him over to his bail bondsman on the outskirts of Tampa. I nodded at him, but didn't accept his hand. After all, he was a punk criminal who'd hurt too many people in the past. His only endearing quality—and the reason I'd agreed to the job of getting him out— was his desire to get away from the lifestyle and go whistle-blower on his gang's activities. His testimony would put a shitload of his friends behind bars. Not as satisfying as if they'd been sitting astride their bikes when I blew them to pieces, but there you go. Still a good result.

It was the small hours of the morning, but the subtropical heat was like a wet hood thrown over my head. An air-conditioned room and comfy bed seemed like a nice idea, but I'd arranged to meet with my friend Jared Rington first. Didn't matter what time it was, Rink would be waiting up for me.

Rink has a condominium up in the wooded lands northeast of Temple Terrace, but he keeps an office for his private investigations business in downtown Tampa. It was outside his office that I parked the Ford. There were few people out on the street, and what traffic there was in the area was reduced to the occasional police cruiser or taxicab. The blinds had been drawn on the window to his office and a closed sign was hanging in the door, but when I stepped up and twisted the handle the door swung open.

Rink was sitting behind his computer tapping keys as I walked in and shed my coat. He just didn't look right at the desk. He should have been in a wrestling ring or octagonal cage. If he were a foot shorter and a hundred pounds lighter he'd look like the hero from a 1970s kung fu movie. He owed the blue-black hair and hooded eyes to his Japanese mother, while his size and muscular build had to have been passed down from his Scottish-Canadian father.

"Got a call thanking us for a job well done," he said. He gave me a grin, his teeth flashing white against his tawny skin. "Course, we might have to do a little damage control over the shitstorm you left at Shuggie's Shack. Did you have to burn down the entire building?"

"It burned down?" I couldn't help the chuckle. "Never mind, it was a pigsty. Shuggie will likely thank us."

If things worked out with Maynard, Shuggie's wouldn't be getting as many customers in the future. The owner would get more from the insurance payout than the place was worth.

Pulling out the envelope that Richard Dean had passed me, I put it down on the desk next to Rink's computer. "What do you know about this client, Rink? Impression I got was he's on paranoia overdrive."

"Just your run-of-the-mill white-collar worker with a mortgage to support," Rink said. His Arkansas drawl always made me think of Wild West heroes, which was apt considering how quick on the draw Rink was with a gun. All that was missing was the white Stetson.

"So how does he come up with that kind of cash?"

On the drive over, I'd pulled into a rest stop. The way Dean had conducted the meeting had set off a worm of unease inside me. Opening the envelope, I'd found it contained a number of photographs and a wad of cash. Twenty thousand dollars, to be precise.

"Maybe he's done a little digging into his daughter's college fund. It ain't like she's gonna be needin' it."

Moving the cash to one side, I laid out the series of five photographs. The first showed a pretty if innocent-looking young girl smiling into the camera. She was slim, her slightly prominent ears emphasized by the way her hair was pulled back into a tight ponytail. She wore only a dab of makeup and her jewelry didn't extend beyond gold studs in her ears and a delicate crucifix on a chain at her throat. Her clothes were a conservative blue cardigan over a white blouse. Richard

Dean's seventeen-year-old daughter, Marianne, looking shy and uncomfortable in front of the lens.

In contrast, the young woman in photos two and three could have been lifted directly from a celebrity gossip magazine. This woman was the type you usually see hanging on to a movie star's arm. If it weren't for the crucifix I wouldn't have immediately made the connection to the insecure child in the first photograph. Marianne had definitely blossomed from drab duckling to radiant swan.

The final two images were those that gave me most concern. The first showed Marianne in the back of a limousine. She was drunk, her hair disarrayed, clothing twisted askew. The man sitting beside her was mugging for the camera as he slipped his hand up the hem of her dress. His face was cruel, mindless of the token effort that Marianne made to push his hand away. Then there was photo number five. A flat portrait shot lifted from a Miami PD file.

Marianne had been crying. Her hair was dark with sweat and clung to her forehead. Mascara was smeared down her cheeks but failed to hide the bruises round both eyes. Her top lip was split in two places, and an earring had been torn from her left lobe, leaving dry blood streaking her neck.

The most poignant thing that was instantly noticeable to me was the lack of her crucifix.

There was a note pinned to the final shot. Handwritten by Richard Dean, it said, "Will the next photograph be taken from the M.E.'s post-mortem report?"

Maybe he had a point.

Recalling his final words to me, I thought about what he expected. *"Please, Mr. Hunter, I need you to get my daughter away from that monster. If it means killing him to do that . . . well . . . I'll pay you any price you want."*

When me and Rink were in the Special Forces together we'd both killed men. Government-sanctioned killings of terrorists and gang lords. I never saw myself as an assassin. Still don't. I saw the death we doled out as a necessary evil. The scum we put down deserved what they got, and it usually made life much better for the innocents who had suffered under their reign. Maybe I'd been a little too quick to deny Dean's assumption that I was a hit man. There were some men in this world that needed killing: Marianne's battered face was all the proof I required.

"The asshole in the limo," I said. "I take it he's Jorgenson?"

Rink swung the computer monitor so that I could see it. The same face smiled out at me from the screen. He was a clean-cut-looking kid, early twenties, reddish hair. Bradley Jorgenson was one of the playboy elite who were gaining media attention on the Miami scene.

"He do that to her?" I tapped the police photograph.

"Marianne wouldn't go through with any official charges. She denied Jorgenson was responsible. So did more than two dozen partygoers at his mansion that night. Course, when they were out of earshot of the police, talk was different. They said Jorgenson must have beaten her for the hell of it. He was pissed off about some deal or another going ass-up: Marianne was the nearest punching bag he could find."

"But she went back to him?"

"Don't think she had a choice in the matter."

"We'll see about that."

Three months ago, moving out here had been a big decision. It had taken me all of about one minute to consider whether I could build a new life in the sunshine of Florida. It meant leaving behind my old life in England, an ex-wife I still cared for, and my two dogs, Hector and Paris. Diane took the German shepherds and I took the first flight out. Rink's offer of work had clinched the deal. When we were in the forces together we'd worked as equals. Although by the sign on his door Rink was at the helm of this PI outfit, we were still equals. So there was no need for an executive meeting to decide what we were going to do about the Marianne Dean situation. I pressed buttons on my cell phone.

"Mr. Dean. You're still awake. Good." I looked down at the portrait of his daughter. The fear behind the flash-washed image couldn't hide. "You still want me, I'm going to take the job."

I'd have taken it whatever his answer.

3 MENTION NEW ORLEANS AND CERTAIN images come to mind. The world-famous Mardi Gras carnival. Jazz musicians. Riverboats plying the wide Mississippi. Then there are the pictures that people wish to cleanse from their minds. Hurricane Katrina. Floods and devastation. The dead and the displaced. Thousands of families still living in transit, suffering for all they had lost when nature unleashed its pent-up fury upon them.

New Orleans is a potent mixture of extravaganza and destruction. Magic and mayhem. Wonder and desolation.

It would be hard to imagine a human equivalent, a poster boy for the city. No one would instantly bring to mind the face of Dantalion. But, in his own estimation, he was the very essence of this contradictory place of enchantment and woe.

Outwardly—he accepted—he was no great shakes to look upon. Some might even say that his unhealthy pallor and emaciated frame spoke of disease and decay. Initially people would avoid him, but always they'd come when he wished. They would bend to his will and give him what he desired. He had that power over them. It was his gift.

It was what had made him a master of his craft.

Why he was much sought after when certain people required other persons dead.

He was meeting *certain people* today.

Not in New Orleans, the place of his birth, but far to the east in Miami. The whisper had gone out among those certain people that he was in town and available. A coded message had come through on his Blackberry, requesting a meeting. This was why he found himself sitting on a bench in Bayfront Park overlooking Biscayne Bay. Nearby the MacArthur and Venetian Causeways carried traffic over the holiday-brochure water toward the island where could be found the world-famous Miami Beach. The Mildred and Claude Pepper Fountain was just visible through the trees, and to his left he could make out the Miami Island Queen at its permanent berth, allegedly Miami's most unforgettable attraction. Dodge Island was a low-slung beast hunkering in the water. Pale against the turquoise sea, it was like a great white whale run aground in the shallow bay. Barnacles on this creature's back were industrial units and storage containers.

He wasn't there to appreciate the sights. Not a tourist. But that was how he would appear to anyone walking by. His pale skin was at risk from the sun, so he'd be forgiven the wide-brimmed hat and dark glasses. His billowing white coat, which brought to mind the cassock of some medieval monk, was a little strange when taken at face value, but not when compared with the costumes of some tourists.

Behind his sunglasses his pale blue eyes were watchful. The stark light pained him, but it was necessary that he be vigilant. Sometimes certain people wished *he* was dead, too.

A group of three men were walking toward him from the mall area next to the marina. One dark-haired man, permatanned, in a cream linen suit, broke off from the other two and headed directly toward Dantalion. The other two, men with guns concealed under their jackets, stood kicking their heels as though admiring the bronze statue commemorating Christopher Columbus. But their eyes never left the man on the bench.

Scanning right, Dantalion saw another two men standing on the parking lot of the Bayfront Park Amphitheater. Not interested in the bandstand, they, too, were more involved in watching him. There could be more, but it was enough to be getting on with. Discreetly Dantalion slipped a hand beneath the tail of his voluminous coat, as though scratching at an itch on his thigh. He unsnapped the holster holding his 90two Beretta semiautomatic. It had the capacity to fire off seventeen 9 mm rounds as rapidly as he could caress the trigger. Enough for the five men and then some.

The tanned man sat down on the bench next to him. There was no preamble. No checking of identities. Both men knew who they were there to see.

"I'll see to your instructions personally. The information you need is already where you asked," said his client. He brushed a speck of lint off his suit. "In return I need something from you."

"I know what you want from me." Dantalion's voice came out in a whisper. It wasn't practiced, merely an effect of his feeble genes. His words were lilting; not effete but androgynous, as though spoken by a prepubescent child. There was no trace of his Cajun heritage in its inflection. "Confirmation of death. One target has been eliminated. The others will soon follow."

"Sooner rather than later would be appreciated," said the client.

"You have a choice," Dantalion pointed out. "If you only wish these people dead, you could send your dogs around"—he nodded at the two nearest the amphitheater, just to let his client know that he was aware of them—"or you can be patient and allow me to do *what I do best*."

"The killings can't be traced back to me," said the man.

"So you choose me." Dantalion nodded slowly. He turned and placed a hand on the man's wrist. He saw the cringe worm its way up the man's arm and into his face. Dantalion smiled faintly and slowly drew back his fingers. His touch caused that reaction in most; something to do with the scaly look of his skin, the thick yellowing nails.

"You know my terms?" Dantalion asked.

"You will be paid half the sum up front. The remainder on confirmation that the targets are dead. You are trusted to do the job. . . . I have no problem with that."

Dantalion's chuckle was like the whisper of bats' wings through the night. "Those are not the terms I'm referring to."

A pale flush crept over the man's features, turning his tan ashen. He sniffed, looked across at the two men keeping Columbus company. He transferred his gaze to his hands where they were folded in his lap. "Along with the targets you have the right to choose how many others die. Yes, I understand. That's up to you."

"Yes," Dantalion agreed. "It's up to me. But, worry not, I don't charge extra for a high body count. I'm just happy with the job satisfaction."

"Just make sure the dead can't be connected to me. You do realize what's at stake here, don't you? *How much* is at stake?"

"I thought you trusted me to do the job?"

"I do. Your record is impeccable. Only"— he coughed—"you can't blame me for being nervous."

"No need to be nervous, is there?" Dantalion smiled, showing the client his caramel-colored teeth. He shifted his sunglasses so that he could lock gazes with the man. "It's not as if I'm coming after *you*."

The man stood up fast. He swayed, looking down at the killer on the bench. His face said it all.

"Please." Dantalion laughed. "Sit down. I'm only funning with you."

"You don't look like the type of man to make jokes," the client said. He didn't sit down again.

His gaze sought Dantalion's hand where it disappeared below his coat.

With a flourish the killer swept his hand out. The man flinched, but then saw what Dantalion was holding. A book, attached to him by a silver chain. With a thumb, he flicked open the book. He rifled through the pages. There were rows of numbers.

"They're all listed," Dantalion said. "The names numbered. Each corresponds to a person I have killed. Do you know how many there are in this book?"

The man stiffened, shook his head.

Dantalion neglected to enlighten him. The plethora of handwritten pages should be evidence enough.

"I am still walking free," Dantalion said. "None of my clients has ever been tied to my work. Does that make *you* happy?"

"I'm happy," said the man. He stuffed his hands into the pockets of his linen jacket, scrunching the cloth between his sweating palms. He took a discreet step away. He glanced around at the men near the statue.

"The alternative is I walk away," offered Dantalion. "The downside of that is, well, you've seen me. You can identify me. If you aren't happy, you'd best set your dogs on me now."

Out on Biscayne Bay a speedboat swept by, throwing out a phosphorescent spray in its wake. Music drifted on the air from the nearby Hard Rock Café. Strolling couples talked in low mur-

murs. The fountain danced to life amid a chorus of wonder from the gathered tourists. It was a strange setting for the standoff that Dantalion had just offered.

Finally the man turned around and walked away. Over his shoulder he said, "I understand your terms, and I trust you. I'm happy, okay?"

"Okay," said Dantalion. "I am happy, too."

Deal done, he stood up. He straightened his long coat over his lean frame, adjusted his hat. He turned and spied the two men over by the amphitheater. They were watching him with their jaws set. Dantalion flicked the brim of his hat at them—just to let them know.

4

IT WAS HOT IN MIAMI. BUT THAT WAS OKAY. I was enjoying the sun on my face and making the most of the sightseeing opportunity. Other times I'd been in Miami, I'd got off a plane, then hightailed it elsewhere. Breezing along the causeway in my Ford Explorer, I had the AC on high and a John Lee Hooker CD belting out of the surround speakers. My idea of cool.

Interstate 195 connects Miami Beach with the mainland. Straddling Biscayne Bay, it's the main route onto the island, and at this time of the day it was relatively free of traffic in both directions. Sometimes people refer to Miami and Miami Beach in the same breath, but Miami Beach is a city in its own right, a distinct municipality of Dade County. I was heading for the South Beach area—again not just a beach, but an urban sprawl. Considered one of the richest commercial areas now, it had suffered from urban blight prior to the fame lavished on it by the TV show *Miami Vice*. I knew it was just a veneer: in SoBe, as it was known, poverty and crime were still rife, just a kick in the ass away.

Cutting across the city, I picked up Washington Avenue and followed it south until I saw the Portofino Tower, a huge terra-cotta-colored edifice that Rink had told me about. Here I swung west, back toward the marina overlooking Baker Island. There's no road across to Baker Island, the rich and famous demanding privacy. The only way across to the island was by boat or helicopter.

Once the Vanderbilts owned exclusive rights to the island, but after it was sold for development in the 1960s, more than two hundred homes had been erected on the artificial land. It still remained exclusive to the superrich set, and once had equaled nearby Fisher Island as one of the richest-per-capita locations in the USA. Maybe it still was. The northern portion of the island was barely settled, but in the southwest it was well developed with megahomes. That was where I hoped to locate Marianne Dean.

Catching a ride over on a water taxi, I arrived at the island among a group of giggling teenagers. It was handy, because there were a couple of bodyguards within the group, and I blended in with the stern-faced men who watched me as though I was a challenge to their employment. Once I was back on dry land, I hired a thing that looked like a beach buggy and drove the short way over to yet another marina on the southwest shore. I met a young lady named Tiffany, my real estate agent, who passed over the keys to the condominium I'd leased. The week-long rental had already snatched a significant portion of the $20K Richard Dean had supplied, but I wasn't there because of the money.

My prime concern was getting Marianne Dean

to a safe place. Richard Dean had painted a pretty ugly picture of Bradley Jorgenson and the way he treated the girl, but there was something about the man's motivation that was giving me cause to question how I'd complete my task. Dean wanted Bradley stopped—no longer a threat to him or any of his family—and I knew exactly what he meant by that. He didn't strike me as being the overly affectionate type, and he seemed more concerned with having Bradley stopped than he was in getting Marianne home.

From the balcony of the condo, I looked over a circular swimming pool, which in turn looked over a palm-fringed garden and down onto the marina. Yachts and motor cruisers seemed to be the preferred mode of travel here.

To my left was the house that Jorgenson had leased for the summer. He had his permanent place of residence up the coast at Neptune Island, and a boat moored at Puerto Banus, near Marbella in Spain, but this was my best chance for getting Marianne away from him.

I was there on a scouting mission. Rink would join me later after he'd finished up a little business of his own in Tampa. Dressed in shades, a cotton short-sleeved shirt, and Bermuda shorts, I set myself up on the private balcony. A glance over the rail and I could see some beautiful bikini-clad women frolicking in the next-door pool. The deck chair was comfortable and the beer cold; it was always mind-numbingly boring on stakeout, but somebody had to do it.

By the time the sun started to set, the bathers had disappeared inside and my beer had grown warm. Even the executive-class sun lounger was beginning to feel like a torture device. The sunset made up for some of my chagrin, though. It was spectacular, setting Miami city and Biscayne Bay aflame with bronze and gold highlights.

Also, as if he were a vampire, Jorgenson made his first appearance.

In a cream linen suit, his reddish hair slicked back and a cell phone to his ear, he wandered out on the tiled area next to his pool. The water was like a mirror, reflecting his downcast face. Bradley didn't seem very happy.

"I've told you," he grunted into his phone, "over and over again. No! When is that going to sink into your stupid fucking head?"

Whoever he was speaking to must have pleaded his or her case. As he listened, Jorgenson chewed his lips, and even from my high vantage point above him I could hear the rasp of his breath.

"You know what I should do to you?" Jorgenson suddenly shouted. "I should have you . . ." His voice suddenly faltered, and his gaze now became nervous as he searched for unseen watchers. His dark eyes flicked my way, but I'd already moved back so I was out of sight. His next words were whispered, and I couldn't hear what was said. But I heard the snap of his phone as he closed it. Then followed the clop of leather heels as he hurried inside. There was more shouting, but it was muffled, then there was a crash of something heavy, and—I'm pretty sure—a female cried out.

I'd made up my mind already, but the man's words and actions only served to confirm what I already knew. Jorgenson was a bully. And anyone who knows Joe Hunter knows I can't abide bullies.

My plan didn't extend to walking up to his front door and ringing the bell, but at that moment I felt the urge to get on the move. It was the stirring of anger that always drove me to violent conclusions. In the past, Rink has accused me of getting a kick out of the violence. But I don't. I only want peace. The problem is, I want that peace to extend to everyone, so if that means cracking the skulls of those causing the rot in the world, then so be it. As a counterterrorism soldier my career was dictated and channeled toward specific targets. Now, free to roam, I could pick and choose who needed sorting. And I'd decided; Bradley Jorgenson required setting right on a point or two.

Marianne Dean—despite the glitz and riches—had to be very unhappy. I'd seen it many, many times before: a woman giving up everything for the man she loves. She will take the beatings and humiliation, won't reach out for help, because, underneath it all, *he loves her.* It must be her own fault.

Domestic violence is a curse on society. Most times it stays hidden, but even when a woman is brave enough to come forward and report what's happening behind closed doors, the finger of blame can be pointed back at her. What was she doing to her man to push him to hurting her? Likely she got exactly what she deserved!

But I wasn't from that school of thought.

The way I look at it, men who hurt women are only a step lower on the ladder of shame than those who hurt children. Sometimes there is no distinction between the two. Marianne had blossomed into a beautiful young woman, but she still remained the shy child captured in that school portrait less than a year ago. Likely she wouldn't thank me for saying so, but to me, Marianne was still a baby. Suddenly I could understand her father's vitriol, his desire to see Jorgenson dead.

In the past I've been accused of many things. Some have called me a vigilante. Fair enough, I can live with that. But I don't see things the same way. I prefer to be seen as someone who can help. When the full weight of the law can't do anything, well then, that's where I step up. I don't take the law into my own hands. Not as such. Not when the law doesn't extend to what is occasionally required.

The thing that stopped me from approaching Jorgenson that instant was one undeniable truth. I still hadn't seen Marianne. I'd no way of knowing if she was inside the house. Introducing myself to her violent beau at this stage could mean that I never saw her.

Better to wait, then.

There would be a time for entering that house, but it would be later, under cover of darkness, and with Rink watching my back.

Jorgenson—notwithstanding his sudden rise to prominence as one of Florida's social elite—was third-generation money. His grandfather had come over from Europe in the late 1950s. He brought with him a pharmaceutical supply company that rocketed along with the post–World War II financial boom. The Korean and Vietnamese conflicts didn't do any harm either, and set Jorgenson's father at the helm of an industry driven by military contracts that were fed by Desert Storm and the more recent campaigns in Iraq and Afghanistan. With his father ailing, Bradley was now poised to step up and take the reins. He was the face of twenty-first-century consumerism.

My worry was, and this was possibly due to my doubts regarding the man's character, he was living a lifestyle usually associated with another kind of pharmaceutical. Those that don't come with a prescription.

Two could play by those rules. Whatever pharmaceuticals he was peddling, I had a painkiller of my own.

I reached for my SIG Sauer.

5

AS A CHILD OF THE MISSISSIPPI DELTA, Dantalion had been raised on the myths and legends surrounding haunted groves and magical ceremonies performed by high priestesses of voodoo. Louisiana voodoo, Haitian *vodou,* or West African *vodun* in its generic form had all appealed to the fertile mind of a child with too much time on his hands. From an early age he had grasped at the tales of spells and enchantment, of living dead men and ritual sacrifice. But in his early teens, he left all that nonsense behind. He turned his studies to other legends, in particular a story everyone knows, though the usual take on the fall from grace was normally mired in the dogma preached by the church.

How could this impressionable youth not grasp at the notion of angels, when his alabaster skin and ice-blue eyes had picked him out and set him above all the other human cattle? His earliest recollection had been his momma cooing that he was her little angel. They were fond memories. Next were the bullies at school stripping him to see if his wings had been cut down to stumps, then beating the shit out of him when their suspicions proved unfounded. Conversely, they were fond memories, too. They were what had confirmed in his mind that he was better than they were. Encouraged him to embrace the reality. The Fallen did not have wings. Their wings were seared from their backs when God cast them into the flames of Hell.

In the subdued darkness of his hotel room in the SoBe district of Miami Beach, Dantalion was not concerned about the stares he received in day-to-day life. In this enlightened age, people were more alert to the feelings of others. Still, people passing him in the street couldn't help the involuntary flicker of their eyes as they tried to probe beneath his coverings, seeking out *what the hell he was*.

They were ignorant of his condition. Most assumed he was an albino, but that was not the case. Vitiligo is an acquired disorder distinguished by patches of unpigmented skin. Ordinarily people with vitiligo have an absence of melanin in the epidermis and form patches of milky- or chalky-white skin. In extreme cases—as in Dantalion's—the hair and the retina of the eye are affected. Various treatments are available, but in cases where depigmentation affects more than half the body, a bleaching agent named monobenzone is applied to the normal skin to match it with the paler areas. The treatment is not usually debilitating, but the skin can become more sensitive to damage caused by the sun. Occasionally, dermatitis can be a side effect of the treatment. As long as he remained covered he was in no danger, and thankfully it was only patches on his hands and face that he had to apply hydrocortisone creams to. Ingestion of immunomodulating drugs was also a necessary precaution, though the risk to his bone density was a potential and serious side effect he could do without.

In this room, though, with the dimmer switch turned to its lowest setting, he felt at peace. He was stripped to the waist, his body faintly luminous against the darkness. He had disdained his dark glasses in order to see what he was writing in his book.

He had people to kill.

He was confident in his abilities.

When he chose to kill, there was only one outcome.

He was so confident, in fact, that he'd already assigned the numbers. Two new figures he jotted down. They were for starters; of course, there were always others he could add if he chose.

6

WATCHING THE BOATS SAILING INTO THE marina, I was acutely aware that nothing was getting done. The buzz of adrenaline I'd experienced earlier was wearing off, and I was beginning to get a slightly nauseated feeling in my gut. The beer I'd drunk on an empty stomach wasn't the best idea I'd ever had. There was no public restaurant on the island that I was aware of and I was starving.

Rink was due soon, though, so I sent him a text requesting a detour to the nearest fast-food joint for something substantial. He replied:

YUR GONNA GET FAT!

So I told him:

I'D PREFER A CHEESEBURGER

Told you stakeouts were boring.

With nothing for it, I returned to my recliner and sat watching the adjoining property. Things were silent in the household now, but I knew that Jorgenson hadn't left. His personal boat was moored off a promontory at the foot of his garden. Assuming that Marianne was with him, my best course of action was to sit and wait. To kill time, I again took out my SIG and for about the fourth time that evening I stripped it down and cleaned it.

That done, I went inside and shucked out of my shorts, pulling on a pair of black jeans and a sweater. Carrying my boots onto the balcony, I laced them up while glancing down into the pool area of Jorgenson's property. I'd only been gone seconds, but already the tableau had changed. A woman was moving through the garden, her arms folded beneath her breasts. Her light brown hair was pulled up in a knot and pinned in place at the back of her head. In pale blue cardigan and blue jeans she looked more like the girl in the school photograph. Without a good look at her face, I was pretty sure it was Marianne Dean.

She seemed to be lost in thought. A soft hum was her singing to herself. Was it a sad song?

Quickly I let myself back into my condominium and took the steps to the lower level two at a time. Exiting into the garden, I did so nonchalantly, whistling loudly to myself as though I was unaware of the woman on the other side of the palm-fringed border which was all that separated us. Armed with a net, I approached the swimming pool and began scooping bugs and nonexistent windblown dross from the surface. I knew that the woman had heard me come outside, and that she was now watching me from between the palm fronds.

I kept up the charade just long enough to make it look natural, then I swung round to place the results of my labor on the garden. Widening my eyes, stepping back, I said, "Oh! Sorry. Didn't see you there. I hope my whistling didn't disturb you?"

Marianne seemed amused. She shook her head. "I didn't know we had neighbors," she said. "Maybe it's us who should apologize about the noise."

Stepping forward so that I was leaning through the fronds, I offered her my most disarming face. Studying her features, I couldn't make out any signs that Bradley had been up to his old tricks. "Just arrived. I haven't heard anything."

Her lips pinched momentarily and I wondered what had flitted through her mind. But she offered, "I had some girlfriends over earlier. Immature idiots, I'm afraid. We had to send them home before they had us run off the island."

Nodding at her wisdom, I said, "Beautiful island, isn't it? Wish I could live here all the time."

"Yeah," she said, but her features smoothed out.

"I'm only here for a few days," I told her. "Couldn't afford this type of lifestyle all year round. As much as I'd like to. What about you? That your parents' place?"

"No," she said, but she didn't expound. There was an uncomfortable second or two between us. To fill it, I stuck out my hand. "Sorry, I'm being rude. Name's Joe."

Her arms were still tucked tight beneath her breasts and it didn't look like she was going to accept my proffered hand of friendship. Her glance skipped toward the house. But then she leaned forward and shook my hand gently.

"Mari," she said. "My name's Mari."

"Nice to meet you, Mari," I said. Mari, not Marianne. The little girl all grown up and demanding her place in the world. Demanding individuality.

"Were you thinking of taking a dip?" she asked me. She was stuck for words now, and they seemed like the first thing that had come to mind. She nodded over at the pool, then looked pointedly at the net I still grasped in my hand.

"No, not just now. Look," I offered, "I didn't mean to disturb you. I've kept you long enough."

"It's okay," she said. "It wasn't as if I was doing anything important. Just thinking about . . . stuff."

"Still, stopped you doing that."

She waved away my concern.

"It's not important," she said. But her arms went back under her breasts. Body language that said she was being defensive.

"Anything I can help with?"

She looked at me strangely. Then her mouth opened slowly. "No."

Nodding once, I told her, "If there's anything, well, you know where I am. You just have to say. I *can* help you, Marianne."

There was confusion on her face now. It wasn't a slip, I'd called her by her given name on purpose, and she'd picked up on that fact. In the past she'd made some bad decisions, yeah, but she wasn't stupid.

"Who are you, *Joe*?"

Staring into her face, exuding honesty, I made her a promise. "I'm someone who can help you."

Marianne wavered. Fear flashed across her features but was replaced instantly by something that looked too much like anger to be ignored. She opened her mouth to speak, but the words didn't come. Before things went any further, I stepped back, hefting my net again. "Well," I said, "I'd better get back to work and let you get on with thinking."

There was a noise from up near Jorgenson's house. A heavy tread on the poolside tiles. "Mari? You out there?"

I could see a heavily built guy in a dark suit. His stomach was large and extended over his belt line. Thick rolls of flesh hung on his jowls and made a hump at the base of his shaved skull. He was like a heavyweight boxer who'd gone to seed. He glanced my way once. Then back to Marianne. "Something wrong, Miss Dean?"

Mari glanced my way, then said, "No. Of course not. Just saying hello to our new neighbor."

The big man—undoubtedly hired muscle—squinted my way. I nodded a greeting at him that he mirrored with no enthusiasm. Back to Marianne he said, "Best you come in now, Mari. Mr. Jorgenson's looking for you."

Marianne gave me the tight-lipped smile again, then wandered back toward the house. I couldn't swear to it, but there seemed less melancholy to her humming than I'd heard at first. I watched her until she was back inside the house. The muscle watched me for a long beat, then he turned away and went inside.

After that, I dropped the net by the pool and wandered back inside. Took up my place on the balcony.

I went there to take Marianne Dean away from Jorgenson. But the opportunity I'd just been given had passed. Obviously I wanted the girl to trust me when I did snatch her out of his hands, and I knew that she didn't yet. But another opportunity would arise, I told myself.

To kill time I cleaned my gun again. And watched the boats coming and going from the marina.

I was watching for Rink, but I saw something else instead.

Good job I'd got the gun ready.

7

As a killer for hire, Dantalion had certain limitations. By his look, the paleness of his skin and hair, the limpidness of his eyes, he stood out in a crowd. It was never good for one who prized anonymity over all else to be seen and remembered. It was one reason why he rarely left anyone alive in his wake. There couldn't be so many angels wandering around in the flesh that he could get away with his trade if anyone should witness his comings and goings.

But because of his individuality he had schooled himself in the art of concealment. He knew how to get in and out of places without alerting even the most vigilant of watchers. He was adept at disguises, could apply theatrical makeup as though born to the movie industry. But sometimes, he knew, boldness and confidence could win the day where all sneaking around would achieve was raised eyebrows and pointed fingers.

Arriving at the Baker Island marina, he did so in style. He made sure that to any observer he was yet another man of the überrich set. The boat—a two-and-a-half-million-dollar cabin cruiser—might not be the most expensive moored in the marina, but it certainly didn't look out of place. He was dressed in the finest silk suit and his face and hands were a light tan, his hair concealed under a sleek black wig. Even his eyes—his greatest giveaway—were disguised by tinted contact lenses. To all intents and purposes, he looked like someone at home on the island. The real boat owner wouldn't mind that Dantalion had stolen his identity; he was currently bleeding out through the hole in his head back at Miami Beach.

Purposefully Dantalion didn't moor the boat anywhere near the target's home; that could alert any minders prowling in the area. Better that he stroll in, a man arrived from the sea, regaining his balance now that he was back on dry land. As he walked he lit a cigar. He didn't smoke, but it was all part of the look. He walked with his free hand tucked into his jacket pocket, where a slit had been cut in the seam so he could reach the sound-suppressed 90two Beretta strapped to his thigh.

Lights arranged along the dockside attracted swarms of gnats: even megamoney couldn't eradicate the presence of pests. Dantalion ignored them. He was too intent on the row of plush houses ahead. The buildings looked pink in the yellow haze of the lights, almost semicircular in construction as they hugged the curve of the land where the marina spilled back into Biscayne Bay. Off to his right was the sprawling length of Dodge Island and beyond it the blazing nightscape that was Miami itself.

The house he was looking for was the one to

the extreme right of the three making up the half-moon structure. The houses, making the most of the view and the afternoon sun, were built so that the gardens and pools faced toward the sea. Entrance to the buildings could be gained from the gardens, but the main doors were at their far side.

Taking in the nightscape of the metropolis across Biscayne Bay, he stood leaning his elbows on a low wall overlooking the promontory that gave private mooring to these three properties. There was a ten-million-dollar-plus craft bobbing on the swells there. Made Dantalion consider the fee he'd set to get this job done; maybe he should have doubled it. Perhaps he still would.

Putting the cigar to his lips, he took smoke into his mouth. Then, exhaling slowly, he turned and leaned his elbows on the wall so that he was looking back toward the houses. It was nonchalant enough that to any observer he would appear simply as a man at peace with the world and enjoying the privileges afforded him. In that brief moment he scanned all three upper balconies of the properties he could see. The left-most building appeared deserted. There was a man, apparently asleep on a reclining chair, on building two. Lights blazed throughout the target house, but he could not immediately detect any movement from within.

His eyes strayed back to the central balcony. He couldn't see much of the man, but he appeared to be relaxed enough that he could be asleep. He watched for long seconds but got no reaction.

He discarded the presence of the man; probably drunk or sleeping off a long flight. He could always pay him a visit after he was done, and make sure that a potential witness was no longer around. Jamming the cigar between his teeth, he pushed off from the wall and wandered along the pathway overlooking the sea. Tiny waves made crystalline splashes on the rocks below. He flicked the cigar away, watching it spiral end-over-end like a tiny meteor before it fizzed out in the ocean.

He then moved inland toward the high wall bordering the garden. To look at him, you wouldn't think he had the strength to catch the top of the wall and swing up as nimble as a cat, but that was what he did. There he crouched, peering over the shrubbery toward the house. He held the pose, crouching gargoylelike as though he were an evil sprite fleeing a European cathedral. Pretty apt, considering.

When he was sure he'd gone undetected, he hopped down into the garden, landing sure-footed amid a stand of palm. Crouching again, he felt for the necessary tools of his trade. Beretta. Check. Book. Check. That was all he needed. He rose up from his crouch and moved forward, staying within the shadows of the trees. Nothing stirred around him; even the endemic bugs had fallen silent.

The bushes ended at a paved terrace, and then there was an open space he had to traverse to get to the door. From this vantage point he could see inside the door where there was a well-appointed foyer. A large, overweight man in a dark suit was sitting on a couch, using a telephone on an adjacent stand. He was giving someone quite express orders judging by the snapping motion of his free hand. The man looked away from the phone and Dantalion followed his gaze. Another man was farther inside, another big man. In trousers and shirt, his shoulder holster was immediately obvious. Two minders at the very least. Could be more on the upper floors.

Calculating figures, Dantalion moved forward. He lifted the silenced Beretta and took aim. There was a noise like someone slapping a catcher's mitt. The light above the entrance went out. Inside the house, neither of the two bodyguards noticed the sudden darkness outside. Dantalion was immediately on the move.

He was across the terrace in seconds. He didn't pause, pulling open the door in one swift motion. The fat man on the couch was the nearest target, but he was sitting down and had his gun hand full of telephone. Dantalion shot the standing man. The 9 mm bullet hit him center mass, going through and putting a hole in the mirror he was standing in front of. Blood spray misted the glass.

It was a heart shot, but experience told Dantalion that sometimes that wasn't enough, so even as the man crumpled, Dantalion shot him a second time, taking off a sizable portion of his skull.

Barely two seconds had passed, but it was the length of mortality for at least one of the men.

The heavy man had hardly registered what was happening. He swung his gaze from his dead companion to the mystery man in the foyer, his mouth hanging open. The Beretta was now aimed his way. This man was more show than substance. His real weapons were his size and his fists. Not much good against an expert with a semiautomatic handgun. His response was to sink back on the couch, bringing up his hands. Dantalion shot him twice. Once in the throat to stop his shout of alarm, once in his tremulous gut, just for good measure.

Both men out of the picture in less time than it took to stalk the length of the foyer. The suppressor—though not as effective as Hollywood would have it—deadened the sounds of the gunshots, but there'd still been a sequence of thuds. Most noise had been from the smashing of the mirror. Still, Dantalion wasn't concerned that the people upstairs had been alerted; they weren't familiar with the sounds of death.

The greatest threat to discovery was that the big guy's voice had fallen silent.

Moving to the foot of a staircase, Dantalion swept the remainder of the foyer with his gun. A door was closed on his right, possibly an entrance to the kitchen area. He stepped forward and twisted the handle. Didn't want to be going up the stairs only for the door to swing open and disgorge more minders. But the kitchen was in darkness, empty of armed guards. He quickly pulled the door to.

The door out into the parking area was closed. No movement beyond it. He returned his attention to the stairs.

There was a young woman walking down them, taking them a step at a time as she clumped downward hefting a heavy suitcase. She saw the dead man on the couch, jerked her stupefied gaze toward Dantalion. Her eyes widened. A scream began to swell. Dantalion shot her in the mouth. No need of a second shot this time, not with half her skull decorating the stairway. She slipped to the stairs, boneless, making hardly a sound. Not the suitcase, though; it rattled and thumped and banged its way over the steps before Dantalion could reach it and halt its fall.

Quizzical voices were raised from above him. Dantalion differentiated one from the others. One female, two male. He glanced at the dead woman on the stairs. Slim and petite with the dusky look of Cuba. She was wearing a white blouse, black skirt, and sensible black shoes. Housemaid, he determined. That would mean the three upstairs were his targets, plus one more probable guard.

Taking their confusion as cover for his own upward charge, he gained the upper floor before any of them had the notion to come and investigate the commotion.

Walking along the landing, he saw another young woman step out of a bedroom. Anglo-Saxon this one. Light brown hair, blue-green eyes, nice figure. Dantalion smiled at her.

"Hello, Marianne," he said.

Then he showed her the gun. The woman immediately yelped and jerked back into the room. Dantalion followed her. He was only a beat in her wake, and he was planning on using her fear against the others.

He blinked, taking in the tableau.

The woman was still running across the room. A young man, reddish hair marking him out, was in midpose pulling on a suit jacket. The second man was older, gray hair, slim, officious looking. Sitting at a desk, he had been bending over a laptop computer. More accountant than bodyguard, perhaps, but still a viable threat. Dantalion lifted the Beretta and blew him out of contention.

To the younger man, Dantalion said, "Bradley, how are you, sir?"

Jorgenson gaped at him. Then he looked down at the dead man, who'd slumped over the computer, his fingers arched over the keys as though writing his own eulogy.

"Dad?" Jorgenson croaked. His face collapsed in on itself and he sobbed.

Dantalion quirked his head. "That was your father? The great Valentin Jorgenson?"

Bradley turned his face away.

"If it's any consolation, your father would probably thank me for killing him. What was it? Cancer? He was in great pain, was he not?" Dantalion stepped closer. He lifted the gun so it was aimed at Bradley's heart. "Do you want a quick and painless death, Bradley? I'm prepared to give you the choice."

Jorgenson stepped back, bringing up placating hands. "Look, whoever you are, whoever put you up to this, I will double the price. Don't kill me."

Dantalion let out a long sigh like an escape of steam. "I'm not averse to being handed heaps of cash, Bradley. However, a deal is a deal and you must die." He turned and sought out the woman. Marianne had pressed herself to the far wall as if, merely by wishing, she could melt through the brick and escape the horror. "You too, Marianne."

Marianne croaked, slipping down the wall and covering her head with both arms.

Turning back to Jorgenson, Dantalion waved him over to the woman with the barrel of his gun. "Go and comfort her, Bradley. She deserves a hug, don't you think?"

"Please," Jorgenson pleaded. "She hasn't done anything wrong. Please don't kill her."

"The deal has been made, Bradley. I must."

Jorgenson was fit and strong. Approaching his prime, before the hedonistic ways the affluence afforded him would make him fat and slow. Dantalion saw him clench his fists.

"Don't be silly, Bradley. The hype is just that. They've dubbed you 'Superman,' but, believe me, you're not faster than a speeding bullet."

"Who sent you?" Jorgenson demanded.

Dantalion tapped the Beretta alongside his nose. "That would be telling."

Jorgenson snapped his gaze on Marianne. There was a flash of anger, but then the hardness melted.

"Let her go," he said.

Dantalion shook his head.

"I will let you choose, Bradley. The woman first?"

"No!"

"Then you first?"

"No!"

Dantalion shook his head. "You just don't seem to have a grasp on this, do you?"

"I'm not going to choose who you kill. How can you expect me to do that?"

"Flip a coin if you wish," Dantalion said. "But if I kill her first, then we go back to my first offer. Quick and painless or long and in untold agony."

Shuddering, Jorgenson looked down at the woman. Her eyes were huge ovals as she looked back at him. "Mari," he said, "I'm sorry I dragged you into this, babe."

"Not . . . your . . . fault," she whispered back.

"Now that's very touching," Dantalion said. Unconsciously he wiped his arm over his chin. A pale patch of skin drew Jorgenson's gaze.

Realizing his error, Dantalion shook his head slowly. "Bang goes the neighborhood! Now there's definitely no choice."

With a lifestyle built on giving commands, Jorgenson wasn't one to give in so easily. The immediate shock of seeing his father gunned down by the weird man threatening him with death was beginning to dissipate. He squared his shoulders.

"You touch either of us, you'll be hunted down. They won't stop. You'll be hounded constantly, and when they get you they will make you *hurt*!"

Dantalion raised an eyebrow. "They? Who are these *they* you have so much faith in? *They* will have to find me first. And if I don't want them to find me, they never will."

"They already have," said a voice from behind him.

8

NOT NORMALLY ONE FOR MOVING IN THE CIR-
cles the people of Baker Island enjoyed,
I could be forgiven for missing *just another rich
man* as he took an evening stroll along the dockside. But as one who had spent fourteen years
hunting terrorists and the last four dealing with
criminals ranging from moneylenders to a bone-
collecting maniac, I recognized a stone killer
when I saw him.

On an island this wealthy, it was probable
that a large portion of the populace was ex-cops,
ex-military—and everything in between—
employed as executive protectors by those that
called Baker Island their home. But there was
something about the sinuous way this man
moved that told me he wasn't the type who celebrated the sanctity of life. For one, he was too
watchful of his surroundings. Even switched-on
security men don't act that way when they aren't
covering their mark.

The cigar was a prop. Too exaggerated, the
way he put it to his mouth, then removed it with
a grand gesture of his sweeping arm. And all
the while the other hand didn't move from his
pocket. It fiddled with something, and I could tell

his hand extended much lower than the confines of his pocket. He was packing.

He flicked the cigar away, watching it with a strange air of fascination as it pinwheeled into the ocean. Leaning back on the wall, the man turned and stared directly at me. I'd been expecting that, so I'd already slunk down against the recliner, tilting my head as though dozing. I watched him through the merest slitting of my eyes. The man ghosted a smile. I'd have missed it in the subdued lighting if I hadn't caught a flash of saliva on teeth.

Out of his line of sight I was already midtext to Rink.

GET HERE FAST. TROUBLE

I hit the send button just as the man turned away and walked along the coast path. His very black hair picked up highlights from the lamps along the path, so I could make out his progress beyond the wall to Jorgenson's garden. I blinked and the man was suddenly crouching on the wall like some unearthly bat. Next instant he was down in the garden and he paused to check his pockets. When next he moved it was as if a snake had sprung out of a coil, fast but sinuous at the same time. Then I couldn't see him because of the angle and the obscuring foliage.

Keeping low, I moved to the edge of my balcony. The lights above the entrance door spilled across Jorgenson's terrace, making for faux daytime. Then came a noise like a sharp cough and the garden went dark.

As soon as it did, I was on the move.

But not without hearing four rapid shots from a silenced handgun, and the smashing of glass.

Going back through my apartment would take too long. I swung over the balcony railing and jumped to the terrace below. Harking back to my parachute days, I tucked and rolled, absorbing the impact, and came up with my SIG leveled toward Jorgenson's house. Then I moved forward. Farther down the garden, only the shrubbery marked the boundary, but here close to the entrances a small wall had been erected to offer privacy to occupants sitting on the terrace. I had to shift a terra-cotta pot containing some fern-type plant. Then I vaulted the wall and landed on Jorgenson's property.

There was another dull thud, then the bang and rattle of something clattering down a staircase. I stepped into the foyer just as the man I'd watched outside earlier raced up the stairs. The big man who'd called Marianne inside earlier was dead. A telephone was still in his hand, but he'd ripped the cord loose as he'd died. Another man sprawled on the floor; his blood decorated the walls and made a crazy pattern on the shattered mirror.

What the fuck have I got myself into this time? I wondered. I couldn't take time to ponder the bad luck that had cast its hand my way. Marianne was up those stairs. Who this killer was I had no idea, but whether or not Marianne was the target, she wouldn't get out of this situation alive if I stood there trying to figure out the age-old question.

The killer was already out of sight. Another gunshot, then muffled talking. I swung onto the stairs and saw another corpse. A young woman with half her head gone. This angered me more than any number of slaughtered bodyguards. It also told me the killer wouldn't hesitate to put a bullet through Marianne as well.

Silent as possible, I made my way up the stairs. The killer and someone I took to be Jorgenson were conversing in low tones. I wasn't concerned about what was said—the threat in the killer's voice was enough to keep me moving.

On the landing now, I moved along the hall. A thick carpet beneath my rubber soles ensured silence, and I was able to move directly to the bedroom door without raising the alarm.

There I readied my gun. Listened.

Jorgenson's voice came sharp and clear now. Anger born from fear. "You touch either of us, you'll be hunted down," he promised. "They won't stop. You'll be hounded constantly, and when they get you they will make you *hurt*!"

"*They?*" the killer asked. "Who are these *they* you have so much faith in? They will have to find me first. And if I don't want them to find me, they never will."

Conceited, overconfident bastard, I thought. I stepped into the room behind him. "They already have," I said.

Should have kept my mouth shut. Conceit and overconfidence can get anyone killed.

The killer spun and fired even before I'd done gloating.

His bullet missed me. Only just. But it made me flinch, and my return fire missed him as well.

Sometimes sudden violence can have a strange effect on the senses. As adrenaline spurts through the system, you can experience a startling slowing of reality so that everything around you seems like a slow-motion, hyperclear shot on a 3-D screen. Really it's your mind racing as it seeks the options for flight or fight, overtaking the responses of the body powered by the engine of the brain.

There was an overriding sense of déjà vu even as I pulled the trigger again and saw the material of the man's suit jacket trail on the wake of the bullet's passing. Unfortunately, there was no blood. Missed the fucker a second time. Then he was lunging to one side and shooting across his body at me. Throwing myself into the room, I fired off a volley of five rounds. Unlike his silenced pistol, my SIG roared like Thor's battle cry.

I was here on the knight errant's quest to save a damsel in distress. I wouldn't be much good to her if I ended up dead.

Swinging round into a sitting position, I leveled my SIG on the killer.

He must have had an equally important reason to live, because he fired back. Burning cold creased my right shoulder. It wasn't a debilitating hit; in fact, having been shot before, I realized that the bullet had barely grazed me. It was enough to draw my aim, though, and my return fire went over his head and struck the door frame as he vaulted back onto the landing. The clatter of his feet down the stairs resounded through the house.

Pretty certain he wasn't going to return to the room in the next second or two, I searched for Marianne. She was unhurt, but still in a state of near collapse. Jorgenson was in a duck's crouch of his own, ass almost touching his heels.

"You okay?" I asked, my words for both of them.

Receiving nods from both, I swung to cover the door. "Jorgenson," I said, "get over here."

Jorgenson blinked at me and half rose from his crouch. Then he sank down again. Not sure why, but not wanting to approach me, either.

I snapped at him, "If you want to get out of here alive, you're gonna have to do what I say. Now get the fuck over here!"

When I came here it was with the understanding that I might have to kill Bradley Jorgenson. It's funny how fate plays out sometimes. The arrival of this would-be killer had changed the dynamics of my mission. In my mind, Bradley had been someone to be loathed, someone to be put down with all the regret of shooting a rabid dog. Yet here I was, offering to be his protector.

"Are you armed?" I asked him.

He shook his head.

"What about him?" I jerked my head toward a man folded over a desk.

Jorgenson's eyes teared up. He shook his head sadly.

"Make sure," I ordered him. "He could be carrying."

"He isn't," Jorgenson said. "My father. He abhorred violence. He was a man who only wanted to stop pain."

Noble, I thought, but misguided. Someone who makes their billions from military contracts can't play the moral card when challenged over his source of income. He could say what he wanted, but Daddy Jorgenson was as much to do with causing pain as curing it.

"Check," I said.

Rising up, I crept over to the door. Keeping low, I bobbed my head round the frame, then back inside again. I didn't see the killer, but he was likely still in the house. When I glanced round, Jorgenson was gently patting around inside his father's jacket. He was looking at me, and his eyes were full of disgust.

"Anything?"

"Nothing," he spat, moving away quickly.

"Get Marianne," I told him. "Take her over there."

Jorgenson helped Marianne up. She looked shaky but unhurt. On rubber legs, she allowed Jorgenson to lead her past the dead man to the far end of the room. Her eyes swooped around like birds chasing insects at dusk, never still, never in one place.

"Do you know that man?" I demanded. I

sneaked a look round the door frame, noticing a play of shadows from below.

"No," Jorgenson said. "And I don't know you. Who the hell are you?"

Surprisingly, it was Marianne who offered an explanation. "He's Joe. He's here to help."

"You've no idea why he wants you dead?" I asked.

No reply. When I looked, Jorgenson was holding Marianne, his hands cupping her head against his chest, and Marianne was sobbing into his shirt. The picture of young love. It didn't look much as if Marianne had ever suffered at his hands. Maybe she'd only traded a lesser terror for a greater one.

There'd be time for resolving the Jorgenson problem later. Right now there was a far greater danger to Marianne's welfare. The killer was downstairs and he was up to no good.

"Is there another way out of here?" Studying the windows, I decided that we could smash one of them and climb out. It would be a fair drop to the ground but we were all capable of it. What I didn't like was the idea of the killer waiting for us, picking us off from below as we clambered from the window.

RINK HOW FAR AWAY

My text was hurried. Thankfully I received his reply in seconds, but it wasn't what I wanted to see.

FIFTEEN MINS

Not soon enough. The killer wasn't going to wait that long.

I heard a clatter and dull thump from below us.

"What's he doing?" Marianne asked.

I'd been wondering the same thing. Sounded like he was in the kitchen.

I sent to Rink:

MEET US SOBE

In her schoolgirl guise, Marianne might not have been much help in these circumstances. But as the sleek trophy Jorgenson had made of her, perhaps there was something she could bring into play.

"Marianne, you have perfume in here?"

Marianne stared at me as if I were mad. In all honesty, she wasn't so far removed from the truth. "Perfume?"

"Good stuff. Concentrated."

She nodded, pulling free from Jorgenson's embrace. She gave the dead man a wide berth and went to a credenza. Pulled open a compartment and grabbed at bottles of scent. Judging by the brands and designs of the bottles, she handed me the makings of a bomb that would cost thousands of dollars.

Checking that the killer wasn't sneaking back along the landing, I again snatched a look. The sounds from below reassured me he was still being industrious in the kitchen. For a second I considered leading Marianne and Jorgenson out of the bedroom, taking our chances on getting down the stairs while he was busy with whatever the hell he was doing. He'd hear us, though, and would pick us off as we came down the stairs.

When I turned back to the bedroom, Jorgenson had joined Marianne beside me.

"This better not be what I'm thinking," Jorgenson said to me. His head-shake was pure denial.

"We have to make a diversion; otherwise we aren't going to get out of here alive." I began unscrewing tops off the perfume bottles. "Find me something larger than these. That wine bottle over there will do."

"But my father . . ." Jorgenson croaked.

"Your father is already dead," I pointed out. "But I'm pretty sure he'd want *you* to live. Now go and fetch me the fucking bottle."

Then I stepped out onto the landing and peered over the railing. The killer immediately shot at me, and I ducked back. I unloaded five bullets directly through the floor. Not really an attempt to hit him—the wooden joists would probably sap much of the velocity of the rounds—but it was enough to force him back into the kitchen.

Two could play at the same game. The killer's bullets drilled upward, lifting tatters of carpet in front of my eyes. I jumped back into the room. Good enough, I thought, I'd got his attention. Plus he was using the kitchen for cover.

"Empty the perfume into the wine bottle, and

get me some sort of rag for a fuse," I whispered to Marianne. She understood my train of thought and nodded. She turned to the bottles I'd set on the floor.

Jorgenson brought the wine bottle. He walked slowly, and his eyes never left the still form of his father. His father was a sick man, dying from cancer, as I recalled, but I don't think that Jorgenson ever expected to be cremating him so soon.

"If there was any other way . . . " I said, by way of apology. His face was set in stone. There'd be no consoling him. Not at that moment. It'd be pointless trying, so I turned away from him, concentrating on keeping the killer at bay.

Behind my back Jorgenson sobbed for his murdered father. It was enough to make him step over a precipice.

The stupid son of a bitch swung the bottle and smashed it over my skull.

9

THE APPEARANCE OF THE MYSTERY GUNMAN was an unfortunate—and unforeseen—complication that Dantalion could have done without. It was the man who'd been dozing on the balcony next door. Dantalion recognized him, but couldn't at first understand his reasons for intervening. It wasn't as if he was in the employ of Jorgenson. The targets had been as surprised by the man's appearance as he'd been. Plus, however much cash you could throw around, you didn't hire a condominium adjacent to the one you were living in and set the guard up as sole occupant. This man had another reason for being here.

Recalling the meeting with his client back in Bayfront Park, Dantalion thought about the subtle threat he'd leveled at the man. Bad idea in hindsight. Maybe his employer had set this man up to kill him after the hit had been completed on his targets. Insurance that Dantalion wouldn't come after him, once in receipt of payment for his services. Or that Dantalion didn't become a liability: someone who could lead back to him, implicating him in the murders.

Fucker! Well, if that was the case, his client better watch his ass. He was numbered now.

But first he had to finish what he'd started here.

Bradley Jorgenson and Marianne Dean must die. So must the gunman. In fact, the gunman took priority because he was what was stopping Dantalion from getting the primary job done.

Time was against him.

He'd come with a silenced gun, but the other man hadn't been so discerning a killer. He'd been shooting off a barrage of loud volleys. Place like this where the populace of the island lived on tightly wound nerves for fear of robbery or kidnap for ransom, dozens of people would be demanding the immediate arrival of the Miami PD. The cops didn't have a station house on the island, but there'd be plenty of rent-a-cops en route. The police wouldn't be far behind.

Weighing his options, there were two possible ways for this to play out. He could get the hell away now and take a second shot at his targets later, or he could try and kill them now and take his chances with the swarm of uniforms bearing down on him.

Optimistic as ever, he wasn't worried about security guards or cops. They'd never been capable of stopping him before.

He made his choice.

He stepped out from the kitchen where he'd been searching for something he needed. Looking up, he saw a head glance over the balcony. Quickly Dantalion lifted his Beretta and fired. The man had seen him, though, and ducked back out of sight. Then Dantalion had to dance to avoid the bullets blasting holes through the balcony above his head. Splinters of wood sifted down on him, but miraculously none of the bullets hit their mark.

Dantalion fired back.

Then he was back in the kitchen. His mind made up. Choice made.

The island wasn't supplied with a gas main. Electricity was the overriding source of power to these houses. However, there were secondary sources, too. Oil tanks. Propane gas. Jorgenson's house was equipped with a full cooking range.

Reaching down alongside the range, he found what he'd expected. A rubber pipe attached to a valve on the wall. Dantalion grabbed at a knife from a nearby cutting block and swiped it through the rubber pipe. He heard the hiss of escaping gas. Then he moved back across the room to the door. Listened. There was a mutter of voices from above. Good, they were in the room still.

Dantalion looked back across at the range. He imagined that there was a haze over it now, but knew that was only fancy. The gas was invisible. But it was there, the cloud growing exponentially by the second. Pretty soon it would be visible.

The scorching flames of Hell would scour this house, do his work for him, suitable to one who fancied himself as one of the Fallen. It would be just like home.

Above him he heard smashing glass. Not a window, something that sounded like a dull thud followed by tinkling. A second, more solid thump followed, and he almost believed that he saw the balcony above him shift under the weight.

He quickly stepped out into the foyer, training his gun on the bedroom door. True enough, two forms raced out, bent low as they charged along the balcony toward the rear of the house. Startled by the direction they'd taken, he was a split second behind them as he fired. His bullets found only plaster; then the two were out of sight behind a turn in the hall above.

A gun poked over the balcony. Firing blind. One of the bullets snicked a bleeding chunk from Dantalion's right thigh and he was forced to swerve away. Back toward the kitchen. In the doorway he searched for the front door. Should have opened it first. But never mind. He'd take his chances. He took from his pocket the lighter he'd used to ignite his cigar earlier. Back out under the balcony, using the wall as a shield, he flipped the top open and spun the wheel of the lighter. A flame guttered, went out. He hissed, spun the wheel again, and this time the flame stood an inch tall.

As he slid the lighter across the floor toward the cooking range, he was already running.

The gas caught with an imploding cough, then expanded as the flames raced through the kitchen.

Two feet from the front door, Dantalion held his breath in anticipation. He grabbed at the handle, tugged open the door, was through it. That was when the flames backed fully down the exposed rubber pipe, found the reserve tank, and exploded like Hiroshima.

The concussion knocked Dantalion sprawling. His ability to hear fled him. His vision was full of raining debris and flames and smoke. His body was pummeled by flying dust and fragments of wood.

But he was happy.

No way the people inside could survive that explosion.

Coming back to his feet, his first concern was for his book. He felt in his pockets as his ears whooshed and squealed, seeking to regain normal function. His book was there, attached to his belt by the ever-present chain.

His next thought: I didn't bring a pen!

There were numbers that needed adding to the list.

10

BRADLEY JORGENSON WAS SOMEONE CA-
pable of beating the woman he suppos-
edly loved, so I should have expected something
like this from him. He didn't want me to burn
down the house where his father's body lay. Fair
enough, I understood that. But my plan to lob
a jury-rigged firebomb at the killer was only to
keep him at bay in the kitchen while we ran
down the stairs. The house was equipped with
a sprinkler system that could handle the local-
ized fire set off by the perfume bomb. In reality
I didn't trust the scent to do more than set off
a sweet-smelling flash, but it would have been
enough to make the killer duck for cover, giving
us the opportunity to get out.

But Jorgenson whacked me over the head with
the goddamn wine bottle, putting paid to those
plans. He hit me hard enough that the bottle
shattered, cutting a strip of flesh from my scalp
and knocking me to the floor. I was disoriented
for a few seconds but not stunned to the point
that I lost my senses. Marianne yelped in dismay
but didn't fight him off as Jorgenson grabbed her
wrists and dragged her past me into the hall. I
made a grab at her but missed, not able to go after

them because of my ignominious position on the floor.

Thankfully they turned to my right. If they'd headed for the stairs the killer would have shot them dead in an instant. In a crouch they ran along the hall. Bullets whacked the wall in their wake, but they managed to gain cover and were— for the moment—safe.

Leaning forward, I hung my SIG over the balcony, shooting blindly at the man below. Then I swung back onto my knees, rolling backward into the bedroom for fear of return fire. My gun was depleted of ammo, so I took the time to eject the magazine, tug a fresh one from my hip pocket, and slam it in place.

I was just coming to my feet when from below me I heard a dull *whumph!* A nanosecond later I was racing across the room, head down, firing repeatedly at the window. The glass was double-glazed and resisted the bullets somewhat. Then I was driving forward, arms folded tight over the top of me. There was one frightening instant when I thought I'd recoil from the window, but then I was through the shattered glass and sailing through space. Around me the air went searing hot, and even though I shouted involuntarily, all the oxygen was sucked out of my lungs.

The sound was deafening, like some angry god had stamped his feet. The concussion of the blast picked me out of the air and sent me somersaulting toward trees. Striking the bole of one of the palms, I'd have split like rotten fruit. Luckily, I hit the hanging fronds first, my body was spun full tilt, and I caromed to the floor through rasping leaves that whipped me mercilessly. Then I slammed the ground with enough force that my internal organs must have gone as flat as pancakes.

For too long I lay there moaning. Glad to be alive, but in agony *everywhere*. It was probably no more than ten seconds in reality, but to my stunned brain it felt like I was prone for a month. The rest and recuperation didn't help. When I finally clawed myself onto my knees, I had to hold that position while my brain tried to right itself in my skull. I needed to vomit, but all that came out was a thin stream of bile. I spat on the mulch to clear my mouth. My eyes were still rattling in my skull, but I saw my SIG lying a few feet away, and trained response made me reach for it.

Making it to my feet, I limped through the bushes, finding my way round the building, looking in hope for any sign that Marianne had got out of there alive. As I went, I wiped the SIG clean on my sweater sleeve.

Jorgenson's house was devastated. The entire upper floor had collapsed onto the ground floor; the roof was a burst-open wreck pushing splintered joists skyward. Flames and smoke broiled against the sky. The condominium I'd leased next door wasn't in much better shape, with the whole front of the building spilling out toward the parking area. The golf buggy I'd rented to get me here from the ferry landing was flattened beneath fallen masonry.

Two cash deposits I wouldn't be getting back, I thought idly.

There was rubble heaped everywhere. Thankfully there weren't any chunks of burned flesh or bones poking from the mounds. That didn't negate the possibility that Marianne was buried beneath the wreckage of the house.

Movement nearby caught my eye. A shadow moving away from me. Wearing a dark suit, neither Jorgenson nor Marianne. The killer, I thought, making his escape. I lifted the SIG, drawing a bead on him. But then I let the barrel drop. The figure had longish fair hair, whereas the killer's had been jet black. For all I knew it was an innocent passerby caught up in the fury of the explosion and staggering away.

Moving back to the side of the building, batting cinders from my hair, I sought where the couple's run would have taken them. The building was still standing here, even if the upper portion now boasted a view to the sky and crenellations that hadn't been there previously. At ground level I saw an open door, steps leading upward. A service stairway down to the Dumpsters stacked against the wall.

The sound of an engine caught my attention.

Spinning on my heels, I ran toward the boundary wall, hooked my elbows over the top, and pulled myself upward. As I cleared the top of the wall, I looked down to where the promontory pushed out into Biscayne Bay.

No sign of Marianne, but I saw Jorgenson

standing in the cabin of his boat. His face was smudged with dirt, but he looked like he'd escaped the explosion without serious injury. I could only hope that Marianne had fared as well. Pulling myself up onto the wall, I shouted to Jorgenson. My voice was lost amid the crackling flames, the creaking of collapsing masonry, the thrum of the boat's engine. But Jorgenson looked my way.

Our eyes met.

Jorgenson snarled something at me. Then the boat was swinging away from the dock, heading for the open water. I watched, feeling more than a little inadequate. Especially when I caught a flash of pale blue sweater and realized that I'd failed to get Marianne away from her abuser.

In my pocket my cell phone vibrated.

Pulling it out, I looked down at the screen. Despite myself, I smiled.

YOU STILL ALIVE?

Pressing buttons, I returned the call.

"Hi, Rink," I said when he answered. "Where are you now?"

"Watching some kinda fireball from out on Biscayne Bay," Rink said. "Don't tell me that was your doing."

"Not responsible," I reassured him.

"But as usual you're smack-dab in the middle of it."

"Who, me?"

Rink laughed to himself. "Glad you're okay, Hunter. Did you get Marianne away?"

"Afraid not," I said. "Something else went down here, Rink. I'm only glad the girl got away safely. We can pick her up later." Then I told him about the killer, and what he'd done.

"Sounds like one desperate son of a bitch," Rink offered. "Any idea who he was? Why he was there?"

"I overheard a little. Sounded like a real sadist: wanted Jorgenson to pick and choose which of them died first."

"Ah, just your typical whacked-out freak with his own agenda, huh?"

"He came across like a psycho killer, Rink. But there was more to it. He was a professional. He wasn't there just to get his kicks. He'd been sent by someone who wants Jorgenson and Marianne dead."

"You said they got away?"

"Yeah. And when this asshole realizes he missed them, he'll be back."

"Yeah," Rink said.

And we'd be waiting.

11 THE DESTRUCTION OF JORGENSON'S HOME WAS all over the news before I even woke up. I was greeted by the early morning paper slapped down on my chest by my big buddy Rink. It had the desired effect of rousing me from troubled dreams where I was engulfed in flames and a demon laughed and tittered at me from behind a wax mask. Sitting bolt upright in my impromptu bed, I found I was on the couch in the front office at Rington Investigations. Took a few seconds of head-shaking to recall the mad flight from Baker Island, dodging police and Coast Guard boats so that I wasn't pulled in as the cause of the conflagration.

Feeling the effects of the evening before in every muscle and bone, I stretched, yawned, then decided I had to get my butt in gear. I could give in to the discomfort, or I could work the kinks out of my aching limbs.

When my eyes were able to focus, I scanned the newspaper. The press had given the explosion all the due of a planet-smashing meteor strike. Speculation was the order of the day. Rescue teams were sifting through the wreckage, but as yet no bodies had been discovered. That simple fact gave us a little breathing space. I threw the paper down and accepted the coffee that Rink held toward me.

The coffee was strong, the rich aroma invading my nigh-empty skull. It was the kick I needed. My injuries were superficial, grazes and scratches, the occasional bruise, and thankfully my bones were intact. The bullet graze on my shoulder hurt like a bitch, but it was more a burn than an open wound. The gash in my scalp had required stitches, and my last memory from the early hours of this morning was Rink coming at me with a tube of Super Glue, a needle, and some catgut. Probing the wound, I decided Rink was no Florence Nightingale, but he'd make the grade at seamstress school.

The difference between the two of us was my ride on an explosion and my crashing fall to the ground, but Rink didn't look to be in much better shape than I was. He had dark smudges beneath his bloodshot eyes like he'd been peeping through keyholes all night. Couldn't have got much sleep, I surmised.

Sometimes Rink seems to read my mind. He nodded me through into his office. His glowing computer monitor cast a cold light on the walls of the otherwise darkened room. Made me feel the chill of the air-conditioning unit. I cupped my mug of coffee in my hands, savoring the steam on my face.

"Been surfing all night, trying to get a handle on who this killer for hire is," he told me. He sat down wearily, his shoulders sinking.

"You look like you could do with some of this."
I held my mug up to him.

"Had a gallon of the stuff already," he said. He
tapped on the keyboard, brought up his e-mail
account. "Been speaking to some people in the
know about these kinds of things."

"Find anything?" I asked. I could tell by the
slump of his shoulders that he hadn't.

"Diddly-squat on the shooter. But there's a guy
here says there's been a bit of a power struggle
going on with the Jorgenson empire. Since Valentin announced his terminal illness and his
impending retirement from the business, people
have been jostling for position. Bradley is in pole
position for taking over the business, as well as
the fortune his family has made over the years.
Couple of runners-up not too happy with the situation. They don't think the company is in safe
hands with Brad. Apparently he hasn't the head
for business his pa and grandpa had."

"You think one of them would go as far as putting out a contract on Bradley? Bit extreme, isn't
it?"

Of course, there maybe wasn't anything extreme about it. Richard Dean had set me on Jorgenson's heels because Jorgenson was a little too
liberal with the amount of contact he was laying
on Dean's daughter. Billions of dollars into the
equation, I didn't doubt it warranted half a dozen
hit men sent his way.

Rink said, "There's any number of people we
could throw into the 'make-Brad-dead' club.

Seems he's pissed off a lot of people. Mainly family."

"What about?"

"The girl. Marianne Dean."

"What? The way he's been treating her?"

"Yeah," Rink said. "But not how you mean. According to some of his nearest and dearest, he should be rid of her. They don't think she meets the high expectations demanded of one in their social circle. He treats her like a princess, and they ain't too happy about it."

"According to her father, Bradley treats her like shit. Beats her and practically keeps her a prisoner. You saw the police report, Rink."

"Saw she had a bashed-up face, but not where it said Bradley was responsible."

"The witnesses. They denied it, too. But if you remember, the gossip was that Bradley beat her after some bad deal went down."

"Someone beat her, that's for sure."

"What're you saying, Rink? That it could've been another one of these disgruntled family members? They beat Marianne so they would get their way with Bradley? Maybe to force him into their line of thinking?"

"Could have been," he said, dismissive. It wasn't like him. He closed down his e-mails. His eyes were downcast. There was something wrong with him, that was for sure.

"You should get some sleep, Rink," I told him.

"No time for sleep," he said, sounding a little like his old self.

"Nothing we can do for now. We don't even know where Jorgenson and Marianne are, let alone the killer." Getting up and leading the way, I hoped that Rink would follow me. He didn't.

"Rink?"

He lowered his face. What is it about men that they don't want to show any weakness? He was my best friend, for Christ's sake. His pain was my pain. I moved back toward him.

"What is it, Rink?"

He coughed. Another male thing. His big fingers, capable of throttling a bullock, trembled over the keyboard. Rink was afraid of something. But I doubted that it had anything to do with hired killers or the dysfunctional state of the Jorgenson family. I'd been there when Rink was going into battle. Like the rest of our Special Forces unit, he was afraid. But he'd practiced the art of compartmentalization—as had I—and could shove that fear to someplace where it didn't inhibit his ability to function. Like the rest of us, he could use that fear to galvanize him. Make him a more efficient soldier. Rink's reticence now, the trembling in his hands, stopped me in my tracks surer than all the bullets ever fired my way.

"I should go to San Francisco, buddy," Rink said.

"Oh."

Rink's parents currently lived in San Francisco. The wheels of trepidation began to churn in my gut. "Tell me, Rink. What's happened?"

"My mother," he said. His eyes closed slowly, and it was all the explanation I required.

"She hasn't . . ."

"Died? No, not yet. But she is very ill." Rink started shutting down the open windows on the computer. "She's had a heart attack, Hunter. I should go to her."

Immediately I said, "I'm coming with you."

Rink shook his head, looked at me with sparkling eyes. "We have a job to do here, Hunter. There's still a girl out there who needs us. There's a chance we can still save her." There was a long pause that was filled only by Rink's harsh breathing. "It's maybe too late to save my mom."

12 DANTALION WAS ON HIS WAY TO NEPTUNE Island, farther up the coast. It wasn't really an island, but a long finger of land separated from the mainland by a marshy inlet bordering the Intracoastal Waterway. At the northern end, a causeway gave access to the island, the causeway constructed so that it was a permanent route and not affected by the tides. At the southernmost tip the coastal highway crossed the inlet on a suspended bridge that attracted weekend naturalists and bird-watchers, who parked on the bridge to watch the wildlife in the estuary below.

It wasn't a densely populated region of Florida.

In fact, one family practically had the sole right to call Neptune its own.

For three generations the Jorgenson estate had claimed much of the land that constituted Neptune's Atlantic shoreline. Since the late 1950s the family had purchased or built twelve family houses on the land. Each house was distinct in itself, but all were enclosed within a single wall that stretched almost three miles down the coast. At intersections every four hundred yards, access to the Jorgenson estate was gained by gates that were under twenty-four-hour surveillance.

CCTV cameras were mounted on tall poles between each gate, so there was nowhere along the three-mile stretch where an intruder could gain entry without a swift visit from the armed security guards who patrolled the grounds.

On the coast side, men in boats patrolled back and forth both night and day and enforced an exclusion zone of almost a quarter mile offshore.

Some would think that the security measures were extreme. But the Jorgensons were implicitly tied to the military, and their secrets were protected almost as though they were a principality that the U.S. military depended upon for its survival.

Dantalion had no worries about getting in. He was too good at his job to doubt himself.

There was always the fuckup last night, but he wouldn't let that ruin his self-confidence. At the end of the day, he'd successfully completed his mission. Killed the targets and then some. It was just a pity he hadn't been able to look into Bradley Jorgenson's face at the end. He always liked to watch as the final grains of life sifted away like sand in an hourglass.

He would have preferred to see the gunman dead, too. His unwelcome arrival had spoiled Dantalion's plans for torturing Jorgenson. He'd been looking forward to killing the girl in front of him, then putting a bullet into each of Jorgenson's limbs. Lastly he'd have gut-shot him, made him squirm in his own spilled innards while Dantalion told him who it was that wanted him dead. It would have been beautiful.

He was driving a minivan. Blacked-out windows helped keep the sun off his exposed limbs, but there was another ulterior motive: they kept CCTV observation to a minimum. The van would be spotted, yes, but not the driver. He could drive by and scout the perimeter without alerting anyone to his identity. Unconcerned, they wouldn't be ready for the visit he'd pay them this evening.

Before arriving at the Jorgenson estate, he pulled into a layover, parking the minivan beneath a copse of trees. Afforded shade, he lowered the window and peered across the marshlands that stretched toward the Atlantic. A flight of birds streaked through the pale blue sky, heading south, as if they had a premonition of what was to come and wanted nothing to do with it.

On the passenger seat next to him, Dantalion laid his book of lists. He was tempted to look at it. Go over the numbers in his head, try to match them to the people he had killed over the twenty-two years he'd been engaged in the murder trade. The first few numbers were easy to recall. First, his abusive uncle. Second, his school friend Tyler. After that things grew a little foggy. The faces tended to meld and swirl in his mind. A week ago he'd murdered Caitlin Moore, her husband, *and* her child. That one stuck in his mind. He regretted having to kill the little girl, but she'd woken from the mild dose of sodium amytal he'd injected into her. Couldn't leave a witness who could describe his appearance, could he? Shame really, after he'd gone with Caitlin's decision, killing Nate, and had promised her that her daughter would be safe.

Then there were those he'd killed on yesterday's mission.

The boat owner was collateral damage. He didn't really count, but he was still given a number. Two bodyguards, a maid, Valentin and Bradley Jorgenson, and Marianne Dean. Last, but not least, the assassin sent to kill him after the job was done. Dantalion touched his thigh where the gunman's bullet had nicked him. The guy had been good, but not as good as he was.

He would show his client the folly of sending someone second-rate after a master killer.

From his deep pockets he pulled out his Blackberry. Bringing up the Internet, he deftly keyed in numbers that would put him in touch with an associate. In code Dantalion inquired as to the successful completion of payment for his services. Was not happy when informed that the client had reneged on the arrangement. Confirmation of death had not been announced.

"What is wrong with these people?" he asked out loud.

After he'd fled the scene of destruction, he had to use all his cunning to avoid the en masse arrival of police and fire department personnel. The fire wouldn't have taken that much dampening down—once the propane tanks were secured and isolated in the adjoining properties, the task of sifting through the rubble would have begun. They had to be pulling out charred corpses by now.

Okay, it was still early, give them a little time. Florida's bravest had a difficult job to do.

Charred corpses often took time to identify.

It just annoyed him that his client hadn't the confidence in him to see that he'd done *exactly* what he'd agreed to do. Just in a more dramatic fashion.

There was, of course, another reason why the fee had not been delivered to his account.

His client had sent a killer after Dantalion. Maybe he thought his gunman had killed him. Why pay money that would end up languishing in an account as dead as the man with the codes to access it?

Dantalion would show Petre Jorgenson the error of such thinking.

13

WHAT SURPRISED ME MOST WAS THAT BRAD-
ley Jorgenson didn't run directly to the
police. He was a man of power and could have
demanded that the weight of the entire police
force be thrown into finding the person responsible for the attack on his home. Instead, he
seemed reluctant to cooperate with the officers
on the case, stonewalling and throwing up bar-
riers in the form of disgustingly highly paid legal
advisers to allow him immunity from the ensu-
ing investigation.

It wouldn't last, but for now Jorgenson and
Marianne Dean were in hiding and refusing to
answer any questions.

Their refusal to talk was a relief in some respects. I didn't want to spend half the day answering questions and denying allegations that I
was anything but a concerned citizen who had
tried to intervene during a murder spree. Marianne could easily have dropped me in it by talking about our meeting in the garden before the
killer's arrival. It would have shown that I had
more than chance involvement. Some could
even read into my presence at the scene something that wasn't true: that I had foreknowledge

of what was about to happen. In some schools of thought, that would make me an accessory to the crime. If that was the case I'd be seeing much more of the inside of police stations than could be achieved in half a day. At the very least my movements would be curtailed, and I would be useless to Marianne. There'd be no way I could save her if I was locked up in the Dade County jail awaiting trial.

Not that the police would immediately link me to the Joseph Evans who'd taken out the lease on the adjoining property, but once the federal government became involved—and for a case of this magnitude I knew that it would—my fingerprints would throw up an interesting connection to certain military records. With my background, my proximity to the scene would raise more than a few eyebrows. There'd be no talk of coincidence. Christ, I'd be lucky if the entire shitstorm wasn't blamed on me.

Rink shut down his office, and taking his Porsche Boxster we traveled across the state. The Ford Explorer would have made traveling more comfortable for two big guys, but I'd had to abandon it last night at Miami Beach. Could be that by now the vehicle was in some chop shop in SoBe and I'd never see it again.

We cut across the state, skirting Bartow, then a series of low-lying lakes and open grasslands with the occasional outcropping of pine, and ended up at Fort Pierce, where we picked up Route 1 south. On our left was a peninsula that hugged the coastline, separated from the mainland by an open stretch of tidal sands.

Another hour or so would get us to the gated community on Neptune Island.

We were on our way to confront Bradley Jorgenson.

We'd made the decision to lay all our cards on the table. Speak to Jorgenson. Brush the punk off if he stood in the way of freedom for Marianne, if in fact that was what she wanted.

I'd begun to have doubts after seeing how she'd clung to him when she thought they were about to die. Her words in response to the killer's demand that Jorgenson chose who died first.

"*Mari,*" Jorgenson had said to her, "*I'm sorry I dragged you into this, babe.*"

"*Not . . . your . . . fault,*" she'd whispered back.

At first I hadn't taken much notice of the words. I was more concerned with what the killer had to say for himself. But thinking back I remembered the softness of her voice. No hint of vehemence or even resignation. She'd meant what she said. They sounded like words spoken by someone deeply in love. Certainly not by one fearful of the person she spoke to.

Then there was Rink's hint that everything might not be as clear-cut as it seemed. That perhaps Marianne's injuries weren't caused by Bradley, that they could be down to another person with a reason to hurt her. Witnesses said that Jorgenson had been arguing with someone else. A family member perhaps? Shortly afterward Marianne had been taken to the emergency room for treatment of her injuries. Two and two were put together. Maybe the witnesses weren't so great at counting.

Then there was the least incriminating detail of all. Something that told me that Bradley perhaps wasn't the worst monster involved here. Maybe it was the same person who wanted them dead that was responsible for hurting Marianne the first time round. When I'd first laid eyes on Bradley at Baker Island, he was arguing with someone on his phone. Had he been under threat then? He'd denied the demands of whoever it was. Perhaps that had been a last-ditch effort at bending Bradley to the caller's wishes. When that hadn't worked, had the hit man been the next course of action?

The killer had arrived at Jorgenson's home on Baker Island at someone's bidding. He was intent on killing not just the heir to the Jorgenson billions, but also Marianne. My appearance had maybe stopped the killer, but when push came to shove, Bradley had gone out of his way to protect his girl. I was still pissed that he had cracked me over the head with the wine bottle, but I couldn't really blame him. I was just another man with a gun placing his woman in danger. If the roles had been reversed, I'd have done the same, and a damn sight more.

Rink was very quiet on the drive over. Even getting closer to Neptune Island he had more on his mind than what our impromptu visit could stir up.

His mother, Yukiko, was possibly dying. He should have been with her for her final days, but he'd chosen to be there with me. If I had it my way he'd have been on the first airplane out to San Francisco. But I knew how Rink's mind worked. Men of duty accept their lot without question.

There's an old samurai adage that when it rains the warrior continues to walk up the center of the road. His path is set, and he must not deviate from it. The untrained run for cover and get soaked anyway by the water pouring from the eaves of the houses they seek shelter beneath. The warrior knows that he will get wet, so allows fate to take its course. He cannot stop the rain. He cannot stop death. So he accepts it.

At a service station outside Port Saint Lucie we stopped to refuel, then ordered takeout from the attached diner. The cheeseburger I'd wished for last night had never transpired, so I ate this latest one with the gusto of a starving man. The fries went down well, too. While I carried my greasy papers over to a trash can, Rink made a telephone call he'd been dreading.

Andrew Rington was of Scottish descent. In his thinking all this samurai shit could take a backseat when it came to family. His clan mentality dictated that there was nothing more important than family ties. I was with him on that one. Rink had inherited his size and build from Andrew's side of the family, but his mind was definitely from that of his mother. Duty would prevail, and his father would come round to the idea. But he'd likely bawl Rink out before coming to that resolution.

When I got back to the Porsche, Rink had finished speaking. I'd picked the farthest trash can I could find, and hung about watching the gnats buzzing round it for more than five minutes. Who knew what anyone watching me would have thought? Amateur entomologist, I'd have told them.

"How's Yukiko?"

"Hanging in there," Rink said. He ghosted a smile, but it was too laden with sadness to be anything but a front.

"She's a tough lady. How's your father handling things?"

"He's a tough guy," Rink said. This time his smile held more spirit. Maybe I was wrong about the balance of genes that made up Jared Rington. For a second there he looked—and sounded—the double of his dad.

Living in Little Rock, Arkansas, Hitomi Yukiko was only five years old when the Imperial Japanese Army declared war on the United States by launching an attack on Pearl Harbor. The little girl named "Snow Child" was interned along with her parents at Rohwer—a Japanese-American "relocation center"—by the very people who for two generations had been her neighbors. Following the devastation wreaked upon the Japanese mainland by the payload of the *Enola Gay*, the Hitomi family might understandably have fled back to their ancestral land with a curse on their lips for the USA. Except that they were here as U.S. citizens and did not want to leave their home. Yukiko was seventeen when she met her husband to be, Andrew Rington, a Scottish-Canadian serviceman returning from the Korean War. Five years later they married. Yukiko bore three children: Yuko, a girl child who died shortly after birth; Ronald, a son who would later die while serving in Kuwait; and then, when she was at an age when she might have been content with nursing memories of the girl she'd lost, she birthed Jared. Nevertheless, both Yukiko and Andrew cherished their baby boy.

They both still did.

As much as Rink cherished them in return.

I had a feeling that, down the line somewhere, Rink's decision to stay and help me would come back to haunt him.

"Told my father I'd be there as soon as we got finished with this," Rink said.

I laid a hand on his shoulder.

"Okay, Rink," I said. "Let's get it done, then."

14

NEPTUNE ISLAND WAS MORE THAN A HOME TO the Jorgenson clan; it was also an integral part of the superstructure of the coastal highway that ran all the way from Key West in Florida to Fort Kent in Maine. The megawealthy family could purchase the island, but they couldn't stop the flow of traffic up and down the coast. The route was an alternative to I-95, the picture-perfect tourist route, so was packed at certain times of the year with vacationers traversing the coastline between Miami and Jacksonville. On the sandbanks and dunes that made up much of the coastal lands, vacationers would often camp out, wandering down onto the beaches and searching for sea turtles in the shallow tropical waters. Overnight camping wasn't permitted on Neptune Island, but there was no law against people stopping for short spells at any of the layovers next to the road.

Slightly farther to the south and west, tropical palms and trees such as mahogany and gumbo-limbo were prolific, but here on the Atlantic shoreline the predominant trees were oaks, pines, and willows. Much of the forest had been cut down to make way for the highways and towns that sprawled up the coast, but out on Neptune some copses had survived. Grass was dominant, in the form of waist-high, sharp-toothed saw grass. Occasional limestone outcrops formed hummocks of higher ground where the indigenous wildlife made their homes. Vacationers, cameras in hand, would traipse through the grasses in hope of snapping pictures of raccoons, marsh rabbits, and—if they were truly lucky—bobcats.

Dantalion had no interest in wildlife, but in the guise of a bird-watching tourist, he found he had free rein to conduct surveillance of the Jorgenson compound without fear of discovery. He was only one of approximately a dozen tourists he'd seen armed with high-powered binoculars. He had dressed appropriately to fit in with the scene. He had on a cream hat and dark glasses. His shirt was a gaudy Hawaiian number, designed apparently by a disciple of Jackson Pollock on a seriously mind-bending LSD trip. He had on long khaki shorts, and on his feet he wore a pair of shabby deck shoes. He'd applied hydrocortisone cream liberally to his exposed arms and shins, but that was in keeping with the smears of high-factor sunscreen he'd seen on others' lily-white skin. He blended in nicely with those first- or second-day Europeans protecting themselves from the scorching sun. Over one shoulder he carried a bag that bounced uncomfortably on his hip with each step. Inside were his 90two Beretta, a half-dozen spare ammunition magazines, and his book of numbers.

The bullet wound he'd taken to his thigh caused him to limp. But that was good, it added to his disguise.

He didn't look at all like a killer.

But he was.

At its southernmost tip, the island had been artificially built up to support the road bridge that then arched toward the mainland. Under the structure of the bridge, Dantalion walked, his deck shoes disappearing beneath the silt. There was a family out on the tidal sands, turning over rocks, a child hoisting a trophy in the air with a shout of glee. The trophy squirmed in his hand, chitinous legs working furiously, and the little boy dropped it with a squawk of alarm. The family laughed at him as he ran away to avoid the crab's fury.

Dantalion paid them only minimal attention. He wasn't one for human interaction. They were beneath him. Good for only two things: doing his bidding and paying him money. Correction, there was a third thing they could do for him: they could die in agony and fear.

Momentarily he considered pulling out his gun and shooting the entire family. Their laughter grated on his bones, reminding him of all the spiteful laughter he'd had to endure growing up. The only thing that saved them was that he wasn't in a counting mood. The formula for writing their individual numbers wasn't the simplest of processes but one that took concentration. Didn't want to spoil his list with incorrect calculations.

Away from the shadows of the bridge, he walked again in direct sunlight. He could feel the prickle on the back of his neck, and his calf muscles felt as if someone was holding a blowtorch to them. Sand stung as it hit and adhered to his skin. He pushed into the tall saw-tooth grass, and if anything, things got worse. The grass snagged him and made tiny itching cuts in his flesh. Enough to send him insane.

But he wasn't insane. He was a professional.

He didn't give in to mild discomforts such as these.

In the past, he'd stoically taken the beatings doled out by the older kids. Smiled at them when they were too exhausted to strike him again. When enduring many hours in hospitals, he hadn't once complained. He accepted the reality of his existence. From birth to death, existence is measured in a series of chapters governed by various levels of pain, some greater than others. Some are easy to recognize. Birth is a screaming, howling experience. Growing, stumbling, taking the knocks in life is a form of physical, mental, and emotional torture. There is loss and then there is grief. Then you die, and it's a lucky one who doesn't perish in agony. In comparison to some things he'd put up with, pressing on through the grasses was almost akin to bliss.

He was a professional.

He wasn't insane. Fair enough, he accepted that his penchant for killing probably was tied to a psychopathic quirk, but he wasn't mad in the sense that other killers were mad. He was not a deviant who killed for the pleasure of collecting trophies, or to sate his need for sexual dominance over a weaker creature. He did not flay the hide from women to make himself a housecoat or lampshade, and he did not keep the petrified remains of his mother locked up in an attic, then run around in her clothes slicing up nubile young women.

He killed because that was what he was good at.

He killed because it paid him well.

He killed because he had a strict purpose.

The others, those whom he personally chose to kill, were merely a by-product of his assumed persona. It didn't take a talented assassin to drive by a victim, poke a gun out of a window, and shoot a man dead as he stepped down from his front porch. Any half-assed idiot with a gun could do that. But such actions quickly got them caught. Or killed. Dantalion murdered in a fashion that was more thoughtful, planned to create impact. The style of his killings mimicked the actions of a deranged serial killer, not of a hired assassin. It wasn't always apparent who his intended victim was. He or she was lost among the body count. Law enforcement and FBI VICAP teams were scratching their heads, searching for elusive maniacs, but the murders would never be tied to him.

Plus, the randomness of the deaths made his clients fear him. It added to his mystery and ensured that his reputation as a master of his craft guaranteed full and prompt payment. No one wanted to chance upsetting him. They knew where that would get them.

Most of his victims were collateral damage. But they served his purpose well. Success bred success. The more he killed, the more often he was sought out. The higher the fee he could set.

He had no reservations about killing those innocents he chose. They were only props for the theater of his schemes. Also, he shared the blame around. Everything shouldn't be ladled onto his conscience. He allowed his victims a choice. Who dies first? How do they die? If they pointed the finger at their loved ones, then so be it, it was out of his hands. He was only the tool that completed *their* wishes. It was fucked-up reasoning, he accepted that, but it was a coping mechanism he embraced. It relieved him of the burden of guilt and allowed him to continue doing what he did best.

No, he wasn't insane.

Crazy men don't know they are crazy. And neither do they question their actions.

Psychopaths don't deliberate over death the way he did. They certainly don't share out the glory. They keep it all to their greedy selves.

Crazy men do take on personas. But so do hired killers. They never use their real names. Not in a craft that demands anonymity and mystery. Jean-Paul St. Pierre wouldn't bring the clients running to pay high fees for his services. When in his teens he'd shed his old Mississippi beliefs, he'd turned to esoteric books and lore for the perfect incarnation of the professional killer he would become.

In *The Book of Enoch* he'd found the perfect match. Dantalion was one of the angels cast out of Heaven by Gabriel and the army of God. The panoply of the Fallen were numbered, and the seventy-first spirit was Dantalion. He was a great and mighty duke of Hell. According to legend, he appeared in the form of a man with many countenances, all men's and all women's faces. For one as androgynous as he, and with his talent for disguise, what better physical description could there be? The angel Dantalion was said to know the thoughts of all men and women. He carried them in a book, and could change them at will. This modern Dantalion also had the knack for bending people's resolve and for jotting down the sum of their lives within his own book. He had the power of life and death over them.

Crossing the grasslands, he paused to bring the binoculars to his eyes. He watched the birds rooting among the reeds for insects, looking like every other bird-watcher in the region. Then he casually swung his view past the turreted gate on the Jorgenson estate wall. Near to the shoreline, this gate wasn't used for access on a daily— possibly not even a yearly—basis. It was a relic from almost half a century ago, a way down to the coast dating from long before the suspended road had been built nearby. He could imagine the folk from simpler times wandering out of their gardens onto the beach here. Perhaps carrying a picnic basket and a blanket to lounge upon. Maybe Valentin Jorgenson had enjoyed boy-hood playtimes on this very portion of the beach. Before he was molded into the successful busi-nessman who would continue the legacy started by his own father. Before the cancer that blighted him in his last few months. Before Dantalion put some well-placed rounds through him last night.

A wrought-iron gate barred progress into the grounds. It was in need of a coat of paint, and the corrosive sea winds had turned the metal rusty. The chain and padlock holding it in place were equally rusted. A sign was riveted to the wall next to the gate.

NO ENTRY WITHOUT PERMISSION—PRIVATE PROPERTY

Like that was going to deter Dantalion.

A fortunate occurrence presented itself. A rare Snail Kite soared through the sky and perched on the wall near the gate. Dantalion, binocu-lars fixed to his face, walked closer. Studying, studying. Not the bird. He could see that the lock would be easily shattered by a 9 mm round from his Beretta. He could be inside in seconds.

The bird streaked away. He wandered away, too. But he'd be back later.

15

"WE'RE HERE TO SPEAK TO BRADLEY JORGENSON."

"Name?"

"He doesn't know my name."

"Then he isn't expecting you?"

"No, he wouldn't be."

"Then you'll have to make an appointment through his office. You have the contact details?"

"No, I don't."

"Then I'm afraid it's impossible to see him. We are currently experiencing unwanted attention from the media and I have express orders to send everyone through Mr. Jorgenson's press office. Good day, sir. Please move your vehicle so it isn't blocking the access drive."

The intercom was switched off, the active green light dying. I leaned away from it back into the Porsche and looked across at Rink. His eyebrows jerked but that was the sum of his contribution.

I pressed the buzzer again.

"Sir, I already told you . . ."

I didn't listen to the guard's words. I swung open the car door and went up to the gate. Peering up at the CCTV camera above it, my hands clenched by my sides, I shouted, "Speak to Jorgenson. Tell the ungrateful son of a bitch that

Joe Hunter is here. He'd have died last night if it wasn't for me."

Turning back to the buzzer on the intercom, I pressed my finger to it. Held the button depressed. Somewhere on the property the buzzer would be shrieking in protestation, probably sending the guard insane.

The tableau held for the best part of two minutes.

Then from within the compound I heard the grumble of approaching engines. Letting go of the buzzer, I said into the speaker, "Now that wasn't so difficult, was it?"

The guard didn't respond. Maybe he was in one of the two dark silver sedans approaching the gate.

The sedans drew to a halt on the road beyond the gate. Men got out. Four big guys with guns under their jackets. They eyed me coolly, the way a pack of jackals would challenge a lion. Together they could likely bring me down, but not one at a time. Rink got out of the car and stood beside me. The odds now tipped the scale firmly in my favor. Rink's presence often had that effect.

One of the guards, a self-appointed delegate, stepped forward. He was a man edging fifty years old, but he still retained a hard body and steady eyes. His brush cut indicated he was ex-army as much as his straight back and staccato movements.

"What is your business here?" he demanded.

"None of yours," I told him.

I wasn't interested in any of Jorgenson's hired

guns. Looking past the man to the second sedan, I called, "You can see me, Bradley. Same guy as last night. You would have died if I wasn't there. The way I see it, you at least owe me a couple minutes of your time."

I waited, and the man with the brush cut continued giving me dead eyes. After what seemed to be an hour, but was only half a minute, the driver's window in the second car slid open. The driver didn't say anything. To Brush Cut he just inclined his head in silent communication. Then the second vehicle began reversing up the drive. There was a turning circle twenty paces back, and the sedan swung around and continued up the road.

"You'll have to step back from the gate," Brush Cut said.

About to argue, I felt Rink's fingers brush my wrist. One of the other guards had stepped over to a box on a pole. He pressed a button and the huge gates began swinging toward us. We were forced to take a couple of steps backward to avoid being swatted aside.

"Come with us," Brush Cut commanded.

"We'll bring our own car," Rink said. His tone said he'd brook no argument.

Brush Cut looked at Rink. Then at me. He sniffed once, then turned on his heel, indicating that the others should get back in the car. Only the man at the gate controls waited.

Back in the Porsche, Rink drove through the gate and past the sedan. He pulled into the turning circle, waiting until the gate guard was back in the sedan and it had gone past us. Then we followed.

"Well, that was easier than we thought," I said to Rink.

"Could be taking us somewhere less public to shoot us," Rink said.

We followed the sedan along the road and came to a collection of houses, almost a village community in itself. We passed them, and I thought they must be on-site housing accommodation for the large number of staff that had to be employed on the estate. At its highest point, Neptune Island was only a few meters above sea level. The ground swelled at its center, then quickly dipped down toward the shoreline. The houses built just above the shoreline were large and impressive, more like the stately homes back in the UK than any I expected to find on the Florida coast. They were set at intervals of perhaps a quarter mile apart, like the forts the Roman Empire once built to guard its frontiers.

The sedan angled toward the largest house of all. It would only be about fifty years old, but the architects had to have drawn inspiration from Victorian times. A bird's-eye view would have seen an immense sprawl of red slate roof, shaped like a capital H. My angle showed me a three-story wing at either side, attached by a cross section that had windows extending from the roofline to a yard or so above the ground. The windows were like those seen in cathedrals, but without the colored glass. Kind of excessive, however much money you had to waste.

The silver sedan that I assumed had held Bradley Jorgenson was already there but was now empty. The driver was sitting on the hood of his vehicle. His arms were crossed, one hand nonchalantly dipping into the folds of his jacket. A second man stood on the far side, and he was a lot more obvious about the way he held an Uzi submachine gun braced across his stomach. The second sedan pulled up next to it, leaving room for Rink's Porsche between the two of them.

Brush Cut and his three companions climbed out of their vehicle, circling like sharks round the Porsche. They were all holding sidearms.

Climbing out, we were clear on our intentions. Our guns remained out of sight and we showed our empty palms. Brush Cut pointed a Glock 17 at my chest.

"You can drop the posturing," I said to Brush Cut. "We're not here to cause trouble. We're here to help Jorgenson."

"We don't need any help." Brush Cut waved us toward the house with a jerk of his gun. "We can handle things, I promise you."

Beside me, Rink grumbled to himself. He wasn't the only one bemoaning how amateur these guys were. What kind of bodyguards allow armed men to bring a vehicle directly up to the house where their principal is in residence? We could have a bomb under the hood for all they knew. Despite their guns, I was pretty sure Rink and I could draw and fire and all six of them would be dead or injured in seconds. Any other time, I imagined, Rink would have laughed in Brush Cut's face. But Rink wasn't in the best of moods. Neither was I.

"Where's Jorgenson?"

"Inside."

He made it sound like an order, but that's where we wanted to be at any rate. We walked quickly toward a large wooden door, causing the others to stumble into a ragged skirmish line behind us. They were like children falling in behind the toughest kids in school.

The door swung open before we reached it, and we were greeted by another couple of rent-a-punks. These two were your typical intimidators, man mountains with shaven heads, broken noses, and tattoos on their depressed knuckles. I brushed by them, not intimidated. It's not guys with smashed-up faces that you have to fear, it's the ones who are unmarked, the ones who win all the fights. Sounds a little pompous, but neither Rink nor I has the face of a second-rate punk.

Jorgenson was waiting for us in a huge room shelved floor to ceiling with a library of books to rival a university for knowledge. A cursory glance showed me that most of the titles were in northern European languages. Jorgenson was sitting behind a huge mahogany desk, elbows splayed, his chin resting in his hands. He watched our entry with a look of bored resignation.

"You made it out of the house, then? I thought I saw you looking over the wall afterward."

"Yeah, I made it out. No thanks to you," I said. "Didn't help being crowned with a bottle just before the place went up."

He sat up a little straighter. His palms fell open. "I couldn't be sure whose side you were really on."

"I wasn't the one shooting at you."

"You were about to burn down the house."

"I think that's academic now," I pointed out, "considering what happened."

A shadow crossed his face. "They still haven't found my father."

Brush Cut and one other had followed us into the room. The others all assumed various poses of menace in the hallway.

"Relax, will you, Jorgenson? If I was going to kill you I'd have done it by now." I held his gaze and he finally gave a nod in return. He waved the pack away, but indicated that Brush Cut and the other man should stay handy. I said, "Better if we spoke in private."

"You haven't killed me yet," Jorgenson replied. "Doesn't mean you won't."

Rink laughed sardonically. "You think these frog-giggin' assholes would stop us?"

"Hey!" Brush Cut said. He stepped up close, realized just how big Rink was, and faltered. Rink turned his head to regard the man as though he were something he'd tracked in on his boots.

"Try it, buddy," Rink said. "Go on. I'm in the right mood for slapping someone down."

Jorgenson smiled at the testosterone-charged atmosphere. "Mr. Seagram is a highly regarded executive protector. He came from the Marine Corps with top recommendations."

"Hurrah," Rink grunted. "What did you do in the service, Seagram? Cook?"

"West Point," Seagram stated.

Rink sniffed, unimpressed. "Yeah, they have cooks there. Decent cooks, I'll give you that."

Seagram looked like he'd been slapped. But I could tell his mind was caught in flux. Rink had insulted him and paid a compliment in the same breath. Rink grinned, showing he was just ragging him. It was one of those forces things where all soldiers put down anyone who wasn't in their own troop. Seagram stepped away, at a loss about how to respond.

"Are we all finished now?" Jorgenson asked.

"We haven't started yet," I told him.

"That's true. I don't even know who you are."

"Where's Marianne?"

"Why do you want to know?"

"Because we're here more for her than for you."

"Can I ask why?"

"You can ask."

He shook his head. "Can I ask who you are?"

"I'm Joe Hunter."

"What about him?" Jorgenson looked at Rink.

"*He* can speak for himself," Rink said. "My friends call me Rink. But you can call me Jared Rington." He turned and shot a wink at Seagram. "Mr. Rington to you."

Seagram hissed something under his breath. He turned his back on us, walked over, and leaned against the bookshelves. The other man, who'd remained silent throughout, blinked rapidly, looking from Seagram to Jorgenson. He was a whip-thin man with spiky, sandy-colored hair and freckles. He wasn't long out of high school, judging by his fresh face. Looked like he wished he were back there instead of here.

"What's your interest in me?" Jorgenson asked.

"Zero. It's Marianne we've come about."

Jorgenson's lips twitched down. "Marianne doesn't know you, either. She told me about speaking to you in the garden. But she says that she's never seen you before. Is that true?"

"Do you doubt her?"

"No." Jorgenson stared into my eyes. "I love her."

"Tough love," Rink muttered.

Jorgenson snapped his gaze on Rink. Color flushed up from his throat, making his cheeks a dapple of red blotches.

"What does *that* mean?" he demanded.

Stepping forward, I leaned one fist on his desk. Time to interject, I thought. Rink wasn't in the best frame of mind to lead the negotiations. "Forget it," I told him. "What I'm concerned with is what happened last night. The man at your house was there to kill the two of you. We're committed to protecting Marianne. Now, you say you love her. If that's the case, you will want Marianne to be protected. Seems to me that we're on the same page."

"We don't need you," Seagram said from the far side of the room.

"You don't?"

Jorgenson said, "I trust my staff to protect us."

"You shouldn't. They opened the gate to men they know nothing about, allowed us to carry guns inside. We parked a car outside that could be packed with Semtex for all they knew."

Jorgenson nodded along with my reasoning. But then his finger came up and wagged in my direction. "But that was after I'd viewed you on the security system. I recognized you. Like you said earlier, if you were going to kill me, you'd have done so by now."

"Fair enough. I would have."

"I take it you have some kind of offer in mind?"

"Not interested in working for you, if that's what you're thinking."

Jorgenson shrugged. He acknowledged Seagram. "I'm happy with who I have already."

"Fine," I said. "But I want to speak to Marianne. If she wants us, then we will work for her."

"And if I don't allow that?"

"Then we're going to have a problem."

16 BACK IN HIS MINIVAN, DANTALION HEADED north. Following the boundary wall of the estate, he scouted out other entry points should his first plan fail. The wall was twelve feet tall in most places. Nothing as crass as razor wire had been installed, but he had the feeling that pressure pads would be laid along the top and numerous more would be sown inside the perimeter. They could prove a problem, but not insurmountable to someone with his skills. The CCTV cameras weren't too much of a concern, either. A well-aimed shot would put a camera out of commission. A system with so many cameras would be prone to occasional malfunction; by the time a maintenance crew had come out to investigate the dysfunctional camera, he'd have been in and out again and his business would be done.

But he had more to worry about than cameras and pressure pads. He could hear distant barking. The estate was guarded by patrol dogs. It would take a master magician to spirit himself in and out of an enemy stronghold where trained attack dogs were running loose. Sometimes he wished his assumed identity came with all the trappings of the original Dantalion. Dark angels have nothing to fear from dogs. Being a mere mortal still, he'd have to come up with a contingency plan.

He took out his Blackberry, checked for messages. Nothing new. Just the same old message from his associate about the nonarrival of his fee. One hand on the wheel, he thumbed in a message, requesting what he needed, then sent the e-mail spinning through cyberspace.

Eyes off the road for a split second, he almost missed seeing the occupants of the car passing him on the other side of the road. However, something subliminal grabbed at his mind, made him glance at the Porsche Boxster in a moment of admiration for the superior vehicle. The small, sleek beauty was the black of glistening tar. The man driving the vehicle was of no concern to him; he was a muscular brute with straight black hair and tawny skin. He had a scar across his chin that was as livid white as was Dantalion's entire body. It was the passenger who caught his attention.

He wasn't as big as the driver, rangier of build than he was muscular, with the broad shoulders of a swimmer or gymnast. His short brown hair had only the faintest hint of gray at the temples. He had the kind of face that could blend in with a crowd, but the intensity of his eyes would forever set him apart. Women would love those eyes; men would fear them.

Dantalion cursed under his breath.

The gunman from last night.

"How the fuck did you survive *that* explosion?" he asked out loud.

But then the Porsche was by him and he was left wondering if perhaps he'd been wrong. Maybe it was someone else. He hadn't got a good look; maybe the man in the passenger seat was merely someone with a passing resemblance to the one who'd almost killed him.

His hand crept to his thigh. The bullet wound was a constant ache radiating through the entire muscle, up his hip to his spine. Conversely, he viewed the wound as being fortunate: if he'd been standing another few inches to the right, the gunman's bullet would have found a more fatal target than his leg.

Whoever that man had been, he couldn't possibly have escaped the exploding building. Dantalion had heard him retreat into the bedroom just as he had brought flame to the lighter. There had only been seconds before detonation.

No. The would-be assassin was as dead as everyone else in the house. He was already numbered in Dantalion's book. Just below Bradley Jorgenson and Marianne Dean. The numbers never, ever lied.

Still, he looked for a place to turn, and then spun the vehicle around and pushed the minivan after the Porsche. The man had the eyes of a killer. Even if he happened to be an unfortunate doppelgänger, Dantalion decided he had to find out. Perhaps he'd even have to kill the man.

Almost a mile later, Dantalion drove by the main entrance to the Jorgenson estate. He was intent on catching up with the Porsche and almost missed it. The vehicle was parked outside the entrance gate. The two from the Porsche were talking to some of Jorgenson's security men who were standing on the far side. He only got a fleeting glance and couldn't be sure if the shorter of the two men from the Porsche was the man from yesterday. He had his back to Dantalion and his clothing was different. One thing he did notice, though: the face of one of the security men. Dantalion recognized it. The one with the brush cut. He'd been one of the men with Petre Jorgenson yesterday. One of those who'd feigned interest in the statue of Christopher Columbus at Bayfront Park in Miami.

Doing the arithmetic in his head, there was only one answer. Brush Cut had been with Petre. His client had asked him to kill Bradley and Marianne Dean. A mystery man had turned up, almost killing Dantalion. A mystery man who bore more than a passing resemblance to the hired killer was now talking to Brush Cut. It could only mean one thing: Dantalion had definitely been set up to die by Petre.

He turned the minivan around.

Sped back northward.

He pressed the button to lower the window. Pulled free his Beretta, hanging it out of the window.

It didn't take a talented assassin to drive by a victim, poke a gun out of a window, and shoot a man dead as he stepped down from his front porch. Any half-assed idiot with a gun could do that. But such actions quickly got them caught. Or killed. Dantalion murdered in a fashion that was more thoughtful than that, planned to create impact. But just now and again a good old drive-by shooting was just what was required.

He slowed down as he again approached the gate. Held the gun steady against the window ledge.

But he was too late.

The Porsche was already inside the compound, following a silver sedan farther into the grounds. Other men were climbing into a second silver sedan. One of them was Brush Cut. A single guard was standing next to a control box, and the gate was swinging shut. Dantalion pulled the Beretta back inside just as the guard glanced his way. Dantalion gave the man a nod, as though he was a tourist enjoying the drive and greeting every other person he met along the way. The guard didn't even notice. Dantalion sped up.

Opportunities like that one didn't present themselves too often. He'd missed it. But this evening he'd make his own opportunities, and this time he would not miss.

17

"WHO ARE YOU?"

The same question kept being asked of me. I suppose this time I owed more of an explanation than simply my name and that I was there to help. Marianne deserved as much.

"My name is Joe Hunter," I said.

"So you weren't lying." I didn't quite catch her meaning, and she went on, "Yesterday, when you introduced yourself, you told me you were called Joe."

"I wasn't lying about what else I said."

"That you were there to help?"

We were in a room adjacent to the library. Rink was keeping Bradley, Seagram, and the third man company. I only hoped that Rink's surliness didn't cause a confrontation before I could reassure Marianne of our good intentions.

She'd changed since I saw her last.

She had on black trousers and pumps, a pale cream blouse. But that's not what I meant.

She looked different.

Her light brown hair was loose, full of body as though recently blown dry. Her skin was pink and she wafted a scent that was more delicate fragrance of soap than expensive perfume. I guessed her shower had been long and very hot. Her flight from the house on Baker Island would have meant her clothes were tinged with the reek of smoke and dust and debris. But that wasn't what she was trying to scrub away. You could wash all you wanted, but to be sure, you had to expunge the memories. It sometimes took that to wash away the stench after witnessing violent death.

She was perched on the edge of a desk, her feet swinging in space. Her arms were crossed beneath her breasts. Her body language was in conflict. She was a young innocent girl, but the folded arms said she was now much wiser than her years dictated, and understood the need to protect herself. She'd experienced something that most adults never have to go through, never mind a child. She had survived where she should have died, and she was suddenly feeling her mortality weighing on her as heavily as the collapsed house that barely missed her.

"How did you know that . . . that monster was coming?"

"I didn't," I said. "I was there for another reason."

She stared down at her feet. They were still now.

"My father?"

"Yes. Your father asked me to bring you home."

"I don't want to go home."

"I understand. You're an adult now. You want to live your own life."

She shook her head slowly. "That's not what I meant. I don't want to go home. My life is here now. With Bradley."

"You don't have to be afraid of him. If you want, I'll take you away right now."

Marianne gave a small laugh. It wasn't humor, though. Nor relief.

"Afraid of him? Yes, you could say that."

"I won't let him hurt you again," I promised.

"If you take me home, there will be no way to stop him. You couldn't be there all the time. He'd get to me sooner or later."

"What has he done to you, Marianne? To make you so afraid? I saw the police photographs of when he assaulted you. Why didn't you go through with an official complaint then? This would be all over now. You'd be free of him."

Marianne gave me a look that assured me she had grown way beyond her years even before the terror she'd endured at Baker Island.

"Love," she said. "It doesn't matter that he hurts me, *I love him*. How could I have him arrested and charged? It would destroy him. I couldn't live with that."

"Men who hurt women don't deserve your love."

"No, maybe they don't. But I can't help my feelings. I can't turn my back on them."

There was a knock at the door. Jorgenson entered without waiting for a reply. When he saw my face, he faltered in his step. It took all my will not to grab him by the throat and throw him through the nearest wall. As it was, I clenched a fist, considering that a gut punch wouldn't be out of order. Marianne saved him from punishment.

She hopped down off her perch and went to

him. She hugged him, tilted up her face, and he kissed her sweetly on the tip of her nose.

"You okay, babe?" he asked her, giving me a hooded glance over the top of her head.

"I'm fine, honey," she told him.

I had to turn away from him.

Love's blind, they say. Must also be an anesthetic.

Rink came in the door, followed by Seagram.

"What's going on, Rink?" I asked.

"Been explaining to Bradley what we think is going on. About who could have sent the hit man after him. Bradley has agreed that we could be helpful in stopping him."

"We're here for Marianne," I said.

"Marianne's with me," Jorgenson said.

I nodded once. A curt lifting of my chin. He could see the anger in my face and wasn't so sure that it would be a good idea to piss me off.

He went on, "But Mari's safety is everything to me." He said to her, "If it's okay with you, babe, I'll let them stay."

Marianne looked at me. Confidant. "I trust them."

"Then we'll stay," I said. I looked across at Rink. Concern for his ailing mother must have been gnawing at him, but he agreed with a lift of his shoulders. Then I studied the room, the huge windows. "This place isn't safe. We should move somewhere less vulnerable."

Jorgenson looked at the windows. The view was phenomenal. Open sky and open sea. "What's to fear?"

"Boat out on the water. Any half-decent sniper could shoot you from half a mile out," I explained. "But that isn't what I was meaning."

"So what do you mean?" Jorgenson asked.

Flicking a glance over at Seagram, I said, "Not now. We'll speak again later. First I want to get Marianne somewhere a little safer."

"My room would be okay, wouldn't it?" Marianne volunteered. "I've things I can be getting on with."

"How many men have you got in the house?" I asked the question directly of Seagram.

He didn't have to think long. "Eight including myself. Then there are five staff members."

"Unlucky thirteen," Rink offered.

"Round them all up, Seagram. Tell them that no one goes near Marianne until this is over."

"Wait a second," Seagram said. "Who put you in charge? I'm head of security here. I decide what happens."

"No," Jorgenson put in. "*I* decide what happens. Hunter is right. The man who tried to kill us last night was in disguise. He could be anyone. Who knows? He could already be in the house."

"I know all of my men personally," Seagram said in outrage. "I can vouch for each and every one of them."

"You care for your men," I said to him. "That's good. If you want to save their lives, you keep them the fuck away from Marianne's room. That goes for you as well."

There wasn't anything subtle in the threat.

It was a full-on challenge. I expected him to
back down, and he did. He turned and walked
away quickly. Back in the hall, I could hear
him shouting angrily at his men. I paid him no
further attention. Seagram was an asshole, and
things would be much better if he kept out of
the way.

"He can see to your personal safety, Jorgenson.
I have no objection to that. But where Marianne
is concerned, it's up to us. If you happen to be
with her, then so be it. We'll protect you, too."

"I'm seeing my legal advisers in an hour," Jorgenson said. "They've arranged a meeting with
the police. I have to explain what happened at
Baker Island."

Complication.

"It's up to you, but I'd deny that I was there.
You were here on Neptune last night, and Marianne was with you."

"You expect me to lie?"

"For the time being." Marianne was looking
at me with her mouth partly open, wondering if
she'd made the wrong decision in trusting me. I
said to her, "If the police believe you were here,
their investigation will be hampered, sure. But
they aren't going to stop this killer. They aren't
going to stop the person who hired him. All that
will happen is that more strangers are allowed
into your home. The killer could infiltrate the
building and get at you. Also, it will be impossible to keep you out of harm's way if you have to
go into Miami to be interviewed."

Jorgenson jammed his hands into his trouser pockets. "My father died. Shot dead in cold blood. How do you expect me to lie about that? I was there and saw the man who did it. So did Marianne. You did. We're all witnesses."

Jorgenson stared at me, almost a mirror image of Marianne the way he watched me with open-mouthed incredulity.

"You're right. But our eye-witness testimony isn't worth shit. The man was in disguise. He will look nothing like the person we can describe."

"How do you know it was a disguise?"

"Something I saw but didn't realize at the time. There was a pale smear on the man's chin. At first I thought it was dust, but I've been thinking about it since. I now think he had darkened his skin. The pale patch was his natural color. His hair isn't black, either." I remembered the person in the dark blue suit stumbling away from the wreckage of the house. At the time I'd thought it was an innocent caught up in the blast as he wandered by. I'd held back from shooting him for that very reason. "The killer had black hair, but it had to have been a wig. Really he has longish blond hair."

"So tell the police that."

"Won't help."

"The police will give us all the protection we need."

"No," I said. "They'll only give the killer more opportunities to get at you. It's better that we do it my way. This man doesn't know that I survived the blast. He doesn't know about Rink. He isn't expecting us. We'll be able to get him."

"What if you don't?" Marianne asked. *"What if he gets you first?"*

"That's when you go to the police and tell them everything."

18 HOBE SOUND IN MARTIN COUNTY, FLORIDA, had a strange history. In the first quarter of the last century, the movie industry was big news in Florida. The goal of the Olympia Improvement Association was to develop Hobe Sound as a permanent movie production center and town in the style of ancient Greece. For a short time, Hobe Sound was renamed Picture City. A hurricane in 1928 put paid to the plans, devastating the area and putting an end to the land boom, and the hopes of the OIA came to nothing. Their legacy remained only in the names of the streets: Zeus, Saturn, Mercury, Apollo, Athena, and others.

Strange names were nothing new to a man who went by the name of a fallen angel, but even he might have drawn the line at the downtown Demeter Plaza. He was sitting on a terrace outside a coffee shop with the name of Pots and Pans—complete with a welcome sign depicting a life-sized goat-legged satyr blowing on a reed pipe with the day's specials chalked across his midriff. Panpipe music played from tinny speakers above the door, but unfortunately it sounded more Peruvian than ancient Greek.

He put up with the place out of necessity. His

associate had arranged what he needed for his assault on Neptune Island and would deliver it here within the hour. In the meantime, he sat gritting his teeth, drinking coffee as strong as sump oil, and moving with the shadows under the parasol above his table.

It was late afternoon but it was still edging ninety degrees Fahrenheit, and under his voluminous coat, sweat was trickling down the small of his back and pooling on the vinyl chair he was sitting in. He was uncomfortable, and the wound in his thigh was screaming in protest. He wasn't very happy.

Banyan trees with their weirdly twisted trunks and branches blocked the traffic noise from nearby Athena Street. Against the harsh afternoon sunlight they were like the silhouettes of deformed giants. The chatter of tourists and locals was muted, as if the heat leached all energy, making speech too difficult a task at anything above a whisper.

He watched the people passing by, conscious of the glances he received in turn. Here, under his parasol, he stood out like a candle flame in a dark pit. He didn't like being so visible, but at the end of the day he wasn't going to kill anyone here. Not if they turned off that damn pipe music!

A fat man approached him. He had on wide flannel trousers and a black shirt with embroidered flames writhing up the sleeves. Sweat stood on his forehead like mountain dew. He carried a knapsack. Dantalion recognized his associate.

The fat man thought he controlled Dantalion, but Dantalion knew otherwise. He was simply the mule who carried Dantalion's necessary supplies.

The man sat down, the chair legs squealing under his weight. He dropped the knapsack at his feet, pushing it farther under the table with a couple of none-too-subtle kicks. Dantalion hooked a strap with an ankle and pulled the bag the rest of the way. It felt heavy.

"You want coffee, Gabe?" Dantalion asked.

Gabe Wellborn swiped at his forehead with the palm of his hand, scattering droplets on the tablecloth. Dantalion scowled at the damp patches, then up at the man's sweaty face.

"Or would you prefer something a little colder?"

"Appreciate it, Dan."

Dantalion waved a waiter over. The man walked as though he had all the time in the world and wasn't about to waste any of it.

"Coffee for me and whatever my friend is having," Dantalion said.

"Soda," Gabe said. "Ice. Lots of it."

The waiter didn't bother scribbling the order into his book. Bad form, Dantalion thought. Then he wandered inside to fetch their drinks. He'd be back in about fifteen minutes, judging by his lack of motivation.

"You have what I asked for?"

Gabe nodded. "In the bag. EMF meter. Gen three night vision goggles. Sound suppressor and ammo for a 90two Beretta. Ketamine plus delivery system. Just as you asked."

"Thank you."

"Be careful, Dan. You're familiar with the suppressor and ammo; I don't have to tell you they're illegal. I wanted to bring the drugs to your attention. Ketamine's become the party drug of choice. If you're found with it, the police will have you down to the precinct quicker than you can think."

"The police have never taken me before, Gabe. Why the concern now? Anyway, ketamine's an animal anesthetic, isn't it?"

"Originally, yeah, but that doesn't stop crackheads from shooting up with it. It's used these days as a human antidepressant, strictly prescription only. Has some serious hallucinogenic side effects if the wrong dosage is administered."

"Don't worry, Gabe, I won't be using it on humans."

"Mind if I ask you what you do want it for?"

"If I told you I'd have to kill you," Dantalion quipped. From the shocked look on his face, Gabe didn't think he was joking.

"That's your business, Dan. I just thought I could give you a nod on the correct dosages you'd need."

"Enough will be enough."

"Planning on a ghost hunt?" Gabe asked. "Electromagnetic field meter. Night vision goggles. They're standard equipment for paranormal researchers these days."

"There might be a few ghosts around after I'm done," Dantalion told him. "Yours for one if you don't stop asking stupid questions."

Gabe stopped the questions. He knew when to keep his mouth shut when he was around Dan-fucking-talion.

The waiter returned. He placed the drinks on the table, slapped down a paper slip. Dantalion scattered a few dollar bills in his direction. The man clucked his tongue. Reached for the notes. Dantalion resisted breaking his arm. That would make the lazy fucker a bit faster on his feet. When the waiter had retreated to a place where he could study his fingernails, Dantalion leaned toward Gabe.

"What's the latest news on Baker Island?"

"Rescue crews are still sifting through the wreckage. They haven't released official num-bers—or names—of those they've found dead yet. There's a lot of speculation by the media, they're throwing names around like rice at a wedding. It's all guesswork 'cause they've noth-ing firm to go on. Bradley Jorgenson's refusing to speak to the police. I'm sure he'll be subpoenaed before long, and then he'll have to come clean."

Dantalion was engaged in lifting his coffee cup to his lips. Some of the coffee slopped down his coat, leaving a stain like a month-old knife wound. "Wait a minute . . . *Bradley Jorgenson*'s re-fusing to speak?"

"Yeah, he's got some top-dollar attorneys hold-ing off the cops with a verbal smokescreen. Of course, that'll only go on so long; doesn't matter how much money he has, the police are conduct-ing a homicide investigation and—"

Dantalion slammed down his cup.

"I killed Bradley Jorgenson," Dantalion hissed. "Have you forgotten, Gabe?"

Gabe blinked rapidly. He slumped backward in his seat, gaining space from the anticipated lunge he could see building in Dantalion. It never came. He hoped that Dantalion—despite his jokes about killing Gabe—valued his associate's help too highly to give in to base anger. Emboldened by that fact, Gabe said, "Not according to CNN. They say that he's currently at his home on Neptune Island."

"And the girl? Marianne Dean?"

"Yeah, she's with him."

"Son of a bitch!"

Dantalion stood up swiftly. He ignored the pull in his wounded leg. Anger overrode the agony.

"I guess that's why the client was remiss in making payment?"

"I guess so," Gabe said. "Sorry, Dan. I thought you knew."

"No, Gabe, I didn't know." He reached into his pocket, toying with the spine of his book. Withdrew his fingers and wiped them on his coat. The book had lied to him. The numbers were all wrong. "But it looks like I'm going to have to do something about that."

He was sure of it now: Jorgenson and Marianne had both survived the explosion. So, too, had the damn gunman who'd been sent to kill him. Now they were all making powwow at Neptune Island. Suddenly he wasn't so clear about how many enemies he was going to have to kill.

"You have access to a thermonuclear device, Gabe?"

Gabe sniggered. "You're joking, right?"

"Do I look like someone with a sense of humor? There are a lot of people on Neptune Island about to die. Maybe every last one of them."

Gabe reached for his soda. He gulped it down in one continuous slurp. Smacking his lips, he said, "Can't get you a nuclear bomb, but call me if you need anything else, Dan."

Dantalion stooped low, hooking the knapsack with one hand.

"I've everything I need right here," he said.

Then he walked quickly away, leaving Gabe to sweat a lot more.

19

JORGENSON'S PEOPLE CONDUCTED A BACK-ground check on us. Rink came back fine. He had a private investigator's license and his business was registered at the address in Tampa. My own legend was a tad more difficult to come up with. I told them they'd just have to take my word for it. No one argued.

Jorgenson left with an entourage of vehicles, heading down to Miami Beach to meet with his legal advisers and then with officers from the Miami PD's homicide unit. His father's body had been pulled from the wreckage, but unlike those on the ground floor, his corpse wasn't so burned or torn to shreds by the blast: it was obvious he'd been shot.

Marianne stayed with us. Just the way I wanted it.

Whatever it was that she had to get on with, she was doing it in her bedroom. I'd conducted a cursory sweep of the room, checking that an intruder couldn't gain access, and had told her to keep the blinds closed so she didn't offer a target to anyone outside.

"We should move her," Rink told me. He'd said the same thing about a dozen times previously.

"I agree." I'd also said the same thing numerous times.

"So what are we waiting for?"

"Marianne doesn't want to move."

"So we convince her."

"She won't budge. Despite everything, she loves Bradley."

We were sitting on chairs in the hall on the second-floor landing. Marianne's room was about three doors up. We could see the entrance to her room, but we'd placed ourselves so we could guard the main stairs and could also see the door that led to a secondary stairwell farther along the hall. Seagram's men were keeping well out of our way.

"While Bradley's outa the way, why not snatch Marianne away and have done with it?" Rink demanded. "She'll get over it. When she comes to her senses and sees what an asshole he is."

"Two things, Rink. We've made ourselves public coming here. Bradley would scream kidnap. We'd be hunted down by law enforcement, despite our good intentions. Plus, there's something going on here we don't know about. I'm beginning to think that Richard Dean hasn't told us everything. Neither has Marianne."

"It's not safe here," Rink said.

There were armed guards in the grounds, armed guards in the house, more CCTV cameras than in the Big Brother house. But he was right.

"I'll speak to her again," I offered. "But we have to respect her wishes, Rink. I know we're looking at her like she's a child, but she is eighteen years old. She has her own mind and a right to make her own decisions."

Rink rolled his shoulders. "She isn't thinking with her head, though, Hunter. She's smitten with Bradley. She's got herself into a position where she's afraid to walk away. She'll take the violence from him, twist it round, blame herself. Try harder to be the good little wife. You know how these things work."

I did. I'd seen it too many times. Women afraid to walk away for fear of losing everything they'd worked so hard to achieve. Not realizing that whatever they did, they'd never be *good enough*, they'd be caught up in the circle of domestic violence that spun on through their lives until one day he wouldn't stop hitting her. Sometimes that was when the woman finally broke. She'd pick up a knife and jam it between her abuser's shoulder blades. Or the man would hit her too hard, and that would be that. More women were killed by their intimate partners—or other family members—than by all the strangers or serial murderers in the world.

"I'll speak to her again," I repeated.

Rink stood up. Walked along the hall. He checked the door to the secondary stairwell. Still locked. He walked back, passed me, then went to the head of the main stairs. Peered down them. Turned and came back. It made sense to stay vigilant, but Rink was conducting a patrol just to be doing something. It wasn't like him. Rink was the type who could sit in the same position for hours on end without giving any extraneous signs that he was anything but an inanimate feature of the landscape. On seek and destroy missions we'd often be dropped miles from our targets. We'd make our way in, find an observation point, then sit tight while gauging enemy strengths and weaknesses. Once we were conducting surveillance on a terrorist training camp in the deserts of Libya. Rink took point and dug himself in less than twenty yards from the enemy base. He was there undetected for seventy-three hours before we launched our assault and wiped the bastards out.

His unease had nothing to do with our current mission.

"You shouldn't be here, Rink."

He looked down at me. "None of us should."

"You know what I mean, buddy. You should be in San Francisco with your family."

He nodded slowly, his gaze staring off to somewhere very distant. "You're family, too, Hunter. My place is here."

"Okay."

I didn't say another word on the subject. The decision was Rink's.

"Maybe we should draw on a few contacts, see if we can find out who this hit man is. We know him, we know his MO. We'll have a better idea of how to stop him."

"I'll get Harvey onto it," Rink said.

Harvey Lucas was our friend farther west. He

was an ex–Army Ranger who now ran his own private investigations outfit in Arkansas. He'd been an invaluable ally during a case we'd been involved with last year. He'd backed us up when the bullets were flying, and he'd got the job done. He was also damn good when it came to gathering the kind of information not generally in the public arena.

"I'll leave you to it. I'll go and speak to Marianne again."

Rink brought out his cell phone and hit a hot key.

I knocked on Marianne's door.

She answered it immediately. Almost as if she'd had her ear to the door, listening to what we'd been saying. Her hair was pinned up again, and she'd changed her clothes. Tight blue jeans and a pale yellow sweater that bared her shoulders and the upper swell of her breasts. Her neck made a long sweeping curve toward the cream skin of her chest. I couldn't help a quick glance.

Marianne caught my look and stirred uncomfortably.

"Come in," she said. She folded her arms, and I couldn't help but notice they went above her breasts this time.

"Mind if I ask you something?" I said as I followed her into the room. It was a well-appointed room, but I was more conscious of the delicate perfume that the space held. The scent of her shampooed hair and freshly scrubbed skin. She'd been showering again. I felt a little awkward. A little like a father who's used to walking into his young daughter's room unannounced, until the day when suddenly he realizes that *she isn't a child anymore. She's a woman that I don't recognize!* After that he always knocks and then hovers in the doorway, shucking off the offer to enter, then hurrying away quickly.

"What would you like to know?"

"Your necklace," I pointed out. "I noticed it was missing."

Her hand crept up to her throat, fluttered there like the beating wings of a butterfly.

"I saw photographs of you. You were wearing a small cross on a chain."

"My mother's necklace," she offered. I thought I saw a shadow flit behind her eyes.

"You aren't wearing it now."

"No," she said. Her voice went to a whisper. "It was broken."

"It couldn't be fixed?"

"I . . . I don't have it anymore."

She didn't want to speak about it. I guessed it had been torn from her throat during the assault. A sore subject that she didn't want to acknowledge, let alone revisit. Quickly I changed tack. "It's not safe to stay here, you do realize that?"

"I'm not leaving without Bradley."

"Bradley can come with us, but I think it would be safer to take you somewhere that isn't associated with the Jorgenson family."

"Not home."

"No, Marianne, not home. Somewhere that can't be connected to you."

"Why is this man after us?" she asked.

"Truthfully? I don't know." I wondered how much of my suspicions I should lay on her. Decided that she had a right to know. "There's been a suggestion that jealousy is rife within Bradley's family. Some people resent the fact that he's been named as sole heir to the business."

"He has the right," Marianne said. "His father gave it to him when he knew he was too ill to continue, just as his father did before him."

"I've no problem with that. But from what we've been able to gather, his father had two brothers. They also have children. They believe that they've been as instrumental in building the family business as Bradley has. They think that the business should have been shared equally among them."

"I know all his cousins. Jack and Simon are brothers. Then there's Petre. He's the eldest. I can't believe they would have anything to do with harming either Bradley or me."

"Petre would stand to inherit the business if anything happened to Bradley?"

"Yes . . . but . . ." She shivered involuntarily.

"Envy among family members is nothing new," I told her. "Under the surface even the closest of siblings can be concealing a deep-seated hatred. It can stay hidden for life and can be taken to the grave with them. Sometimes it erupts into anger and violence. Especially where huge amounts of money are concerned."

"And you think Petre may be responsible?"

"Petre doesn't like you, does he?"

"No." I saw her fiddle again with the nonexistent cross. Wondered why she wouldn't just come out with it and tell me the truth. She asked, "Do you think Petre would really go that far?"

"Could be any one of the cousins. Or all," I said. "Maybe I'm wrong and it's none of them. Regardless, there is a man who has tried, and will try again, to kill you and Bradley."

"When he came to the house last night, he shot Bradley's father. He didn't know who Valentin was. That doesn't sound like someone working for any member of the family."

"Maybe he knew," I pointed out, "but he just didn't care."

"But why kill the man whose wealth is the bone of contention? Surely by killing him it only speeds up the process of dropping it into Bradley's lap?"

"Good point," I conceded. "Perhaps the killer has nothing to do with any of Bradley's family. Maybe it's got nothing at all to do with his inheritance of the business. Can you think of anyone else who would want the two of you dead?"

"No," she said, but I could tell she wasn't being truthful. Something about the way her fingers again went to her throat, seeking solace from the missing crucifix, told me so.

20

DANTALION WAS UNDER THE SAME BRIDGE ON the same beach, but the family with the crabby kid had long gone. The sun was a bloody slash on the western horizon. Out to the east, the first stars were twinkling in the purple evening. Above him day fought night but was rapidly losing ground. Dantalion wished night would get on with it, sucker punch day, and then stamp it into surrender. He needed the darkness. It was his greatest ally.

He was sitting on a hummock of grass, his feet sunk in sand. Around him was the flotsam cast up by the sea, sun-bleached twigs and the cast-off shells of crustaceans. There was also the ubiquitous plastic bag, dropped by someone careless or simply uncaring. A soda can, ferrous red around its lip, was buried to the shoulders in the sand. Between Dantalion's splayed feet was the knapsack delivered to him by Gabe Wellborn.

From the bag he pulled out the sound suppressor. The one he had used last night was useless now. Suppressors didn't have an infinite life span; each successive shot fired through them robbed them of some effectiveness to deaden sound. He screwed this fresh one into place on his specially adapted Beretta. He disengaged the magazine from his gun, inserted a new one, slid the loading mechanism to place a round into the firing chamber, then fed a round into the magazine so that he had the full seventeen-round load ready to go.

Placing the gun across his left thigh, he reached back into the bag and took out a second gun. This wasn't nearly as effective a man killer as the Beretta, but it was as he'd said to his associate, *"Don't worry, Gabe, I won't be using it on humans."* The gun looked like something patched together from a plumber's castoffs. A pipe, a valve, and a canister. A simple trigger mechanism was the only part that looked as though it had been gleaned from a genuine firearm. It was a dart gun powered by compressed gas and could deliver the ketamine cartridges over a space of fifty yards.

Next came the night vision goggles. They were advanced Generation 3 goggles, military grade, with image intensifier capacity, bright source protection, and wide exit pupil design. They came with a fully adjustable, padded head rig to allow hands-free operation. With these in place he would have the ability to move through the darkness as though it was high noon. His enemies would be blind to his presence even when he was standing in front of them.

Last out of the bag was the EMF meter, a device for measuring electrical and magnetic fields. This particular device was distinct in its very wide frequency response and sensitivity. Any pressure pads or trip wires hidden in the grounds of the compound would set off an audio sounder not unlike a Geiger counter, increasing in intensity the closer he approached the hidden alarms.

The sun was almost down now. Under the bridge the shadows had thickened and swarmed around him like furtive confederates. He slipped out of his coat, bundled it, and placed it in the knapsack. In went his hat and sunglasses, and he strapped the goggles onto his head, flipping up the dual tubular optics so that he could still use his own vision for now. He was dressed in close-fitting sweatshirt and cargo pants—the type with numerous deep pockets—tucked into laced-up boots. In the daytime Dantalion dressed in white or cream clothing, but his current garb was as black as the night folding around him. He holstered the Beretta on his hip. The wound in his thigh made it too uncomfortable to carry the gun in its normal position. Extra magazines were fed into the deep pockets on his left thigh. The EMF meter had a clip that he fixed to his belt. He swung the knapsack across his shoulders and cinched the straps tight. Lastly he picked up the compressed-gas gun and inserted a ketamine-charged dart, then thumbed the canister control.

He straightened and took a couple of steps so he could peer from under the bridge toward the gate he'd reconnoitered earlier. He couldn't make it out in the dark. Not until he slipped the goggles in place. Twinkling green light played on the interior of the goggles. Now he could clearly see the dark bulk of the boundary wall on the horizon to his left.

Ready now, he set off, keeping low so that he was nothing but an amorphous shape against the swaying grasses. Earlier he'd picked his way painfully through the tall grass, but now he went more swiftly. The sunlight on his delicate skin was no longer an issue, and the cargo trousers staved off the prickling edges of the grass stems.

Cars moved along the coastal highway, their lights streaking across the elevated bridge like a flight of UFOs. Their sound was hushed by the fall of night; even the Atlantic made only the faintest of whispers where it caressed the shoreline.

Dantalion made his way through the grasslands, coming to the wall slightly east of the gate. Using the magnifying capacity of the goggles, he studied the CCTV camera mounted over the gate. The camera was angled away from him, seemingly static, as though the controller within the grounds was taking a nap. The likelihood was that with a system having this number of cameras, the controller rarely used this one. Wasn't much to look at during the dark hours. He'd probably be concentrating on the traffic outside the estate, or taking voyeuristic peeks into the bedchambers of the Jorgenson women.

Dantalion decided against shooting out the camera. Whereas a malfunctioning camera along the wall near the road wouldn't be of immediate concern, a broken camera at this remote corner of the grounds could call for immediate investigation. He scanned to the right toward the beach end of the wall and saw that the wall ended in a right angle but that a tall fence extended out across the sand and disappeared into the Atlantic. The gate remained his best choice for entry unless he wanted to swim a couple of hundred yards. The salt water would destroy his equipment, and his book, which was tucked inside his sweater.

He tested the rusty chain and lock and found that they were still very strong in spite of the corrosion. Taking out his Beretta, he aimed at the lock. Fired once. Fired again. The lock shattered, but it was a task to twist it out of the links and unwind the chain from the metal bars. All the while he kept a discreet eye on the CCTV camera, anticipating its swinging his way. It never did.

Hauling one side of the gate toward him, he slipped through the gap. Then he tugged the gate shut behind him. Immediately he took out the EMF meter and switched it on. Lights danced across the top of the device as it ran through a calibration sequence. He cupped a hand over it to smother the lights. It made a soft *beep*, then a green pinpoint held steady. Ready to go.

Beretta back in its holster, he held the dart gun in his right hand, the EMF meter in his left, sweeping the ground as he moved forward. Through the enhanced lenses of his night vision goggles the nearest houses were black-green hulks, but lights from within the rooms were exaggerated, causing flare that looked like cold flames. The heavens above were aflame with twinkling stars. Mist off the Atlantic swirled like translucent phantoms.

"Planning on a ghost hunt?"

Gabe Wellborn's attempt at humor came back to him. Dantalion smiled whimsically. It was as if he were traversing a haunted landscape. He remembered his own words: *"There might be a few ghosts around after I'm done."* Everything going to plan, his lists would be corrected, and there'd be further numbers to be added.

Keeping close to the beach where the tall grass had been left to nature, he continued past the first few structures. They didn't mean anything to him. He needed to walk the best part of a mile to reach his destination. He had plenty of time, so he wasn't frustrated by his slow pace. Just because he hadn't yet come across hidden security devices didn't mean that they weren't there. He was vigilant with the EMF meter, and scanned with the goggles in continuous arcs of vision.

Almost twenty minutes later he had to crouch down among the reeds. A motor launch crept through the shallow water, a searchlight sweeping the beach for interlopers. The boat continued to the south, and Dantalion came out of his crouch, moving inland now. The long grass gave way to a low wall, beyond which was a manicured lawn, and beyond that a statue-dotted garden.

The EMF meter finally warranted the effort of bringing it. The clicking started the moment he approached the low wall. Dantalion searched for the source of electrical disturbance. What he found wasn't a buried pressure pad; it was a motion detector mounted on the wall itself. Further along the wall would be a second motion detector. A laser beam fired between the contraptions, and anything breaking the beam would set off an alarm inside the house. It was a sneaky alarm, designed to catch out anyone stepping over the wall, but it wouldn't stop him if he vaulted over the top of it. Which was exactly what he did.

If the security-conscious Jorgensons were clever they'd have placed pressure pads just inside the wall where a person jumping over the motion detector beam would be caught out by the secondary appliance. But Dantalion knew that dogs roamed the grounds after dark, so pressure pads would be useless. Being careful, though, he swept the lawn in front of him. The EMF meter remained silent. He moved forward, looking for cameras. The house in front of him was huge. Cameras stood out from the roofline, but the two he could see scanned the areas at the sides of the building. There were other cameras mounted above the grand entrance door, but these faced down at the threshold itself, and he wouldn't be going in that way.

Staying out of the visual arcs of the cameras, he moved close to the building, shaped like a giant letter H laid on its back. The left wing of the building extended out from the entrance portal.

He crept up to it, keeping below the line of the windows, and then used the angle of the building to move directly beneath the CCTV camera. It would have a wide lens, but he doubted that he'd be visible when pressed close to the wall; the cameras were placed to spot anyone moving toward the building, not actually against it. He drew the Beretta, stretched upward, and fired a single shot into the camera housing. Sparks showered and the camera swung lazily to one side, then dipped in its final throes of mechanical life.

Dantalion sped along the side of the building. At the far corner he paused, peeking around toward the back of the house. Glad that he'd brought the ketamine, he lifted the gas-powered gun.

The dogs were penned in a compound. This early in the night it wasn't yet time for their handlers to start their patrols, and the two German shepherds were lying with their heads on their paws, staring back toward the house with a patience that had to be seen as virtuous. Dantalion took aim, vectoring in the slight breeze, the loss of velocity of the dart over the intervening space. He checked the gas pressure, flicked it higher. Aimed again. He squeezed the trigger and the gun gave a soft bark. In response both dogs' ears twitched. One of them yelped, swinging up from its crouch, inspecting the tasseled object embedded in its rump.

Within the next second the dog dropped to the ground, one paw scrabbling uselessly at the earth. Dantalion had charged the dart with enough ketamine to fell a buffalo, or to give a dozen crack-heads the trip of a lifetime.

The second dog was confused by the conflict-ing stimuli. It had heard the gun discharge, and duty bade it set off a racket, but it had also seen its pack mate collapse to the ground, and moved to inspect it. Dantalion's dart struck it just below its left shoulder. Angrily the dog turned on the stinging missile, trying futilely to pull the barbed dart from its flesh. It collapsed midsnap.

Dantalion hurriedly slung the gun over his shoulder and moved forward, drawing his Be-retta. Beyond the dogs, he came into a space where cars were parked. He moved among them, tempted to shoot out the tires but deciding not to. He would need the ammunition for something far more important.

21

BRADLEY JORGENSON RETURNED FROM MIAMI looking worn and harassed. Immaculately presented when I'd seen him earlier, he now looked as unkempt as a person who'd slept overnight on a park bench.

He was pale, and his reddish hair was dark with perspiration and stood up at weird angles as though he'd been pushing his sweating palms through it at regular intervals. His trousers were rumpled, and I could tell he'd spent a lot of time sitting in uncomfortable chairs. Moisture dampened his shirt beneath his armpits and at his lower back. His tie was slightly askew, and the top button of his shirt was open.

Marianne went to him as if he were a hero returning from war. He held her, and they cooed to each other. It would have been sickening if it weren't for the situation. Bradley's father had been brutally murdered, after all. I couldn't deny him the measure of comfort.

"We're going to have to make some decisions," I told him when they finally parted.

Jorgenson nodded in resignation. It was as though the return to Miami had brought the enormity of what had happened yesterday back to the forefront of his mind. Someone had tried to kill him and Marianne. In doing that the killer had murdered four others—one of them his own father—destroyed a multimillion-dollar house, and would have killed the two of them if I hadn't showed up. This killer wasn't about to stop. When he discovered that his targets had thwarted him, he'd be coming again. Who knew what lengths he'd go to this time to achieve his aim?

"The police didn't believe that I wasn't at the house on Baker Island. Witnesses saw my boat. I'm under suspicion." Tears sprang into his eyes and he turned away and wrenched out a sob. He batted at his face with his hands, scrubbing them up and through his hair. When he turned back to me, he said, "We can't leave the house. My attorney agreed to that, and I can't go against the agreement. If I run away it'll look like I'm guilty."

"Stay here and you'll die."

"I can't run."

"You can," I said. "And you will."

Taking Bradley by his elbow I led him to the far side of the room. Marianne watched us and almost made to follow until Rink interjected himself between us. While she was distracted, I pushed Bradley through the open door and into the en suite bathroom.

"Let's get a couple of things straight," I said to him. To spare Marianne, I kept my voice low. "I don't like you, Bradley. In fact, I'm struggling hard not to put a bullet in your skull. You're scum, in my estimation. Do you understand?"

His mouth had fallen open and the blood was draining from his face, making mottled patterns in his flesh. He tried to step away, but my fingers dug into the nerve at the back of his elbow. He squirmed against the pain but was unable to escape.

"I don't like what you did to Marianne. Not one bit. Normally I treat men like you like the shit you are. I scrape you off the sole of my boot. But the truth is, I believe that there's someone out there who means Marianne more harm than you've already done her."

"Marianne? She told you that I—"

"Shut it! Let me finish." I leaned in, placing my mouth very close to his right ear. "I came here with the intention of taking Marianne away from you. I'm still going to do that."

He began to shake his head and I grabbed his arm even tighter, probing for the radial nerve in his arm. When I'd gained his compliance, I added, "And you're going to give me your blessing."

"What do you mean?"

"You are going to make Marianne come with me. She's smitten by you, afraid to go against you. I want you to tell her it's best that she goes somewhere safe until this is over with."

"You're not taking her home."

"I'll take her where I want, but no, I won't be taking her home."

His shoulders relaxed a little. Was that relief in his eyes? I wondered. I said, "The man who tried to kill you last night will come again. I can guarantee you that. It would be best that you went somewhere safe as well."

"The estate is like a fortress," Bradley said. "Where would be safer than here?"

I snorted out a laugh. "If I'd wanted to kill you I could've done it anytime I pleased. The man from last night was good. He could get to you, too."

"I'll strengthen my security, bring in more men."

"The killer could be among them for all you'd know." Leaning close again, I whispered in his ear, "Take my advice, Bradley. Don't strengthen your security. Strengthen your options. Take some of your most trusted men and get the hell away from here. Go somewhere you can't be found—it's the only way to stay safe."

"Why do you care about my safety? You've just made it clear that you don't like me."

"You're right, Bradley. I don't like you. The only reason I'm interested in keeping you alive is for Marianne's sake. Things are bad enough; I don't want to have to contend with a distraught woman grieving for her dead lover as well."

Letting him go, I watched him work his sore arm. There was a scent coming off him that I recognized as fear. The patches under his armpits had grown.

"Where will you take Mari?"

"I can't tell you that."

"Why not? I—"

"If the killer gets to you he could make you tell him where she is. Do you want that, Bradley?"

"No. No, of course not. I . . . I . . ."

"Love her?" My mouth twisted into a knot around the words. "If you do love her, you'll let her go. The most important thing in the world to you should be her safety."

"It is."

"Then we're in agreement?"

He nodded acquiescence.

I shoved him toward the door. "Go and do it, Bradley. Convince her."

He paused, looked back at me. "I will. But there's something that you've got wrong, Hunter."

"Yeah? What would that be?"

"Whatever you were told, you're wrong about me."

"We'll see," I said.

He lifted a finger and pointed it at me. "Ask her. Ask Mari, and she'll tell you."

"Put the finger down, Bradley, or I'll break it," I snapped. He dropped his hand to his side, but the challenge remained in the set of his shoulders. I shook my head at him. Pathetic bastard didn't frighten me. "Marianne will only tell me what you've ordered her to say."

He exhaled. "Believe what you want. But you'll learn the truth in the end."

"Yes, Bradley, I will." Placing my hand on the butt of my SIG Sauer, I said, "And when I do, it will be the end."

22

DANTALION IS A GREAT AND MIGHTY DUKE OF HELL. He knows the thoughts of all men and women and can change them at will. Or so it was written in the fabled *Book of Enoch*. Nothing can stand in his way.

After sedating the dogs, he'd walked through the rear entrance unchallenged. In a vestibule he'd come across a man sitting reading a newspaper and had shot him in the throat. Then he'd moved on. At the front of the house he came across another man sitting in a small room that was in darkness but for the glow from numerous CCTV monitors. The man was dozing, and Dantalion killed him without the man ever coming awake. Next he'd checked the opposite wing of the house where he shot two guards in the back. They'd crumpled on plush carpets that absorbed the shock of their landing.

And then he was on the stairs, moving upward, intent on the task he'd set himself. The numbers in his book required correction, and there was only one way to rectify that.

Numbers are the building blocks of equations, he reminded himself. Equations are formulas with a strict resolution. They gave him the answers to his existence.

Answers. That was why he was there. He wanted answers.

At the head of the stairs he heard the murmur of voices from within a room to his left. He took a spare magazine out of his trouser pocket, ejected the one from his gun that was almost half depleted, and fed in the fresh one. He racked the slide. Continued up the stairs with new resolve. He moved along the hall toward the bedroom. The tugging sensation in his wounded thigh was a reminder of what mistakes can get you. There would be no mistakes this time. He stepped immediately into the room, the gun leveled at chest height.

And found himself staring down the barrels of five guns pointed directly at him.

"Ah, Dantalion. We've been expecting you. Please come in," said a voice he recognized.

He didn't look at Petre Jorgenson. Instead he looked at the fat man sitting in a chair behind the armed men. The fat man wouldn't return his gaze.

"You betrayed me, Gabe?"

Gabe Wellborn shifted in his chair, looking to Petre for support.

Petre stepped forward, his gun pointed at Dantalion's midriff. "Best you drop the weapon, then we'll explain."

Dantalion kept his gun exactly where it was.

"If that's your choice," he said. Then he allowed the gun to lower to his side.

"All the way," the client ordered. "Put the gun on the floor and kick it away."

"No," said Dantalion.

"Then we'll shoot you, and you'll never know why you had to die."

Dantalion dropped the Beretta. Kicked it from him with the side of his foot. "Explain."

Petre moved away. He approached Gabe and placed a hand on his shoulder. Squeezed reassuringly.

"Mr. Wellborn has done us all a great service."

"He has?" Dantalion said. He twisted the corner of his mouth into a sneer.

"Yes, he has." Petre looked at him oddly. Nodded at the night vision goggles. "Are you going to take off that ridiculous contraption?"

Dantalion made do with flicking the dual tubes upward so that they stood up from his forehead like a ram's horns. Symbolic in its own way, but lost to the others in the room. Petre waved a hand. "Take a seat. We may as well be comfortable."

"I'll stand."

"Okay, but I insist that you be searched for any weapons. You can lose the dart gun, for a start."

Dantalion allowed two of the armed men to strip the gun from him, then the knapsack. His Beretta was scooped off the floor. One of the men, tall, thin, and Cuban-looking, touched the book concealed beneath his sweater. Dantalion grasped his wrist. "You don't touch that! Nobody touches that."

The man pulled his wrist free, but it was an effort. Dantalion's spindly fingers held more strength than his emaciated frame would suggest. The man looked at his boss for direction.

Petre said to the Cuban, "Leave it." Then to Dantalion, "I take it that's the book you showed me at Bayfront Park. Mr. Wellborn has already explained to me how important your book is to you. You may keep it, Dantalion."

"I was going to," Dantalion said.

The armed men moved away, giving him space. Not for his benefit—it was so they could hold him in their line of fire without blocking the other two guards. Petre stepped behind a desk and sat down. He laid his Glock 19 on the desktop within easy reach of his hand.

Normally the position of power is held by the standing person. It forces those seated to look up at him, see him as the dominant figure in the room. It didn't seem to perturb Petre Jorgenson. He appeared at ease. But then again, the illusion of Dantalion's dominant position was severely corrupted by having four automatic weapons aimed at him.

Dantalion looked from Petre to Gabe. He blinked very slowly. "You betrayed me, Gabe. How could that be a great service to me?"

Gabe swallowed noisily.

But it was Petre who answered. "Mr. Wellborn was concerned about your intentions. He believed that your decision to come here was not based upon professional logic but on some crazy notion of misguided revenge. Revenge is never good for business."

"My decisions are neither crazy nor mis-guided," Dantalion said.

Petre folded his hands, tapped his little fingers on the desktop. "Okay. So let's call it a misinformed decision."

Dantalion didn't reply. The tapping sound set off a tic in his jawline.

Petre said, "Mr. Wellborn—as you know—is an asset to both of us. He brokers deals, organizes payment, supplies necessary equipment and intelligence. After he spoke to you earlier, he contacted me. He feared that you were acting a little irrationally. When you heard your targets had survived last night, he believed you might do something to rectify it. I applaud that—you have pride in your work. But he also gained the impression that there was an underlying problem."

"You could say that," Dantalion grunted.

"You thought I'd reneged on the deal." Petre lifted his bunched hands, steepled them against his lips. "I can see how you could have come to that conclusion. But that wasn't the case. I was merely awaiting confirmation."

"Yes," Dantalion said. "Confirmation that I was dead."

The skin on Petre's brow creased. "Why would you think that?"

"My words when we spoke at Bayfront Park."

Petre sat back in the chair. He shook his head, a smile on his tanned face. "I took them as the words of someone bolstering his negotiating position, not as a direct threat. I hear their type day in and day out at all levels of my business."

"It's one thing receiving veiled threats from *ordinary* business associates," Dantalion pointed out. "Quite different when dealing with a professional killer, wouldn't you agree?"

Petre put up a hand, as though waving away Dantalion's words. "Nevertheless, I did not take them seriously. Your credentials are superb; I had no doubt that you would deliver. I never perceived you as a threat to me."

"So why send a man to kill me?"

Sitting back in his chair again, Petre rested his hands in his lap. At ease. Nothing to hide. "I didn't," he said.

Dantalion watched him. Then he glanced round the room, taking in the positions of the other armed men. They, too, had visibly relaxed. Their guns were still aimed at him, but only loosely.

"How do you explain this man turning up, then? He was prepared for me, almost got me. Only I happened to be better than him."

"Mr. Seagram? Please come in now," said Petre. Dantalion made a quarter turn, watching as the man with the brush-cut hair walked into the room. He skirted around Dantalion so that he was standing next to Petre's desk. Petre raised his palm, giving him the go-ahead. "Explain, Mr. Seagram."

"The man's name is Joe Hunter. He's freelance."

"So you hired outside the network." Dantalion directed his words at Petre, shrugging his shoulders as if to say "So what?" Dantalion wasn't in Petre Jorgenson's network, either, so this was no major surprise.

Seagram said, "He wasn't hired by us."

"You want me to believe that?" Dantalion

asked. "Don't lie to me. I saw you talking to this Hunter earlier. At the front gate."

Seagram made an apologetic nod toward Petre. "No offense, sir. My allegiance lies here, but *officially* I work for Bradley Jorgenson. I was with Bradley when Hunter and his partner turned up at the front gate. Unannounced, I may add."

"So it was Bradley who hired him?" Despite his misgivings, Dantalion could see how that could work.

"No."

"No?" asked Dantalion. "Then who?"

"Like I said, Hunter is a freelance. Someone else sent him. Our best guess is that he was sent by Marianne Dean's father. He's there to protect Marianne."

"How would her father know I was coming?"

"He wouldn't," Petre put in. "Hunter turning up was a coincidence, that's all. He has come here for reasons of his own."

Placing one hand across his middle, Dantalion gently stroked the book beneath the material of his sweater.

Seagram went on. "There's no love lost between Bradley and Hunter. However, Bradley is doing everything he says. Hunter's moved in and practically taken over the security arrangements in the house. Him and his partner, some asshole who goes by the name of Rink."

"Two of them. Is that all?"

"I'm still in charge of security, whatever Hunter thinks," Seagram said, his face rigid. "I command all the others in Bradley's house. I can assure you that there's just the two of them."

Dantalion looked away from the man. He was a disgrace, a turncoat with no honor. His gaze slipped over Gabe Wellborn. Check him into the same box. He returned his attention to his client. This was a man who desired his own cousin dead. He was no better than Gabe or Seagram— but for one important fact. He was the man with the money.

Petre Jorgenson said to Seagram, "Thanks for your input, Mr. Seagram. Best you get back to Bradley before you are missed."

Dantalion watched the man as he made his way to the door. Seagram wouldn't return the look.

After he was gone, Petre said, "So how does this play out, Dantalion? Now that you know we aren't enemies."

"I'd be dead by now if you weren't considering some new arrangement," Dantalion said. "Double the money. Half up front for services already rendered. The remainder when I kill Bradley, Marianne, and Rink. I'll kill Hunter for free."

Petre nodded. Satisfied in part. "How do we know that we won't be in this self-same position after you are done with Bradley and the others?"

"It wouldn't be good for business if I went around killing my clients, would it?" He gave a slow smile that would have curdled milk. "Now, I see Gabe has his laptop with him. He can patch into your system, transfer the money across to my account. Once that's done, you can count me in. Deal?"

"Deal," Petre said.

They didn't shake hands. By the look of things, Petre recalled the scaly touch of Dantalion's fingers and wanted no part of that.

"Five hundred thousand now, Gabe. Five hundred on completion," Petre ordered. Double again the price just requested. To Dantalion he said, "Call it a token of my sincerity."

Gabe flipped open the laptop and set to it with a speed that belied his bulk. Dantalion guessed that this had been the anticipated outcome. He smiled inwardly. Not too bad a resolution when all was said and done.

"That's it! It's done," Gabe said with a final flourish. "The money has been transferred to your offshore account."

Pointing to the man who held his Beretta, Dantalion said, "I'll need my gun."

The man wasn't so sure. He looked across at his boss for assurance. Petre gestured with a hand, sitting back in his seat.

"Relax," Dantalion told the guard as he accepted the Beretta into his hand. "We're on the same side again."

Then he shot the guard point-blank in the face.

Hollywood glamorizes gun battles. They would have it that there are bunches of men loosing bullets while remaining cool and objective throughout. Every bullet finds a mark in the bad guys, while the hero dodges and whirls and avoids injury. Dantalion didn't mind that scenario. In his mind, he was the hero. The only man of honor in this pit of filth. But he was also a realist.

Gun battles are down and dirty. No getting away from it.

He would accept the risk of debilitating injury—perhaps even death—to get the job done.

One guard dead. Three with guns in their hands. Petre Jorgenson already reaching for his. Gabe was just a fat useless lump in the corner.

Dantalion fired again. Not at anyone. He shot out the light bulb above his head. There remained enough light-spill from the hall that he could still be seen, but that was okay. He slammed the door shut.

The Cuban-looking guard brought up his gun and fired. The bullet made a hole in the door that sent a shaft of light across the room. It was as good as a laser guide back to the man who'd fired the gun. Dantalion fired twice, both bullets striking the man's body. Droplets of blood rained through the narrow beam of light.

Bullets punched the wall next to Dantalion, but he was already moving. Dodging and whirling and avoiding injury like the best that Hollywood could offer. Snapping the night vision goggles over his face. Firing 9 mm ammunition at the guards. One he got in the head, the other in his chest. Then, with no more than five seconds gone since he'd killed the first guard, he moved across the room toward his client.

Petre Jorgenson shot at him.

Dantalion felt the displacement of air by his

left ear and realized how close the bullet had come to taking his head off. He shot back, and his bullet didn't miss. Petre slumped into his seat, the Glock 19 falling from his hand and clumping across the desk to spill onto the floor at Dantalion's feet.

Petre Jorgenson wasn't dead. Not yet. Dantalion had deliberately shot him in the gut. The man would last, but his final minutes on earth would be in extreme torment. Petre screamed.

So did Gabe Wellborn.

He cried like a baby, knowing exactly what was coming.

"You betrayed me, Gabe."

"No, I didn't betray you. I got you the money, Dan. You would have blown everything if it wasn't for me!"

"You're right, Gabe. I thank you for that. But don't call me Dan."

He shot Gabe between his eyes.

Turning back to Petre Jorgenson, he leveled the gun on the man's face. Petre couldn't possibly see him in the dark, but he would know how close death hovered over him.

"We made a deal," Petre croaked.

"I made a deal to kill the original targets. You can rest assured that I will do that. I did not make a deal not to kill you."

"Bastard . . ." Petre hissed. "Not . . . good . . . business . . ."

"To kill my client?" Dantalion exhaled. "You're right, Petre. Except I haven't killed my client, have I? I made a choice. This was personal. I am the client."

He shot Petre Jorgenson in the heart.

By now the suppressor was almost useless. The sound was very loud. An exclamation point in this latest recorded chapter of Dantalion's book.

23

SEAGRAM CAME INTO THE ROOM YELLING.

We were in the downstairs library again. Me, Rink, Marianne, and Bradley. I almost shot the security man as he burst in. I thought he'd lost it and had gambled his lot on a mad charge into the room. But then I saw the terror on his face and the blood on his hands.

Some professional, I thought scornfully. Ex–West Point? Made me wonder if Rink's estimation of the man had been about right, except cooks aren't normally upset by the sight of blood.

Marianne had been against the idea of splitting up from Bradley, but the combined effort of the three of us had convinced her that it was in her best interests. Probably more important was my argument that Bradley would be safer without the added worry that she could come to harm or—worse still—be used against him. She was just gathering up the last few possessions she couldn't do without when Seagram came running into the room.

"What the hell?" Rink intercepted the older man, barring his way with one hand. Seagram twisted, tried to get by, and Rink grabbed him round the neck, spinning him into the crook of his elbow and giving his throat a squeeze. The pressure of Rink's corded muscles could easily have throttled Seagram within seconds, but that wasn't the intent. Rink only held him, hissing into his ear, "Calm down, Seagram. You're good to nobody like this."

The blood on his hands wasn't his own. Neither were the smears he'd wiped on his trouser legs. But to look at him, you'd think he was mortally wounded. His face was pale and his lips had a faint blue tinge to them. He was shivering uncontrollably. Shock, I decided.

Rink maneuvered Seagram to a chair, pressed him down into it.

"Now, tell us what's going on," Rink said.

Hands twisted together, shivering wildly, Seagram looked past Rink. Bradley had moved to cover Marianne, but now that he'd realized there was no immediate danger, he'd crept closer to Seagram. He also asked, "What's going on, Seagram?"

Seagram moaned.

In the end, Rink lost patience. "Call yourself a fucking soldier? Suck it up, man. You're a goddamn disgrace."

The older man's reaction was to slump, his head going into his hands. His knees bounced with the fear coursing through his frame, making the chair creak with each movement. Sounded ear-piercing. Enough to make my mouth flood with saliva.

Rink grabbed at him again, forcing the man's head up by gripping the longer hair at the front of his brush cut. "Goddamnit! Are you going to tell us what's wrong or do I have to beat the freakin' words outa you?"

Finally Seagram appeared to take stock of where he was. Color began to sweep through his features like a morning tide racing to shore. He reached up, batting at Rink's hand. "Get off me, for Christ's sake!"

Rink released him and took a step back but held his hand ready to smack Seagram should the necessity arise.

Seagram rocked back in the chair. He studied his hands, then turned them palms out like a magician about to perform sleight of hand. To Bradley he said, "This is Petre's blood."

Petre Jorgenson. Recalling Marianne's words from earlier, I remembered that Petre was Bradley's eldest cousin. One of those she couldn't believe would have anything to do with harming Bradley or her. Maybe she'd been right, if the killer had murdered him.

"Is he hurt?" Bradley asked.

Judging by the amount of blood on Seagram and the way he was reacting, the question was pretty redundant. But to be fair, the same words had been on the tip of my tongue. Instead, I changed the emphasis. I asked, "Is he dead?"

Seagram's face twisted into something akin to a leering gargoyle. He stared at the floor in front of him as if the answer to some great riddle was to be found within the weave of the carpet. When he looked up, he had a touch of mania in his eyes. "They're all dead. Every last one of them. Murdered by the same man who's after you!"

Behind me I heard Marianne moan. Bradley, too. Rink did what I did; we took out our guns.

"Tell us what happened," I demanded.

Seagram shook his head. It wasn't in denial; he was trying to regiment the words in his head. That, or come up with a plausible lie. I've dealt with too many self-serving assholes in my lifetime not to recognize another when I saw him. The story he was about to unfold—I guessed— would be only partly true. As long as it was the important details, I didn't mind. We could deal with the lies at another time.

"Don't be mad at me, Bradley," he began. "I only went to speak with Petre out of concern for you. You haven't been getting on that well lately, but . . ." His eyes flickered once to Marianne, then back to Bradley. He shook his head. "But I thought that he could help. He has his own security team, and I thought that if we pooled our resources—"

"There'd be an even larger bunch of amateurs running around the place with guns," Rink offered.

Seagram's face darkened. But he ignored the insult. He went on, "When I got there I could hear talking upstairs. I couldn't see any of his staff around, so I made my way up the stairs to where Petre has his office. Suddenly there were guns going off. The door slammed. There was more shooting. Then silence. I'm ashamed to say that I didn't immediately go into the room to help, but my first loyalty was to you. I thought about running back to raise the alarm then and there."

"Very noble," Rink said. My friend turned away, and I could see he was buying Seagram's tale about as much as I was. The only part that rang true was that he didn't try to help.

"What was I supposed to do?" Seagram asked. "I had no idea who was in the room. No idea of the numbers or the firepower. I waited. Hid myself. That's when I saw a man come out of the room and run down the stairs. I was going to follow him, stop him, but I realized that Petre maybe needed help."

"Petre was dead?" Bradley asked.

Seagram again looked at his hands.

"I tried to save him. But it was no good. The man had shot him twice. He was gone."

"Who else?" I asked.

Seagram looked at me as though I were a stranger who'd just sprung into their midst.

"Tell me," I ordered. "Who else was dead? Numbers, specifically."

"Petre. Some computer geek I'd never seen before. Four of Petre's guards." He made as if to wipe his hands over his mouth, but then realized they were covered in blood and made do with scrubbing them down the front of his trousers. "There were others, too. The security staff downstairs were dead. At least another four."

"So a man kills ten people single-handedly?" My question was pure rhetoric; I was merely weighing up the ability of the man, not questioning the figures.

"Perhaps more," Seagram said. "But that's how many I saw."

"Weapons?" I asked.

"Just a handgun, I think."

"You saw it? Describe it."

"I didn't get a good look."

"Useless," Rink said.

"What did he look like?" I asked. "You saw him, tell me about him."

Seagram chewed his lips. It was like he wanted to tell all but also wanted to hold something in reserve for later. Like it was his GET OUT OF JAIL FREE card.

"White male. Midthirties. Tall but thin. One fifty pounds at most. Dressed like a cat burglar."

"Anything else?"

"Yes. He had on night vision goggles."

"And he managed to shoot dead five men in that one room?"

"In the space of seconds," Seagram confirmed.

Damn good shooting, I had to give him that.

"We have to leave," I announced. Marianne didn't appear so reluctant now. She took a couple of steps toward me, and I nodded her on. Took her hand in mine. "Don't worry, you'll be fine. I won't let him harm you. I won't let anyone harm you."

She flicked a glance toward Bradley, her lips pinching. Then they moved together and held on.

"How long ago is it since you saw the killer?" Rink asked Seagram.

"Ten . . . fifteen minutes," Seagram offered. "I can't be sure."

"How far away is Petre's house?"

"Two down. Maybe a little over a half mile."

"So he could already be here."

"I was inside the house a few minutes after he left. But I drove here. He was on foot."

Rink shot me a glance and I nodded. We'd both caught something very obvious in Seagram's words. But we both let it go.

"Seagram," I said, "among your supplies, do you have any Kevlar vests?"

He thought a moment. "Yes. I think we do."

"Go get them."

"There's one at least," he said.

"Then go get it."

"I should be here with Mr. Jorgenson," he said. "To protect him."

"Punk!" Rink called him. "Tell me where the fucking thing is and I'll get it."

"No," Seagram said, an attempt at regaining face. His eyelids were flickering wildly, so his words didn't do the trick. "I'll get it. Just make sure Bradley is safe."

"Just get the vest, then get back here," I snapped. "Round up any of your men that aren't already dead."

Seagram got up from his chair looking a little unsteady on his feet. He moved toward the door, faltered, grappled with his shoulder holster to pull out a gun. A Colt Mark III .38 special. Double action revolver. The famous law enforcement gun. It looked large and cumbersome in Seagram's shaking hand.

He ducked out the door, disappearing along the corridor to our left. I turned to Bradley. "After this is done, you should take a serious look at the caliber of staff you employ."

Bradley's lips pinched. But he wasn't thinking about the ineptitude of Seagram. He'd lost his father. Now a cousin had died. The Jorgenson family was dwindling fast, and he was wondering if he was going to be next.

Not my problem, I decided. Marianne was the only reason I was there. Bradley should thank his lucky stars that I hadn't killed him at the first opportunity. Rink's suggestion of waiting until Bradley's back was turned, then spiriting Marianne away from him maybe hadn't been a bad idea after all. She'd have been angry, more than reluctant to go with us, but it would have saved us this latest trouble.

May as well make the most of the situation, I thought.

"Bradley, you're going to help us get Marianne to safety," I told him.

Then I related the rest of my plan.

At the end of it, everyone was in agreement.

Seagram returned with the Kevlar vest.

I took it off him and handed it to Marianne.

"Put it on," I said.

Seagram reared up. "But that's for Mr. Jorgenson."

"Shut up, Seagram, you asshole!" Bradley said,

and the man took a step up in my estimation. Bradley snatched the bulletproof vest from him, turned, and held it out to Marianne. She accepted it as if he'd just gone down on one knee and presented her with a diamond ring. Bradley helped her into it.

The vest was designed for a man, not a young woman, so it was a little big and clumsy looking on her. But it had adjustable Velcro straps. I stepped in close and cinched them tight.

"Can barely breathe," Marianne said.

"You'll breathe less if a stray round makes its way between the vest and your body," I pointed out.

She turned back to Bradley and he smiled at her. Touched her chin with his cupped palm. She tilted her head and kissed his palm. Sweet.

"Let's get moving," I grunted.

"Sheesh! Thank fuck for that," Rink said.

24

THE NIGHT VISION GOGGLES WERE AN ENCUM-brance now that Dantalion was close to Bradley Jorgenson's house. Lights had come on all over. Floodlights spilled out from the building like it was the finale of a rock concert. Bugs swarmed in the beams, making swirling patterns around the floodlight housings.

"Good move," he whispered to himself. The people inside knew he was there, and what he'd come equipped with. They were trying to take away the advantage of his goggles by making the area as bright as day.

Old-type goggles had the problem that when a sudden intrusion of light struck the lenses, the wearer could be momentarily blinded. These Generation 3 goggles had integrated flare protection to combat that problem. Still, with the bright lights surrounding the building, the contraption did feel a little redundant. He took it off. Dropped it on the ground next to him. He moved toward the house.

His Beretta was in his right hand, Petre Jorgenson's appropriated Glock 19 in his left. The extra firepower wouldn't come amiss.

He was still outside Petre's house when Seagram had come running out. The man looked ready to vomit. His face was white. He'd jumped into a silver sedan and streaked off toward Bradley's house. Dantalion should have shot the man when he had the opportunity, but he'd decided to wait. In some respects he regretted that decision now. With Petre gone, Seagram would be Bradley's boy again.

Concluding that Seagram had returned to Bradley, he had to assume that the man had spilled everything. They knew he was coming and were setting themselves up to defend the house.

Hunter and Rink.

He hadn't heard the names before. Not associated with his line of business. They had to come from some other discipline. The only yardstick he had to measure their ability with was how Hunter had fared the night before. He'd done well—even if it hurt to admit it. The man had stopped him killing his targets, shot him in the leg, and then survived an explosion that should have put anyone in a casket. Likely Rink would be as good.

He had to be very careful from here on in.

Careful but not cautious, he told himself.

Caution breeds fear; fear builds an inability to react. Lack of movement would kill him.

He crept forward.

This house was very similar in design to that owned by Petre Jorgenson. The sideways H design. Dantalion had decided on the same approach as before. From the beach to the front of the house. To hell with the EMF meter, he didn't need it. They knew he was coming anyway. This time his advantage wasn't in stealth but in full-on assault. Movement and noise. Shock and awe.

He came out of his crouch and ran forward.

From inside the front door a gun opened up in his direction. Dantalion swerved right, then left, bullets punching turf from the ground behind him. He kept moving, bringing up the two guns and firing as rapidly as he could pull the triggers. Three shots from each gun. A half-dozen high-velocity rounds into the partly open doorway.

Unaware whether he'd hit the shooter or not, he continued to zigzag his way across the lawn until he had the corner of the left wing between him and the gunman. There he didn't stop. His painful leg wasn't a hindrance now. Adrenaline was too good an anesthetic, better than all the ketamine in the world.

He ran along the front of the building, stooped over but peering sideways through the windows. The rooms were deserted. He kept going. Came to the corner. The camera above him was swinging wildly, trying to get a bead on him, but he was below its arc of movement. The camera swung along the side of the building, just as he'd thought it might, and he immediately spun around, running back the way he'd come.

Alerted by whoever was controlling the cameras, the people inside the house had expected him to rush to the back of the building. But here he was approaching the front door again. The lack of bullets fired his way meant he'd hit the person who'd been guarding the door earlier, or that his ploy had worked and the guard was even now rushing through the house to add reinforcement to the troops there.

Fortune favors the bold. Sometimes a full-on assault could achieve more than any amount of sneaking around. Bravery, or downright recklessness, had the ability to disarm the enemy.

Dantalion had never been of a timid disposition. He ran at the front door, lifted a boot, and kicked the partially open door back on its hinges. He was through in an instant, moving sideways with his back to the wall as he probed the entrance hall for movement. Nobody. But there was blood on the floor, a trail of drops leading farther inside the house. Stepping forward, he lifted his guns, one to the front, one to the side, exchanging positions as he moved along the hall, passing doorways.

Farther back in the house he could hear voices and the thump of feet. The sound of a vehicle roaring to life. Dantalion sprang onward. He passed through a doorway and into a kitchen. The sounds were now farther to his right, and he charged through the kitchen, seeking the far door. A shadow lurched across the doorway and Dantalion fired. No time for differentiating one target from another when everyone in the building was a viable kill. If the man falling across the threshold was Hunter or Rink or Bradley Jorgenson, then so be it. In the event that it turned out to be none of them, well, that was all right, too. He'd get them soon enough.

When he gained the doorway he saw that the man was none of them. His bullet had struck the man in the throat, and he was gagging on his own blood. The gun had fallen from his hand, but Dantalion wasn't of a mind to leave an enemy behind him who might yet have the capacity to put a bullet in his spine. He shot him a second time, and the man's skull and brain matter spilled across the floor.

Another vehicle started. A lower roar, as the vehicle was driven away at speed. Dantalion cursed under his breath. He stepped into a second vestibule beyond the kitchen. There were three men blocking his exit. They turned on him even as he ran at them. He fired. They fired. A bullet tugged at his left arm—a searing pain—but he ignored it. His arm was still up and his hand was still pulling the trigger of the Glock 19. These things his mind processed without inhibiting his ability to perform. He continued toward the men, and they scattered, seeking cover. He shot one of them in the side and the man went to his knees. The other two had the sense to put the door frame between them. One on each side of the opening.

Bottleneck.

He couldn't go through the doorway without being cut down by the crossfire of the two guns. But it didn't stop his forward dash. He merely swerved, going left toward the window.

He jumped, crashing through it, taking shards of glass and wood with him. He landed on his feet— his injured leg protesting but not giving in—and spun, already firing both guns.

These were anonymous men. No one he recognized. But he killed them anyway, without discrimination. One of them, the man farthest away, who didn't have to turn around to fire on him, got off a shot, but it zinged away into the bug-filled night.

Dantalion ignored them; he was more intent on seeking out the two vehicles speeding away from him along the drive. The workers' village was a jumble of silhouettes on the near horizon, but neither car was headed in that direction. They were going for the exit gate out onto the coastal highway. Even if his leg weren't paining him, he wasn't about to catch them on foot. He required transport.

A silver sedan was still parked in the area at the back of the house. The two making off were a second sedan and a Porsche. The three cars he'd seen at the gate earlier in the day. Dantalion approached the vehicle, wary that others might be lurking about. He stuffed the Glock 19 into his waistband but kept the Beretta ready should anyone attempt to take him as he tried the car door. The door opened and he leaned in, checking the rear seat. Didn't want to be caught out by a silent assassin popping up behind him and putting a bullet in the nape of his neck. No one there. He reached under the steering column, feeling around. It wouldn't be the first car he'd hot-wired during his eventful life. Then he forgot that idea, reached instead for the sun visor, and flipped it down. A bunch of keys dropped into his palm, one of them the new card-key type. He would never have been able to hot-wire the vehicle.

Getting in, he placed the Beretta on the seat beside him. He started the engine, pulled away, swung the car around in a tight circle, and headed up the exit drive after the taillights of the Porsche.

The car was this year's Lincoln Town Car, with a V-8 engine capable of 289 horsepower and complete with electronic traction control and an automatic rear suspension leveling facility. The vehicle was built with comfort in mind, but it was also built for speed and maneuverability. Dantalion could have done far worse.

Pushing the car up to seventy miles an hour, he felt the Lincoln respond beneath him. He pressed the accelerator and the car continued to pick up speed. The Porsche had a lead on him that he couldn't hope to reduce on this straight, but the electronic gate at the exit would slow them. He'd catch them there.

Behind him, pulling out from the blind corner of Jorgenson's house, came a fourth vehicle. It was driven without lights and joined the procession of speeding vehicles without Dantalion noticing.

25 RINK'S BOXSTER WAS NOT AS FAST AS THE SIM-
ilar 911 Turbo Coupe model Porsche that
I'd once had the pleasure of driving, but I couldn't
complain. Not when it accelerated from zero to
sixty miles an hour in under six seconds and had
a top speed approaching 160. Ten seconds later I
was up to one hundred and gaining on the sedan
in front of me. I flashed my headlights, exhort-
ing Seagram to greater speed, but he held steady,
and I had to slow down and follow at a moderate
speed of ninety-five.

Passing the cluster of buildings that made up
the homes of the estate staff, we kept going on
our planned route toward the highway. Glancing
in my mirrors, I saw another car peel round in a
circle and take up the chase. That would be the
killer, then.

Beside me Marianne had her eyes closed, and
she was gripping the seat belt across her chest as
she might once have gripped her crucifix at times
of stress. Made me recall her words.

"My mother's necklace," she'd offered. Something had bothered her at the time. A sad
thought, perhaps.

"You aren't wearing it now," I'd pointed out.

"*No*," she'd said in a voice verging on a whisper. "*It was broken.*"

"*It couldn't be fixed?*"

I'd asked the question only to confirm my suspicions, and her next words had done just that.

"*I . . . I don't have it anymore.*"

Made me wonder who did.

One thing I was pretty sure of now: it wasn't Bradley Jorgenson. I recalled his words, too. When I'd been putting the fear of God into him earlier, he had implicitly denied ever harming Marianne, and he'd been oddly convincing.

I'd originally taken on this job with the intention of taking Marianne away from him. If that meant killing him, I'd even prepared myself for that. I'd been led to believe that Marianne was in a violent relationship—which the police photographs proved—but I now believed that it wasn't Bradley who'd done that to her. Domestic violence often hides behind lies and deceit, but in Bradley and Marianne I'd only witnessed genuine tenderness. He loved her the way she deserved to be loved. He hadn't hurt her. It was the person who now had her cross. Marianne hadn't confirmed who that was, but I had an idea. And if my suspicions were proved correct, he'd be made to pay.

First, though, I had to get her to safety. There was a far greater threat to her than the person who'd blacked her eyes and slapped her around. The crazy fucker who was third in line in this cavalcade.

We still didn't know who the killer was. But I had to pay him his due: the son of a bitch was good. He must have gone through Seagram's security team like a dose of salts. Otherwise he wouldn't be chasing us now.

Approaching the highway, I saw the brake lights flare on the vehicle I was following. Seagram decelerating rapidly. I braked as well, cursing under my breath.

Marianne's eyes snapped open. Full of terror.

"It's okay," I lied. "Nothing to worry about."

We'd had a good lead on the sedan racing after us, but we'd forgotten one thing. The gate that gave exit onto the highway was closed. We should have thought ahead, had it opened from the control room back at the house. As it was, I saw Seagram jump out of the car in front and race to the control panel in the grounds. He stabbed buttons and was running back to the sedan even as the gate began its slow crawl outward.

A noise like an angry hornet buzzed by my right shoulder, and the windshield starred. From somewhere behind me I heard the retort of a gun as the sound finally caught up with the supersonic bullet.

Out of the window, I roared at Seagram, "Get that fucking car moving!"

Another bullet swept through the interior of Rink's Porsche and lodged itself in the fancy console. Rink was going to be royally pissed off, but that would teach him. He should have taken more time selecting his wheels of choice, considering the business he was in. The Porsche's soft top was no defense against a hard-flung knife, let alone high-velocity rounds.

Back in the sedan, Seagram booted the throttle and pushed the heavy car through the opening gate. He blasted the front fender against the gate, sending the gate flying but also tearing loose a good portion of the fender. Half a million dollars' worth of car was nothing to consider when the alternative was a swift and violent death.

As we'd agreed, Seagram swung the sedan to the right. Seconds later, I went left, straight along the four-lane highway on the wrong side of the road. Two hundred yards on—and immensely thankful that no one had been heading along the road at that time—I powered the Porsche across the gravel bed separating the two roadways and onto the correct side of the road. The Porsche spat gravel and sand as I accelerated away. On our right was the Intracoastal Waterway, and beyond it the lights of the mainland.

"Is he still coming?"

Marianne's words caused me to glance in the rearview mirror.

"Yeah."

"Dear God," she whispered.

The killer had been given two options: right or left. He'd chosen to continue left. I'd have preferred it if he'd gone after Seagram and his passenger rather than me and mine. I was better fixed to protect my charge than Seagram was, but I'd rather have got Marianne well away from harm before turning on the bastard and showing him just who he was messing with.

Speed was my best weapon.

I pushed the Porsche up to 150 miles an hour. Just a little way behind, I saw that the Lincoln matched me for speed. Maybe it even gained a little. The driver hung his hand out the window. I saw the muzzle flash, but the bark of the gun was lost as we sped on.

I pressed Marianne down. "Unclip your belt," I told her. "Get down in the footwell. Undo your vest and pull it over your head if you can."

The trunk and seats wouldn't stop the bullets, but I guessed that the shooter would aim that little bit higher, shooting where he'd expect a hit. Comparatively safer than I was, Marianne would be very unlucky if a bullet found her. But that possibility wasn't out of the question.

The gun fired again, and sparks jumped along the door frame next to my elbow. I couldn't return fire, didn't have the angle. All that trying to twist round and fire would achieve was deceleration and possibly a high-speed collision with the guideposts on my right, then a flipping, rolling, body-tearing wreck that would achieve more than the killer's bullets ever could.

I concentrated instead on pushing the car to the limits of its performance. Technical specifications of the Porsche Boxster boast a top speed edging 160 miles per hour, but I saw the odometer register 165, then 170, then 175. Still, the RPM needle was hovering dangerously in the red zone.

Pushing the vehicle to these extremes could do untold damage to the engine, but then again, so could the killer's bullets.

The road was preformed concrete, and every so often a seam projected above the surface, causing a bumping noise to sound from the tires. Rocketing along at high speed, the bumping rattled like a drumroll. The accompanying *ting* of bullets off metal and Marianne's yowls of fear made for ungodly tympani.

Approaching the southern extremes of Neptune Island, I made out the sweep of the bridge that took the road across the waterway. It looked like a humpback whale had breached the depths and would at any second flip up its gargantuan tail and send us flying into space. I pressed the Porsche on.

The Lincoln behind couldn't match the Porsche for acceleration, but the heavier sedan was gaining along the straight. There was a slight sway in the way it went from one side of the carriageway to the other, but that was more to do with the killer driving with only one hand on the wheel. He continued to shoot. This time he sent a volley of five bullets. Two of them lifted concrete shards from the road ahead, but three of them impacted the Porsche. None hit me, but I snatched a glance at Marianne. She looked up at me from beneath her Kevlar shield with big round eyes. She was okay.

"Hold tight," I told her.

Then I stomped on the brake.

The Lincoln was a much heavier vehicle, but I was counting on the killer's reaction to do more damage than the Porsche could. True to my expectation, he swerved. The front fender clipped the back of the Porsche, lifting us from the road for the space of a very long two seconds or more. I felt weightless, and a tiny portion of my mind expected the car to flip over and disintegrate in a billion pieces. Then the rear tires found traction again and I pushed the Porsche forward, gaining distance on the killer, who had to struggle to control the Lincoln.

The daring maneuver only bought us a few seconds respite from the bullets. But it slowed the pursuit somewhat. We were now averaging only 140 miles per hour.

The bridge swept upward, then curved to the right. There was no median strip on the bridge, only collapsible plastic markers. A U-Haul truck went by on the other side. The driver swerved in dismay. Distractedly I wondered what he'd think of the Lincoln behind, with the gun poking past the door frame and raining 9 mm Parabellum ammo at me.

On my right, all that protected us from launching into the sea was a waist-high barrier. Every so often along the way, I saw evidence of where other cars had clipped the barrier, gouging paint but causing little other damage. I doubted they'd been doing twice the average speed when they'd collided, though. I swung the Porsche to the left, straddling the central markers of the two southbound lanes.

Behind us, I saw the Lincoln roaring toward our back end. When I'd braked, the killer had been forced to control his vehicle. Now he'd decided it was our turn. He rammed the Lincoln into the rear end of the Porsche, jamming us forward. He rammed us again. I could feel some of the traction go from beneath me. I dropped a gear, pressed the throttle, and surged forward, taking control again. In response, the gun came out the window once more and another bullet went through the Porsche. The windshield had had enough. It exploded, some of the glass collapsing inside so that I got a lap full of tiny, grainy squares. I closed my eyes to avoid the splinters and glass particles I felt on my skin.

It was little more than an exaggerated blink. But when I opened my eyes once more, the Lincoln was surging up alongside the Porsche on my left, scattering the plastic markers as though they were ten pins, flattening them or throwing them into the air. I swung the Porsche at the Lincoln, but all that achieved was to lock us together momentarily. There was a squeal of buckling metal.

Then I got my first look at the man behind the wheel. My first thought was that I'd been right about the pale smear on his chin. The guy had the face of a ghost or some other more evil ethereal creature. His thin blond hair knitted a pattern over his features from the wind driving in through the open window, and I only caught a glimpse of his eyes. Pale blue slits. It was enough to see that he was as psychopathic as every other nutcase who killed out of enjoyment.

He nodded at me, as if in recognition.

Here, I thought, do you recognize this?

I lifted my SIG Sauer left-handed and fired at him, unloading half the clip as fast as I could pull the trigger. The noise inside the Porsche was deafening. I didn't hear my rounds smack his car, but I saw his windshield implode. Sparks and particles of metal flew off the hood. Something burst in the engine and there was a gout of steam. No blood, unfortunately.

The Lincoln dipped on its suspension. He was braking. Then he was behind me and I couldn't see to shoot anymore. A quick glance at the odometer showed me I'd decelerated almost forty miles an hour. But we were still traveling at over one hundred. It was insane. Something else— our collision had taken us back toward the barrier on my right. The rearview mirror had been snatched off and went tinkling into the darkness behind us. I jinked left, to get away from the metal barrier.

Now the Lincoln was nosing up to my trunk. He nudged the Porsche. We slewed. Almost had me with the PIT maneuver police patrol vehicles occasionally employed to stop fugitive vehicles. Unfortunately for him—and very fortunately for us—his vehicle hadn't been in the optimum position to spin us out. But it did make the Porsche's back end swerve toward the median, blasting more of the plastic markers out of commission, the front end juddering for traction on the concrete.

Marianne wasn't the only one yelling. I probably had the edge on anger, though. I grappled with the steering, righting the Porsche, but the Lincoln was now alongside me again, and this time the killer was directly in line with me. In his left hand I saw a Beretta 90two. In the split second it took to register the make and model of the gun I also calculated my chances of avoiding the bullet aimed at my skull. Zero or nil. Take your pick.

He mouthed something at me, but I didn't catch it.

In one of those slow-motion moments of ultra-clarity, I saw his index finger caress the trigger. In reflex I started to duck. But, even in slow motion, the bullet wouldn't register.

26

HE'D LOST COUNT OF THE TIMES HE'D BEEN back and forth, over and under this self-same bridge in the last day, but Dantalion had a feeling that this wouldn't be the last. Even after he finished Hunter and his unseen passenger, he knew he was going to have to go back after the second vehicle that had headed off up the coastline toward Jupiter Island.

He'd recognized the tactic immediately as the sedan turned right while Hunter headed left. They were attempting to split his targets with the hope that he'd be frustrated and give up the chase. He wasn't the kind of man to back down, so they'd assume he'd continue hunting Jorgenson and Dean, but not until he rallied and got his act together. Likely they'd thought that would give them the opportunity to prepare for his next assault. They couldn't have expected that he'd chase one of them with unabated determination.

If Seagram had been telling the truth earlier, Hunter would be Marianne Dean's chaperon, so it was probable that the woman was in the Porsche with him. She was probably hunkered down in the footwell so she made a smaller target. He didn't mind killing Marianne first.

That had always been the plan. What he'd almost forced Jorgenson into agreeing to yesterday on Baker Island. And he definitely didn't mind killing Hunter.

It had been an exhilarating chase until now. But it was time to end it. Dantalion saw his opportunity. Hunter was a damn good defensive driver to have controlled the Porsche after he'd rammed it into a sidelong skid. Hunter had controlled the car, yes, but in doing so he'd lost some of his forward momentum. Plus he couldn't have managed to do so while holding a gun in one hand. Dantalion swerved round the Porsche and came parallel with the driver's door, smiling as his theory was proved.

Both Hunter's hands were back on the wheel, the gun out of sight. Dantalion smiled to himself. He wasn't unarmed. He lifted the Beretta. Aimed it directly at Hunter's face as it swung to look at him. The man didn't look alarmed, he just had a grim set to his jaw.

"Hello, Hunter," he said. "And good-bye!"

Hunter made a token attempt at saving himself, but a bullet would always be faster than a human reaction.

He pulled the trigger.

And heard only an empty click.

"Shit!" he snapped, more at himself than at anything.

He was a man governed by numbers and yet he had to have miscounted. He was positive that there had been one bullet remaining in the gun.

Seventeen rounds. But then he remembered. When he'd reloaded, shoved in the fresh magazine, he hadn't racked one into the firing chamber as he had when first loading the gun. He hadn't miscounted. He'd made an error of guncraft that should never have caught him out.

A bigger mistake would be to dwell on the fact. He quickly put the Beretta down, trading it for the Glock 19. Lifted the gun. It was a matter of no more than two seconds, but as he tracked his vision on Hunter, the man was no longer in sight. Neither was the Porsche!

Hunter had braked, and the Lincoln had sailed on by.

Worse than that, Hunter was now behind him, and a glance over his shoulder showed that the man was lifting his own gun. Through the gaping hole in the windshield Hunter fired. The flash of the gun was like a strobe light. Bullets zinged through the Lincoln. Three missed, lifting padding from the headrest on the passenger seat. One of them scored a hot line along the flesh of Dantalion's jaw just below his left ear.

It was as if someone had hit him with a hammer, and his mind flashed with scarlet agony. The pain was excruciating, sense-numbing.

Darkness descended over him for the briefest of moments, and his hands slipped from the steering wheel.

And that was all it took.

In the next instant his mind was full of flashes and bangs, and he was rocked sideways, jerked upright, then slammed back in his seat. The volume of noise was horrendous and seemed to go on and on. Around him the Lincoln shuddered like a dying behemoth. Finally, he blinked, and silence surrounded him.

Stunned, he was only vaguely aware that the Porsche was now passing him, then in front of him, moving away at speed over the arch of the bridge and out of sight.

He was sitting in the seat, and both his hands were in his lap. He'd lost his grip on the Glock, and it was now somewhere out of view in the footwell. The partly inflated airbag that had erupted from the steering column didn't help. He wasn't concerned about the Glock. He could soon pick it up again, as with the Beretta. First he had to check that he was able. Both arms were all right. They responded to the messages sent from his brain, fluttering up his midriff to find the comforting bulge made by his book beneath his sweater. His toes wiggled at command. His legs ached, primarily the one that was already injured, but he detected no broken bones. His jaw hurt more than anything. Tremulously he lifted his fingers to check the wound. Part of his mind expected a gaping wound through which would project shattered teeth, but his fingers found only a groove in the meat itself. It oozed blood, but it wasn't going to kill him.

He looked out the open window.

He had lost control and the Lincoln had collided with the barrier at the edge of the bridge.

The metal barrier was mangled into a twisted heap. But it had done its job. It had stopped the Lincoln from sailing out unchecked into the Intracoastal Waterway. Still, the front of the Lincoln hung a precarious two feet out into space, only one loose portion of the barrier holding the sedan in place.

He laughed. There was a slightly manic edge to the sound: realization of how close the car had come to going right through the barrier and into the sea a long way below him.

But that was when he heard the roar of an approaching engine.

Swinging around to stare at the vehicle barreling toward him, he had only a second or so to register the face of the driver. It was enough.

Rink, Seagram had called him.

Black hair, hooded eyes, livid scar across his chin.

Rink made no attempt to shoot him. Neither did he stop the car. He kept on coming and rammed the car into the side of the Lincoln.

Dantalion was rocked and slammed yet again. There was the rending of metal all around him. The front wheels went through the barrier and the car abruptly dipped forward. Rink continued to force his vehicle against the Lincoln. Then the world tilted as the back wheels of the Lincoln were forced over the demolished barrier.

What had happened barely registered in Dantalion's mind.

All he saw was the solid black wall that reared

into his field of vision. It approached him at speed. And it was only when it was a few yards away that he made out sparkling highlights on the wall. A second after that he recognized the highlights for undulating waves casting back the reflections of his own headlights as the Lincoln hurtled down toward the sea.

27

"SON OF A BITCH." RINK SIGHED. "THERE GOES my no claims discount."

We were in a beauty spot, but he wasn't interested. He was standing with his hands on his hips, surveying what remained of his Porsche.

We'd stopped at a parking lot on the northern side of the Jupiter Inlet, near a terra-cotta tower over a hundred feet tall that served as a lighthouse to steer boats into the Loxahatchee River. The beacon itself stood on a mound almost fifty feet high, so it was a definite landmark that I'd been able to pick out. Rink arrived minutes after Marianne and me.

While Rink bemoaned the death of his pride and joy, we stood shoulder to shoulder. On the shoreline, we looked south, watching traffic zoom by on something called the Federal Bridge, and even more traffic on the A1A highway bridge beyond that. Across the water was yet another marina, and I couldn't help but think that you couldn't live in Florida without owning a boat. I saw my first mangroves, but in the darkness they just looked like a bundle of twisted branches dumped on the water. Which, I supposed, was exactly what they were.

The lot was next to a visitor center that served the lighthouse. Throughout the day the place would be a jumble of vehicles and bustling tourists snapping photographs. At this hour we were the only ones there. I'd parked the Porsche beneath a stand of palm trees so that it was hidden from the nearby road. Rink had parked adjacent to us. The big gray Ford Crown Victoria he had been driving wasn't as bashed up as the Porsche, and hadn't been the target of numerous bullets. Nevertheless, it did have a crumpled fender, and one of the headlights was smashed. Any cop snooping around would immediately associate the two cars with the high-speed gun battle that had taken place at nearby Neptune Island.

"What happens now?" Marianne asked.

"We take you somewhere safe," I said.

"But that madman is dead, isn't he? Didn't your friend say he rammed him right off the bridge and into the sea?"

"I did just that," Rink said, coming over to join us. "But he's not the only danger we have to contend with."

"If he's dead, can't we just go to the police?"

"Not yet," I told her. "We still don't know who sent the hit man after you. Whoever did could try to get at you again."

"All the more reason to tell the police what's going on. Why do we have to keep running away? It's *him* who should be punished, not me and Bradley."

"You're right. But we're not ready to get the police involved yet."

"Why?" she asked.

"They'd take you away from us," Rink explained. "And we don't want that to happen. We're committed to protecting you, and that won't happen if you're kept away from us."

"I don't get it," she said. Then she looked directly at me. "Yesterday on Baker Island you said you were there to help me, Joe. But I don't understand how you could have known that I was in danger. You aren't doing this for nothing. Someone is paying you. Who sent you?" Then she closed her eyes, shook her head. "No. Don't answer. I know who it must be."

So I didn't answer.

Marianne said, "How could my father have known this was going to happen? No, wait . . . he couldn't have. He sent you to take me away from Bradley like you said. I can't believe that he just won't let things go."

Rink said, "Doesn't matter who sent us. Or why. Truth is we're here, and that should give you peace of mind. We ain't gonna leave you till we're sure this damn thing is over with." He turned and scanned his Porsche again. His lips turned down. I looked at him. That was quite a mouthful from my usually taciturn friend, and I guessed he was saying it for my benefit as much as Marianne's.

"Sorry about your wheels, Rink," I said to him.

He shrugged. "S'okay, Hunter. I was about due to trade it in anyway. C'mon, better get moving, folks."

We weren't talking cars. Not as such. I was expressing my regret at keeping him away from his mum's sickbed. He was telling me that material objects didn't mean much to him. Ergo, his mind was fully on his mum, and nothing would change that. Except getting this job done.

"Better take the Crown Vic," Rink said. "Porsche is done, you ask me."

"We leaving the car as it is?" I asked. The Porsche was full of trace evidence—fingerprints, fibers, spent rounds—and would be tied to us even faster when a CSI team got to it.

Rink took out a cigarette lighter and flicked back the lid. He turned the wheel and orange flame sprouted.

"Like I said, I was about to trade it in anyway."

We drove away in the Crown Vic, the guttering inferno that once was a Porsche lighting up the parking lot. The flames were reflected on the hundred-foot lighthouse and bounced back off the lens at the top like a ghost light.

Rink was in the driver's seat. Marianne and I took up positions in the back. She sat in the far corner of the seat, her legs pulled up and her feet tucked under, arms hugged round her knees. For safety's sake I'd made her put the Kevlar vest back on. It swamped her, the collar riding up almost to her ears, so that only the upper portion of her face above the tip of her nose was visible. Cute in its own way. Desperately sad in another. She was lost in her own thoughts, so I concentrated on what we were going to do next.

Rink had called our mutual friend Harvey Lucas. It was about time to find out what he'd come up with. I had his number stored in my cell phone and hit the hot key. Harvey picked up in seconds, his mellifluous tones rich in my ear. I put the call onto speaker so that Rink could catch what was said.

"You guys are up to your necks in it as usual," Harvey said.

"Tell us about it," I said. From the front seat Rink grunted agreement. He was navigating an interchange that was taking us up and over the A1A highway bridge toward West Indiantown Road, crossing the broad Loxahatchee River inlet.

"Don't have much on your shooter," Harvey said without preamble. "Seems he's a bit of a ghost."

"He is now," Rink said.

"You got him?" Harvey asked.

"Pushed him into the sea from a great height," I said. But the eternal cynic in me wouldn't believe he was dead until I saw him laid out all white and shiny on a coroner's slab.

"So the heat's off?" Harvey asked.

"Not yet. Don't know how many other players we have," I said. "What've you found out about who hired him?"

"Nothing yet, but I have done a bit of digging around regarding the Jorgenson business."

I glanced across at Marianne, but she was lost inside her own head. She didn't even look my way, and didn't appear to be listening to the conversation. Thinking of other things: Bradley, for sure.

"Go on, Harve," I prompted.

"You want the full history or just the potted version?"

I checked the charge on my phone. Down to two bars. "Best just give me the main points."

"Okay, then." Harvey paused, as though he was ordering his thoughts. Not that he needed to. I believed he knew exactly what he wanted to say. "First off, you know the family business goes back three generations here in the U.S., right? Since Korea, Vietnam, and up to the modern day, the Jorgensons have been working hand in glove with the Pentagon. The partnership has been a rosy deal and brought millions—actually billions—of dollars into the Jorgenson coffers. Problem is, it seems that for the last half-dozen years, Valentin Jorgenson has been ruffling a few feathers. On both sides. His company has been responsible for the development and production of vaccines for the use of the military. Well, you remember the fuss following Desert Storm, don't you? Gulf War Syndrome, it was sometimes referred to. Soldiers returning from war complained about debilitating problems brought on by the inoculations they were given before going out there. Well, Valentin wanted no part of the fallout from that. Seems like old news now, but with the current rumblings in Iraq and Afghanistan, there are new questions being raised in Congress about the chemical soup our troops are being fed these days."

"The chemical soup that the Jorgensons are supplying?" I clarified.

"One and the same. The Jorgensons certainly

don't have a monopoly on government supply, but they do develop some of the vaccines. Valentin didn't want any involvement in the same kind of scandal that went down first time round, so, basically, he's pulled the plug."

"And the other Jorgensons aren't happy?" I thought back to when Bradley had defended his father in the room at Baker Island. What he'd said then, *"My father. He abhorred violence. He was a man who only wanted to stop pain."*

Harvey said, "His ethical decision could cost them billions in lost revenue."

"You're saying *could* cost them? So the contracts haven't been severed yet?"

"No. As in all businesses, Valentin hasn't got the ultimate say. Has to be a majority agreement. And he's had some stiff opposition in the form of his partners."

"These being his nephews and son?"

"Yeah." Harvey sounded like he was riffling through papers. "Petre, Simon, and Jack. His son, Bradley."

"I'm guessing that Valentin had a majority share in the business?"

"No, just a little over the quarter mark."

"So how come he was outvoted? Oh, wait, I get it. Bradley?"

"Yeah, Bradley's vote went his cousins' way. Between them they own a little over seventy percent of the vote. With Bradley on their side, the decision was made to honor their agreement with the government."

"So why, if that's the case, is someone trying to kill Bradley? Are you saying that our shooter might belong to some group opposing the supply? Some Gulf War Syndrome support group?"

"Not at all," Harvey said.

I was relieved by Harvey's answer. I had some friends from back in the day who had suffered badly on their return from Desert Storm, could sympathize with them in a big way. Didn't really want to go up against anyone with the same fundamental belief that I had on the subject. Apart from the fact that their decisions could mean death for innocents like Marianne. On that I'd fight them tooth and nail.

Harvey went on: "Bradley has changed his outlook these past few months."

"He's gone across to his father's way of thinking?"

"He has. Valentin was dying—you knew that, huh?—and he'd recently bequeathed his share of the company to Bradley. Added to his own shares, that gives Bradley a majority sway. He hasn't done it yet, but when Bradley takes over, the military contracts will be dropped. It'll cost the company billions of dollars."

Marianne was rocking in place, humming that same sad tune I'd first heard in the garden at Baker Island. Suddenly I knew where Harvey was going with this.

"Someone has Bradley's ear? That's what you're suggesting?"

"His opinion changed round about the time his new girlfriend came onto the scene."

I noticed Marianne's eyes flick my way, but she didn't add anything. Neither did she argue.

"It's starting to make a little sense now," I said. "So Bradley's gone against his cousins, and that's pissed them off. If Bradley is killed, they inherit his voting power and keep on with the billions the government is happily handing them." I again looked at Marianne and saw that her eyes had closed. Confirmation of my theory. To her I said, "And that's the reason the killer wants you as badly as your boyfriend. You're the reason Bradley has changed his way of thinking."

She didn't answer, but her nose dipped below the neckline of the bulletproof vest.

From the front, Rink asked, "Where are you now, Harvey?"

"Where I said I'd be," Harvey said.

"Okay, buddy, we'll see you in a short while."

"Gotcha, Rink," Harvey said.

"Keep on digging in the meantime," I added. "See if you can find out anything on the shooter. You might want to listen in to what's going on at Neptune Island. By all accounts, the crazy fucker paid Petre Jorgenson a visit before he came for Bradley and Marianne again."

"Reading between the lines, I take it that Petre didn't survive?"

"No one survived," I said. "Except some pussy that goes by the name of Seagram. Bradley's bodyguard. Maybe you can do a little digging on him, too. West Point's a good place to start."

"Leave it with me, Hunter."

"Thanks, Harvey."

"Pleasure."

I clicked off the phone, pushed it into my pocket.

We'd come off the highway onto surface streets. Nice enough area. Low single-level houses with pretty gardens. No one around, as though people here lived only for the sun and disappeared when darkness fell. On our right was a tributary of the Loxahatchee. The water was slow and still. I wondered if alligators sometimes crawled up out of the river and wandered these lonely streets. That would explain the lack of domesticated animals prowling through the night. There were no cats, no dogs, but then again, there were no alligators, either.

We had agreed to meet Harvey up at Hobe Sound. That meant taking a circuitous route that would lead us up past Neptune while avoiding the coast road. There'd be an army of law enforcement personnel converging on the Jorgenson estate by now, and I didn't want to run a cordon of blue lights. The only way I trusted that Marianne would be safe was if she stayed with us. Okay, it appeared that Petre Jorgenson was now shaking hands with his murdered uncle, and it would take a very lucky man to survive the fall from the bridge into the sea, but that didn't mean that other attempts wouldn't be made on her life. It didn't take a rocket scientist to work out the probability that Petre and the shooter were in cahoots. Something had happened between them that had left Petre dead. But that didn't mean all our enemies were done with. There were still two cousins alive who had a reason to wish that both Bradley and Marianne were no longer around.

28 FOLLOWING OUR DETOUR ROUND THE BACK streets of the suburbs of Jupiter, Rink found a slip road that took us to Florida's Turnpike, where we picked up I-95 north. He drove on through the darkness in silence, and eventually we arrived at a motel on the edge of Seabranch Preserve State Park. Here I saw my second lot of mangrove, as well as many trees I didn't recognize growing round wild sandy hummocks the Atlantic had molded into weird shapes.

Harvey's rental was in the lot outside the motel entrance. It was a Ford Explorer, not unlike the one I'd been forced to abandon down at SoBe. For our purposes it wasn't the most discreet of vehicles, but it was still less obvious than the bashed-up Crown Vic. Rink pulled into the parking lot, and I accompanied Marianne toward the room that Harvey had booked. Rink drove off again, heading for the nearby state park on a short errand to get rid of the Crown Vic. Maybe it would turn up one of these days when the shifting and squeezing of the earth's crust forced it out of the mangrove swamp like a corroded leviathan rising from the depths.

The motel celebrated the local Native American culture, but spoiled it somewhat with a fake totem pole, copied from one I'd seen a few years ago commemorating the great chief Seattle in the northwest city of the same name. This totem pole was midcenter on a swath of grass in front of the motel office. Standing nine feet tall, it almost dwarfed Harvey Lucas where he leaned against it. Almost, but not quite. Harvey is a huge man. He doesn't have the musculature of Rink, but he's still a physical specimen who would make most men envious. He stands well above my nearly six feet. His skin is so black and sleek that he looks like he's been carved from jet by a master of sculpture. Broad shouldered, slim of waist, his clothes hang on him the way clothes are meant to hang. At forty years old he could give men half his age a run for their money on the football field, as well as a lesson in style.

We greeted each other the way old soldiers do—a masculine hug of the left arm, our right hands hooked together at our thumbs, a bump of chests.

"Looking good, Harve," I told him.

His jeans and shirt weren't that different from mine, only he looked like he'd just stepped out of a Hollywood gossip magazine, while I looked like something that people gossiped about for all the wrong reasons.

He touched the wound in my scalp, shaking his head in amusement. "Rink been practicing his field dressings on you? Never could see straight, that one," he said.

I'd forgotten about the slash on my head. But now that Harvey mentioned it, the damn thing reminded me it was still there with an itch that demanded scratching.

"Brought some supplies with me," Harvey said, nodding over his shoulder toward his room. "Better get that cleaned and apply some antiseptic cream. Don't want it getting infected."

"What're they going to do if it does? Cut my head off?"

"Sure would be an improvement." Harvey grinned.

Marianne was standing in our shadow. She was looking up at Harvey as if he were a demigod come down from Mount Olympus on a cloud. There was trepidation in her gaze, and not a little awe.

"You must be Marianne," Harvey said, putting out his hand.

"Mari," she answered shyly.

"Mari," he repeated, and he took her hand in his, giving it a gentle squeeze. Her smile made her look like the girl I'd seen in those first couple of photographs. So did the way she turned her eyes down and away.

She said, "You're not what I . . ."

"Not what you expected. Yeah, I know. You thought I was gonna be as ugly as these two brutes you've been stuck with?" He shot me a wink, and I grinned behind Marianne's back.

"Joe isn't ugly," she said, and that made me grin even more. I should have maybe defended Rink, but to some he did look like he'd be more at home dressed in skins and wielding a club. Then there were others who found his rugged face and scarred chin attractive: the epitome of the bad boy look.

Harvey asked me, "How is Rink?"

"Holding it together."

"He shouldn't be here."

"Tell me about it," I said. And that was the end of it. Harvey turned back to Marianne. He touched the shoulder of the Kevlar vest. "Come on, girl. Let's get you inside and out of that fashion disaster, huh?"

Harvey led us toward his room. The motel was the type that has a stand-alone office with the rooms located in adjacent wings. It was constructed like a loose crescent, the parking lot nearest the road, then the grassed area with the faux totem pole, and the rooms curving round on either side. Harvey had rented the room farthest away on the right-hand horn.

It was a standard room in a standard motel. Twin beds. Couple of chairs. A desk. A credenza with a pay-per-view TV sitting on top of it. Instructions for dialing up porn on a card on the wall. Harvey's laptop computer was plugged into a socket in the wall and resting half open on the nearest bed. A partly open door on the left showed a glimpse of a standard bathroom. Marianne's eyes widened, but then a shadow crossed over them.

"I've checked it out," Harvey told Marianne. "No creepy-crawlies. Shower's hot and the towels are clean. Why don't you go ahead? Make you feel better."

Marianne agreed with a slight nod of her head, then walked toward the bathroom, tugging at the straps of the vest. She dumped the heavy vest by the open door, then slipped inside. I heard the locks engaging. Not that she'd need them with us there, but it made sense. She was shutting out the horror of the last couple of days. I suppose that we were as much a reminder of that horror as anything that had happened.

The shower went on.

Harvey closed the door to the outside.

"Got anything for us, Harvey?" I asked.

He picked up a bag, delved in it, and tossed me a tube of antiseptic cream. "That for starters," he said. Then, going over to the laptop, he pushed open the screen and tapped a few buttons. "Plus this."

"Who's he?" I asked.

There was a profile photograph of a fat man on the screen. Then a portrait. Then a profile from the opposite side. Police mug shots, all of the same man. He had dark hair, sweaty and hanging in bangs on his forehead. His jowls were blotchy with broken veins, and his eyes were the type you normally see on bloodhounds. He was smiling, but it was just bravado for the camera. His eyes weren't smiling. They were fearful.

"Dead, for a start," said Harvey. "He's one of the guys shot dead inside Petre Jorgenson's house."

"Got a name for him?"

"Gabriel Wellborn. Goes by Gabe. Not the kind

of character you'd normally expect to move in the same circles as the Jorgensons." He held his hand at shoulder height. "On the social ladder, the Jorgensons rate a nine." He dropped his hand way down. "Gabe Wellborn scores a minus two if he's lucky."

"So what's his deal?"

"Officially? He has a Web design business. Small potatoes, not so many clients. Just a front, if you ask me."

I nodded. "Unofficially?"

"Go-getter."

I didn't catch his meaning at first. Then I said, "Go get me this, go get me that?"

"Yeah," Harvey said. "You want something, Gabe's your man. Particularly if the thing you want is illegal. Guns, drugs, underage sex . . . you know his type."

"Maybe there's an argument for justifiable homicide. Pleased to hear he's dead," I said. Then, "These things he gets for people, does that include killers for hire?"

"Unconfirmed rumor. But, yeah. He's been on and off the FBI radar for years, but nothing's been able to stick. He recruits through these soldier of fortune sites that have sprung up all over the Web. Takes on mercenaries who are after a quick buck. Very discreet operation. All coded to protect their anonymity. Works for anyone who can pay, not just a select clientele."

"How is his operation run?"

"I spoke to an FBI contact. It's only a theory of

theirs, and up to now they've been unable to prove it. It's so simple it goes way beyond sophisticated."

"Usually the way. Hide in plain sight and people don't recognize what's right under their own noses. So how is he doing it?"

"All via the Web, using untraceable URLs. Hosting by ex–Eastern Bloc companies. Firewalls that would rival Homeland Security. Until now, the FBI has been unable to crack it. His employees use disposable cell phones with Internet connections to keep in touch. Gabe gives them their instructions under the guise of a fantasy role-playing game based on the war between Heaven and Hell."

My snort of derision was like the air brakes on an eighteen-wheeler. "And he's the Archangel Gabriel, no doubt?"

Harvey smiled at my astuteness. "Got it in one. But what about the others?"

"Named after the fallen angels?" I asked.

Harvey patted me on my shoulder. "See, I knew there was a reason why Rink took you on as his partner."

"Got a name for the shooter yet?"

"Nope. But I got this." He started pressing keys on the laptop. The screen changed to a list of names. They were all picked out in magenta, underlined. Shortcuts to Web pages, I guessed. Alphabetical, beginning with Amdusias and ending with Zagan. Weird names from a forgotten language or a cheap sci-fi movie. There were eighteen names in all.

"Names of all the fallen angels?"

"Not all," Harvey said. "There are many more than this. I lifted this list from the FBI. These are all names assumed by the players in Gabe Well-born's game."

"So we could be up against this many shooters?" I asked.

Harvey shook his head. "No. You don't have to worry. Only one of these assholes has been active in recent months."

With a manicured fingernail he tapped the screen.

"Dantalion?" I tasted the name. It was like bile in the back of my throat. "What do we know about him?"

Harvey double-clicked the blue line under the name and the computer flickered between screens. First came words written in flame. They said:

> *The seventy-first spirit is Dantalion.*
> *He is a great and mighty duke, who governs 36*
> *legions of spirits. He appears in the form of a*
> *man with many countenances, all men's and all*
> *women's faces. Dantalion knows the thoughts of*
> *all men and women, and can change them at will.*

Next, I saw a stylized painting of a man in a long white coat. His skin was white and he had flowing white hair. He held a book open in one palm and a sword in the other. I stared at the face. Androgynous, it could have been male or female. Beautiful but cruel. The eyes were like slivers of arctic ice.

I'd seen that creature before. Not so beautiful, but even more evil. Right now it was lying at the bottom of the sea with a Lincoln sedan as its tomb.

Or that was my hope.

29 FIRST CAME WEIGHTLESSNESS AS THE LINCOLN fell through space.

Then a crushing force as it slammed the water.

Next came pain.

Hopelessness.

Bubbles frothing, red flashes across his vision.

Weightlessness again as he sank.

And blackness.

The blackness was complete.

Then there were bubbles again and the taste of salt on his tongue. Not salt from the sea but salt from his blood. Sanguine and bitter, like sucking on a copper spoon.

He tried to move. But the weight of the world was on his shoulders, as if he were the Atlas of the fables. No, not the world, just the roof of the Lincoln. But it felt as heavy as the planet. And he was no Atlas to support it.

He blinked, trying to make sense of his thoughts. Now there was sea salt, and it made his weak eyes smart. He rubbed at them, realized that he was fully submerged in water, and gave up. He groped instead for something tangible to hold on to. He found a circular bar, recognizing it in his confused mind as the steering wheel of the car he was trapped within. The steering wheel was below him, almost at his knees. It took him a moment to realize that the car was standing up on end, nose downward. Bubbles raced by through the gloom, and the surroundings were getting darker by the second. The car had not yet come to rest, it was still sinking. The smashed windshield, the open windows, had allowed the sea to rush in instantly.

Good and bad.

Good because it meant he wouldn't have to fight the pressure of the sea to open the door. He'd learned once that when a car is submerged, people fight at the doors in a losing battle. Only when the pressure inside equals the pressure outside can the doors be opened. Advice under those circumstances is to sit tight. Allow the water to flood in while breathing deeply from the air trapped in the body of the car. Lungs full and the pressure equalized, it's a simple task to open a door and strike out for the surface.

Bad because the water had rushed in on impact. The car was on a steep angle as it dove deeper, and the bubbles were the trapped oxygen escaping through the smashed windows and bullet holes. There was no air pocket.

Add to that the fact he was doubled over, ass lifted by the buoyancy of air trapped inside his clothing, head down, staring through the smashed windshield so that the rushing water battered his features, and he could be forgiven for panicking.

But Dantalion didn't panic. He was a professional. He was calm and practiced.

That was the theory, at least.

Like many caught in a life-or-death predicament, he opened his mouth to shout. And all that did was empty his lungs of what precious oxygen was left to him. Then he was thrashing and pulling and he was half out of the open driver's window. The car continued to drag him down, his legs caught behind the knees by the window frame.

He kicked and kicked and then he was free. But his lungs were screaming, and there was a foggy blackness at the edges of his vision that was even deeper than the darkness around him. He was tumbling in space, arms and legs pulling and pushing but not moving him toward the surface. He didn't even know which way the surface was.

He had a moment of epiphany.

The single remaining headlight of the Lincoln pointed into the depths below him. The last few bubbles escaping his lips streaked upward over his head. Follow the bubbles, he told himself.

He set off after the bubbles. It was a race he couldn't win. But he wasn't going to give in. He struck out after them, clawing handfuls of water.

He had no recollection of his time submerged beneath the water after that.

His next conscious thought was when he was lifted from the water by strong hands. He was laid out on a pitching deck that even in his confused state he recognized as the bowed bottom of a small boat.

His vision swam.

The star-filled heavens were above him. And a pale gray blob that swam in and out of focus. Something like leather smacked against his face.

"You still with me, buddy?" a voice asked. "Hey! Hey! Are you with me?"

Dantalion lifted a hand and grabbed the wrist of the man slapping his face.

"Lay off me, will you?" Dantalion said.

"Hey, you're alive! You all right?"

"I will be when you stop slapping my damn face!"

"Oh, sorry, buddy. I thought I was too late getting to you. I thought you were dead."

Dantalion let go of the wrist. His fingernails snagged in the cuff of a leather glove. Pulled the nail at the quick, but that was the least of his troubles. He dropped his hand to his waist, patting for the bulge. Found his book. He finally exhaled. Then he started coughing, and in reflex he rolled onto his side, vomiting sea water onto the planks.

A hand patted him between the shoulder blades, and he pushed back with an elbow. Then the hands were at his shoulders, supporting him through his final spluttering coughs.

"Easy now, buddy, easy," said the Good Samaritan. "You'll be fine in a minute or two."

Through spittle Dantalion said, "I'm fine now. You can lay off with the helping hand, goddamnit."

But the man wouldn't listen. He helped Dantalion to his feet, letting him rock backward so that his butt dropped onto a bench.

"Can't believe you survived that," the man said. He was standing with his legs braced, hands on hips as he peered upward. Above him—way, way above him—was the dark underbelly of the bridge. Mangled wreckage marked where Dantalion's Lincoln had been rammed through the barrier. A drop of more than a hundred feet. Bubbles still fizzed and popped ten yards out, where his submerged vehicle continued to give up its final hold on the oxygen caught in its subframe.

Dantalion didn't have the strength to look any longer. He dropped his head between his knees, spitting out a long string of salty saliva.

"I saw it all, buddy. I'm your witness. I saw that lunatic hit your car and push you over the edge. He didn't even stop. Just took off like nothing was the matter." The man turned round to look down at his patient. "What kind of madman does that to someone?"

"Beats me," Dantalion muttered. He looked up. Finally getting a good look at his benefactor.

The guy was about seventy but in good shape for his years, short and stocky, face bronzed by the sun but a deep blue in the dark. His hair was as white as Dantalion's, but it was thick and wavy. He had a sturdy build, thick forearms, and bowed legs. Wearing a T-shirt and shorts. Leather gloves. There was a fishing pole on the bow of the boat, forgotten now.

"What are you doing out here in the dark?" Dantalion asked.

"Night fishing," the man answered, indicating the pole. "Best time, if you ask me."

Dantalion raised his brows. He wasn't the only one who preferred hunting in the dark. "No argument from me," he said.

"Good job I was here," the man added. "Otherwise no one would have seen you hit the water. They wouldn't have pulled you out in time."

Dantalion noted that the man's clothes were as wet as his were.

"You jumped in and pulled me out?" Dantalion stood up and extended his hand. "You saved my life?"

"It was nothing," said the man, accepting the hand.

"I thank you for that," Dantalion said. "I really do. And it pains me to have to kill you now."

Midhandshake the man jerked.

"Uh?" he said.

"Yes," said Dantalion. Then he snatched the hand toward him, dropping his forehead so that it struck the man flush in the face. The sound was loud, like a hammer smacking a watermelon. The man dropped onto his backside, hands going to his smashed nose. Dantalion's head swam. Not from the force of the blow but from the lack of oxygen. He had to suck in a couple of lungsful of air before he felt strong enough to reach down and grab the man's arms.

"Now, in gratitude for your selfless help, I'm going to give you a choice," he said.

The man was heavy, his sturdy little body a dead weight, not helped by the fact that he was swimming in and out of consciousness. "Wha!" was all he managed to say.

"I'm going to give you a choice about how you die," Dantalion explained. "Fast or slow?"

"Go to hell," the man slurred. He tried to pull away from Dantalion. His hands were slick with blood and his knees weak. Dantalion let go of him and he fell to his knees, bumping along the bottom of the boat. Dantalion caught him by the collar of his T-shirt. It stretched. Not good for controlling him. He grabbed at the nape of the man's neck instead.

"So it's slow, then?" Dantalion asked. "Okay . . . *buddy.*"

He swung the man round on his knees, pushing his head over the side of the boat. The man tried to resist, and Dantalion punched his free hand into the man's kidneys. He bent him over again, pushing now with both hands at the back of the man's head. Forcing his face underwater. The man yelled in terror. Bubbles frothed. But not for long.

When he was still, Dantalion pushed him overboard. Held him submerged beneath the water with both hands. Counted to one hundred. Numbers, always numbers.

Then he gently prodded the man away from him, watched as he slowly sank, aimed at the place the car went down. Maybe the police who were due to arrive would think he was the driver of the crashed Lincoln and their search for him wouldn't be so exhaustive, giving Dantalion the opportunity to sort himself out. With that breathing space, he would soon be ready to complete his mission.

But then he had to think again. Above him on the bridge, other motorists had stopped. They were peering over the balustrade. Looking down at him. He didn't think they could have seen what just occurred between him and his would-be savior, but it wasn't a chance he was about to take.

The boat was equipped with an outboard motor. He quickly set to it, pulling the starter cord. The engine coughed to life, and he sat down, aiming the prow of the boat toward the shoreline of Neptune Island.

He could hear distant voices. It didn't sound like shouts of accusation, more like concerned witnesses calling out for survivors. Dantalion didn't answer. He just angled the boat along the shoreline, heading farther away. Looking for where he'd left the minivan.

He was angry.

Angry that Bradley Jorgenson had escaped him.

Angry that Marianne Dean had escaped him.

But more than that, he was angry that Hunter and Rink had defeated him.

But the thing that angered him most was the seeping wetness at his waistline. His book was sodden. It pained him to look. He dreaded what he might find. The book was precious to him, but more than that, so were the numbers written inside.

They were the sum of his life's work.

30

RINK CAME BACK WITHIN THE HOUR, LOOK-ing more morose than ever. He had dark mud on his boots and spattered up the back of his jeans. There were even droplets of mud sticking to his black T-shirt and on his face and forearms.

"Almost ended up in the swamp with the god-damn car," he announced. And then he smiled, and it was good to see. It was the first ray of light through the cloud that had been hanging over his head since the news about his mother's illness.

He was holding his cell phone cupped in his left hand.

"You've heard something?"

"Yeah, Hunter," Rink said. He glanced round the room, taking in Harvey and Marianne, noting that they, too, wore expectant faces. "Doctors have stabilized my mom and she's going to be all right. She's feeling much better. Must be; she's been giving my father a hard time for trying to pull me away from my work."

I went over and held my friend.

"Thanks, Joe," he said. It's not often he uses my given name. Only in moments of tenderness like this. It means a lot. Strengthens our brother-like bond.

Harvey came over, too. He hugged Rink and they said their bit to each other.

Marianne didn't know what to do. She just sat down on the unoccupied bed and put her elbows on her knees and smiled up at Rink. My friend isn't the shy and retiring type around young women. He went over and sat down next to her. Patted her on her knee and said, "Okay, Marianne. Now that that's over with, we can get on with sorting out your problems."

Marianne bobbed her head. Smiled sadly. Then asked, "Is your mom ill?"

"Yeah," Rink told her. He didn't expound, but he didn't have to. The gravity of the situation must have been clear in our reaction to the good news.

"And she's all the way across the country?"

"Yeah."

Tears welled in Marianne's eyes with the realization that some people weren't as selfish as she'd always thought. Confirmation that there was still good in the world. Here were three men ready to put their lives at risk for her. Pushing aside their own needs and desires to see to her safety. "Thanks, Rink," she whispered. Then lifting her head, she looked at me and Harvey. "Thanks to you all."

"Don't worry about it," Rink told her on all our behalf. He patted her on the knee again, then stood up smoothly. He nodded at the door to the bathroom. Steam still pervaded the space beyond the open door. He glanced down at his muddy arms. "Unless you've used all the goddamn hot water," he said to her in mock anger.

Marianne smiled again, but this time not so sadly.

"Marianne's safe for now," I told Rink. Looking across at Harvey and receiving a nod of confirmation, I said, "Harvey can take her to the safe house. It's time you got on that plane, buddy."

Rink shook his head.

"You aren't going to miss anything, Rink. Catch the red-eye out of Miami. You can be there and back again in a few hours. Go on. Go see your mother and father."

"You sure?" he asked. All three of us made shooing motions, which got us a smile. "Best get that shower, then, huh?"

Feeling much better, I looked over at Harvey. He had been industrious with the computer.

"Hunter. Come take a look at this," he said.

I went over to him.

He had the CNN news site on the screen.

It showed a story about the mysterious slaying of a young family. Nathaniel and Caitlin Moore and their eight-year-old daughter, Cassandra, had been murdered in their home in the suburbs of Miami.

Yes, it was sad. A terrible reality in today's world where a family can be wiped off the face of the earth to appease one man's sick fantasy. It was exactly this kind of story that made me do the things I did.

"What're you getting at, Harvey?" I asked.

"You said the shooter used a Beretta 90two," Harvey said.

I remembered looking down the barrel of it

and thinking there was no way to avoid the 9 mm bullet headed my way. In that moment of clarity I'd identified the gun. "Yeah," I agreed. "This murderer used a Beretta as well? Doesn't mean much. Popular gun."

"You're right. Taken singly, it wouldn't mean anything." He tapped the screen. "But a witness also saw a tall man with long white hair leaving the house in the early hours. Sounds like your shooter, doesn't it?"

More interested now, I leaned down, placing my hands flat on the bed so I could get a clearer look at the screen.

"Then there's this," Harvey added. He high-lighted a block of text in the story so I could better read it.

"The thunders of judgment and wrath are numbered," I read out loud. "Written in Cassandra's blood on the living room wall. Jesus!"

"Sounds like your usual whacked-out religious freak," Harvey agreed. "Until I did a search on those words."

He brought up another site he'd been holding in a bank along the bottom of the screen. Emblazoned across the page was

A History of Enochian Ritual

"Black magic?" I asked.

"Goetic magic," Harvey corrected. "Something taken from a grimoire written hundreds of years ago by an Elizabethan astrologer named Dr. John Dee."

I'd heard of John Dee. He was the court astrologer to the first Queen Elizabeth. Purportedly he was also her top spymaster, and something of a legend among the security community. He went by the code number of 007; and maybe there was no coincidence when Ian Fleming was developing his fictional James Bond character.

"I think I know where this is going now," I said to Harvey.

He pressed a few more keys. A page came on the screen and there were the same words the murderer of the Moore family had scrawled on a wall in an eight-year-old child's blood:

The thunders of judgment and wrath are numbered.

"It's a quote from *The Book of Enoch*," Harvey pointed out. "A line from the Bornless Ritual. Something referred to as a 'Calling of the Aethyr.' All mumbo jumbo bullshit, I agree. But translated, it refers to the summoning of a dark angel."

"Dantalion," I said.

Harvey's fingers tapped keys yet again, bringing up another link, to a table full of weird symbols next to names and descriptions. Dantalion was eighth down.

"Shit," I hissed.

"*Shit* about sums things up," Harvey said. "This guy's one crazy motherfucker."

"But why kill a family?" I wondered. "What have the Moores got to do with this?"

Throughout our discourse, Marianne had kept her thoughts firmly to herself. But at the mention of the family name, I heard her croak. I looked at her and she stood up slowly. She came to stand at my shoulder and stared at the screen.

"Did you say *Moore*?"

I nodded to Harvey and he brought us back to the CNN screen.

Marianne's hands went to her mouth. "Oh, dear God!"

"What is it?" I asked.

"Caitlin Moore," she said. "She was my teacher at Collinwood High School. It was Caitlin who introduced me to Bradley."

Harvey quickly clicked off the CNN screen. Marianne turned slowly, dropping back on the bed. Her hands worked down from her mouth and plucked at an imaginary crucifix at her throat.

"Back in 2002," she said, her voice barely above a whisper, "my brother Stephen was among the first marines to be deployed to Iraq. There was a fear that Saddam Hussein had weapons of mass destruction hidden away, and Stephen was among those sent in to try to locate them."

Uh-oh, I thought, having a feeling where this was going. Richard Dean had never mentioned having an older son. Neither had Marianne mentioned a brother before. Or that he was a soldier. Even when Rink had done a background check on Dean, it hadn't been mentioned.

"He was given inoculations to protect him from ABC warfare?" I offered, thinking back to how many times I had stood in a line baring my shoulder for a nurse or doctor with a huge syringe. Never questioning, just taking the injections as protection from the atomic, bacterial, and chemical weapons that could be coming our way.

"Yes," Marianne said, her voice barely audible. She sucked in a ragged breath. Her next words were a little stronger. "And it was pointless. As you know, those weapons were never found. Stephen came back from his tour sick. No one would accept that his sickness was a result of the medication he'd been given. They still won't.

"They said that his illness was merely psychosomatic. He was imagining his problems. Fatigue, a loss of feeling in his extremities, blinding headaches. It drove him to throw himself off a ten-story building during an antiwar rally."

"I'm sorry," I muttered, feeling very awkward. "It's a terrible thing to lose someone. Especially under those circumstances."

"I miss him dearly. Five years have gone by and there hasn't been a day when I haven't thought about him."

"Yet you're in love with a man responsible for his death?" I asked.

"Bradley isn't responsible. I don't blame him. Not one little bit."

"It was medication developed by the Jorgensons that you believe caused Stephen's illness?"

Marianne simply nodded. Then she said, "Mrs. Moore was one of my teachers at school, but she was also a trained counselor. She spoke to me after my brother's death. We shared common ideas on the wars in Iraq and Afghanistan. Our servicemen and -women are dying needlessly, and all for the wrong reasons." She blinked at me, realizing that I had been one of those self-same servicemen, albeit with a different army, and had fought in the same war as her brother. "I'm very supportive of all our brave servicemen and -women. I'm not against the military at all. I just wanted to do my bit to see that our troops were given the respect they were due. I joined a protest group that Mrs. Moore had set up to express our views."

"You attended a meeting with the Jorgenson family?"

"Yes. That's where I first met Brad. He was very charming, and he was open to our opinions. He was a good listener. We talked quite a lot afterward."

"And that was when you started dating him?"

"Yes."

"But your father didn't approve?"

"My father is still very angry. He hates Bradley. He blames Bradley for Stephen's death, just as he blames everyone else involved."

"Maybe he has a right to hate Bradley. Your father showed me photographs of you," I told her. "One of you fighting off Bradley in the back of a car. It looked like he was taking advantage of you."

She shook her head in incredulity. "Show me

any celebrity that hasn't had a similar photograph taken. We were just playing up to the cameras, Joe giving the paparazzi something to get excited about. It was a prank. It was a bad idea in hindsight."

"He showed me a police photo where you had been a victim of assault."

Her lips pinched.

"Yes."

"But it wasn't Bradley who beat you up, was it?"

"No, of course not. Bradley loves me, and I love him."

"Yeah," I said. And Bradley had been telling the truth. Made me feel a bit of a shit.

"So who was it?" I asked. "I thought maybe one of his family was involved. Petre, maybe. But it wasn't him, was it?"

"No." A quake ran the full length of her body. "It was my dad."

I'd already come to that conclusion. It had been obvious, when I thought about it. I remembered our first meeting in the grimy roadhouse. As I'd walked away from the bar in Shuggie's Shack, Richard Dean had been fiddling with something in his hand. I recalled now that it had flashed in the subdued light. Something metallic. Her crucifix. He'd quickly stuffed it into his pocket before feeding me a line of bullshit a mile wide.

"He came to Bradley's house to take me home. He accused me of betraying my brother's memory. Said I'd made myself a whore of my brother's murderers. He couldn't see that he was wrong, that Bradley was actually on our side and was prepared to withdraw all contracts with the military." Her fingers went to her throat, teasing the imaginary cross. She began to weep. "He told me that I'd betrayed our family. That my mother would be turning in her grave. He tore my mother's necklace from my throat. When I tried to take it back, he struck me. He was in a rage, and he struck me again and again. He didn't know what he was doing, he was just mad."

"That's no excuse," I told her.

"I forgive him," she said. "I still love him."

Thinking back to when we'd first broached this subject, I'd assumed that she was referring to Bradley when she'd said similar words. She hadn't been, I saw now. She'd forgiven her father for his actions and his words. But Richard Dean hadn't forgiven anyone.

He had sent me here to take Marianne back to him under false pretenses. He had another reason for sending me. I was supposed to stop Bradley from coming after her. *"The balance will be paid as soon as I get the proof that Jorgenson is no longer a threat to me or any of my family,"* he'd said. His meaning had been explicit. Stop him for good. Kill him.

That wasn't going to happen.

I was going to protect Bradley.

Then I would see to the problem that was Marianne's father.

Rink came out of the bathroom, whistling and scrubbing his hair with a towel.

He stopped and looked at us all.

"What did I miss?" he asked.

Where the hell do I start? I thought.

"Nothing important," I told him. "Go and catch that plane, Rink."

31 THERE WERE ONLY TWO THINGS STOPPING DAN-
talion from immediately returning to the
Jorgenson estate on Neptune Island.

First, he was unarmed. He'd lost both the Beretta and the Glock in the water. He didn't doubt
that he could take a weapon from one of the two-
bit guards the Jorgensons had in their employ,
but then there was the second thing that was
stopping him.

It was as if half the Martin County Sheriff's
Office had turned out, along with officers from
the Miami PD, and he was pretty sure that some
of the men and women in stylish business suits
were from the FBI. There were even officers from
the Hostage Rescue Team in attendance, dressed
in black jumpsuits and helmets and armed with
assault rifles. Add to that the proliferation of CSI
technicians, ambulances from Hobe Sound and
Jupiter, and various other supporting agencies,
and the estate was a no-go area for the foresee-
able future.

Or was it?

A man of his abilities should be able to wander
among so many people who were not used to
working together and be missed among the

throng. Hide in plain sight. Become one of them. Look like he had the right to be there.

Except he was soaked through and didn't have a change of clothing. He'd dumped his knapsack with his kit prior to the assault on Bradley Jorgenson's house. In hindsight that had been a bad idea. Though it freed him up to move more easily during the anticipated gun battle, he had never intended leaving his bag behind. His expectation was that he'd kill them all and then return for the bag at his leisure. But then came the high-speed car chase, his subsequent near drowning, and the killing of the fisherman. It wasn't until he returned to the minivan and drove away—passing the first blue lights and sirens hurtling toward the island—that he'd recognized his error. Right now his bag and clothing would be in the hands of a CSI tech, sealed in an evidence bag and en route to the nearest lab for forensic examination. They'd find DNA, hair fibers, and other trace evidence, but that didn't concern him. They'd tie the forensics to some of the hits he'd carried out, but that was all. They wouldn't be able to tie the evidence to him.

Not unless he was caught.

But that wasn't going to happen.

More worrying was the laptop he'd left at Petre Jorgenson's house. He hadn't even thought to turn the damn thing off. He didn't doubt that Gabe Wellborn had taken precautions that the transactions he'd performed through that computer couldn't be easily traced. But to be sure,

Dantalion would prefer to have destroyed the damn thing entirely after Gabe had transferred the half-million dollars into his offshore account. His account wouldn't lead back to him. It was a numbered account only, and the Bahamian bank that he used wasn't famous for bending to the demands of the American law enforcement community.

The FBI had some very clever computer wizards. No doubt about it, somewhere someone would break the codes. It would show his history. Maybe even lead back to him and his true identity. After that he would be forever on the run. Not that they would find him. Jean-Paul St. Pierre would simply cease to exist.

On top of the money he'd already earned from previous jobs, the half-million dollars would make him a wealthy man. He could go anywhere. But that wasn't a consideration right now. He still had a mission to complete.

He'd driven the van north to get past any roadblocks the police might have put up. A little part of him had hoped to intercept Bradley Jorgenson on his return to the island, but he knew there was a small chance of that happening.

Approaching Hobe Sound on the Southeast Dixie Highway, he looked for an appropriate place to turn off. He found it after a couple of minutes and angled the vehicle down a cross street that headed inland toward the Jonathan Dickinson State Park. He was looking for somewhere secluded. A place he could rest up and consider his next course of action. Somewhere to dry out his book.

The road wound through a picture of suburban tranquillity. Beautiful houses in beautiful gardens snoozed away the nighttime hours, at rest and at peace with the world. Inside, families young and old would be sleeping, dreaming their dreams and murmuring in contentment. No one would expect a professional killer to come to Aurora Village, let alone take up temporary residence there.

The village ended abruptly, giving way to swamp and scrubland. Irrigation channels— or more likely drainage—appeared at intervals along the way, and he found himself on a dirt track with a series of short wooden bridges. His tires bumped over the wood, making a double thump that sounded like a faltering heartbeat. He could smell the swamp, the cloying odors of decaying vegetation and stagnant water, but thought the smell could have been coming from his soaked clothes and body. Sea salt had invaded his clothing, and his skin had begun to itch.

To his left he noted the squat silhouettes of buildings. Agriculture wasn't the largest industry here, but the buildings looked like some kind of farm. He found a turning off the track and drove the minivan into it. The track was little more than a series of ruts and potholes, and he decided this probably wasn't the main route to the farm. Nevertheless, he switched off the van's lights so that he approached in darkness. He didn't want to alert anyone to his arrival until it was on his terms.

He stopped the vehicle a hundred yards short of the buildings. Turned off the engine and slipped out of the door. He didn't close the door fully, only pushed it gently to. Then he moved toward the buildings at a steady lope. The bullet wound in his leg was knitting, but with each step it felt as if his skin cracked open. Ordinarily such a minor wound wouldn't be a distraction to him, but now, added to his other problems, it made him chew his lips against the pain. The limp became more pronounced the nearer he got to the buildings.

In his black clothing, his face stark and smudged with blood, hair hanging in colorless ribbons, he felt like a B-movie vampire skulking through the night. Not a bad image—it would add to the fear in the hearts of those he might come across. Fear would be his greatest weapon without the aid of his gun.

He scanned the buildings. Two of them were little more than lean-tos, while one was an enclosed barn. There were a couple of adobe-style outhouses and then a small, single-story house. The house was adobe as well, more like the ones he'd seen in Santa Fe than those indigenous to this part of Florida. He was approaching from the back of the house, but he got the impression of large windows in all the rooms. Because of its remote location, with no discernible neighbors, the drapes hadn't been drawn when the occupants had retired for the evening. The only light he could see was from a dull bulb in a porch at the rear door.

It was hot here through the day, so he could guarantee that the house was temperature-controlled by AC units. For them to work to their best ability, windows and doors would be kept shut during the sultry hours of the night. Shut but not necessarily locked.

The obvious door to try would be the back door. People who lived and worked in the area of the outbuildings would use that door on a regular basis. The front door would hardly ever be unlocked. Still, he bypassed the rear of the property to fully reconnoiter the building. When he got to the front of the house, it was in darkness. His peek through the large picture window showed a simple living space with sturdy wooden furniture and an old-fashioned record player built into a cabinet. Trinket-type ornaments were on shelves on the wall. Framed photographs lined one wall, but in the darkness he couldn't make them out. Portraits for sure; sons and daughters and grandkids, more than likely.

Continuing around the far edge of the building, he found a carport. Only one vehicle. A Dodge pickup. Dusty and scraped from hard toil in the fields. He found the door unlocked and opened it. No alarm. He wasn't expecting one: an alarm or central locking system would have armed itself by now and made the doors secure. He searched the interior for a weapon, but there was nothing. He did note something, though. The driver's seat was misshapen and tattered, but the passenger seat was as smooth as the day it came off the assembly line. Only one person ever rode in this vehicle. No Mrs. Farmer to contend with inside the house. Whoever lived in the house did so alone.

He poked around in the back of the truck and came away with a large lug wrench from a box of tools. Heavy and blunt, it was a formidable weapon. Also, he pushed a screwdriver into his waistband. It wasn't dagger quality, but it could still be rammed through flesh if the need arose.

As he made his way back across the front of the house the scene hadn't changed. The lights were still off, the living room devoid of life. He kept going and gained the back of the house once more. Gnats swarmed on the screen of the porch, seeking the light bulb within. Dantalion opened the screen very slowly so that it didn't squeak, then stepped inside, accompanied by many of the darting insects. Some of them bounced off his features and clung to his hair, and he shivered involuntarily. He wiped them away. Reaching for the door handle, he turned it. The thing resisted him. The person inside was security conscious after all. But that was a good thing, could mean he also had what Dantalion had come seeking.

He took the screwdriver out of his waistband, inserted it alongside the lock, and levered against the frame. With his other hand he gradually forced open the door. The lock was no use when the door frame was made of weathered wood. He was happy that the noise of his breaking and entering was minimal, that it wouldn't have woken even the lightest of sleepers. He stepped inside. A utility area with a stack of washing waiting for the iron greeted him. Checked shirts and jeans, a pair of tan nylon trousers, socks and underwear for a conservative man. His assumption of a single occupant was taking on more validity. A man of middle age, judging by the style of clothes. He picked up the nylon trousers—a fashion faux pas to anyone under the age of fifty—and checked the size. Not that he was going to wear them himself; he wanted to get a picture of the man he would have to kill. They were narrow around the waist, short in the leg. Small, skinny man, then? He lifted one of the shirts and found that it was surprisingly bulky. Who was this guy, Dantalion wondered, a goddamn trained ape?

There was only one way to find out. He stepped through into a kitchen. As bare as the living room, this kitchen had only the most basic of utilities. Stove. Sink with a couple of neatly stacked dishes on the drainboard. One cup ringed with coffee stains waiting for washing under the faucet. A drawer in a cupboard disclosed cutlery. Dantalion took out a heavy-bladed bread knife. It was better for stabbing than the screwdriver, and he kept it fisted in his right hand.

Moving toward the living area, he passed an upright vacuum cleaner standing in the hall. Ambient light came in through the front door, so he avoided tripping over the hose that lay at his feet like the coils of a boa constrictor. On his right now was the living room. He gave it only brief attention, happy to see it still as it was before. Then he turned to the door on his left.

Placing an ear to the door, he listened.

From within came the telltale sounds of snoring. Just a light buzz, but it appeared to be coming from only one person. He tried the handle and the door swung inward silently. He followed the opening of the door by stepping inside and squaring his feet on the carpet. The person lying on his back beneath a sheet didn't even stir. Dantalion was a child of the night; his condition had ensured that, so he had no problems with the darkness. He could make out the man's sleep-relaxed features where they rose from beneath the sheet. Younger than he thought. The man had a shaved head and a thin moustache that hooked around the corners of his mouth. One shoulder looked muscular where the sheet had dropped away. Strong, farm strong, but maybe something to do with gymnasiums and heavy weights, too. Could be a handful in a hand-to-hand tussle.

A quick stab to the carotid artery would do it.

The man would wake, thrash about, his blood jetting around the room, growing less with each failing heartbeat.

Maybe not the best way to kill him, then?

Club him senseless with the lug wrench, then cut his throat? Less thrashing but still copious amounts of blood.

A single stab to the heart would be best. Very

little blood if the heart died instantly. The only problem was he couldn't be sure of an immediate hit. The man had a sheet over his upper torso and it appeared that one of his arms was draped across his chest. It would mean lifting the sheet to get a clear view. The man could wake up, and then there would surely be a fight.

Choices, choices, Dantalion thought, always choices.

And with each choice a myriad of tangents to choose from.

The man muttered in his sleep. Maybe some primal instinct was warning him about the presence of danger hovering so close by.

Maybe I should wake him, Dantalion thought. Let him choose how to die.

But he decided not to. This killing wasn't for pleasure.

Dantalion lifted the lug wrench with his left hand. Brought it down in a sweeping arc. It struck the man's head on the left temple, made a deep depression in the skull above his ear. That could prove a killing blow in itself. The man's eyes shot open, but his pupils didn't contract, they stayed wide and bewildered. He didn't even see the knife that Dantalion drove through his chest. And that wound definitely killed him.

Dantalion leaned over and flicked on the bedside lamp. Pearlescent light shone. He pulled back the sheet until it snagged against the shaft of steel protruding from the man's chest. Just left of dead center. Dantalion smiled at his precise stab, thought that maybe he didn't need a gun after all. But he discarded that notion immediately. He was going up against men who had guns, and he had to at least even his chances of a fair fight.

He checked the bedside table. No gun.

He checked the closet but found only more of those checked shirts and jeans. Another pair of cream nylon trousers, too. These were sheathed in plastic, as though kept for good. He took them out and saw that the leg length was much longer than the worn pair he'd seen in the utility area. These hadn't seen a trip to a seamstress yet. He held them alongside his own legs and found that they stopped a full inch above his ankles, but though he'd probably look like Pee-wee Herman, they would do in a pinch. He set them on the bed at the foot of the mattress. He selected the least gaudy of the shirts. Pale blue-and-white checks. There was also a battered Stetson hat on a shelf at the top of the cupboard. That joined his growing pile of clothes. He found socks, too. He'd be going commando, however, because there was no way he was going to wear the man's underwear.

He drew the knife from the man's chest, wiped it clean on the sheet, then threw the remainder of the sheet over the man's ceiling-staring face. He lifted the pile of clothes and went in search of the shower.

On his way, he poked his head into the living room. Glancing around, he searched for what he wanted and noticed a wooden chest pressed up against the wall below the photographs. Switching on the overhead light, he placed his supplies on a worn settee and approached the chest. It was held closed by a flimsy hasp and cheap padlock. One smack of the lug wrench was all it took to break the lock off and he threw back the lid.

He bared his teeth in a grin of pleasure as his eyes took in the contents.

32 As dawn broke over the Atlantic Ocean, Harvey headed northwest toward Tampa. He took the Ford and he also took Marianne. Harvey was one of the two people on the planet I felt easy handing the girl over to. The other, Rink, was already in San Francisco. He'd left last night. He called me to tell me he was going to fly back as soon as his parents stopped hugging him. I asked him to hug his mum for me. For my part, I had another job to do. Several, actually, but all involved locating Bradley Jorgenson and delivering him to the same safe house where Marianne would be waiting.

While I waited for my rental car to be delivered, I took a run through the state park. A tourist pamphlet in the motel room said that there were more than four and a half miles of trails through the swamps and hummocks of brush. By the time I was finished I'd have covered twice that distance. I needed the exercise. In my line of work you had to remain at a peak level of fitness. All being equal in all other areas, it was always the man with the greatest endurance and conditioning who would win a fight. I pushed myself hard. My lungs labored for the first mile, but then

I settled into a rhythm and my breathing evened out so that I was running at a steady gait and my breathing came easy.

Finding myself on a stretch of sand overlooking the ocean, I stopped for a while. Watched the sun come up while performing a yoga exercise called Salute the Sun. Stretching my muscles, limbering up. I dropped and did two hundred pushups and the same amount of crunches. Then I spent ten minutes going through a series of movements that involved punching, kicking, and elbow and knee strikes. Nothing fancy; not karate or tai chi or anything so stylized. The moves I did were short and brutal and designed along the lines of a simple equation:

$$\text{MINIMUM EFFORT} \times \text{MAXIMUM IMPACT} = \text{DEVASTATING EFFECT}$$

Sweating like a pig in a sauna, I ran back through the swamp, detoured so I completed the course again, then headed back to the motel room. My rental was waiting for me, and I signed an assumed name and showed the delivery guy a fake driver's license courtesy of Harvey Lucas.

Taking the keys for the imported Audi A8 from him, I went inside and immediately checked that my SIG Sauer was still where I'd left it inside a tissue box stuffed behind the TV.

Dripping from my workout, I stepped into the bathroom and turned on the shower. Then I stripped out of my damp clothes and stepped gratefully under the hot water. My muscles were pumped with blood from the exercise, and I relaxed under the steaming flow, working the kinks out of my body with a soaped-up sponge. When I stepped out of the shower my mind was back on the job.

I slipped into fresh boxer shorts and pulled on a pair of crisp denims that clung to my damp body. Shirtless, I retrieved my SIG from its hiding place and sat on the bed to clean it. I had rags and oil and I stripped down the gun so that I had all the working parts laid out on the bed. When I was done, I inserted a full clip and racked the slide so that I was good to go. Police forces the world over teach a method of safe gun handling. They absolutely will not condone carrying a gun with a bullet in the firing chamber. Safety against lawsuits, that was. Or to avoid a fumbling cop shooting off his toes. I came from a different school of thought and practiced a method called "point shooting." A bit like the quick-draw heroes from Western movies, I could draw, point, and fire in an instant. The thinking behind the system was that there was no natural wastage of time. And it would be a waste of a precious second if I had to rack a bullet into place before I fired. In that time I could already be dead.

The SIG I used was specially modified, with no safety switch or sights on the barrel to snag on my clothing. It was a steel-bodied anti-blowback model that barely recoiled in the fist. Handy when the 9 mm soft-nosed Parabellums it fired were a powerful enough load to stop most men dead in their tracks. I didn't want a gun that I had to constantly fight to control and to retarget after every shot.

Harvey had brought plenty of spare ammunition. He'd also supplied me with a military issue Ka-bar knife coated in black epoxy. There was also a new pay-and-go cell phone for use during the operation ahead.

Standing, I caught sight of myself in a mirror at the back of the room. Most people would see a taller than average man on his way to forty years old but with the hard body of someone ten years younger. They'd see the short brown hair with only a hint of gray at the temples and the eyes that flashed between blue and green depending on my mood. They'd notice the tattoo on my right shoulder and wonder what it represented. Only if they looked closely enough would they notice the story of my life etched into my skin in the form of a tapestry of scars that I'd picked up during fourteen years as a counterterrorism officer and the four years since. On my right pectoral muscle is a tiny white indentation where I was shot when on patrol in Northern Ireland. The scar where the bullet exited was a puckered mass of scar tissue an inch or so from the tattoo.

I touched a recent scar, running my fingers over the pink ridge in my chest just to the left of my heart. That was courtesy of a fight with an ex–Secret Service agent named Martin Maxwell who had taken to killing people and stripping the bones from their corpses, then taking the bones to Jubal's Hollow, his secret repository in the Mojave Desert. Maxwell, dubbed the Harvestman by the FBI, made a mistake when he took my brother, John. I hunted the bastard down and rammed one of those bones into his throat. He got me good, though, and it was pure chance that he missed my heart and found only the meat of my pectoral muscle.

Thinking of the Harvestman, I couldn't help but draw parallels between him and this latest maniac I'd gone up against. Why was it that they had to take assumed names? And often from the Bible? Martin Maxwell had believed himself Tubal Cain reincarnated, and now I had some lunatic who thought he had fallen from heaven with Lucifer and his crew. Well, he'd certainly taken a fall, rammed off the bridge at Neptune Island and sent to a watery hell in the sea below.

Ever the pessimist, though, I was prepared to accept that I hadn't seen him die. He could still be out there someplace. With that in mind I pushed the SIG into my waistband at the back and felt around for fresh socks. I pulled on my boots—still dusty from my run—then slipped the Ka-bar alongside my right ankle. A plain black V-neck T went on, with a loose canvas jacket over that. It was too warm for outerwear, but I needed something to cover the bulge that my SIG made at the small of my back. I had a license to carry, but not in my real name. Fundamentally, the cops were on the same side as I was, but it wouldn't stop them running me in if they realized the license was as bogus as the name on it.

A man of many resources, Harvey had already paid up the bill for the room. But I still had to hand back the keys before leaving. Pulling all my belongings into a pile, I shoved them into a plastic garbage bag and knotted the top. I slung them into the backseat on passing the Audi, then went and deposited the key to the room through the flap provided. Back in the car, I headed toward the Southeast Dixie Highway, watching the totem pole grow small in the rearview mirror as I pulled away.

The Southeast Dixie Highway went through Hobe Sound. It was still early, not yet eight o'clock, and the road wasn't so busy. There were only a few people out on the palm-lined streets. Out of Hobe Sound the road hugged the coast. A short distance later, I found the turnpike that allowed me onto the road that traversed first Jupiter, then Neptune Island.

As I drove I watched the boats sailing up and down the Intracoastal Waterway. The sea was turquoise against pale sand. In places I could see all the way to the bottom. The sky was equally clear, with only a haze on the southern horizon that wasn't cloud but pollution from the cities of Miami and Miami Beach. A mile overhead a passenger plane headed out over the ocean, and I imagined vacationers sitting with glum faces as they took their last look down on paradise. They wouldn't think it was paradise if they knew what had gone on down here the evening before.

Arriving at Neptune, I slowed the Audi and pulled into a layover next to a picnic area. There were already families in attendance, but they were too busy enjoying the scenery and the glorious weather to pay attention to a single man making a telephone call. Harvey was driving, so it was Marianne Dean who answered. She put the call on speakerphone so that the two of them could listen.

"I hope Harvey's treating you well, Mari?" I said, to keep things light between us. Purposefully I used the name she wished to go by, a way of reassuring her that I was fully on her side.

"Don't worry, Joe, Harvey's being the perfect gentleman," Marianne said. Her voice sounded musical, as if some of the worry had been expunged from her soul. I only hoped my next question wouldn't send her two steps backward.

"What has hit the news about last night, Harve?"

Harvey grunted. "World War Three, the way the networks are handling it."

"Anything specific?"

"If you're asking if the shooter has turned up, the answer's no. But some old guy was found floating near the crash scene. Unless he was unlucky and the Lincoln landed on him, I think Dantalion did the poor guy in."

"What was he doing out there?"

"At a guess? Fishing. And before you ask, the water's too deep for wading; he had to have had a boat with him. Looks like Dantalion survived. Worse than that, he got clean away."

We should have made sure. It's a pity Rink

didn't get to put a couple of rounds in his ugly face before pushing him into the sea.

But the news didn't exactly surprise me.

"So he's still out there," I said. "But if we were right about Gabe Wellborn being his handler, then I'm guessing he's been cut free. He has no support network to back him up."

"Has to be resilient," Harvey said, "surviving the crash and getting away. I don't think he's about to crawl away and hide under a rock someplace. He's probably got himself holed up somewhere and is planning his next move."

"Okay," I said. "This is what we're going to do. You go ahead with getting Marianne to the safe house; I'm going to try to get hold of Bradley. I don't trust that asshole Seagram to protect him. Only time that piece of shit would stop a bullet was if he tripped over his own feet and fell into the line of fire."

"Can help you there," Harvey said. "We spoke to Bradley a few minutes ago. Marianne guessed where he'd be. They used to use a motel when they were first seeing one another."

In the background I heard Marianne saying something about their rendezvous all being innocent, that they'd only meet there before going on to some movie or bar. There was no funny business.

"Where is he?" I asked.

"On his way back to Neptune by now. We caught him on his way out. Tried to convince him to keep well away, but he wasn't having any."

"Idiot," I said.

"He has to be concerned," Marianne said in his defense. "Don't forget that we're talking about his home. His family."

"Yeah," I agreed. The same family that was trying its damnedest to kill Bradley and her off. I didn't mention that, though, just went on, "The place will be swarming with cops. It's not going to be easy getting in touch with him."

Then Marianne piped up. "I can always give you his phone number."

"He's carrying a cell phone?" I asked.

"No, I don't think so. We spoke to him on the motel phone. But if he's home I can give you a direct line through to his private office."

"Sounds good."

Marianne reeled off the number, and I memorized it to put into my phone's address book later.

"Okay, guys," I said. "I'll let you get on with your bit. I'll ring you when I know what's happening. Watch your backs. If this crazy is still out there, we have no idea where he'll pop up next."

"Don't worry," Harvey said. "Next time there'll be no mistakes."

"Yeah," I said. My sentiment exactly.

"Take it easy, Hunter," Harvey said.

"Yeah, look after Marianne," I said.

Even Marianne got in her thoughts. "Please be careful, Joe. And bring Bradley safely back to me."

"I will," I told her. Then I pressed the button to end the call. And stabbed in the number that Marianne had narrated.

The ringtone came back at me. And kept on coming.

Deciding I was a little premature in ringing Bradley, I got out of the car and stretched my limbs. From where I was standing I could see the beginning of the Jorgenson estate. The wall that encompassed the landward side of the grounds was a smudge on the horizon. Beyond it I could just make out a hint of the first of the family homes beyond it. A steepled roof with turrets at each corner. But the heat haze was building, so the turrets could simply have been a play of the shifting light.

There were quite a large number of tourists about now. Some had brought blankets. Some had fishing poles and were wandering across the sand dunes that swayed with saw-tooth grass, heading toward the inlet. Others came armed with binoculars, and I thought there were an inordinate number of ornithologists unless there were some special birds hereabouts. A noisy group of college-aged guys played volleyball on a stretch of open sand. Some of them had bottles of beer in their hands and were posturing for the young ladies who watched them from their beach towels. I had no beer: I'd brought mineral water with me and slaked my thirst directly from the bottle.

I should have thought to ask Marianne how far away the hotel was that Bradley was traveling from. It would have given me a clearer idea of how long he would be on the road. I didn't even know which direction he'd be coming from. Okay, when they'd taken off last night, Seagram had driven north. But the hotel they'd ended up at could have been in any direction. My plan was to cut him off before he arrived back at the estate and take him back to Marianne. Then the problem posed by Dantalion's apparent survival could be dealt with without having someone I had to protect along for the ride. With that in mind, my only recourse would be to park up next to the main entrance gate, but that would bring the police down on me in seconds. They'd have been there all night, and there would be more coming and going throughout the day and perhaps for many more to come. A strange vehicle with a gun-toting driver would raise the eyebrow of any cop worth his salt.

I decided to wait where I was.

I had a good view of the road and would recognize the silver sedan Bradley and Seagram had taken off in the night before. If by chance I didn't see them, I'd ring the number for his office every quarter hour. I hoped to have made contact with him by midmorning at the latest.

While I waited I watched the traffic heading south. I didn't bother with those coming toward me, as none of them would have Bradley on board. Streams of vehicles drove by. Some stopped at the layover, but none of them was a silver Lincoln. I tried Bradley's number. No answer. A quarter hour and about two hundred vehicles later, I tried it again. Still no answer.

I wondered if Seagram would be clever enough to ditch the sedan and bring Bradley home in a less conspicuous vehicle. Something like an older-model station wagon or the black mini-van with tinted windows I watched sail past. But then I recalled his panic of last night and decided he wasn't fully suited to his chosen career. He would drive the sedan back because that was what bodyguards obviously drove when they had an important passenger.

I tried the number again, and someone picked up. A female voice. Officious. Cop, I thought, and hung up quickly.

It didn't surprise me that the police were in Bradley's office. They'd be trying to make sense of the mayhem that had gone down at two of Bradley Jorgenson's homes, plus that of his cousin Petre, and would quickly tie the family business dealings to the attempts made on their lives. Police officers would be going through the records in Bradley's office in an attempt to identify who had attacked the houses.

I regretted standing outside the gate when we'd first arrived, challenging the security by shouting angrily at the CCTV camera. The cops would most likely be reviewing those recordings by now. Two angry guys demanding entrance, obviously armed and pissed off, would be immediate suspects in their investigation. If they weren't already, mine and Rink's images would be flashing across the country to the FBI VICAP HQ at Quantico to try to identify us from their store of mug shots. Not that they'd find us there, but someone with a bit of savvy might think to interrogate military records, and that would finally give us up.

Hindsight's a wonderful thing.

33

THE WOODEN CHEST IN THE DEAD MAN'S LIVING room disgorged its secrets.

It would have been nice to have discovered a cache of weapons, but what he found instead were the makings of a disguise that could get him close to Bradley Jorgenson. Each item he lifted out was folded neatly, preserved within layers of tissue paper the way he knew some couples preserved their wedding suits and dresses. Not that the man he'd killed in his bed appeared to have been married—not to a woman, at any rate—but he had been married to his career. The love and care with which he'd saved his uniform told him so. As did the proliferation of photographs that showed him standing alone, or with groups of colleagues, proudly grinning toward the camera.

Dantalion wondered where things had gone wrong for the dead man. Perhaps he'd been injured or had become sick, or perhaps he'd merely grown jaded with the day-to-day, but he seemed to have taken early retirement from his career. He guessed it was likely that the man had left on good terms; otherwise he might have destroyed his uniform in protest.

The uniform was complete. Even down to belts and equipment.

The only things missing were the tools of his trade, but Dantalion believed a more thorough search would turn them up.

The trousers might present a problem, the man being shorter in the leg than Dantalion, but he saw a way around that. The shirts might be a little large, but again, not too great a worry. He would only have to fool Jorgenson long enough to take him out, and then he wouldn't be concerned by how many people saw through the disguise.

First, though, he had to get out of his wet clothes. Take a shower. He had no hydrocortisone cream with him to salve his itching skin, but he hoped the dead man would have moisturizing lotions of some kind in his bathroom. And he didn't know of a farm that didn't have a rudimentary first-aid kit. Or weapons, he reminded himself. There were always guns on a farm.

He had a tepid shower. Not hot, his skin was too raw. Then he dried off with the softest towel he could find. He used the man's stock of body lotion to dab over the exposed areas of skin on his face and hands but decided that the rest of his body would be fine as long as he kept covered up and away from direct sunlight. He found antiseptic cream in the same bathroom cupboard and cleaned his bullet wounds. The wounds on his arm and cheek were inconsequential. However, the one on his leg was particularly angry looking, the flesh at the edges red and swollen like botoxed lips. He wondered about the effects the infection could be having on him. But he discarded the notion. *He* was fully in charge, he told himself.

Then he took to his hair with a pair of scissors, trimming the long strands away so that he had a crew cut. His hair was sparse and tufted in places, and he'd never get by a thorough inspection, but he thought that with the hat in place the haircut would suffice.

With the same scissors, he unpicked the hems on the trouser legs, letting them down a full inch. Not too bad, he thought, but tucked them into the tops of his boots like some people wore them in the field. With the shirt on, he folded the back over twice and tucked it into the waistband of his trousers, cinching it in place with a thin leather belt. A clip-on tie. The collar sagged a little, and he looked like someone who'd been on a drastic diet and hadn't gotten around to replacing his wardrobe yet, but overall he didn't look too bad. He pulled on the jacket and adjusted the widebrimmed hat to a jaunty angle, admiring himself in a mirror on the bathroom wall. The mark on his jaw was just a graze, not that noticeable if he kept his chin tucked down.

He found a utility closet. Cleaning fluids and brushes and rags were stacked in boxes. On a shelf at head height he found a strongbox. On the shelf next to it was a key. When he popped the lock he found what he'd been looking for.

The gun was a Taurus 85, a five-shot revolver.

One of the 38-caliber specials worn by some law enforcement officers as a backup weapon. There were two rapid loaders filled with standard .38 bullets. This time he wouldn't be conducting a full-on assault of the Jorgenson estate, so if ten rounds weren't sufficient, then there was something wrong with his plan.

He couldn't find a holster, so assumed the dead man had kept this gun purely for home defense. Not that it had proved much use to him locked in a metal container two rooms away from where he'd died. Dantalion loaded the revolver, then slipped it into his jacket pocket alongside the spare rapid loader.

Then he saw to the most pressing task of all.

He'd been afraid to look at his book.

But when he opened it, he found that the sea water hadn't invaded the interior beyond a broad margin. Flicking through the pages he discovered that most of his lists of numbers were still legible. The ink had spread a little, causing an auric light effect around the figures, but in its own way it made the numbers seem more ethereal and magical and was somewhat to his liking. Only the final numbers troubled him. They told a lie. The three he'd written down pertaining to Bradley, Marianne, and Hunter held no power. He could offset that by entering the numbers of those he'd killed since: Petre Jorgenson, Gabe Wellborn, and upward of half a dozen bodyguards, but that could throw off the value of the figures. The numerology system he used demanded that he be exact at all times. The three he'd already written down must die before he could tally the others' numbers.

In the pantheon of the Fallen, Dantalion is the seventy-first spirit. He is a great and mighty duke, who governs thirty-six legions of spirits. A legion is a subjective figure, whichever way you look at it. In ancient Rome, a legion was a division of soldiers numbering between three and six thousand. That would give Dantalion dominion over the spirits of between 108,000 and 216,000 people. However you approached those figures, it was a largely unattainable sum for any single killer who did not have the power of an army behind him, or his finger on the button of a nuclear arsenal.

But numerology is relative. Dantalion had found that by adding up each victim's personally calculated three-digit number, he was quickly approaching those kinds of figures. Once his targets were dead, and he added those from earlier, he'd only need another few victims and he would be truly treading in the original Dantalion's shoes.

He used a hair dryer from the bathroom to dry the book off. Inevitably the paper had grown warped along the edges, but again it added to the esoteric look of the book. He wrapped it in cellophane—just in case. The silver of the chain was tarnished, but that was okay. The antique look was all the rage. He clipped the free end of the chain to a belt loop and fed the book into his opposite jacket pocket.

Then he lay down on the bed next to the dead man and fell asleep. When he awoke, he ate food from the man's refrigerator. Not that he was hungry, but he knew he had to keep up his strength for what he must do. He chose some fast- and some slow-release carbohydrates and munched them without tasting them. Afterward he couldn't recall what he'd eaten, but he had a full stomach and was ready to go.

He checked himself out in the mirror again. His clothes were rumpled from the nap, but that just made them appear like work clothes, not some he'd taken fully pressed from a storage chest.

He left the lug wrench and screwdriver, but the knife could still prove handy, so he wrapped it in a cloth and took it with him when he left the house. He went out the same way he'd entered and was surprised to find that he'd been in the house much longer than he'd thought. He didn't think he'd slept that long, but he must have. It was dawn, and he could see mist rising from the surrounding fields and swamps as the early-morning sunshine set to burning off the dew.

He crossed the yard, went past the outbuildings, and approached the minivan where he'd abandoned it in the lane. Checking inside, he found that some of his supplies were still there—not everything had been dumped during his assault on Neptune Island. That made his plan for taking out Bradley Jorgenson even more viable than before.

The minivan started first try. Rather than

trying to reverse it the length of the rutted trail, he drove into the farmyard, spun around, then headed out the way he'd come, making his way back through Aurora Village and seeking the highway.

As far as Bradley Jorgenson would know, the attacker who'd come for him yesterday was now sleeping with the fishes and no further threat to him. Under those circumstances, the man would want to return home to survey the damage and whisper condolences to the families and friends of those who'd been killed. He'd also be made to answer the questions of the police investigators who would be on the scene. Dantalion would be waiting for him when he arrived back at the estate.

He picked up the Southeast Dixie Highway, then the coast road, and approached the island from the north. The roadblocks he anticipated weren't there. In all likelihood, they all thought he was dead and were busy looking for him at the crash scene. Cautious, though, he watched for anyone following behind, anyone in front of him. He also looked for a silver sedan but didn't see anything obvious. He skimmed his eyes over vehicles parked on layovers along the way, watching for unmarked police vehicles keeping watch for unwanted visitors. He didn't see anything. A black Audi A8 parked on a wide layover caught his eye, but it looked too nice to be a government-financed vehicle. More probable that the vehicle belonged to a businessman on the commute to

Miami who'd stopped to enjoy a few minutes of peace and quiet before hitting the Babel of the big city.

He continued south, driving adjacent to the wall that enclosed the estate. Parked opposite the main entrance was a group of assorted vehicles that reminded him of the caravans that traversed the country in the late 1960s. Vans back then were decorated with flowers and peace symbols and antiwar slogans. These vehicles were equally emblazoned, but the signs on these vans and cars declared affiliation to a greater movement than flower power. These were agents of the new media-hungry age, and their labels were the names of their respective TV or radio stations.

Turning off the road, he wound his way through the assembled vehicles, parking as far as he could get from the highway. Stepping out of the minivan, he settled his hat on his head, shadowing his face with a tilt of the brim. Then he walked among the vehicles. No one took much notice of him, and no one questioned why he hadn't arrived in an official vehicle.

Walking by a TV crew who were passing the time of day in sarcastic banter while awaiting entry to the estate, he touched the brim of his hat in greeting. Eyes skimmed over him, but no one approached him for a comment. Leaving the throng behind, he approached the highway. He stayed there, directing other arriving vehicles onto the layover, looking fully part of the scene in his Florida Park Service ranger's uniform.

The cops guarding entry to the Jorgenson estate didn't give him as much as a sour look.

Within fifteen minutes he was just background to the scene, and went unnoticed as he walked away along the road, seeking a way into the grounds. When he'd checked out the area yesterday morning, he'd been concerned about CCTV cameras and motion detectors and pressure pads, but with the exception of the cameras, all would now have been isolated. There were too many interlopers present for the security devices to be viable. Also, no one would be expecting him to wander inside among dozens of police officers, so the cameras wouldn't be scrutinized as thoroughly as before. In fact, anyone watching the cameras would be concentrating on recordings from the previous evening.

A five-minute stroll found him a good distance along the wall. Vehicles drove past him, but in his uniform he was a familiar sight. He found an empty oil drum partly concealed in the long grass on the untended no-man's-land between the highway and the wall. He dragged it upright, then pushed it end over end so that the accumulated sand and vegetation spilled out on the ground. Then he set it upright against the wall. Just a warden looking after the countryside should anyone see him. Then he waited for a break in the traffic. When it came, he hopped up onto the drum, then reached upward and got a grip on the top of the wall. He was over it in seconds.

Striking out across the grounds, he headed for Bradley Jorgenson's house. He strolled as if he were at home there—just another official among many others—and he went unchallenged.

He touched the book in his pocket.

Keen to balance the total again.

34 PUSHING ON DOWN THE COAST ROAD, I QUICKLY discovered that the next layover was full to capacity with TV and radio crews. Space was at such a premium that a state park ranger had been drafted to keep the traffic in order. Any vehicles that didn't belong to the media were waved on by the curt man in the stupid-looking hat.

Driving south, I looked for somewhere to park in solitude. Lines painted on the road surface forbade parking where the flow of traffic would be affected, but there were plenty of wide, sandy layovers along the way. Each one I drove by had an abundance of tourists' vehicles already encamped on the parking lots, their occupants disgorged across the saw grass above the beach or walking on the sands themselves. A regatta of boats made their way through the Intracoastal Waterway, and I understood why there was so much activity. The crowds had turned out to watch some sort of big boat race.

I finally found a spot to myself and drove off the road and onto the grass itself. The Audi was equipped with a four-wheel-drive function, so I wasn't concerned about bogging down in the soft ground.

I tried Bradley's office number again, but the phone was answered a second time by the same brisk-voiced woman.

"Who is this?" she demanded when I kept my silence.

I hung up. Then decided it was time to call in a few favors.

Dialing a number that was committed to my memory, I waited while the call was shunted through various relays. It was some time before the call was picked up and I was asked to punch in a numeric sequence on my phone. I was asked to confirm the number, which I did, and then was transferred to another telephone at CIA headquarters, up the coast in Virginia.

Already a member of the British Special Forces, I had been drafted into a specialist counterterrorism team that drew on the finest soldiers from all the member countries of the United Nations. Rink belonged to the same unit. We were ultimately governed by our commanders at a base code-named Arrowsake after one of the locations where William Melville, head of the original British Secret Service Bureau, allegedly trained his new recruits in the fight against German spies. However, because we were drawn from a number of allies, we had facilitators in each country. My handler in the U.S. was Walter Hayes Conrad IV, a subdivision controller in the CIA.

When the face of modern terrorism changed after 9/11, so did the methods of fighting the war. Public relations campaigns and scrutinizing bank accounts became more important than assaults on terrorist enclaves. In some eyes my unit was a dinosaur and belonged buried in history. Our fate was sealed, as the original dinosaurs' had been, and I retired shortly before my unit was disbanded. Our handlers were absorbed back into their own security communities, where most of them still had great influence. As did Walter.

"I need a favor, Walter," I said.

"Why do you only ever call when you want something, Hunter?" he asked.

"Because I know you'll always come through," I said.

"Flattery, as you should know, will get you nowhere."

"Better flattery than bribes, huh?" I said.

Walter owed me big-time. For one, I'd been instrumental in stopping the rogue Secret Service agent Martin Maxwell, who had managed to stay one step ahead of those hunting him. More than that, though, I'd kept the name of Tubal Cain—the Harvestman—secret, avoiding a massive embarrassment for both Walter and the U.S. government. Tubal Cain had gone to his grave as Robert Swan, and I'd made no one any wiser.

"So what is it you want?"

"Cooperation from the local feds," I told him.

My location must have been thrown up by some sort of Global Positioning Satellite screen on his computer monitor.

"Martin County, Florida," he confirmed to himself. "What are you doing there?"

"Up until now? Not a whole lot of good," I said.

"Tell me."

I gave him the brief version.

"I heard about the explosion on Baker Island. Homeland Security flagged it. Thought at first it was some kind of terrorist attack on the rich and deserving. When it came to light it was a good ol' gas explosion it was thrown back to Miami PD. Then bodies started turning up and the FBI jumped on board." Walter ruminated a moment. "Now you're saying that a contract killer's involved and it's all to do with the Jorgenson pharmaceutical contracts with *our* military?"

"That's as much as we've gathered," I agreed.

"And you're up to your neck in it as usual."

"You know me, Walt. Never can keep my nose out of other peoples' business."

"Not where there's a damsel in distress, eh?"

"Doesn't matter who's in distress," I corrected.

"You want me to put men on it?" Walter asked. "Catch this killer before he gets at your mark again?"

"Suit yourself; I'm not interested in the killer. It isn't personal this time. All I want is a green light to speak with Bradley Jorgenson. The family estate is shut down as tight as a duck's ass. Can't think of a way to get in there without having to put some good people to sleep, and I don't want to do that."

"No, not a good idea, Hunter." Walter tapped his fingers on something. Thinking deeply. "Can I ask why you need to speak to the Jorgenson kid?"

"I want to get him out of there."

"Why?"

"Because I promised his girlfriend I would. He's not safe there."

"And you think you can protect him better than the police and FBI can?"

"Walt?"

"Yeah, I know. It was a stupid question." He was tapping again, and I guessed he was already onto someone in law enforcement. While he did that, I told him what we'd patched together concerning Gabriel Wellborn and his network of contract killers named after the mythological fallen angels. I told him about Dantalion. Walter asked, "But you don't know his true identity yet?"

"No. Only that he's decent at his job. I don't think he's military or police. He's, I don't know . . . different."

"Self-taught?"

"Or privately taught," I put in. "Look, this guy looks weird. Very pale-skinned, white-haired, has some sort of condition with his skin."

"Albino?"

"Perhaps, but I don't think so. Something else. But you might want to check historical medical records; it might throw up his identity." I thought about something else from the first time I'd seen Dantalion on Baker Island. "He's also very good with disguises, Walter. Maybe he has a background in theater or the movie industry."

"I'll pass all that on to the FBI," Walter said. "Okay, all done. Go to the front gate; ask to speak with SAC Kaufman. He'll give you what you need."

"Thanks, Walter," I said.

"Say nothing of it," he said. To some it would be a throwaway remark. But I knew exactly what he meant. It was a reminder, and literal in its meaning. Say nothing of it. The Harvestman.

Pressing the end button, I pushed the phone into my jacket pocket. No sooner had I had done that than it vibrated and I pulled it out again. A text message from Harvey.

HOME AND DRY

Good, they'd made it to the safe house. Time for me to get on with delivering Bradley there.

35 THERE WERE OBVIOUS DISADVANTAGES TO THE disguise Dantalion had affected on this occasion. For example, what was a state park ranger's interest in the case? If anyone had thought to ask, or to scrutinize his uniform, they'd have easily seen through the charade. He had no jurisdiction on the private estate and would not be required to attend for official business or otherwise. On the other hand, his uniform was official, and therefore he was able to move among all the other officials without attracting undue questions. In fact, there were other advantages to his disguise. If, say, he had been wearing the uniform of a cop or medic, then maybe he would not have remained invisible for long. There were too many senior officers milling around throwing orders back and forth, demanding tasks from their people. But there were no other park rangers in attendance. No one to question just who the hell he was or what he was doing or to send him off on some errand that would divert him from his task.

By keeping his eyes averted and walking as if he had somewhere to be, he was able to walk directly past officers from the local sheriff's office and toward Bradley Jorgenson's house. Commandoes from the FBI Hostage Rescue Team had secured the area. With no viable threat evident in the area, they had stood down. Dantalion saw a group of them standing around with their helmets off and their assault rifles slung from their shoulders. Talking and enjoying the sunshine. A couple of them smoked cigarettes around the side of the building, out of sight of their superiors, who would still be inside. Most of the traffic in and out of the building was in the form of ambulance crews and people from the Martin County Medical Examiner's Office. Apparently the thirteen-hours-old crime scene had been thoroughly picked through by the CSI technicians and had now been handed over to the men with the body bags.

Dantalion thought he'd be pushing his luck if he went inside the building, but his anonymity would be secure while in the grounds. As yet he wasn't even sure that Bradley had returned to the house. In fact, would it not be a better idea if Bradley went to another of the family houses where there hadn't been blood and mayhem? To one of the other family members who hadn't been in on the plot to have Bradley and Marianne murdered, for instance? That ruled out the houses of both Simon and Jack, but there were plenty of other houses to choose from. Was there a sympathetic aunt or uncle he would go to? Or would the officers in charge of the investigation have picked a house at random, commandeered it while they questioned Bradley and any other survivors about what had happened here?

He decided not to hang around either crime scene too long. The proliferation of law enforcement officers around both Bradley's and Petre Jorgenson's houses meant that the odds of blowing his cover were great. Though he'd remained invisible until now, all it took was one eagle-eyed cop to challenge him, ask for identification, and that would be it. Contrary to all their faults as a collective beast, singly the officers were still trained professionals, and not to be underestimated.

Happy that there was no sign of the silver Lincoln sedan that Bradley and Seagram had made off in last night, he headed northward, toward the other half-dozen houses that lay strung out along the coast in that direction.

The next house belonged to Valentin's eldest sister, Hetti. A Jorgenson by birth, she now went by her deceased husband's name of Gorman. The family business meant little to her as she had made her own fortune in real estate. From the documentation supplied by Petre Jorgenson when he still remained Dantalion's client, Dantalion knew that Hetti was aloof to the squabble between Valentin and her nephews. Aloof and unsympathetic; he doubted that Bradley would seek her out for comfort or support. Nevertheless, he checked around her property for signs of the sedan. It wasn't parked there. He continued on.

Christened Jan Jorgenson but taking the

Americanized form of John for the purposes of the business, Bradley's youngest cousin had always been referred to by the less formal name of Jack. His family home was next in line. He had no wife or children, and the house was somewhat excessive in size for the single man.

Simon, his brother, and five years older at twenty-eight, did have a wife and a baby girl. However, the wife had taken the baby girl along with an out-of-court settlement of twenty million dollars when they'd divorced one year earlier. She'd moved with the child to her own place on Fisher's Island off Miami Beach. Like Jack, Simon also lived alone, but there was a transient population of women coming and going at all times, something that had begun before the acrimonious divorce and had ultimately led to the breakdown of the marriage.

Dantalion bypassed both the brothers' houses.

He stuck to the coastline. The going was a little more difficult than if he'd walked along the road that connected the houses, but it was more in keeping with his disguise.

A full half mile from Bradley's house, he found what he'd been looking for. Not the silver Lincoln, but a helicopter on the broad lawn of the next house. The helicopter was a Bell JetRanger, and it was decorated with the logo of the FBI. The only reason Dantalion could think of for the presence of the helicopter was that it had some pretty important passengers. The special agent in charge from the local FBI office. He would be overall commander of the investigation, and there was only one reason why he'd be at this location. Bradley had come here for tea and sympathy from his elderly great-aunt, Eunice.

From where he was standing, Dantalion could see the pilot on board the helicopter. He was passing time by going through a series of checks, flicking buttons and reading dials. Dantalion quickly walked toward the house, striding purposefully. The pilot glanced his way, but didn't appear concerned and continued with his preflight checks. Dantalion kept going, rounding the house and approaching the walled yard at the back.

This house was in no way as impressive as those the cousins lived in but was probably still worth a couple of million dollars. A two-story wooden house with porch and railings and a steepled roof and attic windows, it reminded Dantalion a little of a house in a movie he enjoyed: *The Amityville Horror*. One of the oldest houses on the island, it looked in need of renovation. Not exactly dilapidated, but a lick of paint wouldn't go amiss. The elderly woman who lived here was in fact one of the first generation of Jorgensons to arrive here back in the 1950s. The house would have been grand in its day, but now it was as dated as the chintz curtains in the windows. It looked as if the old woman was just sitting out her time. When she passed, the house would likely go to one of the younger generation, possibly to be torn down and rebuilt.

He paused at the corner, studying the cars

parked at the rear of the house. There was an older model Chrysler station wagon. Plus, there it was: the silver Lincoln sedan. He took a deep breath. Felt for the Taurus 38. Touched his book. Then quickly took a step backward as he heard the rear door opening. The sound was followed by muted conversation. He couldn't quite make out what was said, but then he detected the crunch of tires as a vehicle approached. Angling himself against the corner of the wall, he watched the approach of a car from the Martin County Sheriff's Office. The squad car drew to a halt, and Dantalion watched as a silver-haired man in a gray suit got into it. The vehicle then did a quick U-turn and headed back along the road. Unsure what that had been about, Dantalion watched the squad car drive away. He waited until it was shielded from sight by a swell in the land.

Yesterday's actions had been governed by fury. He saw that now. He'd acted recklessly and without much thought of the repercussions. His thirst for vengeance had led him to slaying his supporters. He'd left himself without backup and the means to obtain the weapons and information he needed to complete his tasks. He was the proverbial lone wolf. But, he reminded himself, hadn't he always preferred it that way?

Gabe Wellborn had been useful, but he had always been a liability. His method of concealing his network of hired mercenaries had never been foolproof. Sooner or later the FBI would chance upon his Web site, put two and two together, and draw correlations between the fantasized murders and those they reflected in the real world. Dantalion had cautioned him. He did not want the names of his brethren used by the other killers for hire on Gabe's books. It cheapened his own identity when other men—nothing but thugs in his estimation—plucked names from the Goetic pantheon with no thought for those who truly owned those names. Dantalion had sought out each of those men in turn. He'd killed them all. He had planned to kill Gabe, too. But not last night. That had been a reaction to the situation he'd found himself in. Gabe had run to Petre, warned him that Dantalion was coming. What other course was there but to put a bullet in him?

Petre Jorgenson had overstepped the mark as well. Drawing Dantalion into an ambush—and at the expense of his men, whom Dantalion had slain on his way in—showed how untrustworthy the man was. As soon as the money had been transferred into his account, it had been prudent to kill the man. Okay, Petre hadn't actually sent Hunter to kill him, but Dantalion wondered when he would have hired other killers to seek him out.

In any case, this time things had to be different. He must be cool and rational. He couldn't go in with guns blazing; he had to use subtlety and guile to take Bradley Jorgenson. Neither would he kill him instantly. He would give him a choice. Tell me where Marianne is and I won't cut off your hands. Tell me where Joe Hunter is and I won't cut off your feet. Ask kindly and maybe I won't chop off your balls and feed them to you.

Good plan, he thought with a laugh, nothing psychopathic about it.

He scouted the building, looking for a positive sign that Bradley was inside. And found him almost immediately. He was sitting in the kitchen, his forearms resting on a tabletop. A man Dantalion did not recognize sat opposite him. A digital voice recorder lay on the table between them. By the cut of the man's suit, his well-groomed hair, and the giveaway clip-on badge on his breast pocket, Dantalion saw that he was FBI. He appeared to be questioning Bradley—the digital recorder there to record the interview.

There were only two others in the room. One was the bodyguard named Seagram, the one who had offered to help him get to Bradley. That, of course, had been before Dantalion had slaughtered Petre, who had most obviously been paying Seagram to switch allegiances. He doubted that Seagram would be so keen now that his sponsor was out of the picture. Now that Bradley had resumed the role of his main employer, it was in Seagram's best interest to keep him alive. The last person was a very elderly lady. She was sitting in a wooden chair, and despite the heat of the Florida sun, she was dressed in thick wool and tweed and had a blanket over her thighs. She looked as if she hadn't a clue what was going on and sat smiling whimsically and nodding at each man's words as Bradley answered the FBI agent's questions.

There did not appear to be anyone else around. No bodyguards, no police, only the one agent and the helicopter pilot to give assistance to Bradley and Seagram.

This was about the best opportunity for taking Bradley that he was going to get.

He quickly walked away from the house. Didn't want to leave himself open to an attack from behind. He walked toward the helicopter. As he approached he heard the engine whine as the pilot continued his preflight preparations. He slipped his hand into his jacket pocket and carefully folded it around a small cylinder.

He made it all the way up to the cockpit before the pilot noticed him. The man saw only the uniform, and he lifted his chin in a nod of greeting.

"Hello," Dantalion said. He smiled. Then flicked the brim of his hat. Sunlight flashed in his eyes. He adjusted the brim so his face was again in shadow. A natural enough action that explained why he kept his hand elevated.

"Hi," said the pilot. "Can I help you?" He leaned out the open door so he could better see his visitor. He was reading the emblem embroidered on Dantalion's shirt. Behind the visor of his flight helmet, Dantalion saw the man's eyes narrow to slivers. He opened his mouth to speak.

That was when Dantalion swung his right hand as though he were holding a hammer. The bottom of his fist struck the man flush on the left side of his neck. The blow in itself could prove fatal if delivered with enough power and precision. Coupled with the needle piercing his carotid artery and pumping in a lethal dose of ketamine, the man was guaranteed a rapid death.

The punch itself stunned him, the drug raced immediately to his heart, and he was dead within seconds. He didn't have the chance to shout or even to lift his hands in defense. Dantalion accepted his sinking weight, catching the man under his armpits and dragging him bodily from the helicopter. Then he slid open the side door and bundled him into the rear compartment. He followed him inside and closed the door behind him.

Minutes later Dantalion emerged a new man.

Wearing the pilot's jumpsuit and helmet, he walked across the lawn toward the house. As he got to the window of the kitchen he saw that the tableau had not changed in the couple of minutes he'd been gone. Boldly he rapped a knuckle on the window, even as he turned aside, gesturing to those within with a gloved hand. All they would see was the recognizable figure of the chopper pilot. They wouldn't be alarmed, but one of them would come to the vestibule inside the door to see what he wanted. He walked toward the door, watching in his peripheral vision as someone— Seagram, he believed, from the shape of the brush cut—moved toward the door to meet him.

He stood very close to the door. It was solid wood, so the person inside would have to open it fully before realizing that there was something familiar about the bogus pilot's face. He readied himself. He preferred giving his victims a choice of how they would die, but this time he didn't have that luxury. Like that of the chopper pilot, this death had to be conducted in silence.

He heard a noise from within.

"Yeah, what is it?" Seagram's voice.

"I need to give my colleague a message," Dantalion said, purposefully speaking a couple of octaves lower than normal.

"What is it? I'll tell him."

"Can't do that, sir," Dantalion said. "Official FBI business, I'm afraid. You don't have clearance. I have to tell him myself."

Seagram muttered something under his breath. He tugged open the door. It squealed on seldom-used hinges.

Seagram stood looking at him for the briefest of moments. Then it was there, the subtle movement of his jaw, the dilating of his pupils. He'd recognized the lie.

"Hello, Seagram," Dantalion said as he stepped forward. The knife he'd brought from the dead warden's house went under Seagram's rib cage. All eight glistening inches of it. Dantalion's other hand covered Seagram's gaping mouth. As the man's knees buckled under him, Dantalion supported him on the blade. He leaned close, placing his lips close to Seagram's ear. "I've come to tell the FBI that the killer is here."

Seagram's terror was palpable. He knew he

was dying, and it was his greed that had brought him to this point. His eyes went large above Dantalion's cupped hand. He tried to shout, but the knife seemed to suck the words down into his throat as Dantalion pulled the blade out of his abdomen.

Dantalion placed Seagram on the floor just inside the door. The man's mouth was still working, and there was always the chance he could get a grip on his senses long enough to shout a warning to Bradley and the FBI agent. Dantalion swiped the blade across his trachea. His mouth still opened and closed like a fish on dry land, but no noises beyond the bubbling blood in his sliced trachea issued forth. Groping under Seagram's jacket, Dantalion pulled out a Glock 17. Not the model 19 he was used to, but still, better equipment for what was to come than the five-shot Taurus.

He fitted his hands around the stocks of both guns. Something about the two-gun assault had a decidedly intimidating effect that Dantalion didn't quite understand. But it worked for him, so he'd go along with it.

He strode down the hall.

The kitchen door was standing open and he could see the old lady sitting with her back to him. That would put the FBI agent on his right, Bradley on his left. The FBI agent was the most dangerous enemy in the room. By rights he should die first. Dantalion, however, had different ideas about rights and wrongs. He fired a single round through the old lady's back even before he was in the room. The Glock punched a 9 mm round directly through her and shattered something on the far wall. The woman toppled toward the table. As she did so her face twisted to one side, and Dantalion would have sworn that she was still smiling at the whimsy of it all.

"Hello," he called in his usual fashion. "I'm Dantalion."

Bradley and the FBI agent were too busy to take note of his words. They were half risen from their seats, Bradley turning away, the agent grabbing for the H & K inside his jacket.

Dantalion fired one shot from the Taurus, one shot from the Glock. Neither of them at Bradley. The 38-caliber bullet hit the agent above his right hip. A split second later the 9 mm struck him directly between the eyes. The opposing forces of the bullets made him jig in place like a disjointed puppet. Then he dropped straight to the floor, knocking over the chair he'd so recently been sitting upon.

Bradley was lurching around the far end of the table, seeking a way out. He had both arms over his head and was yelling something reminiscent of a bull's defeated bellow as the matador serves the coup de grâce.

Aiming left-handedly, Dantalion fired the Taurus. The bullet struck the wall directly in front of Bradley, who responded by dropping down and covering his head with his hands. He shouted something, but Dantalion's ears were ringing with the echo of his own guns.

"Surprised to see me, Bradley?" Dantalion asked. "You thought I was dead, eh? Must piss you off that the big bold Hunter failed to stop me?"

Bradley could only moan.

"Stand up, Bradley," Dantalion ordered.

Bradley didn't. Terror kept him exactly where he was.

"I said, '*Stand up!*'" Dantalion yelled. "Or I'll shoot you where you are. Cowering on the ground like a dog!"

Bradley came partly to his feet, but nature prevented him from fully straightening and his knees dipped again. Dantalion stalked over, stepping over the dead FBI agent to get at him. He pushed the hot muzzle of the Taurus under Bradley's ear. "Stand up. That's the only choice I'm giving you right now, so you'd better take it."

Cringing like a wounded animal, Bradley came to his feet. He continued to cover himself with his arms, and Dantalion struck at the meat of his forearms, forcing the hands away. Then he pushed Bradley back so that his hips bumped against the kitchen counter and he was forced to bend backward away from the pressure of the gun.

"Now, Bradley, it's choices time again. Do you die instantly, or would you prefer it if I kept you alive and used you as bait to bring Marianne to me?" Dantalion pushed the muzzle of the Glock under Bradley's chin. "Come on, speak up. I'm giving you the opportunity of living a little longer."

"Please," Bradley croaked. His plea never came to any kind of conclusion, and Dantalion was left wondering what decision Bradley had actually come to.

Then he heard a car pull up in front of the house.

So he made up his own mind.

He slipped the Glock in his pocket and pulled out a second object. A hypodermic syringe. Given in the same dosage, ketamine would kill Bradley as instantly as it had the pilot, but this syringe didn't contain ketamine. He'd brought this ampoule from the minivan: sodium amytal left over from his hit on the Moore household. In small doses it caused the drugged person to become compliant. A higher dose caused unconsciousness. Too much and the person would die. Dantalion administered just enough so that Bradley would have no will of his own but still have the use of his legs. He didn't want to have to carry him out of there.

36

SPECIAL AGENT IN CHARGE TAYLOR KAUFMAN wasn't exactly pleased to see me. He extended his hand, but his shake was abrupt. As abrupt as his words: "Walter Conrad said you're the best in the business."

"Depends what business he was referring to," I answered.

The silver-haired SAC studied me with eyes the color of tarnished brass. He didn't appear impressed. Something about my accent seemed to irk him as well. I guessed it was because he'd already fought a jurisdictional war with the Miami PD and Martin County Sheriff's Office, which he'd indubitably won, only to have a Brit standing before him now with carte blanche to take over his position of power. He straightened the lines in his gray suit. Nodded toward the squad car.

"You'd better get in. I'll take you to Jorgenson."

"Go ahead," I told him. "I'll bring my own car."

I was going to require the Audi, and it was no good to me a half mile away.

"Prefer it if you came with us," SAC Kaufman said slowly. "I'll also have to ask you to hand over your sidearm."

"Isn't going to happen," I told him. I challenged

him with my stare, and to give him his due, he didn't immediately falter.

"I've got a man down there who has already survived two attempts on his life. Don't want to risk that again," he said.

"I'm here to protect him, not harm him."

"I don't know that."

"Walter Conrad vouched for me," I reminded him.

"Walter is CIA," Kaufman said in reply, "and we all know what *they're* famous for."

"I'm not CIA," I said.

"No. But that's the problem . . . I'm not sure what you are." Then he turned his back to me and walked toward the sheriff's car.

"Kaufman."

He turned around and his burnished gaze fell on me.

I said, "I'm not here to usurp your power. We're on the same side."

His mouth made a thin line, and he turned away from me again. I shook my head at his back, then climbed into the Audi. The cop at the gate gave me room to bring the car in, and I followed the police vehicle back onto the Jorgenson estate.

Approaching the village made up of estate staff lodgings, I was surprised when we took a left, skirted the village, and approached a lone wooden house standing on the Atlantic shore. This house wasn't like the others; it was older, more homely. Less forbidding than the brick monstrosities the younger Jorgensons had erected.

Why we were headed there instead of directly toward Bradley's house I didn't quite get, but then I saw the silver Lincoln parked at the back of the house and it made sense. Bradley had gone somewhere he felt safe.

SAC Kaufman climbed out of the police car. He leaned in and said something to the uniformed driver. The driver shook his head, then peeled away, heading back along the road toward Bradley's house. I parked the Audi next to the Lincoln that Seagram had been driving the day before. Climbing from my car, I felt the phone vibrate in my pocket. I pulled it out and Rink said, "I'm back from San Francisco. Harvey's got Mari tucked up safe and sound. He's going to look after her. I'm on my way back to you now."

"Pleased to hear it, Rink," I said. "Your mom?"

"On the mend. She smacked me round the head for leaving you alone and told me to get my ass back here. How could I argue with that?"

"You know better than that."

"You ain't kidding." He laughed. Then his tone grew more serious. Back to business once more. "The punk survived, huh?"

"Unfortunately, yes."

"Where are you?"

"I'm back at the estate," I told him. "Had to pull a few strings via Walter Conrad, but I should be with Bradley in a minute or two."

"Walter came through, huh?"

"He owes us big-time, Rink. He had no option, did he?"

"No," Rink rumbled. I imagined him touching the scar on his chin. Like the knife wound in my chest, Rink's scar was courtesy of Tubal Cain.

"I'll wait here until you arrive, then we'll move Bradley between us."

"Give me an hour or two, okay?"

"Should take that long to sort things out at this end," I told him. "I've got a fed here with a stick up his ass."

"Nothing new there, then," Rink said.

I hung up.

"I heard what you just said," SAC Kaufman said.

"You were meant to, Kaufman," I said. "We started out on the wrong foot back there. Can we try this again? We're both here for the same reason, so let's agree to work together on this, huh? Truth is, I'm not going anywhere, so we may as well be civil to each other."

Kaufman nodded at my words. He swept the surroundings with one look. "Would be a whole lot easier without *this* stick up my ass."

We shook hands again, this time with meaning.

"Walter Conrad told me what you'd managed to piece together about the shooter. Not bad work." He gestured me toward the house. As we walked side by side, he said, "I've passed the information along to my people. Got someone on the skin-complaint angle, another on this demon stuff. Hopefully we'll have something useful before long."

"He's unorthodox. I don't think he's been trained through the usual channels."

Kaufman paused in midstep. "That in itself could point us toward him. Maybe one of these private CQB courses or something?"

"Nah, close quarter battle's about protection. This guy comes from a different school of thought. Maybe he has roots in one of these paramilitary home defense groups or something similar."

Kaufman considered my last, continued walking.

My step after him turned into a lunge.

I grabbed him by his shoulders and powered my chest against him, taking us both down hard on the pavement.

Through the space we'd just vacated whistled two high-velocity rounds.

For all he was wearing an expensive suit, Kaufman was no slouch at crawling. He was off, scurrying for the cover of a wall bordering a flower garden. He reached the wall within seconds and went over it, landing on his back on soil.

I had gone the other direction, rolling sideways. Another round chipped concrete from the paving stones, throwing splinters toward my face. Blinking to clear my vision, I continued rolling and got myself under a parked station wagon. Somewhere along the way, I'd drawn my SIG and was looking for targets.

My first reaction was to aim for the window where the shooter had fired. It was the subtle shifting of his shadow, the pale face looming above it that had warned me of his presence. If my mind hadn't been tuned to recognize the danger of that ghoulish sight, Dantalion would have got us cold.

The window had been smashed by his bullets, but I saw no movement there. He'd moved, possibly to get a clearer angle on me.

Just as I thought that, a round struck the front tire next to my head, and the hiss of air sounded like an angry snake. The car dipped slowly toward me, and I wormed my way farther away from the collapsing corner of the chassis.

"FBI," Kaufman shouted. He had one arm propped on the low wall, his service revolver aiming toward the empty window. "Drop your weapon and come out."

The FBI SAC wasn't a stranger to action. The only problem was that it was likely some years since he'd engaged in a gun battle. His face was almost as pale as that of the man who was trying to kill us.

"Keep your head down, Kaufman," I shouted across the intervening space. His gaze jumped to me, back to the house. I knew he was going to shout again even before his mouth opened.

"Come out with your hands in the air and you will not be harmed."

Bullets smacked the wall beside him and I saw his gun arm snatched away. He cursed loudly, and I wasn't sure if he'd been wounded or not.

My position was not the best for shooting back. I could now see only a small portion of the house, and most of that was blank wall. On my belly, I used my feet to push me toward the station wagon's engine. It was a slightly better position, but most of my view remained obscured by the sunken front end of the car. It took me about a nanosecond to decide I wasn't staying there. All the shooter had to do was fire under the car and the ricochets would probably kill me. I scooted away, rolled out from under the car, and came up on the far side.

In the movies you will often see a cop hunkered down behind an open car door, but 9 mm Parabellums will pass through the shell of a car with no problem whatsoever. Some more enlightened moviemakers have their good guys place the engine block between themselves and the shooter, but again there are too many open spaces and fragile components in an engine to stop most bullets. The reality is, a car isn't a safe object to hide behind. Neither are trees or concrete walls. The only thing that will stop a high-caliber bullet is about six inches of solid brick or steel. Kaufman had the best hiding place. My own, other than offering a little cover so the shooter couldn't get a bead on me, was third-rate at best.

As if he had read my mind, the man in the house fired again. He unloaded an entire clip from a semiautomatic. Not randomly, either: he began at the front of the car, fired, moved his hand a fraction, fired, moved his hand a fraction, and so on. Some of the rounds did flatten inside the engine, but for as many as were stopped, at least one got through. The hood buckled as rounds ricocheted under it. Holes appeared in the fender close by my body. I had no choice but run backward, keeping my head down as bullets cut through the car and struck lumps from the ground beyond me.

Kaufman—jurisdictional battle or not—wasn't about to let me die. He bopped up, firing back at the house. He couldn't see his target, only hoped to offer covering fire while I raced for cover behind my Audi. I did so, sliding like I was headed for first base on a baseball field.

The retort of the shooter's gun changed. A lighter bore, but still enough to kill. I'd got myself all the way to the rear of the Audi, and with its nose pointed toward the shooter it gave me much more cover than the other car had. Nonetheless, bullets punched through the galvanized steel body and lifted padding from the seats within. There was a loud pop—a tire going. The semiautomatic was firing again and I had no option but to drop as low as I could to the ground.

Then there was a cessation of rounds. I quickly snapped a glance over the trunk of the car. The door was opening, and my first response was to shoot through it. Nevertheless, I held my fire, waving over to Kaufman to do the same. Only someone with no sense would put themselves behind that door during a gun battle, and for all that I thought Dantalion was as crazy as any other psycho out there, he did appear to be knowledgeable about guns and their effects.

The door swung open, and there stood Bradley Jorgenson.

He swayed like he'd been out on a particularly heavy night's partying. His mouth hung open and I could see a string of saliva knitting together his splayed teeth. He was heavy-lidded, and even from a distance his eyes were unfocused. Drugged.

Bradley was a fair-sized guy. Maybe my height, but heavier. He was ample cover for the slim man crouching behind him. I could only catch a glimpse of the man's white hair, an ear, one gloved hand that was under Bradley's arm and jammed into his armpit. Room under there for a .38 special. Over Bradley's shoulder I saw the muzzle of a Glock.

"Anyone moves and I kill Bradley," shouted the shooter.

"Put down the gun and move away slowly," Kaufman shouted in return. He was again propped over the wall. No way could he take a shot, though.

The shooter twisted Bradley toward him. Fired once from the Glock. The bullet missed Kaufman but was enough motivation for him to drop down out of sight.

I watched, waiting for my opportunity.

"There are only two choices here," the shooter yelled. "Drop your weapons or Bradley dies."

There were actually three choices. I could shoot straight through Bradley and kill the fucker as well. Yesterday, before I knew the truth, that's possibly what I'd have done. And, heaven forbid, if he did shoot Bradley, that was exactly what I was going to do.

"What's it going to be, FBI man? Do you want me to kill this innocent boy?"

I was pleased to hear that Kaufman didn't reply. That put the ball back in my court.

"You aren't going to do that, Dantalion," I said. Then I stood up. It was putting myself at risk, but also giving me a clear shot through Bradley and into the shooter's central mass.

"Oh, you know my name?" Dantalion swung a fraction back my way. Still no clear shot, though. "Touché, Mr. Hunter."

"I know the pussy name you hide behind," I told him. "What is it with all you deadbeats, huh? Why the stupid names? All you sick-in-the-head motherfuckers do that."

Hoping to anger him, to force him out of hiding for even the briefest of moments, I failed. Instead of riling him as I'd intended, my words seemed to please Dantalion. He chuckled to himself, even as he pressed Bradley to take a slow step forward. I matched his step, moving away from the Audi.

"You're looking for an opportunity to shoot," Dantalion pointed out. "Go on. Shoot, then." He dropped the barrel of his Glock so he could pull aside Bradley's jacket. Under it was a bullet-proof vest. Something Seagram had demanded his mark wear after it was too late. Momentarily I wondered where the bodyguard had got to. Hell, I decided. Dantalion went on, "See, the only problem now is that you'll have to shoot through Bradley's head. Are you prepared to do that?"

"Yes," I said.

That caused the psycho to falter in his next step. But then he shoved Bradley on once more. "You would have done so by now," he said, but there was a hint of wariness in his words now.

For effect I allowed my knees to bend slightly, exaggerating my shooter's stance. It was a gamble, a very big one. But Dantalion didn't shove Bradley to one side and come out shooting as I'd hoped. If anything he took a tighter hold on the younger man. His face was barely visible beyond Bradley's lolling head.

"Good. Now that's settled, this is what's going to happen." His Glock was steady as it pointed my way, but I got the impression that he'd turned his head to one side. As he did, I took a step back toward the Audi. His gun was now pointing a yard to the right of my shoulder. He didn't note the subtle shift of my body, calling instead to Kaufman, "FBI man, throw your gun over the wall. You have three seconds to comply or Bradley here will be as dead as your buddy inside."

"Not giving up my gun," Kaufman shouted in denial.

"Your choice. One. Two . . ."

Kaufman's service revolver clattered on the pavement next to Dantalion's feet. I swore under my breath. We'd lost a major advantage, and Dantalion knew it. But he didn't see me shift my weight to the side, moving an extra foot from the trajectory of his first shot.

"Same goes for you, Hunter."

"No."

"Three seconds."

"When you reach three you'll be dead."

"One. Two . . ."

"Three!" I said.

Neither of us fired.

"So, how do things go now, asshole?" I asked him. "You sound like you're a fair man. You like giving choices, don't you? How about you choose to put down your weapons, let Bradley go, and maybe you'll get a comfortable prison cell instead of a hole in your head."

"Don't care too much for prison," Dantalion said. He continued to edge forward, and Bradley continued to be a compliant partner in their slow dance.

"You look like you've spent a long time out of the sunlight already, but I guess you would, seeing as you must've crawled out from under a rock someplace."

"You're wasting your time, Hunter. You can goad me all you want, but I'm not biting."

"So you choose the bullet in the head?" I continued unabated. "Not that I blame you. Pretty little white ass like yours would have them queuing up down at the state penitentiary."

Dantalion didn't reply, and it made me wonder if I'd perhaps come a little too close to the truth for his liking.

"Where'd you do your time?" I asked him. "You've obviously done a stretch before."

"What makes you ask that?"

"Don't care too much for prison," I mimicked in an effeminate voice.

He didn't answer again, only kept moving. I wondered what the hell Kaufman was up to. Where the hell was his backup weapon, anyway? We had Dantalion nicely triangulated now, and Kaufman could have put a bullet in his spine at any time. Only he wasn't making his play. He *had* been off the streets too long.

Dantalion was that much closer to Kaufman. He heard something that I didn't. "The fucking cell phone, FBI. Throw it to me now!"

Kaufman's cell came sailing over the wall, and Dantalion caught it under the sole of his foot and stamped it into fragments.

Dantalion was angry now. But it wasn't the senseless anger that I wanted to force him into. His rage was controlled. More dangerous. He jammed the revolver hard into Bradley's armpit, and although deeply under the influence of some narcotic, Bradley squirmed against the agony.

"I'm done playing games. Hunter, get your ass out of my way or—so help me God!—I'm going to shoot this punk and then you."

"I don't think God is on your side," I told him. Purposefully I didn't move an inch. "You're forgetting that he chose to elevate man above his angels. Whose side do you think he's gonna pick today?"

"Think I believe all that stupidity?" Dantalion snapped.

"Yeah," I said slowly. "I think you do."

"Think again!"

Dantalion fired at me.

I didn't have a shot, so I had to leap away.

His first shot missed by a mile, but he was turning, following me, vectoring in on my running form.

Now I fired. Not at him. Despite what I'd told him, there was no way I could shoot Bradley through the head. Not now. I fired so that my bullet passed over their heads. But it was enough to cause him to flinch, and his second shot missed its mark, too.

Then I was back behind the station wagon and twisting round for a shot. Point. Shoot. That was what had been ingrained into my psyche during the hundreds of hours' training I'd undergone at Arrowsake. My bullet went true, hit dead center. Only it wasn't Dantalion I'd hit, but Bradley. The Kevlar vest absorbed the killing power, but it was still like he'd been kicked by a mule. His body collided with Dantalion's, knocking his third shot astray.

It was one of those do-or-die moments when everything can play out on the basis of a snap decision. I decided just to go for it. He was off-kilter now, and if I charged him he wouldn't waste time shooting Bradley, he'd turn all his attention to me. And I'd blast the fucker's face off the second he lifted it above Bradley's shoulder.

Then something happened that I still find difficult to credit. Seagram stumbled out of the house

looking like the victim from a slasher movie.
His shirt front was dark with blood; a mass of it
had pooled around his waistband and was even
now seeping down the front of his trousers. He
had taken a serious wound to his abdomen. He
also had one hand cupped around his throat,
and there was blood there, too. Not as much as
was coming from his guts, but I knew that it was
going to prove fatal. In his other hand he held
a Heckler & Koch semiautomatic pistol. His face
was ashen and fixed into a rictuslike mask. There
was no recognition when he looked first at Bradley and Dantalion, then at me.

He lifted the H & K.

And pointed it at me.

He fired, but I was already on the move. The
problem was I had to dodge away, so I could no
longer rush at Dantalion.

Seagram didn't see me. Not as Joe Hunter.
He was looking into a gulf he was about to fall
into on a one-way trip. The human body is a mi-
raculous feat of nature. It can take horrendous
wounds and survive and learn to function in new
ways. Pity our minds aren't always as resilient.
Seagram was gone from inside his own head, and
whether it was terror or hatred or sheer natural
instinct to come out shooting, that was all he was
capable of. He pulled the trigger again, and then
again.

I was loathe to shoot the man, but I wasn't
about to take a blind shot from him. I lifted my
SIG and squared it on his forehead. I paused for a

fraction of a second, then watched as a tiny rose-bud blossomed in the center of his face. In comparison, the back of his head exploded in a welter of blood, skull, and brain matter.

I hadn't taken the shot. When I looked, Dantalion had his arm extended over Bradley's shoulder and there was smoke coming from the barrel of the Glock.

Then he was swinging it toward me, and I had no option now but to look for cover. I got to the front of the station wagon, and had to trust that the engine block would be enough to save me.

Dantalion's next shot didn't come. In the few seconds I'd kept my head down, he'd moved backward, and I saw then what he was aiming for. The silver Lincoln that Seagram had used was the only car in a drivable condition. He opened the driver's door and shoved Bradley inside, encouraging him to move faster with added slaps in the face. Bradley scooted over into the passenger seat and then Dantalion was starting the car. Realizing that Dantalion must have been responsible for stabbing Seagram, I concluded that he must also have taken the car keys from him.

I rose up from my crouch.

I could fire, but I was afraid I'd hit Bradley.

So I had no recourse but to watch the Lincoln screeching away up the road.

"Knowles? Knowles!" I heard Kaufman shout. He came over the wall like an Olympic hurdler. Then he lunged forward to pick up his service revolver and raced toward the house. He stepped over the remains of Seagram to get inside. I took a last look at the Lincoln powering toward the exit drive, then at my Audi and the station wagon. Both cars were Edam cheese. Both had deflated tires. No way was I going to catch Dantalion now.

I followed Kaufman inside. The trail of Seagram's blood led us into a kitchen, and what I saw broke my heart. A man was on his back, eyes fixed in a cataract stare. The agent—Knowles—that Kaufman had been concerned about. Bad enough that this man had died, but he was a professional, and death was sometimes a downside of the job. What made my heart shrivel was the elderly lady lying across the table. Her mouth was crooked in an eternal bow. She had been no threat to anyone. Dantalion did not need to kill her and had done it only from a thirst for blood.

Earlier, I'd told Walter that it wasn't personal this time. Well, I was wrong. When Dantalion killed that harmless old lady, he'd ensured that I wouldn't stop until I tore the last breath from his throat.

Kaufman was gingerly probing through the dead agent's clothing. Looking for his cell phone to call for backup, no doubt. I took out my own phone and called all the backup I required.

"Rink."

"I'm here, Hunter."

"Change of plan, buddy."

I told him what had gone down and he swore under his breath. I stood by the window, staring out across the lawn toward the bright sea. A dark silhouette hunkered on the lawn.

When I was done giving my instructions to Rink, I looked back over at Kaufman. He was still yelling animatedly into Knowles's phone.

"Kaufman," I said loudly.

My voice came as a surprise to him, as if he'd forgotten I was there. He blinked over at me.

My finger pointed out the window.

"Can you fly that thing?"

37

JEAN-PAUL ST. PIERRE—DESPITE WHAT EVeryone said—wasn't a sickly child. His vitiligo condition was purely cosmetic, and though it earned him the cruel taunts of other children, even the occasional beating, it had never affected his physical boundaries. So long as he was careful under the Louisiana sun and took his medication at the dosage prescribed, he could live a life of normality and happiness. His mother loved him dearly, cherished him. Her little angel boy. She gave him all the kindness and support he needed. And he loved his mother in return.

He never knew his father, never had any desire to know the man who'd abandoned him before he was born. Maybe he hadn't intentionally abandoned his son, but it was through his selfishness that Dantalion had never known a father figure in his life. His mother told him that his father had died. In a drunken stupor he'd been flattened under the wheels of an express train when his alcohol-addled brain told him he had right of way at a rail crossing. Dantalion didn't think that was a great loss. He'd got on fine without him.

He blamed his father for his condition. It was his father's seed that had cursed him. But he didn't hold it against the faceless man. In a way, his father's curse was also the gift responsible for making Dantalion the man he would become. His father didn't purposefully pass on the degenerate gene that affected him, and even if he had, he wouldn't have intended his son to live with the consequences. Not through any kind of love for the boy, but simply through a lack of empathy. Daddy simply did not care one way or another about anything that didn't come from a bottle. Or so his mother had told him when he was old enough to inquire. He couldn't understand why she cried all alone at night over someone like that.

He wasn't a sickly child. No.

He was strong and resilient, and he looked after his mother as any son should. When it came time to give his mother her greatest wish, he'd had the fortitude to do so. Willingly and without an ounce of selfishness or self-pity. She had longed for it, asked for it, begged her uncaring God for it. So he couldn't understand why he'd been taken away and placed under guard at Juvenile Hall. Everyone had said that he had to be some kind of monster. They obviously didn't understand him. He'd only been doing what his mother had begged for on each of those occasions that he'd found her crying. His mother was infinitely sad, had been since the day of his father's death, and Jean-Paul had only wished to make her happy. He was even mindful that he caused her as little pain as possible when he shot her in the back of her head with his grandpapa's old coon rifle.

Sociopathic, his doctors had called him. Psychopathic. Others called him even worse names. More personal and hurtful. But he wasn't any of those things. He wasn't sick. Physically or mentally. Couldn't understand why they'd kept him locked away for eight years.

"I know the pussy name you hide behind," Joe Hunter had most recently said to him. *"What is it with all you deadbeats, huh? Why the stupid names? All you sick-in-the-head motherfuckers do that."*

He had smiled at the inanity of it. He'd been hearing similar accusations all his life. Throughout all his years, insults just like that had been his bread and butter. They had sustained him, nourished him, made him even more determined to show his doubters just how much further up the evolutionary ladder he was than they. They could not understand his singular take on reality, because they were blind. No one seemed to see it but him.

He had shown Hunter.

He was better than Hunter.

Primarily because he did not share Hunter's base weaknesses.

Where he would not have faltered in shooting through another person's head to kill his enemy, Hunter had paused. That was the difference between them, what made him better at killing than Hunter would ever be. Hunter was trained. His military masters had ingrained in him the technicalities of killing, but they had never fully eradicated that human foible, the reluctance to murder another human being in cold blood. Empathy and guilt are stronger than the finger that pulls the trigger.

That was why his doctors had proclaimed Jean-Paul a sociopath. No empathy, no guilt, they said. Just like his father, he supposed.

Hunter, on the other hand, did have empathy. He had it in bucket-loads when compared with Jean-Paul.

It wasn't that he couldn't feel guilt; just that he was able to divert that guilt away from himself. He gave those he killed a choice. Their choice equaled their guilt, in his estimation.

He guessed that Joe Hunter dealt with the enormous remorse he carried around by constantly throwing himself into the line of fire, offering up his own life in lieu of all the lives he'd taken. He would sacrifice himself for the sake of others, thinking that would correct the balance in his soul.

Dantalion thought he could use Hunter's weakness to bring all of his targets to him. And he would kill them all. He would leave Hunter until last, so that his guilt was magnified tenfold. And, he thought, looking sideways at his hostage, he would start with Bradley Jorgenson.

His escape from the island was easier than he'd first thought possible. When Hunter and the FBI agent had turned up, things had looked like they were stacking against him. Especially when Hunter surprised him by shooting at Bradley and knocking his aim awry. Only the fortuitous arrival of Seagram stumbling around like something from a zombie movie had allowed him to get away. He hadn't cut deep enough when slicing the man's throat, but things had turned out well in the end. The bullet he'd fired through Seagram's head had diverted Hunter long enough to allow him to make it to the Lincoln. Then the Lincoln, the only roadworthy vehicle at the location, had given him the speed and power to ram his way out through the metal gates. They were designed to keep intruders out, not in. The cop who'd tried to halt him by standing in the way and pointing his gun would have been better served if he'd actually fired the thing. He was less of an obstacle than the gate had proved, although his skull had managed to star the windshield as his body was catapulted over the hood and onto the roof of the sedan.

Now Dantalion was ten miles north, traveling at high speed, slaloming in and out of the traffic heading up the coast toward Jupiter. He was actually enjoying the freedom the huge Town Car demanded from the other road users. The Southeast Dixie Highway was somewhere ahead, as he recalled. He had to get off the coast onto the main route, then find a way across country. When the FBI agent got over his initial reaction to finding his murdered colleague, he would have all the available manpower on his trail. Roadblocks would be in place somewhere ahead of him, and already there could be a convoy of blue lights and sirens rushing in his wake. There was no sign of it yet, but the pursuit would definitely come.

Within half a minute he found the turnpike.

Cars were backed up on the off ramp. He just went around them, forcing the car along the shoulder and leaving several vehicles minus their side-view mirrors behind him. He swung into cross traffic, causing cars to swerve and brake and a refrigerated truck to jackknife into oncoming traffic, effectively closing the road behind him. Dantalion watched the carnage in his mirrors, wondering what tally he should add to his book from the pileup that ensued.

He sped up the highway, found a second turn-off on his left, blasted his way across the median, across the path of the oncoming traffic, and cut into it at over sixty miles an hour. He almost lost control of the vehicle, but steered into the slide of the rear tires, righted the sedan, and then took off at speed. The road he was on wasn't anywhere he'd been before, and the collection of houses he passed went unnamed in his mind as he sped by them. The road went under another highway and swung north and then west, through another mysterious community. Then he was rocketing along a single-lane blacktop road, headed into the swampy lands of Florida's interior.

The road hadn't been designed for speed. It was ridged at its center and there were more bumps and potholes than there were smooth patches. He slowed down, thinking it prudent now that he'd lost any possible pursuers. He looked over at Bradley Jorgenson. The young man was oblivious to all that had occurred since Dantalion had jabbed him with the needle.

Dantalion backhanded him across the face.

"Wake up, Brad," he said. "You aren't going to be any help with your head in the clouds."

Bradley's reply was to loll his head toward Dantalion. His eyes opened, but there was no recognition in their depths. He was mindless of the blood trickling from his nose and into the corner of his mouth.

Sodium amytal is sometimes incorrectly referred to as a truth serum. Movies show those who are drugged with it answering probing questions in a dull monotone, unable to deny their questioners. Dantalion knew that was ridiculous. The drug did reduce a person's resistance to suggestion and had the effect of lowering inhibitions, but it would never cause a man to give up his most closely guarded secrets. At a higher dosage it was no different from any other anesthetic: it put you to sleep. Dantalion wanted answers from Bradley, but he had other ways of forcing them from the man than relying on a wonder drug. He wanted him awake and able to recognize the dilemma he was in.

He slapped him again.

Bradley muttered under his breath, turned his face away, and promptly fell back to sleep.

Bradley would have to be awakened by pain. Once, Dantalion had considered threatening Bradley with the amputation of his extremities followed by a meal to remember. Now he thought that perhaps his plan might actually come to pass.

On either side of the road was scrubland interspersed with occasional irrigated fields. Tributaries of a swamp lying to the north were like the twisted fingers of an arthritic crone. Mangrove grew in dense clumps on hillocks standing above the streams. Birds broke from cover, startled by the passage of the Lincoln. Not the most densely populated area Dantalion had ever seen but less wild than the swamps he'd known along the flooded banks of the Mississippi.

He continued on for another few minutes. Bradley stirred beside him.

"Back with us yet?" Dantalion asked.

"Mmmmff!" was all that Bradley managed.

"Not yet, huh?"

Up ahead was a crossroads, giving him three choices. South, north, or continue heading west. Dantalion was all for choices, but occasionally you just had to throw the dice and go along with fate. He sped through the junction, the tires kicking up gravel deposited there by previous vehicles turning off the ill-maintained route to his left. The road ahead was as straight as an arrow. Tall grass that would conceal an elephant grew at both sides of the road, the upper reaches hanging over so that it looked as if he was driving through a tunnel.

The grass tunnel went on for the best part of a mile. It began to disconcert Dantalion in a way he was unfamiliar with. Something akin to claustrophobia wormed at the base of his stomach, making him feel nauseated and struggling to draw a breath. He didn't like the sensation and

was relieved when the Lincoln passed into open
space once more. There was a lake on his right-
hand side. Thousands of birds, myriad species
he could not name, made the lake their home.
Something large splashed beneath the surface
and moved away through the lake, leaving a wide
wake on the surface.

There were trees ahead, then another of those
damn grass tunnels. Dantalion slowed the vehicle down. Brought it to a halt. Not for fear of
entering the tunnel again—he'd seen something
to his liking across the marshy field on his left.
It was a collection of large red cubes surrounded
by metal masts that glinted gold in the sunlight.
Huge transmission towers made a forest of steel
in the background. Power cables streaked away
into the distant haze, and also toward him and
over the Lincoln and across the lake. He could see
another tower on the far bank of the lake, standing tall above the slowly undulating marsh grass.

Dantalion nodded to himself, pushed the vehicle into drive, and headed for the next grass
tunnel. He had barely entered the green twilight when he nosed the Lincoln off the road and
down the slight descent to the field of tall grasses.
A flimsy wire fence was crushed under the tires
as he pushed the sedan into the grass's embrace.
He didn't get far, feeling the car settling down
almost immediately in the boggy earth. But he
made it far enough into the tall grass so that the
car wouldn't be immediately evident to anyone
passing along the road. To make sure, he clam-

bered out, wading through twisted stalks toward the road. His feet sank into the loam and were snagged by the tough grass, but he made it back to where he'd pushed over the fence. He righted the fence, even though it sagged from the nearby posts. Then he grabbed armfuls of the bent-over grass and stood them upright against the wire. It wouldn't fool a determined tracker but was good enough under the circumstances.

When he got back to the car, Bradley was gone.

38 BACK IN THE DAY, I'D FREQUENTLY BEEN A PAS-
senger on various helicopters, primarily
Sea Kings and Chinooks, AH-6 Defenders and
HueyCobras. On those occasions I'd been flying
out on missions, usually into hot zones where I'd
rappel from the guts of the choppers alongside
Rink and the rest of my team on reconnaissance
or seek and destroy missions. I'd never been in
a JetRanger before, and this helicopter was the
equivalent of a sleek limousine next to some of
the cramped flying buses I'd been in.

The FBI chopper was a five-seater, two up front
and three in the back. When we'd clambered
inside, with Kaufman reaching for the controls,
we'd discovered the pilot dead across the back-
seats. His undressed state explained where Dantalion had stolen his costume. I couldn't find any
sign of injury on the man's body but located a
small puncture wound on his neck.

Kaufman was someone who'd once been familiar with helicopters, but—like his on-the-
street days—it had been some time ago.

"Don't worry," he told me. "It's like riding a
bicycle—you never forget."

"I don't mind falling off a bike," I told him as

I settled into the passenger position next to him, "only not from hundreds of feet in the air."

Kaufman laughed.

Then he was flicking buttons and pulling levers and I heard a whine that grew rapidly to a shriek. Over our heads, the rotors began to turn lazily, scything the air as though cutting through molasses. Then the engine noises changed and the rotors became a blur and we were lifting off the ground. I experienced a moment of weightlessness, then it was as though my stomach pressed down into my pelvis, and we were going straight upward. "Welcome home, Hunter," I whispered under my breath.

Kaufman banked to the right, and as we turned, the world tilted on its axis. The sea was a blue wall over Kaufman's shoulder, while the Florida sky stretched away into the hazy west over mine. Then we banked left and the view was reversed. Next moment we were past the house and the bird righted itself and we were streaking toward the highway about fifty feet up in the air.

"See, I told you. Piece of cake," Kaufman crowed.

"I'll take your word for it."

We flew past the village, then used the exit drive as a locator for the gate. Before we'd even arrived I knew which way Dantalion had taken Bradley. The traffic was backed up on both sides of the highway, but I could see a broad smear of blood where some hapless cop had been hit by the fleeing car. People were crowding around the dead officer. The TV crews encamped on the lay-over opposite the gate were charging across the road, pointing their cameras at the victim. He'd been dragged about ten yards along the highway to our right.

"North," I told Kaufman.

He'd seen the same thing himself and was already turning the JetRanger in pursuit of the Lincoln. The nose of the chopper dipped, and then we were scooting along at top speed. Dantalion had a good lead on us, but not for long.

When we'd boarded the chopper, Kaufman had grabbed the copilot headphones. That left me without ear protection, and the sound was terrific. But I was fine; my head was ringing loudly with a jumble of chaotic thoughts anyway. Rather than recording Bradley's testament on paper, the dead FBI agent, Leighton Knowles, had been taping the interview. When Dantalion had burst in on them, the recorder had borne witness to the murders. It became apparent that Dantalion had noticed it but neglected to turn it off. In fact, it appeared that he didn't switch off the recorder on purpose, instead leaning close to it to say, "The thunders of judgment and wrath are numbered. As are you, Bradley. Pretty Marianne Dean as well. All numbered. The same goes for your turn-coat bodyguard. Hunter and Rink, too." He had paused, and his voice had grown louder still. "Do you hear me? Come to me, bring Marianne. Let's get things over with."

When I'd been considering the chopper as a

means of chasing Dantalion, Kaufman had found the tape. Hollow-eyed, he'd made me listen to it. When he snapped off the recording, he said to me, "Let's go get the bastard."

When I first heard the recording I'd been taken aback. Couldn't understand how Dantalion would know either my or Rink's names. But it didn't take too long to draw conclusions. *Your turncoat bodyguard*, he'd said. Seagram had obviously been involved with the plot to kill Bradley and Marianne. It explained why he'd been at Petre's house when Dantalion went on his initial killing spree. It was more feasible than the excuse he'd tried to feed us that he'd gone there to request assistance. I knew the man couldn't be trusted, that I should have had him cut loose the first time I saw him. It was apparent then that he was bitter about us usurping his status as top dog in the Jorgenson household. Worst thing, I'd missed taking Dantalion down because of his arrival, and maybe he hadn't been so blind with impending death when he'd started shooting at me. His actions had been his final desperate attempt at killing a man he hated. The only thing I regretted now was that it was Dantalion and not me who'd put a bullet through the asshole's head.

When Dantalion had spoken directly into the recorder, he must have known I was coming. Perhaps he'd even seen me outside with Kaufman and that was what prompted him to do the speech. His words were a direct threat. He didn't say as much, but he was inviting me to try and take him down. He was confident. But that in itself was no bad thing.

He must have taken what had happened outside the house as a minor victory. He'd beaten me, yes. But minor victories never win the war. They breed self-confidence, which in turn leads to complacency. And as any soldier will remind you, complacency will bring on your destruction.

Before boarding the chopper, I'd called Harvey. Now I used my cell phone to call Rink. Shouting over the whine of the exhaust vents, I asked him if Harvey had done as I'd asked earlier.

"Yeah," he told me. "You know Harvey; he loves all that technical stuff."

It was a ruse we'd employed once before to track the Harvestman. On that occasion, it had been doubtful if our idea would even work. But it had, until Tubal Cain discovered the cell phone that we were tracking via satellite technology. He'd thrown the phone away, but that was okay; by then we already had him in our sights. Pretty soon after that I'd rammed a broken bone from his collection of skeletal parts through the monster's windpipe. Had Cain recognized the ploy earlier, maybe we would never have found him. Not until it was too late to save my brother, John.

This time there was no concern about the killer spotting our makeshift tracking device. It was the phone I was holding that Harvey and Rink were vectoring in on. All I had to do was locate Danta- lion, and even if I failed to stop him, at least Rink would get the opportunity to avenge me.

"You in some kind of aircraft?" Rink asked me. "I'm watching my GPS and the land's scrolling along quicker than I can keep up with."

"Chopper," I told him. "Remember that FBI agent I was telling you about?"

"The one with the stick up his ass?"

"That's him. Well, maybe I was a little judgmental when first we met. He's a good guy. Flew UH-60s on a couple tours in Somalia before becoming a fed."

"UH-60s?" Rink said. "You're talking Black Hawks?"

"Like I said, he's a good guy," I said. "Could even have been your pilot on a mission or two."

The UH-60 Black Hawk is the helicopter of choice of the U.S. Special Forces. Delta and U.S. Rangers, primarily. Before joining my team, Rink had belonged to the Rangers. Kaufman had just won kudos in both our eyes.

"Dantalion got away from us, Rink. He has Bradley with him as a hostage. I intend getting him back."

Beside me, Kaufman indicated the road ahead.

I saw a major pileup of traffic at an intersection of the highway. Then more importantly, a silver Lincoln streaking west. Kaufman banked, following. He knew what I intended, so kept far enough back that we weren't obvious to the fleeing driver. To Rink, I added, "Got him in sight now, buddy. Get to us as soon as you can."

"Keep heading this way, and I'll be with you sooner than you think," Rink said.

I put the phone safely in my pocket. Took out my SIG and reloaded it.

Kaufman was also busy talking. Calling up his own people. Nothing I could do about that. I only hoped I could get to Dantalion before the FBI arrived in force and made a siege of wherever Dantalion intended holing up. Kaufman was an ex–army aviator, used to working alongside the Special Forces. But now he was an FBI SAC and was governed by different rules. I had to give him his lead on this, as long as he gave me a few minutes' latitude before calling the shots direct from the FBI manual.

The Lincoln continued westward, passing through a couple of small towns, blew under the I-95, then continued out toward the wild lands that separated the coastal towns from Lake Okeechobee. The lake itself was a dark line on the horizon as we sped after the sedan.

Dantalion drove the Lincoln like a crazy man, careless of meeting any oncoming traffic on the single lane of tarmac. Anyone unfortunate enough to be heading the other way would be forced to give way, and that meant taking a dip in one of the many sinkholes that potted the land on either side of the road. From our aerial perspective the land looked as if it had undergone a barrage of meteors—like a lush green version of the surface of the moon.

Fields of very tall grass spread out beneath us, and for a minute or so the Lincoln was hidden from view where the grass became a knitted roof over the road. But then the car was onto a clear stretch of road again and passing a lake. The Lincoln looked like it was slowing. I nudged Kaufman's shoulder and he banked away, taking the helicopter out of Dantalion's line of sight. We hovered where we could just make out a flash of silver.

"He's moving again," Kaufman announced. He dipped the nose of the chopper and we moved forward once more. Much slower than before. The Lincoln disappeared beneath a second field of that long grass.

"You think he saw us?" I asked.

"Not likely," Kaufman replied. "He maybe stopped to get his bearings. Now he's happy and he's set off again."

"Do you know where that road takes us?"

"All the way to Okeechobee. There he has only three choices. North, south, or to the bottom of the lake."

This latest field wasn't quite as large as the first. It should take Dantalion less than a minute to pass through it and once more come back in sight. We hung back, cautious, waiting for the Lincoln to reappear. I counted out sixty seconds in my head.

"He must have stopped again," I announced.

"We can't be sure of that," Kaufman replied. "He could simply be driving slower than he was before. Hold on, I'll get a little closer, see what's what."

He put the chopper into a hover, then took us

sideways very slowly. The helicopter began to rotate through a half circle. It gave us a view of the entire field and where sunlight broke on the blacktop about three-quarters of a mile ahead.

"Don't see anything," he concurred. "I think you're right, Hunter. He's stopped somewhere along the way."

"Can you put me down somewhere?" I asked. "This end would be best. You can go to the far side and see if you can backtrack along the road."

"Can do," Kaufman agreed, "but he'll hear us coming. He could be waiting for us."

"That's fine by me. There's no Seagram to fuck things up this time."

"Walter Conrad said that you were one of the best that he ever worked with, but I can't help but think we should wait for backup. I've got a couple McDonnell Douglas 530s on their way here. We could round Dantalion up between us, no sweat."

McDonnell Douglas 530s are commonly known as "Little Birds." They're the gunships employed by the FBI during aerial assaults, the type you see in movies with rocket launchers and men in black hanging out the side with sniper rifles. If Dantalion caught a glimpse of any of those, he'd kill Bradley there and then.

"Can't wait for backup," I said. "He's stopped for a reason. Maybe he doesn't see Bradley as a hostage anymore and wants to lighten the load. We need to stop him now, Kaufman."

He knew I was right, but I could tell he was considering all the ramifications his agreement would have on his future career with the FBI. His decisions would be severely scrutinized by his bosses up at Quantico and Washington, D.C., but in the end, I was my own man and not under his direct jurisdiction. He knew that if he didn't put me down where I asked, I'd make him.

"Careful of those power lines," I cautioned him as we swung back to the open area next to the big lake we'd passed.

"I see them, Hunter," he said. "The ground is too boggy to land here. I'm going to have to look for somewhere firmer."

"No time," I said. I took the Ka-bar out of my boot and tucked it through a belt loop of my jeans. "Just get us low enough so I can jump."

He looked at me like I was the insane one, shaking his head. He probably had it in mind that I'd disappear up to my neck in a sinkhole. But then it was as if that wasn't too bad an idea; it would save him from the bureaucratic nightmare he'd have to face for allowing me to conduct my own vigilante action against Dantalion.

Suit yourself, Hunter, his face said. Then he was going through the routine of bringing us down toward the ground. I pushed open the cockpit door and it slammed back against the side of the chopper. The downwash from the rotor blades flattened the deep grass beneath me and lifted loose debris that swirled around us like we were in the midst of a cyclone.

"This is low enough," I told him and swung my legs out of the cockpit. I took out the cell phone, held it tight in my left hand, and took my SIG Sauer in my right. Over the noise of the engine I shouted, "My friend Rink is on his way here. Don't let any of your boys stand in his way. He's not as patient with people as I am and will probably kick their asses."

Kaufman gave me a tight-lipped smile. "Just watch your own ass, Hunter."

I winked. Then dropped out of the chopper. Hoping I didn't land in the gaping jaws of an alligator.

39 BRADLEY JORGENSON COULD NOT HAVE GOT FAR in the time Dantalion had spent concealing the Lincoln from the road. A couple of minutes had passed, and that was all. In his drugged and disoriented state, it was a high probability that he'd managed to get as far into the long grass as one determined rush would take him before he'd fallen facedown and gone back to sleep. His trail was easy enough to see: the bent and broken stems of the bamboolike grass angling away from the front of the Lincoln into the green twilight.

Dantalion took out the Glock 17 he'd liberated from Seagram and checked the load. He fed spare rounds into the magazine as he started after Bradley. From somewhere ahead the sound of a body pushing through the long grass came to his ears. Only one person it could be. Then another sound came to him: the *whup, whup, whup* of rotor blades.

He craned around attempting to see the helicopter, but he was surrounded by the tall grass, looking up at only a tiny patch of blue sky. The walls of this maze had the effect of distorting and redirecting the source of the noise and made it difficult to pinpoint where the rotor sound was coming from. He couldn't tell where it was now, but he had the feeling he knew exactly where the helicopter had originated—back on the lawn outside Eunice Jorgenson's ramshackle home. Hunter was proving to be one resourceful dude. Dantalion wasn't overly concerned that the man had managed to follow him here; it saved him the trouble of contacting him and drawing him to his death later.

Bradley Jorgenson was still alive only because Dantalion planned to use him to bait a larger trap. Marianne Dean had been spirited away from him, and he'd hoped to torture the woman's whereabouts from her lover, contact her, and then demand that she come to a prearranged location where he'd finish the two of them. That would obviously mean that Hunter and his friend Rink would be along for the ride, but Dantalion thought himself capable of killing them all. He'd beaten Hunter every other time they'd met—discounting the fall into the sea, but even that he'd survived, which in itself had been a victory when viewed in hindsight—and felt sure he would do so again. He could kill Bradley now and be shot of him. Hunter would give up Marianne's location as readily as the Jorgenson brat would. Then he could kill Marianne and Rink at his leisure.

The sound of the chopper receded, and he assumed that Hunter was confused about his sudden disappearance and would continue on toward Okeechobee before backtracking this way again. It would give him all the time he needed to catch up and dispense with Bradley Jorgenson.

Sure enough, he heard the drone of the chopper as it swung away to the west. Dantalion smiled to himself, then stepped into the tall grass.

Small biting insects called this grass home.

So did serpents and lizards and all manner of crawling things.

Not a place that Dantalion would normally choose to frequent. But he pushed through the grass happily, feeling that all was going to be right in his world. The numerological equations in his book would soon be back in balance. He could write up the numbers of those he'd dispatched in the meantime, and he even made himself a silent bet that he was close to meeting the tally of the original Dantalion and his command of thirty-six legions of spirits.

The going was tough. The grass grew in great hummocks but sent out feelers at ankle level that stretched taut across the clear areas, creating trip wires as effective as any he'd ever laid. The grass itself was as strong and coarse as hemp rope. Sheaves on the stems made long prickly spines where they frayed and split from the main growth, and they scratched and plucked at his flesh and clothing with each step. He was glad he was still dressed in the helicopter pilot's jumpsuit, because anything less would have allowed the bristles to invade his clothing and make abrasions all over his body. His hands were protected from the spearing grass, but his face was bared now that he'd ditched the helmet. His short hair was a boon at least; if he'd come in here when it was still long, he fancied he'd have been tangled up in the grasses many meters back and have had to tear his hair out in clumps to make his escape.

He couldn't hear the helicopter now, but he could hear Bradley's stumbling progress. Everything else was still and silent, the indigenous creatures of this sea of grass fleeing before the presence of alien invaders. To Dantalion's senses came an almost overpowering stench of rotting vegetation. A breeze touched his face like the caress of the lover he'd never known. Instead of following Bradley, he swung to the left and pushed through the grass toward an open space. He found himself standing by a wide-open field. Separating him from the cultivated land was a sluggish stream that had been cut out of the earth to help drain the swamp this field had once been. The stream was the source of the stench. It was clogged with black mud and decaying foliage. Across the field he could see the buildings he'd earlier noticed from the road. Closer now, he could make out doors in one building, as well as machinery and spools of cable. Strange place to have a factory, he thought, and decided it was some sort of electrical substation that served the nearby towns.

Following the edge of the drainage channel, he could gain time and distance on the fleeing Bradley. He took off at a lope, peering back over his shoulder as he did so. Giving up the cover of the field of long grass was great for maneuverability, but it put him out in the open for anyone who could be chasing him. He couldn't hear the helicopter anymore, but he had the feeling it would be back. He didn't want to find himself in the sights of an FBI sharpshooter, whether that man be on the ground or up in the air. Bradley's crashing flight through the grass was all he needed to tell he was still on his trail. He moved along parallel to the sounds, seeing every now and then a flash of clothing through the thinner stands of reeds.

In all that had happened in the past few days, Dantalion had forgotten that he was injured. Three bullet wounds were nothing to be trifled with. The one in his leg was the most troubling, the most likely to become infected if he didn't keep it clean. The problem was that he had no way of keeping it clean for long, not in this environment of clinging roots and decaying vegetable matter. A fall in the mud was only one stumble away. His leg had begun to trouble him again.

But he pressed on regardless.

Holding the Glock 17 parallel to his uninjured thigh, he made his way quickly along the edge of the irrigation channel, stepping gamely across secondary ditches hewn from the marsh. He was so close now that he could hear the rasp of Bradley's breath and his sobs of sheer terror. Still under the influence of the sodium amytal but rapidly shaking it off, Bradley would be in a state of severe confusion. His last lucid memory would be when Dantalion shot the FBI man and then jabbed the syringe into Bradley's skin. The rest would be a foggy recollection of disjointed images interspersed with black gulfs of nothingness. He would slowly be coming awake in this world of green and brown prison bars, knowing that he must escape but without understanding fully why or from whom he was running—only that he must do so or die.

Dantalion thought that perhaps he should simply put a bullet through Bradley's head and have done with it, get out of this stinking marsh, and contemplate less muddy alternatives for luring Hunter, Rink, and Marianne Dean to him. But then he decided that since he had come this far, he should see out his original plan. Bradley would be no more difficult to control now that he was resurfacing from drug-induced delirium. Dantalion had a gun, and that was all he'd need to ensure that the privileged brat, scion of the Jorgenson empire, would do exactly as he commanded. All it would take was a harsh word and a nasty promise, and Bradley would give up his flight for freedom.

Dantalion loped on a few extra yards. Deciding that now was the time to get control again, he swung around so that he was facing the young man blindly thrashing his way through the long grass.

"Okay, enough is enough, Bradley. Come on out now." He lifted the semiautomatic handgun to add emphasis to the implied promise that, should Bradley ignore the request, there would be no second chances.

Bradley came to a halt. He held his breath, hunched over like a prey animal caught in the sights of an eagle. It would be as though Dantalion's voice had resounded from the grass all around him. Dantalion fancied his words would have carried like those God spoke to Moses from within a burning bush—only a little wetter.

"You have three seconds to comply," Dantalion added. "One . . ."

Bradley turned and crashed back the way he'd come, yowling something unintelligible.

Dantalion had no recourse but to run after Bradley a second time, following his progress from the less cumbersome route beside the irrigation ditch. He charged along making ground, then, as he overtook the fleeing man, pushed his way through the bamboolike stalks to intercept him. Bradley saw him coming, and there was recognition in his face that no amount of sodium amytal could conceal. Dantalion brought up the Glock, aiming it directly at Bradley's throat. Bradley skidded on his heels, coming to a halt. But he was too afraid of the nightmare images his brain had conjured these past minutes, and even the dark unwinking eye of a handgun couldn't compel him to stop and face his nemesis. He lurched sideways, dodging past Dantalion's left arm, which groped in empty space as it tried to snag him. He was sinuous in his ability to avoid the clutching fingers with their long, discolored nails and scaly flesh. And even in his disappointment at not catching hold of Bradley, Dantalion felt that pang that occasionally accompanied his realization that people found his touch repulsive. The aversion that most people experienced when Dantalion laid his hands upon them had often been a major weapon in his favor, but if the truth be known, he'd always longed for that singular encounter when someone would reach out and take his hand without squirming or an averted gaze. The last person to do so had been his mother, moments before he'd pushed his grandfather's rifle against her medulla oblongata and sent her to the longed-for reunion with his father by a swift jerk of the trigger.

Bradley charged deeper into the grass before twisting to the side and racing for the open ground he'd spotted. Dantalion kept pace with him, so that Bradley was mere yards ahead when he burst through the last stand of grass and onto the embankment above the foul-smelling ditch. Dantalion lifted the Glock. His finger danced on the trigger, but he did not shoot. He wished to be facing Bradley when the boy died. He wanted to look into his eyes and watch the soul die behind them. He wanted to hear the final exhalation of breath, wanted to taste it on his lips.

"You are prolonging your death, Bradley. Is that really what you want? Do you wish to run in terror, or would you prefer to turn around and face your fate head-on like an honorable man?" Dantalion managed all that between huffing breaths as he continued to run after Bradley. "Turn around, Bradley. Turn around and I'll kill you cleanly and painlessly. Should you prefer to continue running, there can be no alternative."

Bradley couldn't possibly have understood the implications of the choices Dantalion offered. He didn't stop running and he didn't turn around.

"So you choose to reject my offer?" Dantalion lifted the Glock so that he was running with his arm extended, legs pumping high to avoid stumbling on the uneven ground. "Okay, then, Bradley. Have it your way!"

Dantalion fired.

The Glock's report was startlingly loud in this wilderness. Animals shocked by the sudden sound gave voice to their fear, and terrified birds broke from the cover of the long grass and launched themselves heavenward.

Bradley crumpled to the ground, his upper body digging a trench in the soft earth from his heavy landing. He gave a groan of agony as he half-rolled with his own momentum, then settled back to the ground where he'd gone down. Then Dantalion was over him and the Glock was pointed directly at the back of his head. Bradley began to mew like a cat, and his fingers elongated as the agony shrieking through his body sought outlet.

"Hurts like hell, doesn't it?" Dantalion asked. Then he pulled the trigger and shot a second bullet through the back of the same knee he'd just demolished. Bradley screamed. Dantalion kicked him so that Bradley rolled onto his back. He turtled up, hugging his damaged knee against his chest.

"Bet you it's even more painful now," Dantalion said.

"You son of a bitch!" Bradley managed in return.

"Don't," Dantalion warned him. "Don't ever say anything about my mother."

Then he shot Bradley again, this time through the bones of the foot of his already injured right leg.

"Do feel free to tell me where Marianne is," Dantalion went on. "Do that and I'll make the next shot count. The pain will end, Bradley."

Bradley was in a place beyond comprehension. Dantalion's whispery voice wasn't registering, not when his entire being was screaming out in agony. Dantalion cocked his head birdlike. He watched the man rolling on the ground, face contorted into an ugly mask, realizing that perhaps taking away Bradley's mobility hadn't been the most prudent of actions after all. He glanced across the irrigation channel toward the distant buildings. He looked down at Bradley again. He could jump the ditch, no problem, but there was no way he could do so with Bradley in tow.

"I'm afraid you've outlived your usefulness," he told the unheeding man. Then he raised the Glock so that it was aimed at the center of Bradley's face. "Last chance, Bradley. Tell me where Marianne is and I'll kill you cleanly." He lowered his aim so it was below the Kevlar vest. "If not, I'll gut-shoot you and leave you for the alligators to find."

In a moment of clarity, Bradley stared up at

him. The young man's face was contorted with pain, but behind that Dantalion saw more revulsion than anyone had ever cast his way. "Go to hell," Bradley spat between his spittle-flecked lips.

"No doubt about it," Dantalion agreed. "But you'll be there before me."

Bradley sneered at him. "Yeah? Well I'll say hello to your mother, shall I? Stands to reason a bitch that gave birth to an animal like you will be there, too."

"I told you not to speak about my mother."

"Tough shit, man!" Bradley yelled. "If she's anything like you she's an evil, ugly old bitch!"

"Don't you say that!"

"Evil, ugly, *diseased* old bitch," Bradley shouted at him.

Dantalion's head swung from side to side. "I'm warning you. One more word . . ."

"What kind of ordinary woman gives birth to a monster like you?" Bradley continued.

"My mother was beautiful," Dantalion said.

"Yeah, right!" Bradley fought himself up to a sitting position. Beads of cold sweat broke along his hairline. "So it must have been your father who was pig-ugly, then."

Dantalion blinked his rheumy eyes.

"Ha! Thought so. You don't even know your father, do you? You're just another bastard born from a drugged-up whore!"

Dantalion lifted the Glock and aimed it squarely between Bradley's eyes. He felt a quiver of rage build in him. He was a professional, he told himself, and should not give in to such animalistic urges. But Bradley's words went beyond the insults he'd endured all his life. Aimed at himself, other people's insults had fueled him, built him into the killer that he'd become, but he could not stand by while this pig of a boy cast aspersions on his mother. He loved his mother more than anything. He had proved the depths of his love when he'd sent her to be with his father rather than keep her all to himself. He could have been selfish, but no. He had done her a kindness, even though he wanted his mother to be his for all eternity.

He pulled the trigger and the Glock barked like an angry dog.

40

THE GUNSHOT SOUNDED SO CLOSE I COULD HAVE sworn I felt the pressure of displaced air in my inner ear. It took less than a moment for it to register that the gun had been fired many yards to my left, and it was an echo effect of the rippling grasses that made it sound so close. The grass stood tall above me, long fronds with featherlike blooms hanging like the heads of bearded wise men. They nodded at me, spurring me to action.

I'd discovered the abandoned car within minutes of disembarking from the chopper. Dantalion had made an effort to conceal the car from the road, but to a man on foot the disguise was pitiful at most. I checked the car for Bradley's corpse and—thankfully—found it to be empty. Two separate trails led away through the tall grass, and at random I chose the nearest to follow. My SIG was in my hand, and I'd also withdrawn the Ka-bar from my belt. When I'd dropped from the helicopter I'd sunk almost to my knees into viscous mud. Water had splashed up my body. I had to take out the knife and wipe it clean on some scrub. The knife was in my left hand now. So I moved through the green ocean in a crouch with both my weapons poised for killing.

The last time I'd stalked an enemy through grasses like these was on an island in the Indian Ocean. Sinhala villagers had been butchered by a faction of terrorists, and my team was sent in to punish those responsible. The terrorists were a particularly devout group of fanatics who were prepared to die for their beliefs. They were known to carry cyanide capsules to avoid capture, preferring suicide instead. It was a good compromise. We caught the murdering pigs and made them chew on their own capsules, but still shot them in their final seconds. Sounds brutal, I know, but the sight of headless women and children is enough to make you forget your humanity.

So does an old lady sprawled across her table with a bullet through her heart.

Moving through the whispering grasses, I thought back to that time. How Rink and I and half a dozen of our comrades had used the cover of the elephant grass to get so close to the men we hunted that we could've reached out and snatched them one by one. It was the same now. I moved to within a couple of yards of Dantalion, and the white-faced freak wasn't even aware of my presence.

He was standing pointing his gun downward, and it took me a moment to realize that Bradley was there, concealed from my view by a dip in the ground. Dantalion leaned over him, and for the briefest time I saw one of Bradley's arms waving him back. He was still alive, but then Dantalion fired his gun again. Bradley began screaming. I lifted my own SIG to shoot, only for the damn thing to jam on me. Bradley was still shouting, even after Dantalion shot him a third time, and I guessed that the man was torturing Bradley by shooting his extremities. I had moments to save Bradley, the seconds ticking down. However, with my gun jammed I had no other weapon than the Ka-bar. I could throw the knife, but there was always the chance that I'd miss. Then it would be my bare hands against Dantalion's gun, and no matter how good I was at unarmed combat, the bullets would be faster than my fists.

It was a huge risk, but I didn't think that Dantalion was ready to kill Bradley yet. I slipped backward into the longer grass, giving me the cover I needed while I disengaged the slide on my gun. I'm a fan of the SIG Sauer primarily because it suits my style of point shooting. It has no safety to snag on clothing, and the sights are removed for the same reason. You could fire a thousand rounds in quick succession and it would never jam. It was pure bad luck that the gun had failed me at the very moment I needed it. Typically, I found that it was the bullet and not the gun that had let me down. I quickly ejected the jammed round, then racked the slide a second time, ejecting a second. Then, happy that the gun was good to go, I moved quickly through the grass back toward Dantalion.

Both their voices were raised. Bradley was more angered by his wounds than he was terrified, and he was belittling Dantalion, goading him with insults about his heritage. By the way Dantalion answered, he was rising to the bait, too. His face looked like molten wax as he stepped toward Bradley. I knew it was now or never.

I fired.

So did Dantalion.

But I had fired first, and my bullet hit him in the meat of his right shoulder. Blood puffed into the air. Dantalion was knocked sidelong and his finger tightened reflexively on the trigger, firing off round after round. He made some sort of high-pitched howl and then toppled out of sight. I heard a splash and saw a gout of dirty water erupt into the air. The stench of rotting vegetation filled my senses.

Immediately I came out of hiding. My bullet had hit the killer, but it wasn't a mortal wound. Only once I had put a wad of lead through his skull or his heart would I relax. Quickly I moved from the grass onto an embankment over a drainage ditch where I saw that Bradley had survived. He was sorely wounded through his right leg, but otherwise looked like he would live. He blinked up at me with an agonized expression on his face.

"Did you get him?" he asked.

"Not badly enough," I said.

Then I stepped toward the ditch.

The water was putrid, murky, and full of weeds. The scum on the surface had been broken and an undulating circle showed where Dantalion had gone under, but there was no sign of him. Part of me hoped he'd been entangled in the weeds and drowned, his lungs filling with the rancid water, but a greater part of me wanted to kill him outright. Things *had* become personal between us.

Three times I fired into the water. It was perhaps a waste of ammunition, but if he was down there I didn't want him coming back up uninjured. I watched for a few seconds, waiting for blood to find its way to the surface, but saw no sign of it. My suspicions played out. Dantalion had used the dirty water for cover. He'd have to come up soon, and close by, but it was awkward when I had to cover two directions at once.

"Where is he?" Bradley croaked from behind me.

"Quiet," I snapped at him. I took a step backward so that I didn't offer a target from below the water, then stood poised with my SIG, waiting for the telltale eruption of water as Dantalion made his play.

But then something else intervened and took away all hope of hearing Dantalion resurface. The shriek of turbines and the *whop, whop, whop* of rotor blades were suddenly horrendously loud above me. My first thought was that Kaufman had finished with his search along the road and returned to give support from the air. But that summation lasted only as long as it took for the pilot on a loud microphone to shout orders at me.

"This is the FBI. Lower your weapon or we will be forced to shoot."

Snatching a glance upward I saw a sleek black craft. One of the McDonnell Douglas 530s that SAC Kaufman had brought in for backup. The

Little Bird hung in the air and an FBI sharp-shooter sat in the doorway with his scope aimed directly at my chest.

"Drop your weapon!" came the order again.

Bad luck seemed to be coming my way in spades that day.

To the chopper crew it must have looked like I was the one standing over a severely wounded man and it was my gun that was responsible for shooting him. It was fair enough under the circumstances, but there was no way I was about to give up my weapon; not when I knew that Dantalion was close by and would be seeking revenge.

That left me only one recourse. I dove head-long into the long grass. The sharpshooter immediately fired, and high-velocity rounds peppered the earth behind me and cut fronds from the grass so that they sifted around me. I could do nothing but run harder. The chopper would have the advantage of a hawk's-eye view, not to mention a heat-seeking scope that would pick me out in seconds, but to stand still meant giving up my weapon and leaving myself vulnerable to the killer under the water. I ran full sprint, slashing at the tough grass with my Ka-bar, trying to get out of the line of sight of the chopper pilot. It would take him the best part of thirty seconds to bring the chopper about, realize I was out of sight, then decide to switch to the heat-seeking camera on the nose of the cockpit. In that time I wanted to be in a more opportune position to protect myself from the overeager sharpshooter.

The loud commands sounded again, but I was only partly aware of what the pilot was saying. Probably it involved giving up, throwing down my weapons, and showing myself. Not that I was about to comply with any of his demands. I intended concealing myself long enough so that they could recognize their error, or for Kaufman to put them right. The McDonnell Douglas swooped overhead, and the downwash of the rotors knitted the grass over my head. As soon as it was beyond me I turned on my heel and sprinted back to where Bradley lay.

Bradley had heaved himself up onto his elbows in the few seconds I'd been gone. I crashed out of the long grass and skidded to a halt at his side. His face was full of pain, and not a little bewilderment.

"What are they doing?" he cried.

"They think I'm the fuckin' bad guy," I told him. And I was going to have to put them right. The problem being I still had a wounded man to protect from his would-be killer. "Sorry, Bradley, but this might hurt."

"What do you mean?"

For answer I grasped him under his armpits and pulled him bodily on top of me so that he was sitting in my lap like an overgrown child. Then I jammed the Ka-bar into the earth beside me and held my right arm high, so that the sharpshooter could see I had my finger through the trigger guard but that my SIG was suspended upside down and no immediate threat.

"Holy shit!" Bradley said. It was an effect of the pain caused by my manhandling of him, but more than that it was the realization that I was going to use him as a shield. "What if they shoot me?"

"Don't worry, they won't do that," I told him, at the same time hoping that I was right. "And anyway, you're wearing a Kevlar vest."

"They could hit my head!"

"Nah, they'll fire for center mass. Only sure way of hitting the target."

"What about the killer? He won't think twice about shooting me in the head."

"Then you'll just have to count on me getting him first."

"Goddamn . . ."

"Yeah," I agreed. "Not good odds, Bradley, but it's all we've got at the moment."

Then I told him what I wanted him to do.

We sat like that until the gunship did a loop and returned to its starting position. The chopper hovered over us, and once again I was in the sights of the sniper scopes. My head was the only visible target, but my emphatic gesturing with the upside-down gun meant that I wasn't going to experience my last moments with the smell of Bradley's fear in my nostrils.

A second Little Bird screamed into view. This one was about two hundred yards out, and it swept over the open field from the west. Passing over the top of the first chopper, it tilted and raced off over the long grass behind me. The combined roar of both choppers drowned out both Bradley's and my exhortations for them to back off.

Out of the side door of the nearest chopper, a black-garbed Hostage Rescue Team trooper rappelled to the ground. He was armed with an assault rifle and he took up a crouched covering position while two more members of the team dropped from the guts of the chopper like large black spiders on fat webs. Once the two exchanged positions with him, the first agent came toward us, his gun braced against his shoulder. The Little Bird swooped away, and finally I could hear myself think.

Also, the FBI agent's voice rang loud and clear.

"Drop the weapon, Hunter. Now!"

I wasn't surprised to find he recognized me. He was one of the men SAC Kaufman had been communicating with from the headset. Whatever Kaufman had told him, he wasn't taking any chances. Truth was, my gun held in an awkward upside-down position or not, I could manipulate it faster than the human eye could follow and could've shot him dead before he could react.

"Lose the fucking weapon," he shouted, and to emphasize the command, he leaned into his rifle as he drew a bead on my forehead.

"The killer is still out there," I shouted back at him. "I wounded him, but he's still dangerous. I'm not dropping my gun."

"The perp's our problem now. I have orders from SAC Kaufman to make you stand down."

Make me stand down?

"Bradley is *my* problem," I told him, "and I

don't stand down until I know he's no longer in any danger."

Switching tack, the anonymous agent said to Bradley, "Mr. Jorgenson, we are here to protect you. You need immediate medical assistance. We can't offer that while Hunter is armed. You tell him to stand down."

Bradley could only make pained gasps, let alone order anything.

"Look," I said. "We're on the same side here. Let's cut the crap and get Bradley the hell away from here. I'm going after Dantalion."

"I agree with you on one thing. But you aren't going after anyone." He'd taken another step forward. The two backup agents had also moved to flank me. I was the proverbial fish in the barrel. But out there in the water was a more dangerous creature in need of spearing.

Rising up from behind Bradley, I lifted the SIG so it was clear to all. "I'm going to holster my weapon, but that's as far as it goes. You can load Bradley into one of those birds, but I'm staying."

"Step away from Mr. Jorgenson," said the first agent, as though I hadn't spoken. "The FBI will deal with this situation now. You do not have official sanction in this matter, Hunter. SAC Kaufman has checked; you are no longer active and do not work with our government's agreement. If you refuse to step away you will be arrested for obstructing a federal agent."

I stepped away.

I pushed the SIG into the waistband at the back

of my jeans. One of the HRT agents stepped in and laid a hand on Bradley's shoulder. He took a grip on the cloth of Bradley's shirt and pulled him around and away from me. As if I were the bad guy. The other two covered me with their rifles, but I was gratified to note that neither intended trying to disarm me. Not immediately.

I indicated the Ka-bar, hilt deep in the silt. "I'm taking that as well."

Without their permission, I stooped and picked up the knife. As I rose from my crouch I was already pivoting. The Ka-bar is a man killer. To kill is its primary function, and all other applications of the fighting knife are by-products of its design. Not that I was about to kill an FBI agent in the execution of his duty. I only used the butt end to thrust into the midriff of the man nearest me. He was wearing armor, but my blow was delivered with all the power of my upswinging arm and the force went directly through the vest and into his internal organs. Wind rushed out of his wide-open mouth, even as I whipped the rifle out of his grasp and turned it on the first agent. Yet again, I couldn't use the weapon on him—not in its conventional sense—but I hurled the rifle at him, end over end. His reaction was to bat it away with the barrel of his own gun. And into the space he'd left me I stepped and launched a kick that caught him at the juncture of his thighs. He was wearing a box, but it didn't make a difference. Not when my shin lifted him a hand's width off the ground. I jumped in as he landed on his face, kicking away his gun with the side of my foot.

One and a half seconds isn't a long time in any violent confrontation. Viewed in afterthought it's amazing how rapidly a tableau can change. But there was yet a third armed agent to deal with. He was well out of range of any sneak attack of my own. Except for the one I'd already planned.

"Now, Bradley," I yelled.

Bradley immediately became less the crippled weight than he seemed. He threw his arms around the man supporting him, grappling the agent's rifle so that it was wedged between them. Bradley continued to drive into the man, and they both went down on the ground, rolling in spongy earth. I charged over and grabbed the man's rifle away from him. Then I spun so that I was covering them all with the leveled rifle.

"Okay, boys," I yelled at them. "The deal's the same as before. You get Bradley out of here, I go after Dantalion."

The first agent was also the first to recover from our attack. "You have assaulted FBI agents in the execution of their duties. It is a federal crime, Hunter. You'll be arrested for this."

"Get a fuckin' life, will you," I snapped at him. "We all know how this is gonna go down. I'm leaving. You lot get the fuck out of here. You tell Kaufman I escaped. I've gone after the demented killer we all want to see dead. Where's the fucking crime in that?"

I threw the gun aside, took out my SIG, and

raced away. None of them lifted a gun to bring me down, so it seemed they'd seen sense in my words.

I'd seen something, too. Way ahead of me. A pale blur of a face turned my way. A dark-garbed figure loping across the field toward the huge buildings on the near horizon.

41

DANTALION HAD BEEN SHOT. THE BULLET HAD clipped his right shoulder just at the point when he was about to shoot Bradley Jorgenson in the face. It had cut away a large chunk of his hide but had missed hitting anything serious like an artery or bone. The wound was numb. Likely very soon it would be screaming in agony, but it wasn't totally debilitating. He could still hold his Glock, he could still shoot, and he could still finish his mission.

The force of the bullet had knocked him off balance and he'd missed his target, but even that might prove to be a boon. It offered him another chance at killing Jorgenson. Next time he would do it with a cool head. It would take much, much longer and involve an infinite amount of pain.

The bullet had also thrown him headlong into the putrescent stream. His initial thoughts were of disgust and an overwhelming sense of failure. But only for as long as it took him to realize that the stream was also his salvation. If he'd fallen on the dry ground, Hunter would have followed up his first bullet and would most definitely have killed him. But the murky water had given him cover while he swam away. He was able to surface many yards west of where he'd fallen. When he came up for air, he was concealed from the eyes of Hunter by overhanging foliage. There he'd been able to catch his breath and check the two things most important to him. The Glock was wet but, he believed, serviceable. After his plunge into the Intracoastal Waterway, he'd taken care to wrap his book in cellophane, so it was barely dampened when he fished it out from the jumpsuit. Everything was A-OK.

Then fortune smiled on him again. The FBI helicopters forced Hunter away from the stream, giving Dantalion the opportunity to make his break for freedom. He heard the roar of the choppers, the hard snap of rifles, and knew that the FBI had confused Hunter with him. Maybe they'd kill the bastard on his behalf and leave the door open for him to get at Bradley a second time. Or maybe not. He couldn't rely on Lady Luck any more than he had up to now. He had to make his own opportunities.

He scrambled along the streambed, found a place to climb out, and crawled up onto the far side. Lying on the embankment, he watched as a chopper set down three armed agents. From this distance he couldn't hear what was said. But he witnessed Hunter dispatching all three in the space of seconds, and for the first time he experienced fear of the man. He wasn't used to the feeling and purposefully thrust it to the back of his mind. Time, he decided, to finish Hunter off.

Glancing back over his shoulder, he spotted

again the buildings he'd first intended taking Bradley to. Closer now, he saw that they were some sort of power station, but they had a decrepit look, as if they hadn't known service in some time. They were bordered by a chain-link fence, but here and there he could make out breaches in the fence as though vandals had broken into the compound many times over the years. One of the nearer buildings had metal coverings over its windows and doors, but he could also see a gaping doorway where the sheet metal had been pried loose.

Rising up, he cast a look backward.

Hunter met his gaze, and he nodded in the direction of the buildings.

Come and get it, asshole, he thought.

Then he took off across the field, heedless of the two McDonnell Douglas choppers circling the nearby field of tall grass. His leg pained him. His arm didn't yet, but it would only be a matter of time. Still, he thought himself capable of reaching the buildings before Hunter could get close enough to shoot.

When next he glanced back, he saw Hunter charging along the far side of the stream. At some point Hunter would have to cross, but before then Dantalion would be safely within the brick building, while Hunter would be without cover as he followed across the open space. Exposed, he would be easy meat for Dantalion's bullets.

A chopper came over the top of the power station, rotors buzzing like an angry hornet. It wasn't one of the black gunships but the Bell JetRanger once piloted by the man whose clothes he was now wearing.

The sun was behind the chopper, but he could make out a single man on board. One of the agents from back at Eunice Jorgenson's home. Probably the asshole tasked with bringing him down.

The pilot saw him. Dantalion came to a standstill and lifted the Glock. The man's eyes widened. Then Dantalion fired. Three rapid bursts of fire that cut a zigzag pattern across the windshield. Behind the starred glass the cockpit changed color, scarlet puffing in the air.

Then the chopper was dipping toward him, and Dantalion was forced to move while the whirling rotors cleaved the air above him as if in a decapitating frenzy. He charged to the left and felt the displacement of air as the chopper rushed to the ground. He didn't look, but the sound behind him was as if the earth had exploded. Dirt and dust and grass showered around him. Then there was the loudest noise he'd ever heard, the screaming of an engine on overload, the *bang! bang! bang!* of rotors churning into the ground, followed by shrieks as chunks of hot metal were torn loose and thrown into the air.

He couldn't help looking back after that.

The Bell JetRanger was reduced to scrap metal. Oily black smoke rose as from a funeral pyre from the burned-out engine components. The rotors had been reduced to gnarly stumps. Still, the dying helicopter was groaning, but only until sparks jumped from the overheated engine into the spilled fuel, and it gave out one final roar as the entire craft went supernova.

The concussion of the explosion sent Dantalion sprawling to the ground. Searing heat washed over him, and for the briefest of moments he felt as though all life was being sucked from his body. An image flashed through his mind: years ago he'd seen photographs of the petrified victims found in the ashes of Pompeii after the eruption of Mount Vesuvius. He'd seen casts of the charred and desiccated corpses twisted into fetal balls when the superheated ash from the volcano had rained down upon them. For the briefest of times, he thought that was how he must now look. Except that now the heat had gone, the ingust taking the flames back toward the wreckage of the chopper, and he realized that—apart from singed hair and a throat that felt as if it burned yet—he was unharmed.

What surprised him more was the realization that he was facedown on the ground with his arms over his head. He had no recollection of adopting the pose. He quickly snapped to attention, wondering how much time his killing of the chopper pilot had taken, and how much of his advantage he'd lost in doing so.

Rolling to his feet, he looked to where he'd last seen Hunter. The man wasn't there. He was two hundred yards nearer and gaining. Then smoke from the doomed chopper rolled across the intervening space and Hunter's charging form was lost from view. Dantalion broke into an ungainly lope, hand slapping at his clothing where he kept his book. The book was there, but it took him a second to register that the hand he'd used should have been holding a Glock. He ground to a halt and turned around, searching for where the explosion had thrown the gun.

He couldn't see it. Smoking debris lay everywhere. Chunks of hot metal and divots of earth obscured the ground all around where he'd fallen.

"Son of a bitch!" he snapped.

Hunter burst through the smoke bank, his seething eyes picking out Dantalion like lasers.

Suddenly, he realized, he wasn't at an advantage any longer and the nearby building offered only one thing: a place to hide.

That was if he could even get there before Hunter got close enough to use his handgun.

When he ran this time, his speed was fueled by adrenaline and all his hurts were forgotten.

42 IT SEEMED MY CIA FRIEND, WALTER HAYES Conrad, wielded only a certain amount of power. He'd pulled enough strings to ensure that I was accepted by Kaufman, so I'd been offered a certain amount of leeway and allowed along for the ride. But SAC Kaufman couldn't have been easy with the arrangement. He had said that I'd only be given free rein until his own men arrived, and he'd been true to his word. All along it had obviously been his plan to take me out of the picture as soon as he had backup at the scene. I'd told Rink that Kaufman was a good guy. But I'd been wrong about him. He was as much a bureaucratic asshole as most others in his position. He was still *the* special agent in charge, and he wasn't about to allow me—a loose cannon, in his estimation—the glory of bringing down the professional hit man who'd killed his colleague back at the Jorgenson estate.

It was bad form taking down Kaufman's men the way I did. I probably hadn't endeared myself to anyone. My only saving grace was that I'd gone easy on them and hadn't left any of them permanently injured. I could foresee that Walter wasn't going to be happy with me, that he was going

to have to kiss a few asses before this was over.
Maybe I would have to as well. But I didn't let
that concern me. I had Dantalion in my sights.

The white-faced killer had a good lead on me.
I jumped the irrigation channel, raced after him,
and could have easily taken him out with a rifle,
but something in me had made me throw down
the FBI agent's gun in favor of my trusty SIG.
Things had grown very personal between the
two of us, and I'd only be happy if I was looking
into the bastard's face when I killed him. Using
my SIG meant I'd be able to see the whites of his
eyes. I only had to catch him first.

It wasn't hard to see where he was heading—a
complex of buildings surrounded by a chain-link
fence beckoned him. My best guess was that he
wanted to find cover and then pick me off while
I was in the open and exposed. So I ran harder,
taking that option away from him.

Then a chopper rose into view from behind the
buildings.

Recognizing it as the Bell JetRanger I'd hitched
a ride here in, I realized that SAC Kaufman was
on an ass-covering expedition of his own. What
the fuck he hoped to achieve, I couldn't imagine. He dropped the chopper low, as if to stop
Dantalion from reaching the buildings. Dantalion stopped, yes. But only to lift his handgun
and stitch a pattern of death directly through the
windshield.

The chopper tilted wildly, then did a slow-
motion dive toward the earth. The rotor blades

churned the ground and the chopper's tail stood high and proud for a long heartbeat. Then the whole construct ripped apart and shards of red hot metal were launched into the air. I saw Dantalion halt and look back. His expression could only be described as awe as he watched the wreckage slump to the ground. Then an explosion rocked me and I staggered against the blast, feeling the heat even as far away as I was.

SAC Kaufman didn't need to worry about answering awkward questions any longer.

I continued to run. The air was full of the stench of aviation fuel, and it felt as viscous as warm syrup on my skin. Smoke billowed, but I caught a glimpse of movement and again saw Dantalion coming to his feet. He set off running. Then stopped, looked back the way he'd come. Then he was running again, and it was more than my approach that lent wings to his heels. The fucker was unarmed. And he was running scared.

The thunders of judgment and wrath are numbered, you freak!

I charged after him. Lifted my SIG and fired a quick volley.

Contrary to popular belief, even a trained gunman like me can't hit targets at a run. Handguns are notoriously poor for killing people unless you are very close to your static target. But that was okay. I didn't expect to hit him from that distance; my only wish was to keep him running and keep him frightened. My bullets kept him moving, and his face when he glanced back at me was a mask of horror.

Dantalion reached the fence and launched himself at a rent in the wires. His clothes snagged and he tore at the wire to free himself. All the while I was gaining on him and I fired again. Sparks marked where my bullets cut through the wires.

Fifty yards or so separated us. But that distance was shortening with each step. So, I told myself, was Dantalion's time left on this earth.

The phone in my pocket vibrated.

Without halting my charge I plucked the phone out of my pocket.

There was only one person it could be.

"Rink?"

"Just lost your signal, buddy. Thought I'd check you were still alive."

Above my head was a tangle of high-voltage cables. The buildings appeared derelict, but I could hear the faint buzz from the wires, felt the hair stirring at the nape of my neck. There was still power surging through the network, so we were lucky to be able to speak at all.

"Still alive, Rink," I huffed as I ran. "If things go to plan, Dantalion won't be for too much longer. Where you at, anyway? Think you'll make it to the party?"

"Can't be far off. I've followed Okeechobee Lake, passed some huge installation, and turned east. I can see vultures circling in the sky, and if I'm not mistaken they're looking for pickings from some big old barbecue."

Snatching a glance over my shoulder, I saw Rink's vultures. The two Little Birds circling the devastation of the Bell JetRanger. The barbecue was SAC Kaufman's funeral pyre.

"Follow the portents," I told Rink. "You ain't too far off. The FBI is playing at assholes now. You think you can keep them off my back long enough for me to finish Dantalion?"

"Don't know what I can do, but I'll do my best. Whatever happens, Hunter, get that mother-fucker."

"Would have liked you with me, Rink, but things are about to come to a head here."

"Just do what you do best. Kill the frog-giggin' asshole so's I can get back to my mom."

"Don't worry, Rink. You'll be headed back to San Francisco this evening."

"Long as you're along for the ride—"

The phone cut out.

I jammed it back in my pocket, then vaulted through the hole in the fence that Dantalion had gone through. While I'd been running and talking, I hadn't lost sight of the fleeing killer. I'd seen exactly where he'd run to. There was a large building directly in front of me and a metal door had been pulled askew. Dantalion had rushed through the door and into the darkness inside.

I was pretty sure he'd lost his gun. But I would have been an idiot if I'd blundered inside and been coldcocked by the man if he was waiting just inside the door. I slowed down. Peripherally I was aware of one of the sleek gunships racing my way. Perhaps they blamed me for the death of their leader. Maybe they were coming to shoot me. But I didn't think so. I waved to the pilot, directing him over the building to cover the exits at that side. The chopper had to swing around the high-voltage cables strung above the compound, but it looked like they were complying with my directions. The other chopper headed away, taking Bradley out of harm's way.

Marianne Dean was safe. Now so was Bradley Jorgenson. There was only one more thing I wanted, and that was to ensure that Dantalion couldn't threaten either of them again.

Pressing myself against the wall to the side of the open door, I drew my Ka-bar. I was entering a dark place. Dantalion could be hiding anywhere, and the knife would be a better weapon than my gun if I stumbled into him in the dark. I shoved the SIG into the waistband at the small of my back, then quickly slipped inside the building.

My first act was to move away from the light seeping in through the door. Randomly choosing to go to the left, I moved silently through the shadows. Then I came to a standstill. I held my breath, closed my eyes against the darkness. As mad as it may seem, even in a pitch-black place the eyes can play tricks on the mind. You see movement in the darkness that isn't there, you jump at images conjured by the mind as the brain attempts to make sense out of the sudden blindness. Far better, I'd been taught, to trust your other senses and shut off the one suffering deprivation. We naturally close our eyes, so the brain does not rebel against the act; instead it heightens your hearing, your senses of smell and taste and touch. I'm also a firm believer in the ability of a sixth sense, that extrasensory perception that warns of impending danger. Maybe it's all the senses working in complete unison, maybe it's something paranormal, but it's there nonetheless. I tuned myself to the dark, listening, smelling, tasting the air. A cool but steady draft wafted from somewhere deep inside the building. It caressed my face, but there was no flutter in the breeze, nothing to indicate that a human body moved nearby, disturbing the flow.

Happy that Dantalion did not lurk close by, I moved farther inside the building. Ten paces on, I paused again. The breeze remained constant. But something plucked at my olfactory senses, and I realized I could smell blood. The coppery tang was faint. But it was there. I moved again, and the smell grew more sanguine.

Following the instincts given us in prehistory, I continued inside the building. I'm no bloodhound, so it wasn't as if I could sniff the killer out, but I was pretty sure I was heading in the right direction. A change in the draft told me that something ahead had occurred to affect the dynamics of the atmosphere. Dantalion had silently opened another door and was seeking refuge in an antechamber.

The smell in the room was now of rusting machinery, and there was a hint of ozone. Somewhere nearby I could detect a static buzz. I tried to tune all these things out, but it was no good. I opened my eyes, and my night vision had adapted so that I could now make out the bulk of machines on either side of me. They squatted like amorphous creatures, as though they silently watched my progress through the building. Ahead of me I could detect a darker shadow than all the others. I edged toward it, the Ka-bar held tight to my body so that Dantalion couldn't strike from the darkness and knock it from my hand. My boot touched a raised platform. Feeling my way upward, I found that I could step easily onto the first of a number of concrete stairs. Grit crunched underfoot. I halted. Listened for a response to my movement.

Nothing came back at me, so I continued up the stairs.

The stairway took me to the door I assumed Dantalion had used to leave the room. Probing for the door with my free hand, I readied the Ka-bar with the other. Touching the edge of the door, I wedged my fingers into the narrow gap between the door and the frame and exerted only the slightest pressure. The door swung silently away from me, and I immediately followed its movement by stepping into the space beyond.

Inside, the walls encroached upon me. I was in a narrow passage, some sort of vestibule that led deeper into the guts of the building. As I continued forward I listened for any hint that Dantalion waited for me. But there was nothing.

The air was close. Like it had been sealed

within this corridor for too long. Dust sifted onto my lips, so delicate, but apparent to my heightened senses. Someone had moved through the corridor very recently, kicked up the motes of dust that were only now beginning to settle. So I pressed on.

Twenty yards farther along I came to a second door. This one was wood. I touched it with my fingertips and they came away sticky. Lifting my fingers to my nose I inhaled, and I smelled Dantalion's blood. He had obviously brushed his injured arm against the door while easing it open. In the darkness I smiled to myself. Then I turned quickly on my heels, bringing up the Ka-bar.

It was an old trick. One I was infinitely familiar with. One where a false trail was laid down, leading a hunter to follow the clues while the pursued person backtracked, waited until the hunter passed by, and then launched an attack at the hunter's exposed back.

Dantalion just wasn't as clever as he thought he was.

As he burst from a doorway to my right I was ready for him.

He came at me, throwing a punch aimed at where he expected to find the nape of my neck. Instead I was facing him and he ran full tilt onto my Ka-bar. The six inches of razor-sharp steel rammed to the hilt into his gut.

I twisted the blade, even as he slapped at me with both hands. His blows were ineffectual, my only injury being what felt like a scratch from one of his ragged fingernails. He slumped on the blade and I grabbed hold of his windpipe, closing my hand into a tight fist to halt his sour breath exploding over my face.

"Die, you freak," I told him.

He couldn't answer. Not with his windpipe crushed in my fist, but I could have sworn the shudder that ran through him was one of laughter. Made me wonder what was so damn funny.

Then I felt a weird rushing in my head.

And I knew immediately.

That was no fingernail that had pricked me. It was something else. A needle. A fucking hypodermic syringe!

Then it was my turn to slump.

43

FROM BRIGHTEST FLORIDA SUNSHINE TO DEEP-est black in an instant. Dantalion rushed inside the semiderelict building. The sudden closing off of the primary senses would disorient most people, but he did not consider himself most people. He was Dantalion. He was elevated above humanity; he moved through planes of existence above and below the ken of mortal man. Darkness did not hinder one who'd looked into the deepest gulfs and soared on divine pinions through the furthest reaches of existence. Or so he told himself.

He stumbled twice as he rushed away from the entrance door, seeking concealment within the shadows. He attributed his ungainliness to the shell of human frailty that his spirit inhabited. It was Jean-Paul St. Pierre who stumbled and almost went down on his face, not the great Dantalion.

Cursing, he staggered on. Feeling the ache in his wounds, reminding himself that until he achieved his goal and the balance of his book was put right, he would continue to suffer the agonies of *ordinary* men. His leg was bad, but the fresh pain now radiating from his most recent wound promised to engulf all else. He had other wounds, too. Another on the flesh of his arm that had not troubled him until now. The one on his jawline. He felt other aches in his limbs and the muscles of his shoulders, products of the car wreck, no doubt, now joining the litany of his troubles to slow him down.

It occurred to him that the racing of his heart, and the endorphins flooding through his system, served to negate most of his pain, and that when he survived this latest encounter with Hunter, he would likely be laid up for the best part of two weeks, unable to function while his body healed itself. He didn't consider that long; he didn't believe that he would exist in this weak shell of mortality any longer. Throughout the journey here, his mind had been working on a subconscious level. It had been calculating formulas, figuring the numerology of all those he had killed, and it had come to a conclusion. The agent he'd most recently killed, he that was piloting the Bell JetRanger, had raised his tally exponentially. He required only the killing of one other to send him into the realms once lorded over by the original Dantalion. To kill Hunter would set him on his throne in Hell, and all his worldly troubles would be shed as though he were casting off the cloak that had concealed his true identity all these years.

He came to a halt.

Hunter wouldn't be far behind. He had to remain silent now. Unarmed he was at a disadvantage, but he could still kill the man if he kept a clear head and single intention.

Dantalion did not fear Hunter now. He was confident in his abilities. He was a professional killer of men. He was an angel, and even one who'd proved as adept as Hunter had was no match for a divine being. He would destroy Hunter; there was no doubt in his mind.

He heard the scuff of feet behind him and Dantalion paused. Turning very slowly, he looked back to the single block of light that marked the entrance to the building. He could detect the outline of a man moving out of the light and into the shadows of the interior.

Hunter.

He must be very careful now.

This man was armed with a handgun while he had nothing.

But that did not faze him. There were more ways to kill a man than with bullets. Guile and trickery could defeat even the most powerful enemy.

His clothing was saturated with the putrid stench of the irrigation channel. First task was to get rid of the jumpsuit that had become a hindrance. Not only did the clinging material constrain some of his movement, but the dripping water would lay down a trail that Hunter could follow. He quickly shed the wet jumpsuit, so he was again in the clothing of the park ranger. He then bundled the jumpsuit in a heap next to a large, archaic-looking machine. He knew that the clothing had covered his bleeding wound, absorbing most of the blood that was seeping down his arm, but he was better off without it. In this inkwell, an occasional spot of blood on the floor would be undetectable, whereas a constant river of foul-smelling water would lead Hunter directly to him.

Once he'd safely tucked away his book, he moved on. He went very, very slowly, so as not to make a sound. He found some stairs and went up them. At the top he waited, listening for any hint of pursuit, but he could detect nothing. Hunter was living up to his name.

Finding a door, he gently opened it. Pent-up air from within wafted over him. He smelled dust and rat droppings. Then he stepped inside, making his way along a narrow corridor. As he went he trailed the fingers of his left hand along the wall, feeling as he did doorways letting into other rooms or secondary passages. He came to a door at the end of the corridor. It faced him, blocking his exit, if indeed it was locked. It could effectively box him in, but that could also be an advantage, because it would also box in anyone who tried to follow him. Here he could make his stand. Finish Hunter once and for all.

He touched the door gently, and felt it give. Not locked, then, but still an obstacle that would make Hunter pause. He would only need a matter of seconds to launch his ambush. He considered briefly before leaning his wounded shoulder against the door and smearing his blood over it. Hunter would find the blood, assume that Dantalion had gone through the doorway. He would halt there a moment while he considered his next move.

Prudence warned Dantalion to keep moving, but he shook the thought loose. Why should he run? I'm better than Hunter is, he thought. I've beaten him every other time. Hunter had shot at him a number of times and his bullets hadn't killed him yet. Why should things be any different this time?

There was always the matter of his injuries, but in the end he decided they didn't enter the equation. Not when he had a way of slowing down Hunter, too.

From his pocket he pulled out the syringe with which he'd controlled Bradley Jorgenson. In the dark he could not see how much of the sodium amytal it still held, but he knew he had not administered all of the drug to Bradley. There would be enough to put Hunter to sleep. When the man was sufficiently immobilized, it would be a simple task to take his gun from him, then use it to ventilate his head in a number of places.

The thought brought a smile to his lips. Gave him comfort. He liked shooting people in the head. There was a finality to it that there was no walking away from.

It was why he'd killed his mother that way.

She wanted to join his father. So he'd granted her wish. The single bullet had instantly severed her spine at the point where it met her brain. She'd died instantly.

So he didn't need to keep on shooting her until he had no bullets left, but he knew now that he'd done that out of inexperience and naïveté. And love. He didn't want to shoot the woman only to find that he'd failed and that she would be a cripple for the rest of her days. So he simply made sure. No walking away, he reminded himself. He wouldn't walk away from Hunter until he was sure he was dead.

He heard a faint crunch.

Recognized the sound as a boot placed gingerly on a stair covered in grit.

Hunter. He was coming.

Dantalion moved quickly to one of the doors he'd found earlier and stepped through it. He readied the syringe in his left hand. Fisted his right, preparing to strike Hunter exactly where he'd placed the bullet that had ended his mother's suffering.

Then he waited.

The man was a capable hunter; he had to give him that.

Hunter moved through the corridor as silently as an errant breeze. Only the shifting of the shadows told Dantalion when he passed his hiding place. Then a slight exhalation of air as Hunter discovered the door blocking his path. Dantalion strained to hear, listened and heard telltale sniffing noises.

"Now," he told himself. "Do it now."

He quickly swept open the door, raising his fist to land the debilitating punch.

And felt the solid thud of Hunter's hand impact with his gut.

Air whooshed out of him.

Then fingers were coiling around his windpipe, effectively halting any hope of an intake of breath.

Weakness assailed him. His punch became a weak slap. His other hand holding the syringe made a feeble attempt at jamming the needle point deep into flesh, but his fingers failed him and he knew instantly that the needle had only raked through the skin on the man's face. Still, he was pretty sure that his thumb had been depressing the plunger at the time. It should be enough.

"Die, you freak."

Dantalion wasn't sure who had spoken those words. Hunter, or himself, he couldn't tell.

Hunter's hand twisted against his abdomen. Dantalion felt a twisting of his gut. Then red searing pain flared and he realized only then that the man had not simply punched him. He had jammed a knife into his body.

So it was Hunter who'd spoken?

Let him have his little moment, he thought. Let him think he's won.

Because Dantalion knew otherwise.

He actually smiled. He felt the man slump and knew that his drug had done its work. So, too, had his book been his salvation. Without checking, he knew that Hunter's blade had pierced his book. It had pushed through the cover and the pages within, exited out the back of it, but there was barely an inch of the blade embedded in his flesh. Not deep enough to reach his internal organs. It wasn't he who was going to die.

The fingers around his windpipe loosened and Dantalion sucked in air. The man in front of him was lying against his shoulder, as though seeking support. Dantalion stepped away and the man went to his knees. His fingers were still on the hilt of the knife, but he didn't possess the strength to use the weapon. Dantalion reached down and teased away each finger individually.

Hunter grunted something unintelligible.

Dantalion snorted. Lifted a foot and kicked the man over backward. Hunter slammed against the door marked with Dantalion's blood, throwing the door open and showing a room much brighter than the dark places they'd already traversed. A raised platform made up the nearest end of the room, then dropped away to ground level. The light was coming from somewhere below.

Dantalion looked down at the knife standing out from his body. It hung suspended in air, held by the wound and the weight of his book, which was caught up in his clothing. Dantalion tugged on the hilt. Winced as he felt the knife pull from his flesh. Warm blood trickled down his abdomen and pooled around his groin. He wasn't overly concerned by the cut in his flesh. Once he finished off Hunter, his flesh would mend as he was transformed into the higher being he'd always been destined to become.

He pulled out his book. In the half-light he

could see that the blade was jammed through the pages. He held the book in one hand, the silver chain looping over his wrist to where he'd fixed it to his belt. Then he wrenched the blade free.

Military issue Ka-bar, he noted. Man killer by definition. Useless against angels, he told himself.

He lifted the knife and stalked toward Hunter.

The man had rolled onto his side in an effort to get up. Dantalion saw the confused expression on his face and was only sorry that Hunter wasn't fully coherent. He would have liked him to be fully aware when he was killed by his own weapon.

Hunter made it to his hands and knees. He crawled away from Dantalion, but he would not escape.

Dantalion stood to his side, lifted the Ka-bar.

Then he saw the gun thrust into the waistband of Hunter's jeans.

The thunders of judgment and wrath are numbered.

It was always about the numbers.

He had been given two ways to kill the man.

He could offer a choice.

"One: knife?" he asked. Then he plucked out the SIG Sauer. "Two: gun? What is it going to be, Hunter? How shall I kill you?"

44

ONE OF THE MORE OBSCURE FACETS OF MY training had been in how to endure torture. I've run the gamut of methods employed by those who find it necessary to pry information from an enemy soldier. Sleep deprivation, mind games, even physical beatings I had to suffer and defeat when a member of the Special Forces. When I was drafted onto the team headed by the shadowy men who became known as Arrowsake, I was introduced to further methods. The Geneva Convention forbids torture. But those I fought didn't give a fuck for conventions in any form. It was only apt, then, that I was exposed to the other methods of extracting secrets that some governments and terrorist groups used with impunity.

As soon as the needle went in and I felt the rushing in my skull, I knew what drug was coursing through my system. I'd felt its effects before. Sodium amytal. Truth serum, as it's sometimes laughably referred to. It's an uninhibitor. It lowers resistance. It makes you feel drunk. But at the low dosage Dantalion had squirted into my face, it wasn't going to kill me. It wasn't even going to send me to sleep.

What it would do was disorient me, take away my strength, and make it difficult to fight back. But I also knew I could shake off the effects. Given time.

Dantalion kicked me over.

He couldn't realize it, but the pain of the blow actually acted in my favor. It shook off some of the debilitating fog in my brain. I rolled onto my side, looking for him.

My eyes rolled in my skull and I saw his silhouette in triplicate as my vision swam.

Aim for the one in the middle, I told myself. The thought struck me as absurdly funny, even as I knew that he was moving forward to kill me.

I rolled onto my hands and knees. A tide rushed through me, and I was almost sick. My heart felt like a massive bellows in my chest as blood pumped supercharged through my veins. Blackness clouded at the edge of my consciousness. I shook my head. Clear the cobwebs, clear the cobwebs, I chanted to myself. Fight the drug, push it aside.

"One: knife?" I heard.

Couldn't quite comprehend his meaning.

"Two: gun?"

Fingers tugged at my back and I realized my mistake. I'd shown him my SIG. I didn't have the strength to keep him from taking it. I barely had the strength to hold myself upright on my locked forearms.

"What is it going to be, Hunter?"

I sucked in air, holding it, making pressure

in my skull to push back the fluttering shadows from my mind.

"How shall I kill you?"

"With boredom," I told him.

Then I kicked out, pistoning from the knee so that my heel crunched into his nearest shin.

Dantalion howled with pain, and the sound did more to clear my mind than all my previous attempts.

Pushing upward, I came to my feet. My head swam, and I felt like I was on the deck of a ship in the storm of the century. But I didn't stop. I slammed the heel of my palm into Dantalion's groin, took hold of anything I could find, and squeezed with all my might.

Now his pain was given voice in a high-pitched way. *Ah-ah-ah-ah-ah*, sounding like he was going to sneeze. To give him something else to think about, I smacked my forehead into his face.

Not the best idea, in hindsight. The effect of bone on bone set off a tsunami inside my own head, and we reeled apart, both of us stunned.

Grabbing for my gun, it wasn't there.

I looked and saw that Dantalion was holding my two weapons.

Have to change that scenario, I thought.

But even as I lunged at him, he brought up my SIG and fired.

Luck rather than skill caused me to dodge at the same time, and the bullet punched through the space beneath my left armpit. I threw a looping right hook and drove my fist into his ribs.

Dantalion was flung around by the force of the blow, but his left arm swept up and the Ka-bar slashed a line through my jacket. He stumbled away from me, but I followed him, chopping at his gun hand with the stiffened edge of my hand. My blow caught him on the mound of his fore-arm, shocking the radial nerve, and his hand opened in reflex spasm. The SIG clattered to the floor. It was out of reach for both of us, and if I lunged for it I'd be inviting a knife in my back. So I threw a punch at his face instead.

Still under the influence of the drug, my punch was neither powerful nor aimed with precision. I didn't knock him out, but I did flatten his nose against his face. Blood splattered, and a torrent ran down his upper lip and into his mouth. He exhaled harshly and droplets of his blood flecked my clothes.

In the next second two things happened: he stabbed out at me and I grabbed his arm. Hold-ing his wrist with both my hands, I hauled him around even as I turned to the side. His ankles bumped against my outstretched leg. It wasn't an expert judo throw by any means, but it was enough to overbalance him and he went down to the floor. I fell on top of him, and loosening one hand from his wrist I drove my clawed fingers into his eyes.

Dantalion fought back. He pushed me off him and I didn't have the strength to resist. We rolled away from each other. Then it was a fight to be first to our feet. Dantalion won the race and he came at me, launching a kick into my ribs. I felt something crack, and white-hot pain flared through my body. He kicked again, but this time I hooked an arm around his heel and swept his leg high into the air. He toppled backward and his fall took him almost to the edge of the platform we were on. Then he rolled back toward me and I saw my own Ka-bar glinting in his hand.

Looking around for a weapon, I had only one option. But my SIG lay on the platform not half a dozen feet from where Dantalion was coming back to his feet. I saw the gun and I glanced at Dantalion. We exchanged stares for less than a heartbeat, and then we were both rushing for the gun. Dantalion got to it first. He snatched at the SIG, even as he scythed the air in front of my throat with the knife.

But I'd never been going for the gun. I simply wanted him in a position where I could finish the bastard off. As he was rising up, swinging the gun toward me, I leaped feetfirst at him. He fired, but he hadn't brought the gun far enough round and the bullet missed by a mile. Both my boots drove into his chest. I slapped down on the edge of the platform, my hip and right shoulder taking the brunt of the fall. It knocked the wind out of me, but nowhere near as much as my dropkick had to Dantalion. He was thrown backward, legs and arms windmilling as he tipped and then disappeared over the edge of the platform. I heard the dull thud of him hitting the ground, and then there was only silence. Painfully, I crawled to the edge of the platform. Looking down, I saw him lying in a pool of light ten feet below. He was squirming as though his spine had shattered during the fall.

Kneeling there, I took stock of my surroundings.

I was in a large room that had once been a loading dock of some kind. A large roll-down shutter dominated one wall. It was partly open, letting in the harsh Florida sunlight. Glancing to my left, I saw a flight of metal steps leading down from the raised platform I was kneeling on. A guardrail would support me going down.

Down was where I wished to be.

Dantalion was injured, but he wasn't dead yet.

Pushing up to my feet, I again had to fight the disorienting effects of the drug in my body. The steps were a challenge, but I went down them hanging on to the rail, my feet making loud clangs on the metal stairs. At the bottom I turned and faced Dantalion.

Apparently his back wasn't broken.

He was now on his hands and knees. His head swung up and he met my stare with a grim smile.

"I cannot die," he told me.

"Want to bet?" I demanded as I moved toward him.

"Yes," he said, raising my SIG.

Suddenly all around us was sound and movement. The light went even harsher as the roller shutter was forced upward and black-garbed men swarmed into the room. Laser scopes stabbed red beams through the air. Men shouted orders and commands.

I kept walking toward Dantalion and he rose up to meet me.

I was aware of the gun aiming at my face, but I just kept going.

Dantalion waited for me. Fisting both hands round my gun, he swayed where he stood, his legs braced wide. Some sort of book was trailing on the floor behind him, attached to him by a chain.

"Don't move!" someone shouted at us.

Neither of us was of a mind to listen.

Dantalion swung toward the FBI commandoes swarming into the room and he fired. The bullet passed above their heads, but it had them dropping for cover. Then he swung back toward me and a smile played across his lips.

One FBI man lifted his rifle and a red dot blossomed on Dantalion's chest.

"Drop your weapon or I'll shoot," yelled the commando.

"No you won't, asshole," said a familiar voice. I heard the racking of a pump-action shotgun. The laser dipped away from Dantalion.

I didn't have to look to know that Rink was there.

As if I'd ever believed otherwise.

Dantalion knew he was there as well. "I owe you for ramming me off that bridge, Rink," he said. "Stick around and I'll kill you, too."

Rink laughed at him.

"He's all yours, Hunter," my friend called.

And I ran at Dantalion.

Dantalion jerked the trigger.

There was only the empty click of a firing pin in an equally empty chamber.

In my mind's eye I saw an innocent old lady lying dead on her table. I thought of Bradley brutally wounded. And, thinking of Marianne Dean—of what this beast intended doing to her—I barreled into him with my shoulder, hooking my arms behind his knees, lifting and throwing him backward at the same time. He slammed down on his back with me on top. The SIG went flying from his hand. I struck him in the chest with an elbow, holding him there even as I crawled up and sat astride him. His arms were free and he gouged at my face with his horrible fingernails, but it was futile. I wasn't going anywhere. I drove my fist into his face, once, twice, three times.

His face was flecked with blood, and his pale eyes rolled up at me from swelling eyelids. His mouth opened and I saw tusklike teeth as he grinned up at me. "You're wasting your time, Hunter. I can't die. But you can."

Peripherally, I caught the blur of movement. Men in the room shouted, and over them all, I heard Rink's warning shout. My brain wasn't so clouded by drugs that it hindered my natural response.

I caught Dantalion's right wrist in my left hand. He continued to push, and he was surprisingly strong. The blade pressed against the flesh below my ribs. I felt the prickle of steel, but that only hardened my determination. Squeezing with all my might, I felt his bones grating together. The pale-faced bastard must have had something wrong with his bones, because I heard them snapping like green twigs.

Dantalion screamed. The knife fell from his nerveless hand.

"You can't die, huh?" I asked him. "Let's see about that."

Reaching down, I snatched at the book trailing like an abnormal appendage between his legs. It was attached to him by a silver chain and I wrenched it from him. He was stunned by the savagery with which I'd broken his arm, but when he saw me holding his book, strength flared in him. He bucked upward, grabbing at the book with both hands.

"Give it back!" he roared.

Hooking my heels under his kidneys, I rode him like a rodeo bronco. Then to stop him I slammed the book against the side of his head and jammed his face against the floor. He squirmed beneath me, spittle shooting from his mouth as he cursed me. His hands clawed toward my face again, so I grabbed his broken wrist and gave it an extra squeeze. He shrieked in agony. Both hands dropped onto the book and touched it spasmodically. I wrenched it from him.

"What's so fucking important about this damn thing?" I demanded. I flicked it open and saw nothing but row upon row of numbers written in a scratchy style.

The numbers meant nothing to me.

Evidently they meant everything to the killer.

So I gave them back to him.

"You want it back, do you? Well, here you are! Have it!"

I tore pages from the book, crumpled them in my fist, then as he shouted in alarm I jammed the wad of paper into his open mouth. He gagged, but I forced the wad farther in. Then I jammed his mouth shut and placed my hand over his sealed lips and nostrils. Adding to the pressure, I threw my weight on top of him and stared into his eyes. We were inches apart and I saw his pupils dilate in the realization that I was right. And he was wrong. He could die.

There were shouts of consternation from behind me. A rush of bodies. Hands clawing at me. But I trusted Rink to keep the FBI off me until it was finished. Dantalion thrashed under me in one final attempt to break free, but there was nothing he could do to stop me now.

It didn't take long.

I wasn't fully sure he was dead until I felt a hand on my shoulder.

"He's dead, Hunter," Rink said. "You can relax."

I looked down at the man beneath me. Marianne and Bradley would be safe now. The old lady was avenged.

His eyes were bugged wide, pale and milky in death.

The flesh round his mouth was blackened, lips blue. Blood vessels had erupted all along his jawline.

"That put a little color in his cheeks," I said.

45 RINK AND I MADE AN UNSCHEDULED VISIT TO the local FBI field office. We were in cuffs and were treated as if we were the ones responsible for slaughtering upward of two dozen people. But then Walter Hayes Conrad IV arrived and a few asses were metaphorically kicked. When we walked out of the FBI building it was with handshakes all round and congratulations on a job well done, even if the plaudits weren't reflected in the faces of the men doing the congratulating. Maybe the way I'd killed Dantalion had something to do with it.

Not that anyone lamented Jean-Paul St. Pierre's passing. He was a psychopathic killer with delusions of grandeur. He was responsible for murder from a very early age. He'd murdered his mother, an uncle, and a school friend when he was only thirteen years old and had spent the next eight years incarcerated in a high-security hospital. At age twenty-one, he'd been released into an unsuspecting world. He had enrolled in a school for performing arts where he'd learned all about theatrical makeup and the assuming of other personas. Later he'd trained to be a stuntman and studied driving, guns, and unarmed combat. He should have stuck to the fantasy world of movies. His training was all make-believe, all fake skills when it came to the very real, very serious world of a contract killer. He thought he was a professional, but he wasn't. He was simply crazy. But that was what had made him so dangerous.

Walter didn't hang around.

He stayed only long enough to remind me that his debt to me was cleared.

"Nothing like this can happen ever again. I can't keep on advocating murder, Hunter," he told me.

"Won't ever come to that again," I promised him. But we both knew our words were hollow.

Violence follows me around like stink on a mangy dog.

Anyway, I didn't see my treatment of Dantalion as murder. I'd simply been winning a bet.

In the end, the fact that I'd stopped a maniac who'd murdered dozens outweighed my "drug-clouded" actions, and I wouldn't be facing any charges.

Rink took a flight out of Miami International and headed across the country chasing the setting sun. I promised him I'd follow in a day or so. As soon as I'd finished up here. I told him to give his mom a kiss for me.

"Kiss her yourself when you get there," Rink told me. "She isn't going anywhere. She's getting stronger all the time."

I called Richard Dean.

We met at a diner a whole lot nicer than Shuggie's Shack. The food must have been good judging by the clatter of cutlery on plates. People talked and laughed with each other. A Patsy Cline song was playing on the jukebox.

It wasn't the kind of atmosphere I desired, so I led him around the back into a service alley. The smell of garbage rotting in a Dumpster was more conducive to setting the scene. It kind of fit my mood.

I felt like smashing him in the face there and then. But I didn't. For all that Marianne had been an inconsequential pawn in his scheme, his daughter still loved him. I wasn't going to hurt her by hurting her father.

Plus, he was a pathetic man when all was said and done. Beating him wouldn't have proved anything.

"When we first met, I told you I wasn't the man you were looking for," I said to him. "I told you I wasn't a hit man. But that's what you wanted."

"I only wanted my daughter back," he said, but his eyes told the lie.

"No, Dean. You wanted your son back. But you knew that couldn't happen. So you wanted the person you blamed for his death to die also. Sending me after your daughter was just an excuse. It was a way you saw to get at Bradley Jorgenson."

"Bradley Jorgenson killed my boy."

"You're wrong."

I explained to him how Bradley opposed the military contracts, how he was working hard to make amends for the mistakes made by his predecessors. I explained how Marianne had brought all this about. How ultimately Stephen's death had brought about the change. How he should be proud of all that his children had done. But my words were falling on deaf ears.

He remained a bitter, twisted man who may never see the truth.

"You lied to me, Dean." I pulled out the photographs he'd falsely used to build his case against Bradley. Then I jammed them into his jacket. All but the one lifted from the police file. I pushed that one under his nose. "I don't know how you managed to get hold of this—it doesn't really matter—but I want you to take a good look at it. This girl loves you, Dean. *And you did that to her.*"

His eyes clouded over as he looked at the photograph. Tears building. I thought he realized that his anger had been misguided. Of all the people in the world, Marianne should have been the last one he struck out at.

"She won't be coming home," I told him. "But it was never about getting Marianne back anyway. You didn't care what happened to her. All you cared about was that Bradley got hurt along the way."

"How do you expect me to feel? She was in bed with the man who killed my son," Dean said. "Marianne betrayed Stephen's memory. She betrayed me."

"No, Dean, you betrayed her. I sympathize with you for the loss of your son. You blamed the

Jorgensons for that, but losing your daughter is all down to you. That I don't sympathize with."

Dean blinked up at me, and I could see that the tears weren't of shame: they were too bitter for that.

"I paid you," he said. "You have to bring her back."

Pulling an envelope from my pocket, I slapped it against his chest.

"It's all there. Every stinking cent of it." When he didn't reach for it, I allowed the twenty thousand dollars to fall at his feet. "Take that as notice of my resignation," I said. "Effective immediately."

"You can't back out. You gave your word." He set his jaw angrily. "You have to finish what you started."

I said, "I just quit, Dean."

"Suit yourself," Dean hissed. He stooped quickly, grabbed the envelope, and waved it in front of me. "I'll send someone else . . ."

Grasping him by his jacket, I pushed him up against the alley wall.

Staring into his eyes, I said, "A short time ago I killed a man who was trying to hurt Marianne. An old friend of mine told me he couldn't advocate murder. I told him it wouldn't happen again. But do you know something, Dean? I'm not sure I can keep that promise."

Releasing him, I smoothed out the collar of his jacket. I fixed his tie and said, "Let it go, Dean. Let it all go."

Then I left him there to consider what would happen if he raised a finger to Marianne again. Or to Bradley.

I was twenty grand down, but it didn't hurt too badly. When I'd been smoothing down Richard Dean's jacket I took payment in another kind.

Later I found Marianne at Bradley Jorgenson's hospital bedside. Bradley was sedated, his leg in splints and raised on some sort of pulley contraption. Marianne leaned close and kissed him on the forehead before she came to me.

We stepped out of Bradley's private room, and I stood there looking down at her uptilted face. She was beautiful. But there still remained a shadow of fear behind her eyes.

"It's over with," I told her.

"How can you be so sure?" she asked.

"Trust me."

"I do."

I told her that the FBI was going to launch an investigation into the attempts on their lives. It was apparent that Petre Jorgenson had been the force behind the plot to have them murdered. He had also ordered the death of Caitlin Moore for no other reason than that she had been instrumental in influencing Marianne, who had in turn influenced Bradley to cancel his involvement in the military contracts. Petre Jorgenson couldn't stand to lose his share of the billions of dollars those contracts meant. He'd preferred to lose family members instead. What no one was sure of was how far the plot had extended and who else among the Jorgenson family had been involved. Jack and Simon were currently answering serious questions.

"Any sniff of trouble, you let me know, okay?"

"I will," she promised. "But what about . . . ?"

"Your father? He knows you won't be coming home."

"He was happy with that?"

"He sends his love," I lied. "He also sent you this."

She held out her hand and I slipped her mother's crucifix into her palm. It was looped on a silver chain.

Marianne studied the chain.

"This isn't mine."

"Souvenir for you," I said.

It was elegant and expensive. An antique piece of jewelry. It had once held the weight of a book containing thirty-six legions of spirits. The weight of the cross would easily balance that out.

Marianne looped it around her neck and lifted the cross between her fingers. She kissed it, and I saw the fear recede from her eyes. Then she stood on tiptoe and pressed her lips to my cheek.

"Thanks, Joe."

All the gratitude I required. I smiled at her. She turned away and reentered Bradley's room. I leaned against the wall next to the door. I could hear her humming something under her breath. The same song she'd been humming in the garden on Baker Island. Only this time it didn't sound so sad.

Acknowledgments and Thanks

There are so many people I am grateful to this time that I'm sure to leave some of them out, but you know who you are, so thank you.

Special thanks go to Jim Hilton, Richard Gnosill, Col Bury, Mark Torrender, and Stu Hall, all of whom have kept my creative juices bubbling in different ways.

As ever, huge thanks to Luigi and Alison Bonomi and all the team at LBA, without whom Joe Hunter wouldn't be the same. Also to George Lucas at Inkwell management, and to everyone at ILA, which champions my books throughout the world.

To Sue Fletcher, Swati, and Eleni at Hodder and Stoughton, and to David Highfill, Gabe, and Sharyn at William Morrow, thank you for all your invaluable editorial advice and support.

Thanks also to Jacky and Val Hilton.

—*Matt Hilton*

If you e

JUDGMENT AN

don't miss

SLASH AND BU

the next Joe Hunter thrille

from Matt Hilton

Available now from Harper

njoyed

D WRATH,

RN,

Prologue

AMERICA. LAND OF THE FREE. WHERE DREAMS CAN come true.

It's a notion that I subscribe to.

The only problem is that most of my dreams are of the darker variety. For fourteen years I was a member of a crack counterterrorism unit, gleaned from the best warriors that the United Nations could field. All those years of hunting and terminating terrorists has left me with horrific memories that often plague my nights. I thought that when I left home and settled in Florida that I could bury those memories along with my past life. But that didn't work out the way I'd planned.

I came here seeking my wayward brother, John. While I was serving my country, John was practicing his gambling skills. I was a better soldier than he was a gambler. In the end his debts grew so large that he chose to flee the people who were intent on taking what he owed them from his hide. He left behind an ex-wife and two small children, and a heap of trouble I had to clean up for him. When I came to the United States looking for him, I wasn't sure if it was to save him or smack the stupidity out of him. It was bad enough when I discovered John was on the run from mob hit men, but there was worse to come. I found John, and when I did, it was under the blade of Tubal Cain, one of the smartest and most demented killers I've ever met. I stopped the murderer—a guy they called the Harvestman because of his penchant for reaping the bones from his victims—but at a great price.

On the upside, I renewed my friendship with Rink, my Asian-American brother in arms, and have acquired bona fide employment with his private investigations business in Tampa, Florida. I've never been much of a detective, though, so I tend to handle the jobs in which my particular skill set is required. The downside to my new life is that it comes with a caveat: I know my battle with Tubal Cain has revived the cold rage that once drove me and now threatens to again.

I hate bullies. Short and simple. I hate that there are people in the world whose lives are made miserable by those willing to murder, rape and trample them underfoot to appease their selfish needs. Tyrants come in all shapes and sizes: a despotic ruler who subjugates his country, all the way down to an insecure person who abuses his spouse and children. In my eyes they are the lowest of the low and I wish nothing more than to show them the error of their ways. Because of that, I've gained a reputation for being the man to come to when there's a problem the cops can't handle. When victims call on my services, I can't look away. That's the duty of all good people. I'm not one to "pass by on the other side of the street": I'm willing to stand up for what's right. Whatever it takes.

For too long, evil has been allowed to flourish. The way I see it, society is broken. Some may call me a vigilante, but I think I've just got problems to fix.

1

IT WAS THE WORST YEAR OF HER LIFE.

She stumbled and fell, her shoulder ramming the bole of a tree, scraping her skin raw beneath her shirt. She cried out in pain, but instantly clamped her teeth down on her lip to stop the sound traveling through the forest. In the next instant she scrambled up and fled again, her breath catching in her throat. She wanted to scream, wanted to howl in terror, but there was only one thing racing through her mind: Get away. Get away now.

She had to run. Leave everything behind. Everything.

But she knew she couldn't do that. There was one thing that she had to keep safe. It was the only thing that would help her end the *worst year of her life.*

It had been a bad, bad year.

Spring had been awful enough. That was when her husband had walked out on her and took up with a girl half his age. Summer was earmarked by the acrimonious divorce. By the time fall came around, Imogen Ballard had decided that things couldn't get any worse.

But then came winter.

And now men were trying to kill her.

Already, blood had been spilled. Thankfully it wasn't hers, but that simple truth was the only chink of light piercing the nightmare she'd found herself in. And, she wondered, how long would that stay true, when the men hunting her through the forest did so armed with rifles and automatic handguns? Sooner or later they would catch up with her, and then there'd be a lot more blood.

She had to run. Hide. Try to stay away from those hunting her with the tenacity of bloodhounds. She was at home in the woods, but she was no Lady Rambo. She didn't know if she was capable of giving them the slip, and she certainly wasn't able to fight back. Not armed as she was with nothing but a digital video camera.

She was thirty-eight years old. Not as fit as she'd been ten years ago when she was regularly competing in triathlons, but she was still lithe and strong. The only problem was, the shock of what she'd witnessed had robbed her of much of the stamina required to maintain the lead she'd set. Her hunters were gaining.

As if to remind her of how close they were, a bullet shrieked by like an angry wasp, cutting a chunk from a tree on her right.

Imogen ducked in reflex. Too late to have saved herself if the bullet was on target, of course, but she couldn't stop the instinctive movement. Then she was pushing forward, her boots driving through mounds of moss and twigs as she clambered over a fallen tree. Another bullet streaked past, galvanizing her to push even harder.

The men chasing her shouted. Maniacal laughter taunted her. Another gun barked, punching the ground in front of her. Imogen spun, turning down a narrow trail, thinking that the men were only toying with her. They were enjoying her terror, and that was the only reason why their bullets hadn't found her yet.

From somewhere ahead she heard a faint rumble. Her first thought was that the men had called in some kind of armored vehicle as backup. That even now some great cannon was vectoring in on her to blow her to smithereens. But, she knew, that thought was sheer madness. The rumble was from Great Wells, the waterfall she'd earlier scaled on her way up the hillside.

She considered running directly to the falls and throwing herself headlong to the mercy of the white water. But that would only kill her as dead as the men chasing her. The falls were 150 feet of steep cliffs. At the bottom wasn't a nice deep pool, but a series of potholes set in jagged rocks. The falls were no means of escape. In fact, they blocked her way more effectively than an electrified fence would.

She spun from the path, hurdling another fallen tree, and crashed through the lower branches of pines that grew from the steep hillside. Her only way out of there was by a route that was unfamiliar to her. And all that she could do was run, and hope that the men gave up before her flagging stamina did.

But she didn't think they would.

2

"MY SISTER MAY VERY WELL BE DEAD."

"Don't see how I can help you, then. I'm sorry."

"But then again, she might not be."

It was one of those surreal conversations that you find yourself striking up with a stranger, and wondering where the hell it was all leading to. I'd been taking a cold Corona on the deck of the beach house I had rented on the Florida Gulf Coast east of Pensacola. I saw the woman approaching me along the curve of the beach. She was walking with the devil-may-care attitude of the tourists that often walked the beach, picking up shells or water-smoothed stones and marvelling at the glory of nature. I noticed her for two reasons. She was obviously beautiful. She was tall for a woman, and willowy of frame. She had the slim hips and broad shoulders I associated with swimmers, but she walked with a ballerina's grace. She had short dark hair and equally dark eyes—kind of Paris chic, I thought. But what struck me most—and the second of my reasons for noticing her—was the way she called out to me like I was an old friend.

"Joe Hunter?" she called, waving a hand. "Is that you?"

She caught me at a time when I was unprepared for visitors. My hair was mussed, I was unshaven. Worse than that, I was stripped to the waist, dressed only in a pair of cut-off denim shorts that were frayed along the hem. My face, neck and forearms were tanned by Florida sunshine, but my upper body was still the pale of one not long arrived from northern England. Since my arrival in the United States I hadn't had too much spare time on my hands—none of it to be spent idling in the sun. My couple of minutes on the sundeck had been an attempt at balancing the deficit out.

Putting down my bottle of beer, I wiped surplus droplets from my chin. Before answering the woman, I discreetly surveyed the beach in each direction. My first thought was, "Who is she?" My second, and more important: "Who is with her?" In my line of work, it was important that I know those kinds of things. Judas betrayed Jesus with a kiss, marking him out to the Romans sent to capture him; a pretty woman calling my name could easily do the same to my enemies.

But there were no enemies lurking in hiding.

She came toward me, her bare feet kicking up golden sand. I saw that a pair of sandals bumped against a shapely thigh, slung from a loop of her shorts.

"You *are* Joe Hunter?" she asked, still ten paces out.

I looked around for my shirt, but it was indoors. I made do with folding my forearms over my chest. My arms covered the unsightly scar next to my heart, but that was about all. Good job that I'd kept up a strict exercise regimen; at least the rest of my body wasn't ugly to look at.

She studied me with interest.

Then her eyes alighted on the tattoo on my shoulder, and it was as if that one symbol confirmed my identity. Not so many people knew about the tattoo, even fewer people wore one like it. There was me and my best friend Rink. Half a dozen others who'd been in the same Special Forces team as us. Everyone else was dead.

"I feel at a disadvantage here," I told the woman. "You seem to know who I am, but . . ."

"I'm Kate," she said, advancing to the deck and looking up at me. "You knew my brother."

Something in her features did look familiar. Jake Piers was a tough, wiry son of a bitch who came to our team from the Navy SEALs. I was there with him when we took down a terrorist training camp in Libya. I carried him back from the raid across my shoulders after he was shredded by machine-gun fire. Jake died in my arms.

"You're Jake's sister?" How could she look so familiar when Jake had been such a pug to look at?

"I'm only *one* of his sisters," she corrected me. "I have an older sister named Imogen."

Wondering where all this was leading, I waved her up onto the deck and offered her a Corona.

She took the beer but declined a glass, drinking directly from the bottle. I watched a bead of amber liquid trace a line down her neck where it shivered momentarily before she wiped it away. She caught me looking and laughed. There was no embarrassment about it.

"I bet you're wondering what I'm doing here."

Leaning against the railing so that the sun was on my back, I ran a hand over my unkempt hair. "Wasn't expecting visitors," I told her.

Her eyes crinkled. She took in my beach house with a sweep of her arm. "It's beautiful here. But lonely, I guess. Do you live out here all alone?"

"Only the last few days," I told her. "That's why I'm surprised you found me."

And I was surprised. There were only two people who knew I had moved into the house, and neither of them were the type to give up my location without a fight. My friend and business partner, Jared "Rink" Rington, and Harvey Lucas, another friend out in Little Rock, Arkansas.

"You didn't get the voice-mail messages Jared sent you?"

I thought about the mobile phone lying somewhere inside the house. I'd slung it aside my first night in my new home. I'd come here for some R and R: why would I want to be disturbed by phone calls? The battery would probably be dead by now.

"Rink sent you here?" It was unlike him. Normally he would have paved the way first. But then, I looked once more at Kate and decided that Rink would see what I saw. Not a threat; just a person in need of help.

"He's tied up with a case at the moment, but he

said that you would be able to help." She looked at me expectantly, but when I didn't say anything, she added, "I've got a problem, Joe. But I knew who to come to. I remembered Jake talking about his friends from his unit. He said that he would trust you all with his life. Even when he died, it was his friends who brought him home. It's why I looked Jared up instead of going to the police."

"And Rink sent you to find me, huh?"

"Said that he was a little busy, but you'd do as a second best."

I shook my head at that.

"What else did Rink tell you about me?"

"Nothing. I already knew from Jake that you were good at your job."

"Jake told you what we did?"

"Not in as many words. But I'm not stupid. I was only thirteen years old when he died, but even I guessed that he was more than just an average soldier. I knew that you were all part of some extra-special unit. It's because I know about your background that I came looking for you."

"If you're looking for a mercenary, you've come to the wrong place," I told her. "I'm retired. Four and a half years."

"Jared said you would help."

"Depends what it is you want from me."

"I want you to find my sister."

"She's missing? You *should have* gone to the cops first."

"My sister may very well be dead." Kate looked at me, bouncing the bottle of beer in her palm.

Frowning, I placed down my own bottle, turning away from her. "Don't see how I can help you, then. I'm sorry."

"But then again, she might not be."

I turned around to look at her again, and she was staring up at me with her chin set with determination. She looked more and more like her brother had—particularly when he grew pigheaded with stubbornness.

"I need someone to come with me and find out which it is," she said. "If Imogen is dead, then I need to know. The alternative is that she's being held against her will and needs help to get away."

Jake Piers wouldn't have survived his wounds. He was shredded, his internal organs torn up. But I wasn't going to leave him behind. There was no way I was about to allow his corpse to be paraded on TV by the terrorists as a sign of victory. I carried him out of there even though it meant slowing down the extraction of my team. No one with me complained; we all owed Jake. It was his actions in saving us from the ambush that killed him. The only way I could repay his selflessness was to help his family now.

So much for rest and recuperation, I thought. I nodded at her.

"I'll get my things together. When do we start?"

"I've booked tickets out of Tampa tomorrow. Can you be ready then?"

I didn't have to look around to know that I already had everything here that I needed. My SIG Sauer P228, with a half dozen spare magazines of

9 mm soft-nosed Parabellums. A change of clothing. Fake air-marshal documents that would get my gun past security. What more would I require?

"Where are we going?"

"Kentucky."

Appalachia. I hadn't been there before. Mountains and valleys were just my thing. It would be picturesque this late in the year. I looked at Kate. The company wouldn't be bad either.

I asked her where she was staying and she smiled up at me. She said she'd booked a room at the Marriott. "Unless there's somewhere else you can suggest?"

"It's handy for the airport. I'll meet you there in the morning."

She turned and placed the empty bottle on the deck. I thought I heard her laugh to herself. Sounded a little ironic. When she stood up, she stepped toward me and laid a cool hand on my chest.

"Thanks, Joe," she said. Then she leaned in and kissed me on the cheek.